# *CHATTERTON*

"A tour de force, a brilliant novel that meditates shrewdly on the act of creativity, on the relation of works of art to the works—and lives—that inspire them."

*USA Today*

"A wildly inventive series of literary allusions."

*The New Republic*

"Deftly entwines fiction and fact while operating on three historical stages ... glints and gleams off many surfaces."

*The Christian Science Monitor*

"A savage and hilarious parable of the increasingly disputed border separating life from literature, told by a connoisseur of literary duplicity."

John Ashbery

OTHER BOOKS BY PETER ACKROYD

*The Last Testament of Oscar Wilde*
*T. S. Eliot* (biography)
*Hawksmoor*

# CHATTERTON

## PETER ACKROYD

Ballantine Books • New York

*For Christopher Sinclair-Stevenson*

Library of Congress Catalog Card Number: 88-91983

ISBN: 0-345-35822-8

This edition published by arrangement with
Grove Press, Inc.

Cover design by James R. Harris
Cover painting: *Chatterton* by Henry Wallis, courtesy
of the Tate Gallery, London.

Manufactured in the United States of America

First Ballantine Books Edition: January 1989

10  9  8  7  6  5  4  3  2

Thomas Chatterton (1752–1770) was born in Bristol; he was educated at Colston's School there and was for a few months apprenticed to a lawyer, but his education was less important than the promptings of his own genius. His father died three months before his son's birth, and from an early age Chatterton had been fascinated by the ancient church of St Mary Redcliffe where his father had once worked as a chorister. He was seven years old when his mother gave him certain scraps of manuscript which had been found in the muniment room of that church, and at once his imagination was formed. He told her that she had 'found a treasure, and he was so glad, nothing could be like it'; 'he fell in love,' his mother said, both with antiquity and with the past of Bristol itself. He began writing poems and then, at the age of fifteen or sixteen, he composed the 'Rowley' sequence: these were verses ostensibly written by a medieval monk, and for many years accepted as such, but they were the work of the young Chatterton who had managed to create an authentic medieval style from a unique conflation of his reading and his own invention.

At last tired of Bristol, and lured by the prospect of literary success, Thomas Chatterton travelled to London at the age of seventeen. But his hopes of fame were to remain unfulfilled, at least within his own life-time; the booksellers were unenthusiastic or indolent, and the London journals declined to publish most of the elegies and verses he offered them. At first he stayed in Shoreditch with relations, but in May 1770 he moved to a small attic room in Brooke Street, Holborn. It was here on the morning of 24 August 1770, apparently worn down by his struggle against poverty and failure, that he swallowed arsenic. When the door of his room was broken open, small scraps of paper – covered with his writing – were found scattered across the floor. An inquest was held and a verdict of felo de se or suicide was announced; the next morning, he was interred in the burying ground of the Shoe Lane Workhouse. Only one contemporary portrait of him is known to exist, but the image of the 'marvellous boy' has been fixed for posterity in the painting, Chatterton, by Henry Wallis. This was completed in 1856, and has the young George Meredith as its model for the dead poet lying in his attic room in Brooke Street.

[1]

'Come,' he said. 'Let us take a walk into the meadow. I have got the cleverest thing for you that ever was. It is worth half a crown merely to have me read it to you.'

He waved the little book at her, but his eager manner frightened the girl and she walked away from him quickly. Then, taking courage from the sight of a friend sitting on the church steps, she called out to him over her shoulder, 'What a poor boy you are, to be sure. And Lord, Tom, how your shoes gape open!'

'I am not so poor that I need pity from such as you!' Chatterton ran out into the open fields, pushing his face against the wind that chilled him; then he stopped short, sat down on the cropped grass and, gazing at the tower of St Mary Redcliffe, muttered the words that had so powerfully swayed him:

> The time of my departure is approaching.
> Nigh is the hurricane that will scatter my leaves.
> Tomorrow, perhaps, the wanderer will appear –
> His eye will search for me round every spot,
> And will, – and will not find me.

He looked at the church and, with a shout, raised his arms above his head.

\*

'Yes, I am a model poet,' Meredith was saying. 'I am pretending to be someone else.'

Wallis put up his hand and stopped him. 'Now the light is right, now it is falling across your face. Put your head back. So.' He twisted his own head to show him the movement he needed. 'No. You are still lying as if you were preparing for sleep. Allow yourself the luxury of death. Go on.'

Meredith closed his eyes and flung his head against the pillow. 'I can endure death. It is the representation of death I *cannot* bear.'

[2]

'You will be immortalised.'

'No doubt. But will it be Meredith or will it be Chatterton? I merely want to know.'

*

Harriet Scrope rose from her chair, eager to deliver her news. 'Cut is the bough,' she said, 'that might have grown full straight.' And she doubled up, as if she were about to be sawn in half.

'Branch.' Sarah Tilt was very deliberate.

'I'm sorry?'

'It was a branch, dear, not a bough. If you were quoting.'

Harriet stood upright. 'Don't you think I know?' She paused before starting up again. 'We poets in our youth begin in gladness. But thereof in the end come despondency and madness.' She stuck her tongue out of the side of her mouth and rolled her eyes. Then she sat down again. 'Of course I know it's a quotation. I've given my life to English literature.'

Sarah was still very cool. 'It's a pity, then, that you didn't get anything in return.' And they both laughed.

*

Charles Wychwood sat with his head bowed. He watched the leaves falling to the ground; they were rustling together and he heard, also, the sound of hammers, of drilling, of workmen calling to each other inside the new building. Then the pain returned and it was only later that he noticed how the leaves had been swept away, the noises stopped. There was a young man standing beside him, gazing at him intently: he put his hand upon Charles's arm as if he were restraining him. 'And so you are sick,' one said. And the other replied, 'I know that I am'. Charles looked down again in despair and, when he glanced up, the figure of Thomas Chatterton had disappeared.

# Part One

Look in his glommed face, his sprighte there scanne;
Howe woe-be-gone, how withered, forwynd, deade!
(*An Excelent Balade of Charitie*. Thomas Chatterton.)

So have I seen a Flower ynn Sommer Tyme
Trodde down and broke and widder ynn ytts pryme.
(*The Story of Wyllyam Canynge*. Thomas Chatterton.)

# 1

A S SOON as he turned the corner, he looked for the House above the Arch. And, when he entered Dodd's Gardens, it seemed that the sun was waiting for him at the end of the long, narrow street. 'There are no souls, only faces,' he said as he looked up at the houses which now enclosed him: the pilasters copied from eighteenth century façades and reproduced in miniature; the small iron balconies, some of them newly painted and others stippled with rust; the pediments so broken or decayed that they were scarcely recognisable above the doors and windows; the curiously moulded fanlights discoloured with age, so that no light could now pass through them; the elaborate stucco work, none of it now without blemish or injury; the wood rotten, and the stone fractured or defaced. This was Dodd's Gardens, London W14 8QT.

But to Charles all these houses seemed alike, all very agreeable family residences. He put his hands deep into the pockets of his khaki greatcoat and whistled, pausing only to stroke a large black dog which was about to lope past him. 'Wouldn't it be nice,' he said, 'to be running in the countryside together?' He bent down in order to talk more confidentially. 'Like Charlie Brown and Snoopy. Like the Indian Boy and Lassie. Like the blind man and Old Dog Tray. The country isn't very far, you know. We could always reach it if we want to. Anyone can.' And with this final message of comfort he walked away; the dog lay down in the filth, and watched Charles as he continued with his jaunty step along the street. Then it saw him stop, take a step back, scratch his head, and disappear.

At first Charles thought that a hole had been blown in the side of Dodd's Gardens; it was only when he stepped back off the pavement that he saw the curve of the arch, and then the house above it. The entire structure was made of stone, so that it seemed much older than the brick houses beside it, and when Charles walked beneath the arch the air became colder. A black silhouette of a face had been daubed against one of the interior walls and, above his head, there were elaborate signs and graffiti sprayed upon the wooden roof and the rusted iron bands which secured it. Beyond the arch was a small courtyard and, as Charles entered it, he noticed a small sign beside a blue door: 'Leno Antiques. Don't Linger. Make Us Very Happy. Walk Up, Do.' This amused him. He took the two books, which he had been carrying under his arm, and put them upon his head; then he tiptoed across the courtyard, balancing them precariously until they fell, and he caught them.

There were two flights of stone stairs, smelling strongly of disinfectant, and as he climbed them he could hear angry voices just above him. He could not make out the words but he could distinguish a woman's high furious shouts and, rising against them, the bellows of a man who seemed to be close to hysteria. Charles reached the first landing, where a door was marked with the sign, 'Yes, You Are Here. Leno's.' He knocked, hesitantly, and there was an immediate silence. He knocked again, and a grave voice from within murmured 'Come'. He opened the door and, peering around it, saw a man busily engaged in dusting the beak of a stuffed eagle. 'I'm looking –'

'Oh yes.'

'I'm looking for Mr Leno.'

'He speaks.' The man still had his back to him, and had now moved down to the claws of the dead bird.

'Hi, I'm Wychwood.' This was Charles's customary greeting.

Mr Leno sounded puzzled. 'Which . . .?'

'Wood. I telephoned this morning. About the books.'

'This is probably true.' Mr Leno turned suddenly to face him and Charles, with some alarm, noticed a bright purple birthmark splayed across his right cheek; it had given him a momentarily savage appearance. 'My darling,' he called into the air. 'My darling, there is a man on the premises.' And Charles realised that the high voice he had heard from the stairs was actually that of Mr Leno himself. 'Mr Witch, be pleased to . . .' He waved his hand but did not complete the sentence, and in the sudden silence Charles glanced around the room with a benevolent, almost proprietorial, interest. From the ceiling to the floor it was filled with ornaments, prints, stuffed animals and miscellaneous bric-à-brac: spoons apparently flung into a cracked fruit dish from a great distance, a row of ivory paperweights placed on some faded sheet music, a heap of large dolls with their various limbs tangled together as if they had been shot and thrown into a mass grave, brightly coloured chess men ranged alongside plaster busts, and on several dusty shelves Charles could see playing cards, books, clay bowls and three small lace umbrellas placed end to end. There were dishes filled with buttons and toothpicks, wooden drawers half-open and bulging with old magazines, and two brass racks in which a number of prints had been filed away. A paraffin stove was burning in one corner of the room (dangerously close to a wooden rocking horse) and for the first time Charles noticed that, in spite of the intense heat emanating from the stove, Mr Leno was wearing a dark three-piece suit. 'Mrs Leno,' he called out again, 'the man is still with us. Come and be mother.'

A metal ramp connected this room to one slightly above it – the difference in height testifying to the great age of the house, which appeared to have tilted or sunk at one end – and now there hurtled down it, as if propelled by a mighty hand, a wheelchair which stopped very suddenly beside a headless torso made of pink plaster. Mrs Leno paid no attention to Charles but leaned forward in her chair and snarled noiselessly at her husband. She was dressed in heavy black, also, but her sombre appearance was modified by the small violet hat which perched precariously on her apparently lustrous brown hair. 'Mr Witch –'

'Wood.'

'Mr Wood has brought books for you, my darling.'

It was only now that she looked up at Charles, almost coyly, and with a sudden movement she stretched out to snatch the two volumes which he held towards her. They were entitled *The Lost Art of Eighteenth Century Flute-Playing* by James Macpherson. She made a small noise in the back of her throat; to Charles it sounded like a joyful hiccup. 'It is the flute, Mr Leno, the divine afflatus.'

'Put it to your lips, my darling. Your metaphorical lips, that is.'

She looked up at Charles, who had been smiling through this brief exchange. 'Are you of a wandering nature? With your bird nest hair and your peach-fuzz moustache, are you a banditto of a minstrel kind? Where is your lovely instrument?'

Charles, not at all surprised by her questions, at once became confidential; he might have known these people all his life. 'I could have been a flautist . . .' In fact he had bought these books from a market barrow in Cambridge some years before; it had been an impulse only, but at that moment he had decided that he was destined to become a flautist. So he had read the first few pages attentively but then he had put the books aside and rarely, if ever, looked at them again. *The Lost Art of Eighteenth Century Flute-Playing* became part of the life which Charles carried about with him from place to place, a permanent reminder that he might still become a great flautist if he ever wished to do so. 'There are no rules,' he used to say. 'Everything is possible.'

But he had woken up that morning in a state of desperation, as if he had spent the night struggling with an enemy that could not

[9]

be overcome, and for the first time in many months he recognised how poor he was and how much poorer he was likely to become. Idly, to quieten these thoughts, he had taken up the two volumes by James Macpherson; and almost at once it occurred to him that he might sell them for a large sum. His depression lifted: he was so impressed by his acumen in business matters that he forgot his poverty and contemplated a new career as a bookseller. 'I could have been a flautist,' he was saying, 'but actually I'm a writer.' He looked straight at her as he said this.

'I knew it, Mr Leno!' Her husband sucked in his cheeks, somehow enlarging the area of his birthmark, and said nothing. 'Are you in the realm of fiction? Or merely the imagination?'

'I'm working on some poems at the moment.'

'Ah, poetry. Bags of fluff!' All the while she was bent over in her wheelchair, scrutinising the books. 'My middle name is poetry. Sibyl Poetry Leno.'

Her husband had returned to the stuffed eagle, and now spoke to her over his shoulder. 'Has Mrs Leno come to any conclusion?'

She emitted a little squeal and pointed to an engraving of an antique flute. 'Look, dearest, look at those golden stops!' But she closed the book before he had any chance to take her advice. 'I can offer fifteen.'

Charles was incredulous. 'Do you mean pounds?'

'No, I didn't mean pounds. I meant iron age monuments.'

Charles took his hands from his pockets, and started twirling a strand of his hair with two fingers. Mrs Leno was once more bowed in meditation, so he addressed her husband. 'Can you go a little higher?'

Mr Leno was polishing the claws with great ferocity, and asked the dead bird. 'Can she go a little higher?'

'She *could* go higher.' Mrs Leno's trance had been broken. 'She could go as high as the Post Office Tower if she had her legs. But not everything is possible. This is not a perfect world.'

Charles was so surprised by the smallness of the offered sum that he lost interest in the subject, and began to wander around the shop with as nonchalant an air as any unseen or unannounced visitor. In any case, he was no longer sure if the Lenos' conversation was directed towards him or merely towards each other. 'Poetry and poverty.' Mrs Leno was declaiming. 'Poetry and poverty.'

'Go on, my darling.'

'What an attic room and a funeral urn they are!'

'She is not to be stopped today,' Mr Leno said, in a tone that managed to combine delight and resentment. 'I see that now.'

Charles believed that this remark, at least, had been addressed to him: he had been examining a pack of Edwardian Tarot cards and, when he turned around, they were indeed both glaring in his direction. 'I would like more, you know. Those are valuable books.'

'He would like more, Mrs Leno.'

'Would he? I would like to run barefoot on Brighton Rock, but what does that signify?'

'With feathers in her hair.' Mr Leno sighed.

Charles was suddenly disgusted by the smell of the paraffin stove, and turned back to the Tarot pack. It was then that he saw the picture. He had the faintest and briefest sensation of being looked at, so he turned his head to one side – and caught the eyes of a middle-aged man who was watching him. For a moment he stood gazing back in astonishment. Then with an effort he walked over and picked up the painting. The canvas had been clumsily tacked upon a light wooden frame, and he held it out at arm's length in order properly to survey it. It was a portrait of a seated figure: there was a certain negligent ease in the man's posture, but then Charles noticed how tightly his left hand gripped some pages of manuscript placed upon his lap, and how indecisively his right hand seemed to hover above a small table where four quarto volumes were piled on top of each other. Perhaps he was about to put out the candle, flickering beside the books and throwing an uncertain light across the right side of his face. He was wearing a dark blue jacket or top-coat and an open-necked white shirt, the large collar of which billowed out over the jacket itself: a costume which might have seemed too Byronic, too young, for a man who had clearly entered middle age. His short white hair was parted to display a high forehead, he had a peculiar snub nose and a large mouth; but Charles particularly noticed the eyes. They seemed to be of different colours, and they gave this unknown man (for there was no legend on the canvas) an expression of sardonic and even unsettling power. And there was something familiar about his face.

Mrs Leno was suddenly beside him. 'We take Access, Visa, American Express –'

'And Co-op Gold Card, my darling.'

'*And* Diners Card. Never forget that.' She tapped Charles on the leg. 'Plastic dulls the pain, I am told. But you know that already. You are a poet.'

On considering the painting once again, Charles decided that he was at least intrigued by it. And at once the idea of simply selling his books became absurd; the money would soon be gone, but this portrait would always remain in his possession. He became cheerful again: 'I would certainly be interested in an exchange.'

'Exchange me, would you, you banditto?' Mrs Leno was very playful.

'But has she the heart to part with it? Speak, Mrs Leno, or forever –' A kettle whistled somewhere in the adjacent room and Mr Leno, turning on his heels, was gone.

Mrs Leno might very well bear to part with this particular portrait, since its presence in the shop had made her uneasy from the beginning. On several occasions she had dragged it from its hiding place and brandished it in front of her husband, saying, 'There is death on that face!' To which his invariable reply was, 'There is death on every face.'

A small cough announced Mr Leno's return, and she wheeled herself around to speak to him: 'Early nineteenth century. No frame. Oil on canvas. Twenty by thirty. Do we or don't we?' Then she added, glancing up at Charles with a wistful expression, 'But can I send it into the outer world? There is majesty there.' She pointed to the picture. 'Like a secret ray.'

There was, perhaps, a slight impatience in her husband's voice. 'Will she part with it for the sake of two bound volumes?'

'A flute for a lord. A flute for a lord. What shall it be, Mr Leno, what shall it be?'

'Shall we finger the flute, my darling?' They looked at each other quickly.

'It is done!' she cried, wheeling her chair towards her husband so that she seemed about to crush him. 'The dirty deed is done! The poet has vanquished me. I am glad to be wearing black today.' Charles followed her, eagerly holding out the canvas, but she shrank back in her chair. 'No, no. It is yours now.'

'I'm sorry.' Charles laughed. 'I just wondered if you could wrap it up.' And he held out his right hand, to show her the dust he had picked up from the side of the painting. She looked at his fingers in horror.

'We have a bag.' Mr Leno stepped between them, and took the picture. 'There is always a bag to be had.'

Mrs Leno doffed her violet hat at the painting, murmured 'Farewell my lovely', and retreated backwards up the ramp into the other room while her husband was trying unsuccessfully to stuff the canvas into a plastic carrier-bag with 'Europe 80' emblazoned in yellow letters on its side.

'Don't worry,' Charles said, taking the painting from him, 'it really doesn't matter.'

'It always matters.' Mr Leno gave a solemn bow, and took Charles to the door. 'But it *is* tea-time.'

As soon as Charles had descended the stairs, and was about to enter the yard, he heard once again the hysterical screams and bellows of the argument which he had interrupted a few minutes

[12]

before. But he was still smiling when he walked back along Dodd's Gardens, carrying the picture in front of him. He was looking out for the black dog, so that he could show it to him, and he hesitated at the spot where he had last seen him. He looked down into the area of the house beside him, but there was nothing there except moss, ragweed, discarded beer-cans and slivers of dark green grass which gleamed in the weak light of the sun. Then he looked up and found himself gazing through the ground-floor window into a bare room; the curtains were half-drawn but he could distinctly see a young child standing upright in a corner of the room. He was holding his arms stiffly against his sides and seemed to be staring back at Charles, who noticed a small bird perched on the child's right shoulder. Then a cloud passed across the sun, and the interior of the room grew dark.

*oh yes*

The Wychwoods lived on the third floor of a house in West London; it had once been a Victorian family residence of some grandeur, but in the Sixties it had been converted into a number of small flats. Certain of the original features had been retained, however – in particular the staircase which, although some of its boards were sagging and many of its banisters were chipped or broken, still curved gracefully from floor to floor. Charles had just turned onto its third landing when he saw his son, Edward, sprawled across the top stair.

'You're late, Dad.' He was resting his chin upon his hands, reading the *Beano*, and did not look up at his father.

'No, I'm not, Edward the Impossible. You're early.' The boy gave a hollow laugh, and carried on reading. 'Where's your key, Edward the Unprepared?'

'You took it from me yesterday. You lost yourn.'

'Yours, Edward the Unexpected, yours. Where *was* you dragged up?' Charles tried to grab his son's spiky brown hair and then, delicately stepping over him, ran laughing to his door. Edward put the comic up to his face and smiled broadly; then he rose and, composing his expression into a scowl, followed his father into the front room of the flat.

This room looked as if it were being occupied by a student, and in fact the orange vinyl chairs, the flimsy pine table, the sagging sofa, and the posters advertising various examples of *film noir* had all come from Charles's lodgings at university. (So, for that matter, had most of his clothes.) Charles had already entered his 'study' – a corner of the room with a wooden screen, painted bright green, placed around it – and Edward tip-toed towards it. Holding his

[13]

breath, he peered through its grooves and was rather surprised to see his father talking to a picture of an old man. 'You are my masterpiece,' he was saying. Edward retreated into the room and remained silent when his father called out, 'Edward the Idolater! Come here for a moment and see what I've got!' No reply. 'It's important, Eddie!' So the boy, with feigned reluctance, walked around the screen. 'What do you think of this?'

Edward glanced briefly at the canvas. 'It's a fake.'

Charles had already half-convinced himself that he had acquired a painting of great value, and he was somewhat disappointed by this response. 'Now where did you learn little words like that, Edward the Ungenerous?'

The boy resisted the temptation to smile. 'Mum'll kill you when she finds out.'

Charles put down the painting and put one hand against his chest. 'What sweeter death to die. I *don't* think.' And at that Edward did laugh; at once Charles made a lunge for him, picked him up and began tickling his legs and ankles. The boy was helpless with laughter but with one great effort he burst out with, 'Mum'll murder you for spending her money!' Charles stopped tickling him and gravely set him down. Edward stepped back, rubbed his eyes and then looked defiantly at his father; but Charles had once more taken up the portrait and started a low, tuneless whistle as he pretended to look it over. In an effort to placate him the boy put his arms around his waist and whispered, 'It's a fake.'

'Haven't you got something to do, Edward the Unemployed?' Charles hesitated on the last word, seemed to his son to be blushing, and went on, 'I'm busy.' Then he added, in languorous voice, 'I want to be alone, Edwardino.'

In fact something really did seem to be occupying him because he put down the canvas, and from a drawer in his small wooden desk he took out a sheet of paper. He rolled it through his portable typewriter, and then wrote

PART THREE
the bridges of contentment

Charles looked out of the window, so lost in thought that he did not realise how his eyes took fright at the endless sky and how they focussed instead upon a sparrow shivering upon a rooftop opposite. Its left wing seemed to have decayed and the air trembled around it; Charles's eyes shifted again, trying to erase that image.

He had been working for some weeks on a long poem, but he was happy to compose it slowly and infrequently: it was just a matter of time before he was recognised, and he did not believe

[14]

himself to be in any particular hurry. He was so certain of his own gifts that he had no intention of yielding to the conventional anxieties about recognition; not yet.

He was pleased with the line he had just written and with a sudden rush of enthusiasm he picked up the painting again and put it on the desk in front of him. His eyes ached, and for a moment he placed his right hand across them. Then he licked the tip of his index finger and passed it slowly over the painted surface of the four volumes beside the mysterious seated figure: there was now a smear in the dust which covered the canvas, and Charles believed that he could see faint traces of lettering on the books themselves. He licked his finger clean as he contemplated them.

'Dad!'

'Hello!'

'What are you doing, Dad?'

'I'm eating the past.'

'What?'

'I'm engaged in an act of research.'

'Can you come here please?'

Charles was not wholly displeased by this fresh interruption of his work, and with a theatrical gesture he got up and moved the screen aside. 'What is it, Edward the Exasperating?' He was about to advance on his son when the front door opened and Vivien Wychwood walked into the room. Charles stopped in mid-stride and looked almost shyly at her, while Edward called out, 'Hello, Mum', took her arm and tried to lead her into the kitchen. He was hungry.

But she held back. 'How's it going?' she asked her husband quietly.

'Oh, it's going.' He had a sudden image of movement which could not be resisted, and of himself as part of that flow.

'Did your headache come back?'

'No. I gave it to Edward. He wants to take it to school with him.'

'Don't joke about it, Charles. You'd joke on your deathbed.' She looked exhausted after her day's work, but still she managed to smile as Charles feigned death and fell across the sofa, with one arm trailing upon the carpet. Edward sprawled on top of him, and they began a mock fight while Vivien watched them. But, as soon as she had taken off her coat and walked into the kitchen, they stopped. Edward turned on the television and lay in front of it, while Charles lingered in the doorway of the kitchen and watched his wife preparing the evening meal.

'I picked up a bargain today,' he said at last.

Vivien closed her eyes for a moment, already fearing the worst. 'Did you get on with your work, Charles?'

[15]

'I found a portrait which might be extremely valuable.'

'Don't forget that Philip is coming for dinner.' She was chopping some carrots with great ferocity; she was used to his enthusiasms, which generally vanished as quickly as they had arrived, but she still became angry when they interfered with his writing.

Edward called out above the sound of the television, 'He's wasting our money, Mum. It's a fake!'

Vivien showed her anger now, but directed it towards her son. 'Don't talk like that about your father! He works very hard!'

Charles went up to her and gently put his arm around her, as if she were the one who needed defending. 'Won't you just come and look at it, Viv? I think you'll like it.' So with a sigh she turned and followed him into the front room; he ducked behind the screen and then sprang out again, holding the painting in front of him so that his face was hidden from her. 'Voilà!' His voice sounded slightly muffled.

And Edward screamed, 'Mange tout!' This was the only French phrase he knew.

Vivien did not seem particularly impressed. 'Who is it?'

'I didn't buy it,' Charles was saying, 'I exchanged it. Do you remember those books about the flute?'

'But who is it?'

Charles's head appeared from behind the canvas, and he peered around to look at the seated figure. 'Don't you see that very intelligent expression? I think he must be a relation.' Edward gave a loud, hollow laugh.

'He looks shifty to me.'

'But doesn't he look familiar? I can't put my finger on it –'

'You did put your finger on it, Dad.' Edward was no longer pretending to be engrossed in the television programme. 'I saw you.'

Already Vivien seemed to have lost interest in the subject. 'Can I see what you've written today?' she asked, going over to Charles's desk.

Apparently he had not heard her. 'I think he may be a great writer. Look at those books beside him.'

Vivien was looking down at the one line which Charles had composed that afternoon and she said, gently, 'Don't worry if you can't write every day, love. Once you've got rid of those headaches –'

Charles was suddenly very angry. 'Will you please stop talking about that?' For some weeks he had been suffering from intermittent headaches, with the loss of peripheral vision in his left eye. He had seen a doctor, who had diagnosed migraine and given him some pain-killers; this had perfectly satisfied Charles, who considered the naming of his condition almost equivalent to the curing of it. 'I am not sick!' He went over to the window, and looked out at the row of early Victorian houses on the other side of the road; and, as the evening sun gleamed on the faded stucco, he had a vision of the street as some unreal thing without depth or volume: if it was Victorian it was only as a diorama, a roll of canvas which unwound and gave the sensation of a moving world. It was like some dream of oppression, and he knew that he had to wake from it before it enclosed him. 'I'm sorry,' he said, turning round, 'I didn't mean to shout.' Edward was looking at him solemnly. 'You and I, Eddie,' he went on, wanting to change the subject quickly, 'are going to investigate that picture. We're going to solve the mystery.'

Edward got up from the floor and took the hands of both parents, exclaiming, 'We'll all do it!'

But this exchange seemed only to depress Vivien who, slowly releasing her hand and bending down to kiss her son on the top of his head, walked back into the kitchen. 'Philip will be here soon,' she said, 'so both of you get ready.'

*if this is real*

Philip Slack stood uncertainly in the middle of the room; he had known Charles for fifteen years (they had been at university together) but, with his head slightly bowed and his hands moving nervously from the pockets of his jacket to the pockets of his trousers, looking for nothing in particular, it was as if he were still unsure of the welcome, if any, he was about to receive.

Edward turned briefly from the television. 'Where did Dad go?'

'Wine.' Philip looked down as he spoke to the boy, rendering his low voice more sepulchral still. 'Opening the wine.' He always brought two bottles with him on his weekly visit and, when he offered them rather sheepishly, Charles was always surprised by the gift.

Edward smiled at him in a friendly sort of way. 'Can I touch your beard, Philip?'

'Oh.' He hesitated, not quite sure how this could be arranged. 'I suppose so.' He bent down a little, and Edward gave it a sharp tug. 'Ouch!'

'It *is* real.' The boy sounded disappointed.

At this moment Charles came out of the kitchen, carrying the opened bottles of wine. 'You might as well sit down, Philip. You're making our Eddie nervous.'

Philip cleared his throat. 'Here?'

'Anywhere you like.' Charles waved the bottles, spilling some

[17]

red wine on the carpet. 'Everything I have is yours.' Philip carefully looked around before choosing his usual and most uncomfortable chair, while Charles was already stretching out upon the sofa. 'Hard day at the office, dear?'

'Computers.' Philip worked as a public librarian.

'Tell me now, what are they?'

Philip was used to his friend's apparent nonchalance. 'Learning computers. You know.'

'No, I don't know.' He was very cheerful. 'It's funny but I don't, Philip. We unemployed people are rather like that. Essentially we are dreamers. We are on a higher plane.' Edward laughed at his father's joke. 'And that reminds me. I've got something to show you.' He jumped up from the sofa and Philip, nervous at the sudden movement, rose slightly from his own chair. Edward noticed this, and smiled. 'What do you think of it?' Charles brought out the canvas with a flourish and held it a few inches from Philip's face.

'What is it?'

'It's a portrait, I believe. What do you think it is?' He took a few steps back and moved the painting from side to side, with a movement like that of a striptease dancer: Philip could only properly focus on the eyes, which seemed to remain quite steady.

'Who?'

'This is the mystery, Holmes. Once I've solved it, I'm a rich man!' But at this moment Vivien came into the room carrying dishes, and Charles quickly put the canvas away. Philip rose awkwardly to greet her, blushing as he did so. He admired Vivien; he admired her for 'saving' Charles, as he often put it to himself. He was quite objective about this: he knew that her resourcefulness protected Charles just as surely as her patience calmed him and now, as he kissed her on the cheek, he breathed in her warm perfume.

Edward was tugging at the side of her dress, wanting attention. 'Don't touch his beard, Mum. It's real. It hurts.'

After a few moments they sat around the small dining table, and Vivien ladled out the soup. 'What's this?' Edward asked, grimacing at the brown liquid being poured into his plate.

Charles laughed at his son's discomfiture. 'Mulligatawny, Eddie. Old Widow Twankey soup, made from little boys. You never know, you might find one of your friends in it.'

'Don't, Charles.' Vivien was not amused. 'You'll give him bad dreams.'

Edward was looking from one to the other, giggling. Charles whispered something in his ear, and the boy was so bent over with laughter that Vivien had to haul him back up to the table. Then, after some prompting from Vivien, Philip began haltingly

[18]

to talk about his work – how there was a prospect of a strike among the cleaners, how there was talk of banning certain books and newspapers which offended the various prejudices of his colleagues. But the subject of Philip's employment never seemed particularly to interest Charles who, allowing his soup to grow cold, began telling a long and involved story about ghosts to his son. It ended when he cried out, in a high voice, 'You all will die!'

In the general silence which followed this, Vivien cleared the table and then brought out the main course of lamb chops, carrots and chips. Now Charles and Philip, as they often did, began to discuss the contemporaries whom they had first met at university. They exchanged the latest news about certain frustrated or unlucky lives, but the sympathy which both men actually felt went largely unstated. Vivien had been an office secretary before she met Charles and this reticence had surprised her at first; now she took their peculiar obliquities for granted. Of their more successful contemporaries they spoke even less and, when they did so, it was with a tentativeness which bordered on indecision; it was as if both men were aware of the risks of seeming envious. There had been a time when Charles spent many agreeable hours with Philip parodying or abusing, light-heartedly, the work of young writers in whom he saw no possible merit. But in more recent years he had stopped doing this. And Philip, more relaxed now with the wine, was saying, 'There's a new Flint.'

Charles suddenly became attentive, and Philip looked down at his plate. 'A novel,' he added more cautiously.

'What's it called?'

'*Mean Time*.' Philip did not know whether he should smile, and looked at Charles for guidance.

'Oh, very fashionable. Very contemporary. Shall I say picturesque?' Charles was imitating Andrew Flint's rather sonorous rhythms; he knew them well, since he and Flint had been friends at university, when Flint's combination of solemnity and facetiousness had in fact appealed to him. Now he went on to say, 'It's a pity he's such a bad writer.'

'Yes.' Philip always deferred to Charles's judgment in such matters, but he volunteered a small addition of his own. 'I'm surprised he sells.'

'Anything can sell, Philip. Anything can sell.'

Bored with this conversation, Vivien and Edward had taken the plates into the kitchen. It was growing dark, and in the sudden silence between the two men Charles Wychwood could hear the sound of plates being cleared away in other rooms, of voices and laughter in the flats close to his own. For a moment it seemed to him

[19]

that all the inhabitants of this house were unwelcome intruders, like distorted images in someone else's head. 'I hate this place,' he said to Philip. In the deepening twilight they were both now in shadow, and they could look at each other steadily. 'But what am I supposed to do? Where else could we go? Where else could we afford to live?'

Vivien came back in the room and, as soon as she had turned on the light, Charles seemed cheerful once again. 'Why don't you put my book in your library?' he was suddenly asking Philip. 'Then I could claim Public Lending Right.'

'Good idea.' Philip stirred the rhubarb which Vivien had given him. He knew that by 'book' Charles meant the series of poems which he and Vivien had xeroxed. They had stapled them together and then left them at several small booksellers where they had gathered dust on the shelves; as far as Philip knew, they were there still. Vivien sensed his discomfort and offered him some double clotted cream for his rhubarb, and they began to talk of other things. Although neither man ascribed to university any special qualities – quite the reverse – Vivien could not help but notice that, at least when they spoke to each other, their references to their lives after that time were more neutral and less enthusiastic. The years since then seemed to exist only as counters in some kind of game, lacking in real significance and sometimes even in interest. They spoke about recent events flippantly, in phrases or broken sentences, as if they did not deserve sustained attention. And all the time they were wondering, as they ate their rhubarb and cream, what had happened to their own lives.

'Scrope,' Philip eventually said in a low tone, looking deeply into his lap where a strand of rhubarb had fled.

'What?' Charles seemed distracted.

'Do you ever see Harriet Scrope?'

Vivien leaned towards her husband. 'Now there's someone who could help to get you published.'

He was visibly annoyed. 'I don't want help!' Then he added, 'I *am* published.' Harriet Scrope was the somewhat elderly novelist for whom Charles had briefly worked as a secretary; he had not been the tidiest or the most efficient of assistants and they had parted company, amicably enough, after six months; that had been four years ago, but still Charles spoke of her with affectionate familiarity – that is, when he remembered that she existed. And already his anger had gone. 'I wonder,' he said, 'how the old girl is. I wonder . . .' He was about to say something else when Edward, now dressed in his pyjamas, burst into the room and began dancing around his father's chair. 'Where's my story?' he shouted. 'It's getting late!'

Vivien was about to carry him away from the table when Charles put his hand upon her arm to stop her. 'No,' he said, 'he must have his story. Everyone needs stories.' So father and son, in single file, marched into the bedroom, leaving Philip and Vivien alone together. Philip cleared his throat; he moved his empty plate an inch to the right and then moved it back again; his eyes roved around the room, trying not to look at Vivien. And then he spotted the portrait which Charles had left by the desk. 'I wonder,' he said out loud, 'I wonder who that is? May I?' Quickly he rose from the table, and walked over to the painting.

*this is him*

Charles enjoyed telling stories to his son; as soon as he sat on the side of his narrow bed, the words seemed to come easily to him. Not like the words of his poetry, which were clear and precise, but different words, vivid, muddy, rich, extravagant; he called them his story words. And this evening he talked softly to Edward, creating a world where rabbits grew to an enormous size and rolled beneath a violet sky, a world where statues moved and water spoke, where stones yawned beneath gigantic trees. In this world children could live for hundreds of years without growing old, as long as they promised to forget the land of their birth . . . Edward was asleep now. But Charles remained there, sitting beside him, watching his vision slowly fade.

When eventually he came back into the front room, Philip was looking at the face on the canvas. 'Chatterton,' he said.

'I'm sorry. I was miles away.'

Philip turned to him, and his eyes were very bright. 'It's Thomas Chatterton.'

Charles was still dreaming of that other country. 'Thou marvellous boy,' he repeated automatically. 'Who perished in his pride –'

'Look at the high forehead and the eyes.' Philip was unusually insistent. 'Don't you remember the picture I have?'

Charles dimly recalled the reproduction of a portrait, of Chatterton as a young man, which hung in Philip's small flat. 'But didn't he die when he was very small? I mean, when he was very young?' He glanced at Vivien, almost apologetically, but she was reading the evening newspaper. 'Didn't he kill himself?'

'Really?' Philip looked mysteriously at his shoes.

'If you don't believe me.' Charles walked quickly over to his bookcase, and took down a large volume. He found the reference he wanted, and read it out. 'Thomas Chatterton, the faker of medieval poetry and perhaps the greatest literary forger of all time. Born in 1752, died by his own hand in 1770.' He closed the book with a flourish.

[21]

'But it's him.'

'Oh, I say. Bloody marvellous.' Both men had come from poor London families, and on occasions Charles amused Philip with his extravagant parodies of an 'upper class' accent.

But Philip was not to be entertained this evening. 'No, really. It is him.'

Impressed by his friend's earnestness, Charles looked at the portrait again and began seriously to consider this new possibility. 'I did say it was familiar, didn't I, Vivie?' She merely nodded, not looking up from her newspaper. Charles's scepticism was dissolving even as he spoke. 'It might be him . . . who knows?' And then he cried out, in mounting excitement, 'Look at the books beside him! The books may tell us!' Philip peered closely at them, as if by an act of will he could pierce through the patina of age and grime which obscured the canvas.

At this point Vivien got up and took the last dishes into the kitchen, unnoticed by the two men. She knew that the picture afforded Charles yet another opportunity of neglecting his work, and this disturbed her since she believed in his poetry just as much as he did. When she had first met him, at a party some twelve years before, she knew at once how extraordinary he was; and that early recognition had never faded from her memory. Even then he had made her laugh but, as he joked and clowned in front of her, she saw how frail he was: when she married him, soon afterwards, it was really to defend him against the world. She closed the kitchen door behind her but she could still hear their excited voices; then Charles ran in, asking for some warm water and a cloth.

When he came back into the front room, Philip had already placed the canvas in the middle of the floor. Now, slowly, Charles moved the damp cloth across the top of the picture: what had seemed to be a shadow, perhaps of some object outside the range of the artist's vision, resolved itself into a cloud of grime and dust which he was able gently to remove; the colours in the curtains behind the seated figure became richer, and the outlines of its folds became more distinct. These fresh colours and contours seemed to issue from Charles's hand, and it was as if he had become the painter – as if the portrait was only now being completed. 'Just there.' Philip was pointing to some darker letters which had become visible in the upper right-hand corner. 'Can you read them now?'

Charles put his face so close that his breath warmed the canvas, and murmured 'Pinxit George Stead. 1802.' Eagerly he drew the cloth down over the rest of the canvas and scrutinised the four volumes which, in the unaccustomed brightness of the paint, seemed to him to be glowing now. And when the titles became visible he recited them to Philip: they were *Kew Gardens*, *The Revenge*, *Aella* and *Vala*.

Philip rolled over on the floor, and stared at the ceiling; then he started rotating his legs in the air, as he were riding an imaginary bicycle upside down.

'So?' Charles was looking at him in astonishment.

'Those are the books,' Philip said to the air.

'What?'

'Those are Chatterton's books.' He was laughing, apparently at some amusing scene which was taking place on the ceiling.

Charles got up quickly and went back to the reference book which he had consulted a few minutes before, and he noticed how his hands were trembling as he read out loud: 'Thomas Chatterton completed the fake medieval poem, *Vala*, a few days before his suicide, although a burletta, *The Revenge*, has some claim to being his last work.' He went over to Philip and gently lifted him up. 'If he was born,' he was saying, 'I mean – if this is right. If he was born in 1752, and the portrait was painted in 1802, that would make him fifty years old.' He looked at the middle-aged man depicted on the canvas.

'Go on.'

'Which would mean – which would mean – that Chatterton didn't die.' Charles paused, to put his confused thoughts in order. 'He kept on writing.'

Philip's voice was very low again. 'So what happened . . . ?'

He did not complete his question, but already Charles knew exactly what he meant. It was then that the truth came to him. 'He faked his own death.' At that moment the telephone rang, and both men clung to each other for a moment in panic. Then Charles laughed, and in his exhilaration picked up the receiver and crooned, 'How do you do, sir? I've been waiting for you.' But his enthusiasm was quickly checked and, when Vivien came in to discover who had called, he put his hand over the mouthpiece and whispered, 'Harriet Scrope.' As he talked to Harriet he performed a noiseless dance on the carpet, bending his knees slightly while going backwards and forwards with tiny steps. 'She wants to see me,' he said to Vivien as he put down the receiver.

'Why?'

'She didn't say, actually.' And in fact he was not particularly interested; he had been distracted only for a moment and now all his exhilaration returned. He put his arm around Philip's shoulder and together they looked into the eyes of Thomas Chatterton. 'Oh yes,' said Charles at last, 'if this is real, this is him.'

[23]

# 2

HARRIET SCROPE was not happy. She shifted in her decaying wicker chair as small pieces of its material dug into her back and buttocks: it was uncomfortable but she was used to its particular kind of discomfort, and now even took pleasure in it. 'Mother is not well,' she said. She leant back and looked around the room with loathing – at the framed photographs on the mantelpiece, the two side-tables of dark oak, the sofa covered with blue silk, the set of Hogarth prints upon the wall, the deep-pile ultramarine carpet from Peter Jones, the Sony television set, the copy of Johnson's Dictionary which was used as a base for the death mask of John Keats reproduced in a limited edition. When I die, she thought, when I die all this will be taken away – and she tried to imagine these objects existing in other houses when she was dead. And the more she considered this, the more it seemed to her that she was no longer in the room . . .

On waking she looked across at her cat, curled up on the bottom shelf of her bookcase; at once it opened one eye in alarm. 'Mother would like to piss on all this,' she said, 'and then she would like to burn it.' It would be like burning her own life, watching the flames brighten the air.

The door opened slightly, and Harriet stiffened. There was a hand, then a forehead, then two eyes and then a tiny voice. 'Oh, Miss Scrope, I thought you were asleep, actually.' This was Mary, Harriet's new assistant.

She rose from her wicker chair with great dignity. 'I wasn't snoring. I was talking to Mr Gaskell.'

'I'm sorry –'

Harriet crossed her hands upon her breast. 'There's no need to be sorry. I haven't been raped and had a stocking stuffed in my mouth, have I darling?'

Mary assumed that she was addressing the cat, and she smiled at it sympathetically as she came into the room. 'Is there anything you would like, Harriet, actually?'

Harriet winced: she had given this young woman permission to call her by her first name, but it was a decision she now regretted. The idea that in fact she would like to see her stripped to her undies, and then severely whipped, passed briefly through what remained of her consciousness; she smiled at her benevolently. 'No thank you, dear. I'm perfectly dressed and I'm very happy.' She bent down and fondled Mr Gaskell's torn left ear. 'Mother *is* perfect, isn't she?'

A sudden gust of air from the opened door sent Harriet's nostrils quivering, and she turned in alarm to Mary: 'Is there a smell in here?' She dropped to her knees and began sniffing the carpet. Mary was momentarily surprised but, in a gesture of goodwill, she knelt down also and put her nose tentatively in the direction of several suspicious corners. She believed that she already understood her employer very well, and was determined not to be upset by anything she said or did. She had read all of her novels, which she described to her friends as 'interesting, actually', although secretly she was appalled by the peculiarities of Harriet's imagination.

Their bottoms knocked against each other as they waded in tandem across the carpet, and Harriet glanced at her sharply. 'What are you doing with my bum? I'm the only one who's allowed down here.' Mary rose awkwardly, still managing to smile at Harriet who was now experimentally licking a stray tuft from the carpet. She would keep the smile in place until Harriet rose and saw it, because she wanted to impress upon her how much she liked and admired her. And at last Harriet stood up, muttering 'I must have imagined it. I imagine so much these days.'

She turned to Mary in relief. 'Shall we listen to a little music?' She winked at her. 'You young people know all about the food of love, don't you?' She pushed the button on her Grundig Party Boy portable radio, and at once the sound of pop music filled the room. 'Mr Gaskell!' she said gently in reproof, as if it had mischievously altered the channel, and with outstretched arms she made a lunge for the cat which, with a shriek, fled from the room. 'Fuck you!' she shouted as it ran around the door. Then, rather ostentatiously, she changed the setting on the dial to that of a classical radio station and they sat in silence for a while listening to one of Schumann's song cycles. Despite the winningly Romantic music, the words of which had something to do with a missing parrot, Harriet's face assumed a more and more stony expression. Absent-mindedly she put out her hand to stroke the cat, and patted the air instead. But this seemed to console her just as well. 'What is

[25]

Mother going to do?' she murmured to the vacant space. 'What is she supposed to do?'

Mary, always eager to respond, decided that for once Harriet was addressing her. 'About the smell, as it were?'

Harriet seemed not to hear this, and turned off the radio with a flourish just as the parrot was about to reappear with a child's shoe in its beak. 'Did you type out the notes, dear?'

At last Mary knew what Harriet was talking about, and immediately she became enthusiastic. 'Yes, of course. And it seems to me that –' Each day for the last month Mary Wilson had sat with a tape-recorder perched demurely if precariously upon her knees (she had for an instant tried to give the impression that she knew nothing of technical or mechanical matters, but one look from Harriet was enough to dispel the impression that this would endear her to her employer), while Harriet reminisced in a loud if on occasions hesitant voice about her literary past. Whether these memories would comprise the autobiography which her publisher, in a moment of desperation, had suggested to her, or whether they would be incorporated into some form of diary, Harriet had yet to decide. If, that is, the question of a decision ever arose.

'And it seems to me that –'

'Oh yes? Exactly how does it *seem* to you?'

Mary did not notice Harriet's tone. She had just finished a course in English Literature at Oxford University, and was eager to display the knowledge she had acquired in tutorials. 'It seems to me that they have seriously misinterpreted Modernism.'

'And who are *they* exactly, dear?' Harriet always pounced upon the pronoun, which in this usage she regularly denounced as being 'as common as muck'.

Mary faltered. 'The academics, as it were, who falsified . . .'

She did not really know what she was trying to say, and Harriet stopped her.

'So you know what is true and what is false, do you?' Mary coloured slightly, and Harriet relented. She put on her cockney landlady voice, which had been her standard 'funny' turn since the Fifties. 'You really tike the biscuit and neow mistike! Ooh 'allo, what you up ter?' This last remark was addressed to Mr Gaskell, who had charged into the room and suddenly stopped short in front of Harriet's chair. 'Wot's bovering you then? Ooh, I know. I know.' Still reciting this litany to herself Harriet got up and walked towards a small alcove in the corner of the room, where a row of bottles could dimly be seen. She poured herself a gin, but not before asking Mary, 'Anyfink for you, petal?' Mary demurred, very gratefully. 'That's a good girl, then.' She returned with her gin and, settling herself once more in the uncomfortable wicker chair, took a silver tea-spoon which was lying on a side-table. Then she began sipping the gin from the spoon; it was her belief that the alcohol's contact with the metal, combined with the small (if numerous) doses required, prevented her from becoming drunk. This theory had not yet been scientifically verified, however, and there were times when Mary had heard her crooning the words of some popular lyric during the quiet hour when she insisted she was 'putting her feet up'. She was looking at Mary over the rim of her spoon. 'So now that you've typed them, I expect you want to put them together.'

'Sorry?'

'My notes.' She paused for a moment. 'Actually.'

Clearly Mary did not understand. 'I bought a file for them . . .'

Harriet laughed very loudly, and once more the image of her assistant being whipped in front of her gleamed somewhat in that wonderful imagination. 'I was hoping for a little more help than that, Miss Wilson.' She seemed to regret her sudden formality. 'Just to save me time, you know. Time past is time future, after all, isn't it, darling?' She made a grotesque face at the cat, distending her mouth sideways with her fingers, before resuming her conversation. 'Didn't I tell you something about Tom Eliot, and how he danced with me in his office at Fabers?' Mary nodded, although she was now rather anxious about her employer's intentions. 'He was so good to me . . .' Harriet was saying; in fact she remembered very little about the poet, and was not at all sure that he had ever known who she was. Mary assumed a reverential expression, and waited while her employer took four sips of gin in quick succession. 'Why don't you link dear Tom with those bits about Fitzrovia?' She licked the alcohol from her upper lip. 'There must be a connection, you know. I can't think of everything.' She went over to the alcove again and filled her glass: Mr Gaskell followed her, weaving its tail between her legs as she stood in front of the bottles, and she bent down to pour a little of the gin into its saucer which had been left there. She straightened herself with difficulty. 'I can't do it myself. I just can't do it.'

'Can't get up, as it were?'

'No, Miss Wilson. I can always rise. I am rather like Lazarus, in that respect at least.' She left her glass, crossed the room and leaned over Mary; she was so close that her assistant could smell the sweet alcohol upon her breath. 'I can't write about the past. Mother's hands are tied, don't you see?' Her hands came out before her, and she placed one on top of the other as if they were bound together with rope. Mary looked down at them in horror, while at the same time Harriet inspected the brown spots on her wrinkled and faded skin. 'There is so much to hide,' she said.

Mary was alarmed. 'But I can't do it either!'

'Can't do what, dear?'

'I can't write it for you. I can't make it up.'

Harriet was stroking her hair. 'But didn't you know? Everything is made up.'

*whereof we cannot speak*

As soon as Mary had left the house, closing the front door gently behind her, Harriet jumped up and once more found the pop-music station on her radio. As the beat reverberated around the room, and the cat shrank back, she executed a few kicks and twirls with a sudden burst of energy. But she stopped as quickly as she had begun, and gazed into the ormolu mirror which hung above the mantelpiece. 'Listen,' she said to her reflection, mouthing the words of the song, 'let me tell you a secret.'

She turned down the radio and, picking up the telephone, slowly dialled a number. She started talking into the air as soon as her call was answered: 'No, Miss Wilson,' she was saying, 'I'll sign that document later.' Whenever she telephoned, she liked to give the impression that she was in the middle of pressing business. 'Hello, darling, is that you?' She was now addressing a real person, her particular friend Sarah Tilt. 'Are you feeling easier in yourself? Some bowel movements, I hope? Good. At last. Listen, darling, Mother was planning a little visit.' There was a pause. 'Yes, it *is* rather important.' She grimaced at Mr Gaskell, and whispered to it, 'Don't tell!' Then she turned back to her friend's increasingly impatient voice. 'What was that, dear? No, I shan't be staying long.' She put down the receiver, slapped it and murmured, 'Bitch!'

As soon as she left the house she felt exhilarated. She lived in a small street off Bryanston Square – the area near Marble Arch which she still insisted on calling Stucconia or, when she was especially playful, Tyburnia. She took particular delight in showing visitors the small plaque which marks the spot where the gallows had once stood: 'They were hanged for sixpence,' she used to say, 'and now there's no such coin! What strange tricks history plays on our pockets.'

But this afternoon she was heading towards Bayswater, where Sarah Tilt lived. Despite a great deal of evidence to the contrary, Harriet still believed that walking 'calmed' her and that something

close to a forced march helped her to 'work things out'. In the
course of these long and erratic journeys she had renamed all the
familiar streets around her, and now it was through The Valley of
Bones, Tarts' Paradise and The Boulevard of Broken Dreams that
she made her way. When she entered The Valley of Bones (so
named because of the gleaming white façades of the Georgian
mansions there), she began to brood upon her inconclusive conversation with Mary. Of course Harriet could not write out everything
herself. If she told the truth, and described the real story of her
life, if she revealed what even to herself she called her 'secret',
there would be an outcry against her, a cleansing and a purification
which, she was sure, would lead to her death . . . And she
trembled with anticipation as she passed The Boulevard of Broken
Dreams (a homosexual pick-up area) and turned into Tarts'
Paradise.

At once she was on the alert, looking out for any signs of 'the
action', as she used to describe it to Sarah Tilt; but it was too early
for any sustained activity from the prostitutes who frequented this
street, and Harriet irritably tried to recall what it was she had
been thinking. But she could not remain introspective for long:
something kept her back, making her attention swerve away from
herself and accelerate in a different direction. She could penetrate
a little way into herself but then the procedure went into reverse
and she was forced upwards again into the world: the experience
was like that of falling.

Her fur hat slipped over the corner of her left eye and with a
sigh she pushed it back again, gently fingering the small stuffed
bird which was pinned to it; now, with both eyes back in action,
she looked about her with renewed interest. A blind man was
walking along Tarts' Paradise; he paused uncertainly a few yards
from her and tapped his stick in a circle in front of him. 'All you
need, old man,' she said to herself, 'is a circle of stage fire.' Eagerly
she went up to him, adopting once again her extravagant cockney
accent. 'Can I 'elp, mite? I'm a pensioner meeself.'

'I want the Post Office.'

'I'm walking that deerection,' she said, 'I'll tike yer.' The man
allowed himself to be grabbed by Harriet, although it seemed to
her that he showed very little sign of gratitude. His face was
impassive, however, and for a moment she glanced with fear at
his white, upturned eyes. If he should be able to see her, after all
. . . 'Where's your dawg, then?'

'He's sick.' The man held out his stick, as if he were still
unaccompanied. 'He's very old.'

They walked for a moment in silence. 'You know I wos goin'

[29]

blind once. I 'ad cataracts.' Harriet enjoyed inventing stories about herself. 'I wos in a right stite abaht it.'

'Is that right?'

'You nevah know, do yer?'

'It's not all bad,' he said. 'The less you see, the more you can imagine.' He turned his face sideways to her, smiling, and she flinched. 'You wouldn't think I knew anything about colours, would you?'

'Oh, I dunno.'

'But I do. I have all these colours in my head.'

'Yeah?'

'Sometimes,' he added, 'it's better not to see.'

They were silent again for a while and Harriet clutched him more tightly, as if she were the one who needed direction. 'Kin you feel that fur?' she asked eventually, putting his hand upon her coat. 'That wos expensive, that wos! And,' she added, expansively, 'I've got a 'at to match. Pity you can't see it, it cost a bomb it did.' She was enjoying her new identity. 'When my old man passed on, 'e left me a bit, you see. 'E woz a taxidermist. Do yer know wot I mean when I siy taxidermy? I mean stuffin wiv odds and bobs.' The old man nodded, but to Harriet he seemed uneasy. Could he tell from the tone of her voice that she was making up a story? And then it occurred to her how strange it was to be looking at someone who could not return that look: the horror of blindness lay less in being unable to see than in not knowing when you were being watched. 'Tell me,' she said, ''ow do yer keep yerself clean?'

'I wash,' he said sharply, 'like everyone else.'

'Yes, but 'ow do yer know . . .' She was going to ask how he could tell what everyone else did, but as she stared into his wounded attentive face she began to enter the darkness which enshrouded him. She began to imagine his life, feeling herself stumble and fall, so she pulled back. ''Ere you are, mite,' she said cheerfully. 'It's just dahn on the right. 'Ave an 'appy diy, luv.' She turned away from him and, for a moment, she closed her eyes and became blind.

*thereof we must be silent*

Harriet was standing demurely in the corridor when Sarah Tilt opened the door. They kissed each on the cheek and then Sarah stepped back: 'I see,' she said, 'that you're wearing your Guards uniform.' And indeed Harriet's fur hat, which had slipped down again to the level of her eyebrows, did in part resemble a bearskin.

[30]

'I thought if I wore fur, you would forgive me.' This remark meant nothing to Sarah, but she was used to her inconsequence. 'You seem to be looking well,' Harriet added.

'Whenever I hear that, I panic.'

'Well, go on then. Panic.' She walked through the hallway into the sitting room.

Sarah followed, poking out her tongue at her old friend's fur-clad back, and then asked her if she would care for 'Coffee?' She waited eagerly for her look of disappointment, which she knew Harriet found impossible to disguise, before going on. 'Or would you prefer something with a spoon?'

Harriet giggled and held up her index finger. 'Just a tot, dear. Give Mother a gin while she's still got the strength to swallow.'

'And I've got the strength to watch.'

Harriet had not heard this muttered aside. She had removed her fur hat, raising it above her head with both hands as if she were taking part in a disrobing ceremony of great antiquity; her capacious fur coat was more of a struggle, requiring a whole repertoire of movements before she could escape from it.

'Finished?' Sarah surveyed the expensive garment with a certain hostility.

'Not finished, dear, just abandoned.' Harriet accepted the glass of gin and the silver tea-spoon which Sarah now offered her, and looked around the room as she took her first lingering sip. 'You know,' she went on, 'this always reminds me of a psychiatrist's office. Not that I've ever been to a psychiatrist, of course. I won't be poked around.' Sarah's flat was furnished in a modern 'functional' style which, together with her collection of paintings in the Fifties abstract tradition, gave the room a somewhat chilling quality. Harriet began to stick the bottom half of her body into a corner, and for one horrible moment Sarah thought that she was about to relieve herself there.

'What is this,' Harriet asked, 'that I am about to lower myself onto?' The object in question resembled a plank sawn in half and mounted on an oil drum.

'It's called a chair.'

'But why is it black? I don't want to sit on black things.'

'Not even your cat?'

'Well, the exception proves the rule.'

Sarah chose not to respond to this particular remark. 'That chair is very good for the posture, although God knows –'

Harriet broke in. 'But it's not very good for a Chanel dress, is it?'

Sarah eyed her once 'chic' red skirt with disapproval. 'Not when

[31]

it's almost in rags, no.' And then she added, not able to stop herself smiling, 'You look like a dog's dinner.'

'Oh yum yum. What's for tea?' Both women laughed, and then sighed deeply.

'Well,' said Harriet, perched now upon the chair, 'let's try to be bright and cheerful. Ask me what I've been doing.'

'I haven't got a strong enough stomach.'

'No. Go on. Ask me.'

Sarah was determined not to be bullied into submission. 'Have a nice banana, dear. You're supposed to be the Queen of Romance, after all.' This was the title Sarah had given her many years ago, although Harriet's novels were generally considered mournful to the point of being macabre.

Harriet looked down at the fruit bowl. 'Where do they come from? The Third World?' She uttered the last phrase with distaste.

'I don't know where they've come from,' Sarah replied. 'But I do know where they're going.' And she took one of them, peeled and began greedily to eat it. It was an old woman's greed and it fascinated Harriet, who had been trying to imagine what she herself looked like when she ate. And she watched as Sarah daintily cleaned her upper lip, above which Harriet thought she could detect the first faint signs of a moustache. 'Bananas help you see in the dark,' Sarah said, putting away her handkerchief. 'Or is that,' she added, smiling furtively at Harriet, 'just an old wives' tale?'

'I wouldn't know, would I? But that does remind me of something.' Harriet sprang out of the chair. 'I met a most peculiar blind man today. He told me he was a taxidermist. I never thought a blind man could *lie*, did you? Except,' she went on after a pause, 'you do get blind poets, don't you?'

'Aren't they generally led by a boy?'

Harriet did not reply to this, and she was already mimicking the actions of the man she had met upon her journey to Sarah's, closing her eyes and feeling her way around the small sitting room. 'Where's my dog?' she moaned. 'Where's Old Dog Tray?'

She was putting her hands over several valuable artefacts, but Sarah resisted the temptation to scream at her. 'You'll give yourself a coronary, dear,' she said gently. She had noticed before how age and relative fame had rendered Harriet less peaceful: the more she wrote, it seemed, the less coherent her personality became. 'Why don't you sit down for a moment?'

Harriet stood in the middle of the room, rolling her eyes towards the back of her head in imitation of the blind man. Then she gazed at Sarah in feigned astonishment: 'What brave new world is this,'

[32]

she said, 'which has such women in it?' Sarah pointed towards the chair, and Harriet sat down. 'I don't like the blind,' she added. 'They make my toes curl.'

'I didn't know,' Sarah said sweetly, 'that you had any feelings in that quarter.'

'Mother has feelings of which you know nothing.' Harriet looked at her sternly. 'She's all heart, and she always has been.'

This was one of her most familiar claims, and it suggested that all other topics of conversation had now been exhausted. Harriet closed her eyes, and tried to stretch out in the chair; but it had no back to it, and she fell against the wall. Sarah was still not sure why Harriet had insisted on visiting her this particular afternoon, but she believed that she had already been given quite enough attention and ignored the squawk which came from her old friend as she toppled backwards. 'Well,' she said out loud. 'Now let's see. What have *I* been doing?'

There was a protracted silence. 'You were stripped and left for dead?' Harriet suggested, struggling slowly towards an upright position. 'Or was it something unpleasant?'

Sarah ignored her. 'I've been working very hard on the book.' There was a note of defiance in her voice.

'Really?' Harriet knew that Sarah had been engaged on this project, a study of the images of death in English painting and provisionally entitled *The Art of Death*, for the last six years and still seemed to be no nearer completing it. 'Still throwing our bucket down that old well, are we?' Sarah looked at her angrily, and Harriet retreated a little. 'I'm sorry,' she said. 'You know that death makes me nervous.'

'Everything makes you nervous.' Sarah was tempted to change the subject at once, since she was in fact afraid of Harriet's scorn, but she needed to speak about it; this book would not let her rest. She had examined the various images of death, from the medieval depiction of the emaciated cadaver to the theatrical richness of Baroque funerary monuments, from the lugubrious narratives of Victorian genre painting to the abstract violence of contemporary art, and so she was now able to chart many of the alterations in the presentation of the death-bed scene, natural or pathetic, violent or solitary. And all the time it had been as if she were watching her own death.

But then Sarah felt compelled to range wider – to understand everything, to recognise and to explain the imagery of death in all of its manifestations. She studied the *artes moriendi* of the seventeenth century; she visited museums in Greece and Italy in order to sketch reliquary urns; she documented the smallest changes in burial rites; she read manuals on dissection and embalming; she investigated the Romantic cult of the dead; in whatever town or city she found herself, she made a point of visiting its cemetery. And, as she did all this, she exorcised her own fears. She turned death into a spectacle. Yet, despite all of her research, she could not bring herself to complete the book; she had written certain chapters, and had made copious notes on the rest, but the final exposition of the subject resisted her. It would not stay still. And she was aware, too, that its completion would reinstate all of her old fears. For this would be her last book.

'I need more time,' she was saying to Harriet. 'I have all the ideas.' She pointed towards her head. 'And I have the pictures –'

'Have you got any new ones?' Harriet was growing impatient with her.

Sarah knew this, and broke off her usual complaints to recite the list of paintings which she had just located. 'The Death of Bunyan, The Death of Voltaire, The Death of –'

Harriet gave a little shudder of pleasure. 'But you don't know,' she said, stopping her in mid-sentence, 'you don't know how they really died, do you?' She was loudly stirring the tea-spoon in her empty glass and Sarah, with a practised air of martyred resignation, rose to refill it. 'They were painted from the imagination, weren't they?' Harriet added as she grabbed the bottle and filled her own glass.

Sarah stared at her: there were occasions when Harriet spoke like a child, and she was never quite sure how deliberate this was. 'They could hardly have done it at the time, darling. Some of these paintings took years to finish. And bodies rot. As you know very well.'

'So what did the artists use?' Again, the child's question.

'They used models, as they were supposed to.'

'Models? Models pretending to be dead?'

'As far as I know, they weren't killed on the spot. What do you want? Blood?'

Harriet was tapping the spoon against the tip of her nose. 'And so the dead can be exalted by others feigning death?'

'The whole point of death is that it can be made beautiful. And the real thing is never very pretty. Think of Chatterton –'

Harriet, now becoming bored by the excessive sobriety of the conversation, sprang up from her black chair. 'Cut is the bough,' she said, 'that might have grown full straight.' And she doubled up, as if she were about to be sawn in half.

'Branch.' Sarah was very deliberate.

'I'm sorry?'

'It was a branch, dear, not a bough. If you were quoting.'

Harriet stood upright again. 'Don't you think I know? I've been quoting all my life!' Then she began again: 'We poets in our youth begin in gladness.' She waved her hands joyfully in the air. 'But thereof in the end come despondency and madness.' She stuck her tongue out of the side of her mouth, and rolled her eyes. Then she sat down, rather heavily, and took another sip of gin. 'Of course I knew it was a quotation,' she added, 'I've given my life to English literature.'

Sarah was still very cool. 'It's a pity, then, that you didn't get anything in return.'

Harriet tried, but failed, to look 'hurt'. 'I am supposed to be famous, at least.'

'Yes, and I hear they're ready to have you stuffed.' Sarah paused. 'Which will be the first time in years.'

Harriet giggled. 'Let the blind man do it.' She put her hands in her lap and squeezed them. 'But he'll have to do it through the mouth. Every other orifice is closed.'

'Well, at least let's hope he begins with the mouth, dear.'

Harriet decided not to reply in kind, and with studied nonchalance she took up an art magazine which was lying upon Sarah's glass table. 'Ah,' she said, 'Seymour. My favourite.' She leafed through the reproductions of Joseph Seymour's most recent paintings, which had been included in a fulsome obituarial tribute. 'What do you think of this?' she asked Sarah, holding up one of them and almost ripping the page in the process. It was of a child standing in front of a ruined building; the child stared out from the canvas, while above him rose a series of small decayed rooms. Seymour had carefully painted the torn wallpaper, the broken pipes, the abandoned furniture, all of which seemed to spiral inwards towards a vanishing point in the middle of the painting; in contrast, the face of the child was featureless, abstract.

Sarah did not share Harriet's admiration for Seymour's work. 'Why don't you buy it? He's one of those realists you seem to like.'

Harriet put down the magazine and walked over to the window. 'But who's to say,' she asked as she stared down into the small courtyard below, 'who's to say what is real and what is unreal?'

'You should know. You're the one who's writing her memoirs.'

'Actually, that's why I came to see you.' Harriet had at last remembered the real purpose of her visit. 'The truth is, you know, that I just can't. I mean –' She hesitated, but she could not resist the little barb. 'I think I'm getting like you, Sarah. I can't finish them. I'm getting nowhere.' Sarah put out her legs and peered down at her stockings, smoothing them with her hand as she did so: it made her feel more comfortable as she waited for Harriet to continue. 'The point is, you see, that I've really got nothing to *say*.' And, with her back still turned, she mimed the open mouth and staring eyes of a simpleton.

'What you really mean is that you have too much to say.'

Harriet turned her head in alarm. 'What do you mean, too much?'

Sarah could sense her anxiety. 'I don't really mean anything –'

'Naturally.'

'– except that you have met a great many people, and written a great many books. And lived,' she paused for emphasis. 'For a relatively long time.'

Harriet could see Seymour's painting of the child standing in front of the ruined building, and for a moment she closed her eyes. 'I wish,' she said, 'that I could begin all over again.'

'Don't be absurd!' The thought of such a rebirth was appalling to Sarah. 'You know it's been a triumph!'

'A triumph? Just look at me.' Harriet turned around, holding out her hands as if in supplication.

Sarah looked down. 'What you need,' she said quietly, 'is an assistant.'

'I have an assistant. I have that silly little bitch, Mary *Wilson*.' She imitated the young woman's high, plaintive voice. 'Who begins every sentence with, *It seems to me*.'

'No, I mean someone who can help you write. You need someone to inspire you.'

It was at this moment that Harriet remembered Charles Wychwood; he had not been the most reliable of secretaries, as far as she could recall, but he was a poet, of sorts, and he had managed to make her laugh.

And it was on the same evening that she telephoned him, just as he was cleaning the portrait he had found in the House Above the Arch. She did not want to discuss the matter on the 'phone, she had said as Charles stared excitedly into the eyes of Thomas Chatterton. 'What did that ridiculous German say?' she went on. 'Whereof we cannot speak, thereof we must be silent?'

# 3

HARRIET SCROPE was preparing a sandwich. 'Mustard!' she shouted, and raised the little yellow pot in triumph. 'Pickles!' She unscrewed the jar. 'Lovely grub!' She dug her knife into a small tin of Gordon's Anchovy Spread, and smeared it over two slices of white bread before adding these seasonings. 'Look at you,' she said to the pungent meal she had created, 'You're so colourful! You're much too good to eat!' Nevertheless she managed to take a large bite and, widening her eyes, swallowed vigorously. But, even though she enjoyed the prospect of eating, she detested the actual physical process: whenever she ate she looked about anxiously and now, as more large pieces of anchovy, pickle and mustard travelled down her alimentary canal, she stared at Mr Gaskell as if she were seeing the cat for the first time. Then she grabbed it and began unmercifully to kiss its whiskers as it struggled in her firm hands. 'I suppose,' she said, 'you want some pickles, my loveliness. But pickles are for human beings. At least I think that's what Mother is.' She held it out at arm's length, and engaged in one of her 'staring matches' with it: Mr Gaskell blinked first, and with a cry of 'Victory!' she kissed it again. As she did so it began sniffing the traces of anchovy on her breath, and she put it down quickly. 'Tell me,' she whispered, 'do you ever dream of Mother?' She closed her eyes for a moment and tried to imagine the cat world: there were walking shadows everywhere, and she saw the large dark outline of one of her own shoes. Then the door bell rang.

She crept down the dark corridor, letting out a soft 'Miaow', and it was only when she had almost reached the door that she remembered she was expecting Charles Wychwood to call. 'Just a minute!' she shouted, and she rushed up the stairs into the bathroom where feverishly she cleaned her teeth. From the small window beside the sink she looked down at him, as he stood on the white-washed stone path that led to her front door: he seemed to be in the middle of a day-dream and, as his pale face flinched under the impulse of some private thought, she pitied him.

Suddenly he looked up and, noticing her at the window, he grinned. 'The Lady of Shalott,' he said.

Instinctively she raised her hand in greeting although the gesture, seen from ground level, might equally have been one of farewell. 'More like Lady Chatterley,' she said to herself as she rushed down the stairs and once more into the hall; but then she skidded to a halt. She opened the front door cautiously in order to make absolutely sure that it was indeed Charles (for there were occasions now when she did not trust the evidence of her own eyes).

Charles, assuming that this was one of Harriet's little jokes, popped his head through the crack and said, 'How's Miss Scrope?'

She gave a little shriek and stepped back, before opening the door properly to let him enter. 'I thought,' she said, 'that you were Mr Punch come to get me.' He did not look well, and she dimly recollected having seen him wear the same clothes four years ago.

'Ah, Racine,' he said as she led him into the front room. 'Have you been reading *Andromaque* or *Bérénice*?'

His speech seemed a little slurred, and for a moment she imagined he had been drinking. Or perhaps the furnishing of the room had reminded him of the French tragedian. 'I don't quite . . .' she began, but Charles was pointing towards a book which lay on the wicker chair. 'Oh,' she said, 'you saw the wrong word. I thought I was going mad for a minute.' On the chair was a form-book for horses with the single title, *RACING*, on its cover. But he seemed not at all discomfited by his mistake, and at once went over to the sofa where he began to caress Mr Gaskell: he and the cat had always enjoyed each other's company, a fact which for a time had led to a certain deterioration in Harriet's own relationship to her pet. She coughed loudly, in order to scare it off. 'And so how are you, Charles?' She hesitated. 'You're looking very well.'

'Am I?' He brightened. 'I've never felt better, as they say.'

'Is that what they say?'

'Yes, that's what they say.' Suddenly he felt depressed, but he knew the mood would never last and decided to ignore it. 'And how are you?' he asked her, putting his hands behind his head and stretching out. He had not been in Harriet's house for four years, but he felt immediately at ease here. 'How long has it been now since we met?'

'Oh, I never change, you know. I'm still good old Harriet.' She restrained an impulse to throttle the cat, which was licking Charles's hand, and instead she started walking around the room, touching various objects with a restless, undirected energy. But when she came to the death mask of John Keats she stopped.

[38]

'Are you still writing poetry?' she asked him in a loud voice.

'Of course.' She had made it sound like a hobby. 'I've brought you my latest book.' From the pocket of his jacket he took out the slim xeroxed pamphlet.

'That is sweet of you. You shouldn't have.' She glanced at the contents and, realising that Charles was watching her carefully, nodded, smiled, turned back one page apparently to re-read one particular stanza, and then gave a little sigh of pleasure before dropping the pamphlet onto the carpet. 'I must introduce you to my publisher,' she went on, for want of anything more constructive to say. 'He's –' she hesitated. 'He's very good with poets.'

Charles leaned back on the sofa, and raised his arms above his head as if he were about to yawn. 'There's plenty of time. I'm in no hurry.' Then he added in a deep, mock-solemn voice, 'My genius will one day be recognised.' Harriet said nothing, and so he went on quickly with, 'Vivien sends you her love.'

'That is nice. Do send her mine.' She could not for the moment remember who Vivien was, but she used her sudden rush of affection for this unknown woman to move on to her prepared speech. 'Charles, the reason I telephoned was, I mean is, that I am not myself.'

'Who are you?'

'No, I'm serious. I need your help. I need bringing out.' He had put his head to one side, and was still smiling. 'I was wondering if you would like to come and work with me again?' She was quite serene as she said this but she kept her hands firmly in her lap, as if without this restraint they might spring to life and carve strange shapes in the air in front of her.

'This is very unexpected,' he said, without looking in the least surprised. In fact he was unsure how to reply. A few days ago he would have responded eagerly to Harriet's offer; but the portrait of Thomas Chatterton had inspired him, and he did not wish to be distracted from his pursuit of its significance. And yet Harriet might be able to help with that, as well . . .

She watched him, remembering how difficult it was for him to come to any decision. 'Just say no,' she murmured, leaning towards him, 'if you don't want to do it.'

'It's not that . . .'

'I know you must be very busy.' She picked up Charles's pamphlet of poems and began to leaf through it. 'With your work, that is.' She looked down at one poem with great interest, while all the time trying to recall the rest of what she had prepared to say. 'You once told me a very beautiful thing, Charles. You told me that reality is the invention of unimaginative people.' In fact she had

[39]

come across the phrase in a book review but Charles smiled, delighted to be reminded of words he must once have used. She pressed home her obvious advantage. 'But can we go one step further? Can we imagine the reality?'

He settled back again on the sofa, quite at ease with the sort of theoretical discussion he had once had at university; in fact, his understanding of such matters had not significantly advanced since that time. 'Oh yes,' he said, 'it's a question of language. Realism is just as artificial as surrealism, after all.' He remembered these phrases perfectly. 'The real world is just a succession of interpretations. Everything which is written down immediately becomes a kind of fiction.'

Harriet leaned forward eagerly, not bothering to understand what he thought he was saying, but looking for another opening. 'That's it, Charles,' she said triumphantly. 'That is precisely why I need you. I need you to *interpret* me!' She stressed the verb, as if it had come as a revelation to her. 'You see I'm trying to write my memoirs –'

'Oh, your memoirs. Memories. Memorials.' He had wanted to keep talking, but now he did not know where these words were coming from. 'Mimosas.' He was puzzled at himself.

'– but I can't put them together. I have all the names and dates. I have my notes and my diaries. But I can't.' She searched for the word. 'Interpret them.'

'But I don't know how . . .'

She cut him off, brandishing his pamphlet. 'You know how to write. Everybody knows that. You write like an angel.' She was watching him carefully. 'And I'll pay you well.'

She regretted saying this almost at once, but Charles did not seem to have heard Harriet's generous offer. He was wondering how so many people already knew that he wrote well: 'everybody' was surely an exaggeration, but if Harriet said so . . . suddenly he was filled with confidence. 'So you want me to write your memoirs for you, do you?'

'I want you to become my ghost writer.'

This phrase appealed to him and, in any case, he prided himself on his ability to take sudden but appropriate decisions. 'Miss Scrope,' he said, 'I will be your ghost.' He smiled at her. 'I will be the finest ghost you ever saw.'

*the first sign*

'Chatterton! Chatterton! Chatterton!' Edward was marching around the room, calling out his favourite new word; he had a piece of toast in his hand, and with it he was writing the letters in the air.

'Edward the Unquiet, you are giving me a headache.' Or, rather, Charles feared one. He was attempting to fix the portrait to the wall, but it would not stay still. Either the nail was too small or the edge of the stretcher too narrow: the canvas slipped in one direction or slid off the nail altogether, and it was only with difficulty that he managed to prevent it falling to the floor. But he was always happy to be busy at this time in the morning, just as Vivien was about to leave for her own work, even though he often returned to bed immediately afterwards. The picture fell against his head, and Edward shrieked with laughter.

'Do you want me to get it framed?' Vivien asked him. She worked as a secretary in Cumberland and Maitland, a small art gallery in New Chester Street: she had taken the job hesitantly since from the early days of their marriage Charles had assured her that they would 'manage', that it was only a 'matter of time' before his writing was successfully published. He had repeated these assurances in the most placid way as they grew poorer and poorer but, when finally she announced that she had taken a job, she expected him to be angry or at least impatient with her for not trusting his judgment. But he had smiled, and said nothing. Since that time he had rarely mentioned her work and, when she had wanted to discuss some problem or argument at the gallery, he assumed a slightly puzzled expression – as if he was not at all sure that he knew what she was talking about.

He had put his head against the canvas in order to balance it, and she repeated her question. 'Framed? No, I don't think so, Vivie. I don't want to leave it with anyone just yet. You know how it is.'

Yes, she did know: she suspected, at least, that Charles did not want to be told that the painting was quite worthless. But she restrained her impatience and bent down towards Edward so that he could fasten the clasp on the back of her pearl necklace; this was always the moment of the morning which her son anticipated and, as he 'did her up', he put his arms around her and smelt the perfume on her neck. She took his hands and kissed them, which always made him laugh. 'And what are you going to do with your holiday, Eddie?'

'I'm going out with Dad.' He still had his face buried in her neck and hair, so that his voice was muffled. 'He says it's important.'

Charles had finally managed to place the canvas on the wall, and he stepped back to look at it. 'We're going to investigate you,' he said to the middle-aged man depicted there, with his right hand resting above his books. 'We're going to find your secrets.'

Vivien gently disengaged herself from her son's arms and stood up: she was about to say something to Charles but, when she saw the enthusiasm on Edward's face, she decided not to. She turned to leave but, before she could reach the door, there was a sudden noise: the portrait came off the wall and fell, face down, upon the carpet.

'Now he's sick!' Edward shouted. 'Chatterton is sick!'

'Will you stop it, Eddie? My head really does ache now.' Then Charles saw the look of anxiety which had passed over Vivien's face and he added, in a theatrical tone, 'And a drowsy numbness pains my sense.'

'I have to go,' Vivien said. 'I'm late. Take care of each other.' But it was with a slight reluctance that she left them together.

Later that morning they set off for the House above the Arch. As soon as he knew in which direction they were meant to go, Edward led the way and occasionally tugged impatiently at his father's sleeve as Charles wandered behind him: whenever he was with his son, outside the house, he became abstracted and uncertain. They were about to turn into Dodd's Gardens when Charles hesitated and then stopped. He looked up at a dusty elm which shuddered as the traffic passed it. 'How many leaves,' he asked his son, 'would you say were on that tree?'

'Seven thousand, four hundred and thirty two. And a half.'

'And how long would it take for the wind to blow them all down?'

But Edward was no longer listening. 'Here we are, Dad.'

'And how long has it been standing here?'

Edward placed his hands against his father's back and propelled him around the corner into the quiet street. They stopped for a moment and Charles pointed to the arch with the decaying stone house above it: 'There it is!' he said, 'that's where all the secrets are buried!'

Edward took his hand; together they passed under the arch and into the small courtyard where now the sign read 'Leno's Antiques. La Crème de la Crème. Come and Taste It.' As they climbed the narrow stairs they could hear a treble voice singing a hymn, or a dirge, and Edward started nervously to giggle.

'Don't laugh!' His father was very stern with him as he knocked. There was a silence, a cough, the sound of a drawer being locked, and then the door was swung violently open.

'Oh yes?' Mr Leno was looking down at Edward, and seemed to be addressing the child. 'Who is this?'

Edward stared back up at him placidly, and they might have

[42]

stood gazing at each other for some time if another voice had not called from within, 'Advance their legions, let them see my eagles and my trumpets!' At this moment Mr Leno stuck out his tongue at the boy, who indignantly returned the gesture before being ushered into the presence of Mrs Leno. 'A sprig,' she said. 'Will he ever grow?'

Edward put his hands into his pockets and scowled at her. 'I'm three inches taller than last year.'

Charles smiled benignly at both of them during this short exchange before turning to Mr Leno. 'Hi, I'm Wychwood. I came here last week and gave you my books for a picture.'

Mr Leno was looking gravely down at Edward. 'I suppose he wants to return it now. What do you think?'

'No,' Charles said quickly, 'I want to keep it. I just want some information.'

Mrs Leno pointed at Edward. 'Does he play an instrument, too, or does he just stand there?' The boy was now blushing miserably and, in his embarrassment, he went over to a corner and peered into a large stone urn which had been placed on top of some old theatrical magazines.

'I was wondering . . .' Charles began again, and at once the Lenos became very still. 'I was wondering if you *did* know anything else about that picture?'

'Does she know anything about it?' Mr Leno addressed the question towards Edward's back.

And for some reason the boy turned around and cried, 'Yes, she does!'

Mrs Leno accelerated backwards in her chair and retreated up the ramp into the room beside the shop. 'She likes you,' her husband said to Edward, who tried to conceal his satisfaction at this news by playing with two ancient puppets he had found propped up against the urn. 'Be careful with my babies,' Mr Leno added, 'they might bite.' And he bared his teeth at Edward.

Now his wife rolled back into the room as abruptly as she had left it, holding out a red ledger in front of her as if it were a warning light of some kind. Then she placed it upon her lap, and folded her hands across it.

'Well?' she asked. 'Tell me about this so-called picture.'

'It was of Chatterton.' Charles was suddenly distracted by Edward, who had dropped one of the puppets into the stone vessel and was vainly trying to reach it. 'I mean it was of a middle-aged man. It was lying over there.'

Mrs Leno opened the ledger with a flourish and began minutely to examine it. 'Portrait of an Unknown Man,' she said at last. 'Early

[43]

nineteenth century. A party by the name of Joynson. Colston's Yard, Bristol, Somerset. Or is it called Avon now?'

'Is that the name of the man in the picture?' Charles sounded dismayed.

'No, that was the vendor.'

He relaxed a little. 'So he sold it to you?'

'You are a poet. Naturally you own a thesaurus. Vendor. Seller. Death of a salesman.'

'And you said the name was . . . ?'

'J as in jabber, o as in orifice, y as in yours truly, n as in nostril, and then son.' She glanced tenderly in Edward's direction, but he had almost completely disappeared inside the stone urn. 'As in unruly son.'

'And did you say Colston's Yard, Bristol?'

'Where else?' Slowly she began to retreat backwards and, mur- muring 'Busy old fool', disappeared once more into the adjoining room.

'Help! Dad!' Edward's voice came from within the urn, where he now found himself trapped after his vain attempt to retrieve the puppet.

Mr Leno turned to Charles. 'May I touch him?' Charles nodded, and with a grim smile the proprietor of the House above the Arch walked over to the urn and grabbed Edward's legs before hauling him out. 'I told you,' he said, 'that they might bite.'

'That thing smells!' Edward was a little shaken.

'Of course it smells. It's a funereal monument.' He gravely shook hands with the boy and Edward gave a little bow in return as his father, taking his shoulder, steered him towards the door.

As they descended the stone steps, they heard once again the sound of high-pitched singing or wailing. Edward gave a little yodel, and Charles stopped him. 'Don't,' he said. 'It's rude to imitate people.'

### real or unreal

There was only one Joynson listed in the Bristol directory, a Cuthbert Joynson of Bramble House, Colston's Yard. And it sounded to Charles as if an elderly man answered when he tele- phoned and asked for the person of that name.

'She's not here. I don't enquire where she is. I don't know where she is. I don't care where she is.'

Charles merely assumed that the old gentleman had misheard him and was talking about his wife, Mrs Joynson.

'No, it was you I wanted. It was about the portrait.'

[44]

'I don't know anything about portraits. I don't know anything about pictures. I don't know anything about art.'

'I think you sold one to Leno's Antiques.'

'Oh never mind about that now.' There was a pause, and Charles thought he heard a rustling sound. 'Did you say you wanted me?' The old gentleman sounded a little more accommodating. 'Come here.' He spoke as if Charles were in the next room.

'I'm in London.'

'A cockney boy, are you? I hope you haven't got any tattoos.' Charles confirmed that he had none. 'Oh well, never mind. Come down anyway.' And he replaced the receiver before Charles had any opportunity to arrange a time for this prospective meeting. Far from finding this conversation unsatisfactory or even unusual, however, he considered it to be a triumph of persuasion and tact: he was already looking forward to his journey to Bristol, when he might resolve the secret of Chatterton's portrait with the help of this sympathetic old gentleman. At least this was how he described it that evening to Philip, who was at once eager to join him.

'The quest begins on Saturday,' Charles said excitedly. 'Oh do not ask what is it. Let us go and make our visit!'

*walk through the gate*

When he woke up, on the following morning, he was alone. He was about to call out 'What time is it?' but something had been stuffed in his mouth, and he choked. It was his tongue and it was not his tongue: someone else was forcing it down his throat. He tried to rise from the bed but his head just lay there and watched, its dull eyes contracting in the glare of the unfamiliar room. There was an odd disturbance beneath his scalp as if it, too, were rearing itself upward to speak. He tried to say Vivien, but the word had grown too long in his mouth and he heard himself calling 'Geranium!' He closed his eyes before the bright knives could reach them.

When he woke up, on the following morning, he was alone. Vivien had left for her work, and Edward was already at school. He knew this and still he needed to call out to them; but his throat ached, as if he had been shouting all night, and it was only with an effort that he was able to part his lips. He was crouched sideways on the bed, the sheets flung off him, and when he rolled out of the position in which he had slept, he saw that the sheet beneath him was dank with someone's brown sweat. It smelt of metal, a sharp inhuman smell. His left eye would not look at this stain; its lid kept on rolling downward, and it was only when Charles put his hand up to his head that he was able to calm it.

[45]

And, as he touched his face with trembling fingers, he could feel the warmth of its continual decay.

He was in the bathroom, retching into the sink. He dared not comb his hair because it was not his hair. He had dressed. He had left the house. He had entered a café, on account of his thirst, and he noticed with delight how bright all the food seemed upon the tables there. He looked around to share his excitement, and he noticed how everyone was feeding off small piles of chemicals: violet, yellow, green and black. Charles was drinking from a cup of tea: the left side of it was cold, and the right side was hot. The world was filled with stripes like brass bands. When he stood up he toppled over, and he was helped out of the café. He walked down the right line, not the left one. Someone stopped him on the street: he had never seen this face before but as he watched the eyebrows, the nose, the lines upon the forehead, the mouth, the pale skin, the side of the neck, the hair, all of it seemed so strange that he broke down and wept.

A blue car passed, and then a red one, their bright colours also bringing sickness into the world. He looked at the houses and the people in the houses, their light merging and becoming a parabola which crept towards the sky. How many faces were there? There were no souls, only faces. And what was this water on his face? The name for it was rain, or cry, or crake. It was a gift. And now all these people, yes they were *people*, were opening their mouths and making noises to each other. They were wearing clothes of different colours, and they moved from one place to the next. Nothing was still. Everything was touching everything else, and Charles watched as the sun moved across the left-hand corner. The world was too bright. I am in prison, he thought, and the brightness is guarding me until I am led out singing. He went into an alley and retched again.

He was sitting beside a small fountain, leaning his back against its round basin. Like a marble oh, he said, and in that moment of inattention he heard the sound of hammers, of drilling, of work-men calling to each other. A building was being erected in the street beyond the small public garden in which he sat, and he considered the plight of the solitary brick. Perhaps it had been taken from the rubble of an older building and was now being used again, and Charles could see all the houses of the world rising and falling with the pressure of his own breathing. Or perhaps the brick had only recently been made, moulded and baked one morning when the happiness of the brick-maker had entered his material. And so, brick by brick, the mood of the new house was formed.

[46]

The noises would not leave his head, and in his pain he leant towards the ground. A wind started up in the tops of the trees and their branches swayed above him, sending their brown leaves drifting to the earth . . .

When he awoke he noticed that the leaves had been swept away, and a young man was standing beside him. He had red hair, brushed back. He was gazing intently at Charles, and he placed his hand upon his arm as if he were restraining him.

One said, 'And so you are sick?'

The other replied, 'I know that I am.'

He was about to rise. 'Not now. Not now. I will come to see you again. Not now.'

Charles was uncertain what to say, and when he looked up again the young man was no longer there. The wind had dropped and, as he listened to the water running from the fountain behind him, he realised that the pain had gone. He stretched out, yawning, and in that movement it was as if the clay had fallen away from his limbs; the strangeness had left him. He stood up quickly, rubbed his eyes, and then scooped some water from the fountain; he did not want to drink it, he just wanted to feel it trembling in his cupped hands. Then he splashed it over his face and hair.

'It's closing time.' The voice came from behind him and Charles turned, hoping to see the same young man who had just woken him. But it was the park attendant, holding open the iron gate which led out into the busy street; he was grinning. 'You shouldn't be talking to yourself,' he said. 'It's the first sign.'

Charles laughed at this. 'A sign of weakness or a sign of woe?' He had come through his illness, even though it had shaken him violently, and in his relief he no longer cared whether the young man had been real or unreal. 'I was sick once,' he said, 'but I'm better now.' Then he walked through the gate.

# 4

'OH, LOOK,' Charles said. 'A Victorian. Doesn't he look sweet?' Philip Slack glanced briefly at the bronze figure of Isambard Kingdom Brunel, with his stove-pipe hat upon his lap. Immediately above his head was an illuminated sign with the words 'Meeting Point' above it, and beside him was the smaller figure of Paddington Bear holding a donation box for the Association of Homeless Families. 'Eighteen hundred and five to eighteen hundred and fifty-one.' Charles was reading the inscription in front of the seated figure. 'He died young, I see.' And they strolled beneath the vaulted glass and iron roof of Paddington towards their platform, the sounds of the old building echoing around them.

By the time Charles had settled himself comfortably in the carriage, spreading out on the table in front of him a bar of Cadbury's milk chocolate, his ticket, two apples and a paperback edition of *Great Expectations*, the 9.15 from London to Bristol was already moving out of the station. Philip stroked his small beard and stared gloomily through the sealed window, while his companion wrote his initials in the dust which already obscured the view. 'Royal Oak,' Charles said. 'What a nice name.'

'Forest once.' Philip looked at the bright red brick offices they were passing, and the ribbon of the motorway curved eastward.

'Westbourne Park?' Charles was very cheerful.

'Fields. In the past.' They were travelling through a canyon of council house flats, which gleamed in the morning light. An old power-station, belching white smoke and debris into the low cloud, flashed by; a lorry passed over a bridge.

'Happy Valley?' Philip looked at him in surprise. 'I made that one up.' Now Charles sat back, visibly enjoying the warmth of the carriage. 'Isn't it nice,' he went on, 'that we're all travelling together to our appointed destination?' He looked around with satisfaction at the other people in the carriage, then he tore a small piece from a page of *Great Expectations*, rolled it into a ball and popped it into his mouth. This was an old habit of his: he could not resist eating books.

Philip still seemed very melancholy as he watched the city and the suburbs of the city rushing past. 'I wish Vivien had come,' he said at last. 'She needs a break.'

'Everyone needs a break, old thing.' Charles had rolled another strip from the paperback, and was already consuming it. 'Would you like some? It's delicious.' He offered the book to Philip, who gracefully declined. 'At least she's not stuck in that flat all day!' Charles suddenly seemed eager to justify himself to his friend. 'I'm the one who looks after Edward, aren't I? And you know how difficult he can be sometimes. Besides . . .' he swallowed the most recent piece of *Great Expectations*. 'Now that I'm working for Harriet, I'll be making some money.'

Philip took the book from his hands. 'It's bad for you,' he said.

'It's not the kind of life I wanted. But I don't see what I can do. What *can* I do? You know how sick I was –' In fact he had not mentioned his illness to Philip and, seeing his friend's startled expression, he smiled. 'But that's all over now. Why are you looking so gloomy, old dear, when we're on our pilgrimage?' He looked across at two people on the opposite side of the compartment. They were playing Scrabble, and he examined the board. 'Occluded,' he said as the train moved on the metal rails towards Bristol Temple Meads.

*

And, when they asked at the station for directions to Colston's Yard, they were told to 'head for the spire' since that particular street lay behind St Mary Redcliffe. 'Chatterton,' Philip said as they walked towards the church. 'He was born there.'

From the station the spire seemed to rise above a group of small houses. 'What lovely purlieus!' Charles said, waving his hand in the general direction of that area. But as soon as they left the precinct of Bristol Temple Meads they became lost in a network of ring-roads and pedestrian 'walk-ways', which took them away from their destination. But Charles was not at all discomfited by this; he seemed positively to relish the distraction. 'Have you noticed,' he said, as they were trying to cross a large junction, 'how many people in Bristol have red hair?' A lorry passed a few inches from his face as the smoke and dust billowed around him. 'Ah, there it is! I saw it between cars.' He put out his hand and stepped into the middle of the traffic, looking neither to the left nor to the right as calmly he crossed the road; Philip followed close behind, nervously signalling and grimacing at the drivers who had only just managed to stop in time. When they reached the other side, and turned the corner, St Mary Redcliffe rose up in front of them.

Far from being in the tranquil locale of Charles's imagination, however, it was set back a little from another busy road. The two men said nothing to each other but made their way across the thoroughfare, and with slow steps walked up a narrow street which passed one of the church's ornate porches. The outer door was surrounded by intricate carvings of saints, skulls, keys, indeterminate animals and small hunched devils; above the door itself the figure of a bearded man had one arm raised in greeting. 'Colston's Yard ahead!' Charles shouted, 'I knew I had a good sense of direction!'

Bramble House itself was not difficult to find, since it was set back from the other houses in a Georgian terrace. There were some iron railings in front of it, from one of which hung a hand-painted sign, 'Beware of the Bitch. She Bites.' Philip stayed back as Charles approached the gate. 'Church,' he said quietly, 'I'll meet you outside the church.'

Charles waved airily, unfastened the gate and walked through. But the front door opened even before he had reached it. 'Oh God,' a voice said. 'Who are you, violating my space?' An old man came out, peering down the street in both directions and not looking at Charles. He was wearing a leopard-skin leotard with the top of a red track-suit hanging over it; he was bald, but from the traces of white stubble still clinging to his pate it seemed to Charles that he must have shaved his head quite recently. 'Isn't that what they say these days? Space?'

'Mr Joynson? Hi, I'm Charles Wychwood.' There was no response, but Charles continued easily, 'I telephoned about the portrait.'

The old man put one hand upon his hip. 'She's gone to think, she's gone to seed, she's gone to hell. So you needn't talk about *her*.' He paused. 'Do you like my sign?' He pointed towards 'Beware of the Bitch'. 'I thought of it last night. Oh, come in and let's have a giggle.' With this he beckoned Charles into the house. 'I love a good giggle, I honestly do.' He had a peculiar wheedling, intimate voice and his breath smelt of throat lozenges. 'I hope you don't smoke,' he said, taking Charles affectionately by the arm and leading him into the hallway. 'I'm on a strict training programme.' He took one more look down both ends of the street before closing the door. 'But you can call me Pat.' And at this point he did, indeed, giggle. 'Massage my neck, will you? I feel tense.'

Charles did not particularly want to touch this old man's flesh, so he put the tips of his fingers on the track-suit top and pressed lightly. 'No, no,' Pat said. 'You're too bony, you young people. Come into the kitchen.' He hurried down the hallway with an old man's blind, baffled energy.

Charles followed and, as Pat opened a can of carrot juice, asked very casually, 'I gather you sold the painting to Leno's Antiques, Mr Joynson?'

Pat suddenly became angry, dribbling some of the carrot juice down his chin. 'I'm *not* Mr Joynson! I told you, she's not here. I can't drink this.' He put down the can. 'I'm in shock. She has threatened me, she has attacked me, she has broken me. There have been guns, there have been knives, there have been explosions. How can I start my training with all that going on?' Charles murmured something vaguely sympathetic and Pat gave him a quick, keen glance. 'I don't think young people ought to wear sweaters or jeans or plimsolls. It is sloppy. It is silly. It is ugly.' Charles was wearing all three of these prohibited items, and looked merely puzzled as Pat went on, 'You see some funny sights, don't you?' He scratched the edge of his leopard-skin leotard as Charles agreed rather more warmly with this. 'Come on,' Pat went on. 'Let's have a run. We can giggle as we go.' He took four pills from the pocket of his track-suit and swallowed them greedily: Charles could see the Adam's apple pulsating within his scrawny neck. Then they left the house, Pat once more affectionately hanging on to Charles's arm. 'I always jog around the church,' he said. 'She *hates* that.'

The old man led the way as they ran towards the north end of St Mary Redcliffe: he kept his chin up and put his elbow close against his sides, making little puffing sounds as he exhaled between each burst of words. 'She hates it. Cringes at it. Blushes at it. Fuck her.'

Charles did not run but, rather, made a series of loping, crab-like motions as he tried to gain Pat's attention. 'But was it you who sold the picture?'

Pat was exultant. 'She doesn't even.' A pause for breath. 'Know yet.' They had passed the north porch and were now moving along a gravel path which curved towards the west end of the church and the Lady Chapel there. 'Miss High and Mighty. She thinks she is. And all she wants. Is a black man.'

'Of course.' Charles had responded to this as if it were the most reasonable statement he had ever heard but, before Pat could begin another breathless tirade, he asked him quickly, 'Where did you find it?'

[51]

Pat put his hand against his left side, as if he had a stitch. 'In. The. Attic.'

'Who is it?' Charles asked as innocently as he dared. He began to slow down the pace, and Pat gratefully followed his lead. 'Who is it in the portrait?'

'Don't ask me. I never question her. I never listen to her. I never understand her.'

Charles kept his eyes on Pat's face, and asked in the most natural possible manner. 'Can I go up to the attic?'

They were passing the south wall and, clutching at the leotard which was in some danger of falling loosely away from him, Pat elegantly picked his way through the stumps of old gravestones until they finally came back into Colston's Yard. Charles repeated his question when they ran back into the kitchen, both of them still panting heavily. 'Can I go up to the attic, Pat?'

The use of his Christian name made the old man hesitate, and he said shyly, 'What do you want to go up there for, when everything you need is down here?' He paused again. 'Are you after a man?'

'Yes. The man in the painting.'

'Oh, her.' He giggled. 'She's probably just a female relative.'

'I just want to see if there are any papers connected with her. Him. It's important to me, Pat.'

'Hold me for a moment while I stretch.' Charles took hold of his left leg while the old man balanced against the sink and delicately performed an arabesque upon the kitchen floor. This seemed to calm him. 'You can have her papers,' he said quietly, 'you can have her notes, you can have her diaries. She can suffer in ignorance.'

'Shall I go up then?' Charles was still very playful.

'Go up what?' Pat was equally playful.

'To get the papers.'

'You don't need to do that, you silly bitch. Pardon my French. Bitchette. I brought everything down. I didn't want anything belonging to her above my head.' He gave an expressive little shiver before executing a small pirouette and gracefully pointing his foot in the direction of two plastic bags. They had 'Body Tech Health Foods' written on the sides and, when Charles went to pick them up, he saw that they had been stuffed with papers and with manuscripts. 'She's been saying for years that she had some family treasures. The only treasure in your family, I said, is me. Well go on, she says, bury yourself in the garden and don't bother to come up in the spring. Come up, I said. Come up? Why should I come up for an old bat like you? I've got better things to do with my time.'

[52]

'So this is the treasure?' Charles held the bags in front of him.

The old man put his finger to his lips. 'Don't tell her. She will kill me, she will hang me, she will butcher me.'

'Why?'

'They're her secret. But I went up there and got them.' He pointed towards the attic. 'I was covered with dust, like some dirty old queen. Do you know what an old queen is? We used to have them years ago.'

'And you don't need them now?'

'What would I need with an old queen? I've forgotten more than they ever learned.'

'I mean, you don't need the papers?'

'They don't bother me. They bore me. They disgust me. They sicken me. But they don't bother me.'

'So I can take them?'

'Did you say your name was Charles?' He nodded. 'You can take anything you want, Charlie. Have you heard the song, Charlie is my darling? I heard that back in nineteen-never-mind.' Pat giggled again. 'You have to go now, Charlie. I need my beauty sleep. Don't you?' He went up and tweaked the bags which Charles was still holding in front of him. 'Like udders, aren't they? Udders from an old *cow*. Which is what she is.' He led Charles towards the door. 'Remember,' he said, 'we never met. We never spoke. We never fell in love. Goodbye for now.'

He watched Charles crossing the road and turning onto the path which led towards the south porch of the church; then, with a sigh, he sat cross-legged upon the floor and waited, despondently but defiantly, for Mr Joynson to return to him.

*Craving & devouring*

Philip Slack had eagerly sought the peace of St Mary Redcliffe. He was aware that both Vivien and Charles were troubled by something, but he was not at all sure what it might be. That was one of the reasons why he had agreed to accompany Charles on this journey: he had wanted to persuade him to speak more openly but, as he had expected, he had not succeeded. And yet over the last few weeks Charles's insouciance had seemed forced and therefore unreal, just as Vivien's customary calm had become over-deliberate; sometimes she seemed to quiver with the strain of remaining her 'usual' self. This distressed him: he thought of the Wychwoods as his family and, in truth, he had no other. But if something should happen . . . and what was this sickness which

[53]

Charles had mentioned on the train? These were the considerations which now sent him towards the old church.

As he walked down the north aisle of the nave his footsteps echoed in the spacious vaults beneath him: it sounded as if someone were walking close behind and with a sudden, child's, fear he crossed the nave to the south transept. He was about to lean back when he touched something; he murmured 'Sorry' and, when he turned around, he saw that his leg had brushed against a reclining stone figure. It was a pilgrim, his hat still tied about his neck and his staff resting in his hand; the face of this pilgrim was in repose but it was impossible to tell, so worn and mottled was the stone, whether the eyes were open or closed.

Philip walked quickly to the back of the church, and sat down upon one of the small wooden chairs placed near the baptistery. From here the worshipper or the casual visitor could look down the entire length of the nave, and Philip became calm once more as he gazed at the glowing blues, reds and yellows of the East Window. The brightness of these colours was such that the stained glass seemed to hover in mid-air, and its rich brocaded light soared across the vaultings of the high roof. And I am seeing again, Philip thought, what Thomas Chatterton himself once saw as a child.

Footsteps broke his reverie, and he glanced at a small boy who was walking with deliberate pace up the narrow aisle which led to the south transept; his head was bowed and he seemed to be scrutinising the flagstones as he went across them. Then he disappeared behind a canopied tomb beside the nave and a few moments later a young man emerged from the other side; it was as if there had been a sudden transformation within this ancient church. Philip was about to rise from his seat in astonishment when he saw both the boy and the young man passing at the top of the nave; they walked by each other without any sign of greeting or recognition, and the light from the window behind them blurred their outlines as they crossed. Philip could see only shadows in front of him, and their footsteps made no noise.

The small boy had gone behind an ironwork screen, and a few moments later some random organ notes echoed around the church: perhaps he had come here to practise, and after a while the stray notes slid into a reverberant low tone of which he seemed particularly fond. Then he launched into the steep harmonies of a hymn, playing it with such care and steadfastness that he must have learned it only recently; and, once again, the church was filled with old music. He had seemed too young to be drawn to so melancholy a pursuit but, when Philip stood up and walked past the ironwork screen, the boy's face was so rapt that he might have been listening to the sounds of his own life echoing back to him. This church would enclose him, and he would play its music until he died. Philip looked away.

He was about to leave when he noticed, on the wall beside the screen, a metal plaque insecurely fastened by rivets. It read: 'In Memory of Thomas Chatterton, 1752–1770, who as a Boy worshipped in this Parish Church.' There were four lines of decayed verse beneath this inscription, and Philip had to peer closely in order to decipher them:

> While yet a boy I sought for ghosts, and sped
> Through many a listening chamber, cave and ruin,
> And starlight wood, with fearful steps pursuing
> Hopes of high talk with the departed dead.

Someone tugged at his sleeve: he looked down in alarm, and an old man was staring up at him with bright eyes. 'He ain't buried here, *he* ain't.' The old man chuckled. 'Oh no, not *him*. No one knows where *he's* gone and buried himself. He's a mystery, that one is.'

Philip said only, 'I suppose so.'

'That's right. You're quite right to suppose *that*. They never found that body. They looked all over, but they never found *him*.' He took Philip's arm and began leading him down the church, towards the north porch. 'You won't find a Chatterton in Brustil. They're long gone, *they* are.' Slowly they approached the baptistery. 'He's all written down, *he* is. Just you have a gander over here.' And in the gently moving light, stained with the colours of the high windows, the old man pored through some pamphlets which had been left for sale beside a 'World in Peril' poster and a scale model of the church itself. 'Here he is,' he said at last, 'I've found *him*.' He held up a pamphlet with the title *Thomas Chatterton: Son of Bristol*. 'That's all *you* need.'

He put his head to one side and waited for Philip, who eventually enquired 'How much?'

'You give what *you* can. This is a church of God, this is.'

Philip searched frantically in the pockets of his jeans, and eventually came out with a pound coin. 'Is that enough?'

'Yes, that will do, *that* will.' The old man quickly took the coin and held it aloft in his right hand as he gave the pamphlet to Philip. Then, in a sudden access of confidence, he took his arm again and said, 'Now that we're all comfy, I'll show you something.' He took him over to the north porch, the light from the half-closed door illuminating the right-hand side of his body, his

[55]

creased neck, his old overcoat, and his trembling hand with the coin still in it. 'There,' he said, opening the door and pointing out into the street beyond, 'There's *his* house. But that's just the frontage, *that* is.' Philip looked in the direction to which he was pointing, and could see what looked like a painted surface raised up beside the main road. 'They've moved it twice, they have. That's just a ruin now.' He put his head to one side again and squinted up at Philip. 'Is there anything else you want to know, is there?'

'No, nothing.' Philip had become vaguely depressed. 'I've seen enough.'

'Then you'll be on your way, will you?' He was still holding the coin in his right hand as he ushered Philip down the steps and into the forecourt. 'Don't forget,' he said, as Philip walked away, 'they'll never find *him*, they won't. He's long gone.'

### *but my Eyes are always upon thee*

Some seagulls were making their usual noise overhead when Philip turned the corner of St Mary Redcliffe and found Charles already waiting for him: he was leaning against the wall of the south porch, his arms folded, whistling to himself. There were two plastic bags lying at his feet, and for a moment Philip wondered if he had been shopping. 'Hello,' he said in a sepulchral tone.

Charles looked up, as if in surprise. 'Well, hello there. Fancy meeting you here. Shall we be on our way?' He kicked a loose stone with his foot, and sent it flying into the graveyard. He was in good spirits after his conversation with Pat, and whistled as he started walking down the path towards the main road.

Philip hastened to catch up with him. 'Food?' he asked, looking thoughtfully at the two plastic bags which Charles was swinging into the air.

'Food for thought. He gave them to me.' He nodded in the direction of Bramble House.

'You saw the owner of the picture?'

'I'm not sure. I think I saw, what is the word, his friend? I think he was a homosexual.' Philip blushed, and Charles laughed out loud. 'He gave me everything.' He swung the bags even higher in the air as they crossed the main road. 'He was dotty. Did you ever see the Ugly Sisters in pantomime?'

Philip was not listening to him. 'House.'

'What?'

'That's Chatterton's house.' Philip pointed at the façade which the old man had just shown him. 'All that's left of it, anyway.'

[56]

They walked over to the wall, which was indeed all that remained: there were four windows with a door, freshly painted, and the wall itself was about six inches thick; it vibrated as the traffic passed. 'A house of cards, no doubt,' Charles said cheerfully as he entered the garden which had been laid out behind this solitary front. There was a sundial here, and Charles bent down to read out the verse which had been inscribed around its base:

> Had restless Time whose harvest is each hour
> Made but a pause to view this poet's flower,
> In pity he'd have turned his scythe away
> And left it blooming to a future day.

'What bad poetry. I hate morbid couplets.' Then he added: 'Let us make haste towards the train. Or else we won't be seen again. We'll find our way to Paddington. And then we'll decode Chatterton.'

### O lovely Delusion

'Thomas Chatterton was born in Pile Street, only a few yards from the parish church of St Mary Redcliffe.' Philip was reading from the pamphlet which he had bought from the old man, stopping only to glance up at the dark red Bovril factory as the train drew out of Bristol Station. 'His father had been a chorister there but he died three months before Thomas was born.'

'That is a pity.' Charles had taken all the material from the plastic bags, and was sorting out the typewritten sheets, old letters and loose papers on the orange plastic table in front of him. 'Is that why they could only afford one wall for their house?'

Philip looked despondently at an abandoned viaduct before continuing. 'Thomas attended the famous Colston's School in Bristol –'

'Of course, Colston's Yard. I think I met his old gym mistress.'

'– but he largely educated himself in the muniment room above the north porch of the church. It was here, in two old wooden coffers, that he discovered certain medieval documents relating the history of Bristol and the construction of St Mary Redcliffe itself. Fired by this knowledge and by his love of the past, he began composing his own medieval poetry. These poems, known as the "Rowley Sequence" after his invention of a medieval monk by the name of Thomas Rowley, heralded the Romantic Movement in England and, although in later years they were discovered to be forgeries contrived by Chatterton, they established the foundations of his everlasting fame.'

[57]

Charles snatched the pamphlet from Philip. 'I hate that phrase, *everlasting fame.'* He raised his voice. 'It's such a cliché.' In fact it depressed him. 'Is there anything new in this?' He turned rapidly to the last page and read out the final sentence of the pamphlet: 'Chatterton knew that original genius consists in forming new and happy combinations, rather than in searching after thoughts and ideas which had never occurred before.'

'True,' murmured Philip gloomily.

'And this,' Charles went on, 'was the foundation of his everlasting fame.'

With a grimace he flung the pamphlet at Philip; then he tore another strip from a page of *Great Expectations*, rolled it into a ball and popped it into his mouth. He settled back into his warm seat and murmured to himself, with increasing cheerfulness, 'New and happy combinations. New and happy combinations. Does that mean,' he asked as he chewed, 'that we just need to switch around the words?'

'Oh God.' Philip was reading the pamphlet and had not heard the question. 'What was the name?' He sounded very grave.

'Legion?'

'What was the name of the man who owns these?' Philip gestured towards the pile of papers which Charles had dumped upon the table.

'I wouldn't say that he owned them exactly. Nobody can own the past –'

'What was his name?'

'Joynson.'

Philip took *Great Expectations* out of Charles's hands before reading out loud from the pamphlet again. 'The boy Chatterton was a great lover of old books, and he became well known among the booksellers of Bristol. In particular he became acquainted with a certain Joynson –' Philip gave the surname an emphasis which was almost melancholy in its detachment – 'who owned a bookshop in Crickle Street; there were many stories of how Chatterton would spend all morning among the dusty shelves of this place, eagerly absorbing all the books which Joynson could show to him. He and the bookseller would often discuss his reading; it has been said, indeed, that Joynson was his true schoolmaster since it was he who apparently introduced the boy to the work of Milton, Cowper, Dyer and many other poets. He was well rewarded for his efforts, however, since Joynson has the distinction of being Chatterton's first publisher. Twenty years after the poet's suicide (this sad young man killed himself at the age of seventeen) –' at this point Philip's voice dived even lower than before – 'twenty

[58]

years after this suicide, it was Joynson who edited and printed the first collection of Chatterton's poetry.'

Charles stared out of the window. 'But he had the painting. He knew that Chatterton didn't kill himself. He knew that he was still alive!'

'So that was their secret,' Philip said very softly. There was a jolt as the train came suddenly to a halt and he went on, more cheerfully, 'Signal failure. We must be stuck at the points.' In his early youth he had been an avid 'spotter' of trains, and had never lost his enthusiasm for the arcana of railway procedure. 'We could be here for a long time.' He was grinning.

Charles was still looking out of the window. 'But why was it their secret? What was the point of pretending that Chatterton was dead?' With more eagerness now he went back to the papers he had taken from Bramble House: the sudden lurch of the compartment had scattered them across the table, and for the first time Charles noticed a large brown envelope with the word 'Fragile' written in red crayon on the side. He ripped it open, in his haste cutting the side of his thumb against its sharp edge, and then removed some sheets of paper. They were of coarse manufacture, stained and darkened at the edges, and some of the papers were spotted with yellow circles like small scorch marks.

Charles put them up to his face in order to smell them. 'Dusty,' he said to Philip, who was watching him curiously. 'I would like to eat a bit of this.' Across each sheet there were many lines of cramped handwriting in brown ink; they had the appearance of having been written at great speed or under the influence of some overpowering emotion, since extra lines had been written vertically down the margin of each page. It was as if the unknown writer had felt compelled to put everything down in the smallest possible space. 'It's difficult,' Charles said, 'I'll need a magnifying glass.' He turned to the last page, and could not keep the excitement from his voice when he read out 'T.C.'

'Oh.' The train had started again, and Philip was momentarily distracted. 'Say it again.'

'The signature at the bottom is T.C.' He noticed a line of blood down the edge of the paper, issuing from his cut, and gingerly he handed the papers over to Philip while he sucked his thumb. And then Philip, leafing through them, read out this: 'like the blind prophet led by the boy, so was antiquity given over to my care. I sold my Verses to the booksellers, also, and though I met with some success in London, for the most part the fame of Thomas Rowley was bruited through Bristol and the trade in my work was very brisk. There was one bookseller who suspected the truth, *viz*

[59]

that these were verses of my own –' Philip broke off. 'I can't read that word. It might be despair. Or desire.'

Charles was still sucking his thumb, occasionally taking it out of his mouth to inspect the small cut. 'Put them back in the envelope. I can't look at them now.' But already, in his imagination, he had solved the secret of Thomas Chatterton and was enjoying the admiration of the world. Carefully he wrapped a piece of Kleenex around his thumb, but then he let the tissue fall to the floor as he picked up another sheet of paper. 'Here it is again!' he said. 'It's the same handwriting.' And then he read out: 'Arise now from thy Past, as from the Dust that environs thee. When Los heard this he rose weeping, uttering the original groan as Enitharmon fell towards dark Confusion.'

'Blake.' Philip looked at the vacant seat beside him, as if someone had just moved into it. 'That's William Blake.'

'I know that.' Charles was suddenly very calm. 'But then why is it signed T.C.?' And as the train took them homewards Charles read out, in mounting excitement, another line from the same page. 'Craving & devouring; but my Eyes are always upon thee, O lovely Delusion.'

# 5

INSTINCTIVELY FINDING her way through the rushing crowd, Vivien Wychwood walked down New Chester Street towards Cumberland and Maitland. In the morning light the world was new again; everything seemed to be freshly painted, gleaming like the sides of salmon already on sale at the Royalty fishmonger on the corner of the street. But she was thinking of Charles and across the bright day was imprinted the image of him, sick and shaking, two nights before. On Saturday evening he had returned from Bristol with Philip; in his enthusiasm he had draped the two plastic bags around Edward's neck and the boy had looked inside them, wrinkling his nose. 'Where did you get this rubbish? It smells dead.'

'Not dead, Edward the Inedible, very much alive. This will make your poor Dad very famous.' But he gazed thoughtfully at his son as soon as he had said this, feeling once more the stirrings of some distant pain within his head.

Vivien came into the room and Philip put up his arm to greet her, blushing as he did so. 'What's all this?' she asked her husband.

'More rubbish!' Edward shouted gleefully, and squeezed the bags with both arms.

Charles took them away from him. 'These are the Chatterton papers,' he said, solemnly. 'I discovered them.'

Vivien, perplexed, looked across at Philip for confirmation of this news but he was staring thoughtfully at Edward's shoes. 'Just like that?' she asked.

'Yes, just like that.' With a sudden furious enthusiasm which alarmed Vivien, he took the bags and emptied their contents onto the sofa. He walked around it, muttering, 'Pieces of eight! Pieces of eight!' And Edward joined him, shouting, 'After Eight mints! After Eight mints!' Then Charles heard a balloon bursting beneath his skull and, suddenly feeling nauseous, he sat down heavily upon the sofa.

Vivien saw how pale he had become and, brushing aside the

papers, sat down next to him in order to soothe him. 'Don't touch the documents,' Charles said. 'Don't damage them. They're very fragile.' And for a few moments he sat with his head bowed as Philip, at a gesture from Vivien, picked up Edward and carried him out of the room.

'What's the matter with Dad?' the boy asked very loudly.

Charles looked up at him. 'It's the curse of Chatterton,' he said gently; he tried to smile but his face did not seem to be moving.

Vivien put her hand against his cold cheek. 'You must see the doctor again,' she said. 'I'm so worried now.'

'I can't see doctors all the time. I have all this to do.' This was at least what he wanted to say as he gestured towards the papers, but the murmured words which Vivien heard were 'Ejis doxon. Fistula don.' He tried to stand up but he could not do so, and a few minutes later Vivien had to lead him towards their bed. 'He's not himself,' she said to Philip. 'He needs rest.'

But by the following morning he seemed to have recovered and, when Vivien tried to explain how alarmed she had become, he merely patted her cheek and laughed. There were times when she thought her husband to be strangely insensitive, but she realised that the insensitivity was principally directed towards himself. Just as in the past he had always seemed able to ignore their poverty, now he was trying to ignore his own sickness.

### the dream unfolds

'He was the greatest artist of the Forties, of course, with the possible exception of Joan Crawford. I don't mean her acting, I mean her hair. It was heroic, if wood *can* be heroic. Good morning, Vivienne.' Cumberland had been talking to Maitland as Vivien entered the gallery. 'Lovely to see you in a solid colour at last. How the pendulum swings.' He was wearing a thinly striped shirt, fastened so tightly that it seemed to hold his neck like a noose; and, when he greeted Vivien, he turned his head very slowly so that he could conceal for as long as possible the large wart which thrust upwards from his thin, pale face. 'But when I see that dress I worry about the human cost of abstract art. Was this the price we all had to pay?' Vivien returned his greeting with no more than a smile; her other employer, Maitland, nodded and said nothing. 'Was that a smile, Vivienne?' Cumberland had turned full circle, so that his wart was invisible to her once more. 'Or did a red creature run quickly across your face?' He fluttered his fingers at her, as if in a form of blessing, and then resumed his conversation with the silent Maitland. 'Anyway, the auctioneer might have come from Dickins and Jones. A brown suit looks so calculating on a man, don't you think? One always suspects that he must have knitted it himself. Still, I could *not* resist those Seymours.'

Vivien, smiling persistently despite the fact that neither man was now paying any attention to her, passed through the gallery towards her small office at the back. She always enjoyed this walk: the gallery was so cool, so pale, so translucent (the paintings seemed to glow on the light grey walls) that it was as if her own feelings were slowly being bleached out of her until she reached her desk as the efficient secretary of Mr Cumberland and Mr Maitland.

This morning, a rather plump young woman was already sitting there. She was filing her nails but, as soon as she saw Vivien, she dropped the file back into her bright red handbag. 'Sorry, old thing,' she said, 'I'm in your saddle, aren't I?' She slid off the desk, and snapped her handbag shut.

'Good morning, Claire.' Vivien had already acquired something of her usual office briskness.

'The Head's very excited, and so's the Deputy.' She was referring to Cumberland and Maitland. 'They've scrumped three Seymours. Three rudies.' Vivien knew that, by this term, Claire meant three nudes; she was accustomed to her colleague's girlish world. 'The other school is furious.'

'Which school is that?'

'Seymour's old dealer, Sadleir. The Head says he was *spitting* at the auction.'

At this point Cumberland's wart put in an appearance around the door. 'There used to be a substance called coffee, Claire, which was considered to be good in emergencies. It had a terrifying effect upon the poor, and caused a revolution in South America.'

Claire positively bounced towards him. 'Yes sir! Can do.' And she vanished from the room, leaving only the faintest odour of face-powder behind.

'She couldn't be nicer, could she, Vivienne? Not even if she tried.' Vivien said nothing; she always felt somewhat uneasy when she was alone with Cumberland, and so she began busily to rearrange the letters and invoices upon her desk. It was a peculiarity of her temperament that, although she considered herself to be very much part of the gallery when she was absent from it, she felt something of an interloper – even an outsider – when she was actually there. 'You look so Edwardian when you're busy, Vivienne. Quite a charming little study, actually. It's just so tragic that you're in the wrong period.'

Vivien was used to her employer's manner, and knew that he

[63]

expected her to respond in kind; it was almost as if he insulted others only to enjoy being insulted in return. 'Would you like to hang me in the gallery?' she asked him.

'Oh no, nothing so professional. Just drawn.'

'And quartered?'

'Let's say halved, just to be on the safe side.' Their complicity in this macabre scene made them both laugh. 'Actually, Vivienne, your country needs you. Someone has a problem.' This was his name for Maitland, and they were both about to walk through to him when Claire returned with the coffee. Cumberland looked down at it in horror. 'This is so black, Claire, I don't know whether to drink it or give it a grant.'

They walked into the gallery, to find Maitland standing against one wall, holding one of the Seymour paintings above his head; he was a short, fat man and his arms reached only a certain way before coming to what seemed an abrupt halt. Vivien did not know how long he had been in that position, but there was a line of sweat across his forehead.

Cumberland saw this, too. 'Quite the noble savage. If I were Vivienne, I would already be dizzy with lust.' Maitland blushed but said nothing and his partner, tip-toeing up to him, moved his arms by an inch or so. 'Vivienne, dare to be learned, dare to be blue. Is someone in the right position now? He will not necessarily be standing there for ever, you understand. Although I suppose we could put a vase on his head and pretend he was a Maenad. The critics would never know.'

Vivien looked at the painting, of a nude upon a beach, as Maitland steadily grew more red in the face. He seemed to be panting slightly. 'It's too small,' she said. 'It's too small for that part of the wall.'

'Oh, Maitland. She says it's too small. It's no good holding it up, if it's too small.' Maitland leaned against the wall, dejected.

'I think perhaps two beside each other . . .' Vivien went on to say.

'Could someone be too good for this world and hold up two oils together?' With a sigh Maitland took one painting in each hand, and held them over his head. The strain of doing so made him slightly pop-eyed, an effect which Cumberland was quick to notice. 'Speak, Vivienne, before someone turns you to stone. He is becoming quite legendary now.'

She saw how his short arms were trembling beneath the weight. 'That's exactly right,' she said quickly.

Maitland, the sweat now pouring off his forehead, looked anxiously at his partner for confirmation of this decision. Cumberland considered the matter, gently stroking his wart as he did so. 'Well,' he said at last, '*I* think she has done wonderfully.' It was as if he were valiantly trying to defend Vivien against a generally hostile world.

Claire clapped her hands. 'Top marks, head girl. Go to the front of the class.'

Maitland slid down the wall, carefully putting both paintings onto the light grey carpet before collapsing. He opened his mouth, about to say something, when the telephone rang in Vivien's office and Claire ran towards it, giggling with excitement at the thought of being the first to reach it. She returned a moment later. 'It's for you, Vivie. It's a man.' Cumberland closed his eyes for a moment and gave a hollow laugh. 'He wouldn't give any name.'

It was Charles. He rarely telephoned Vivien here but, when he did so, he always managed to sound as if he were calling from another country. 'Hello? Viv? Are you there?'

'Yes, it's me. Is there anything the matter?' All her fears suddenly returned, and she heard the panic in her own voice as she leaned forward across her desk.

Charles did not seem to have noticed it, however. 'Absolutely not. Everything's fine.' She said nothing, and waited for him to continue. 'I was just wondering,' he went on, 'when I was supposed to start working for Harriet Scrope. Did I happen to mention it to you?'

She sensed that this was not the real reason for his call. 'You were meant to start this morning. I reminded you last night.'

'That's right! I knew I was late for something.' He paused, trying to gauge her mood. 'Oh, by the way. Could you pick up the shopping on the way home? Now that I'm busy?' Vivien agreed that she would. 'Good. That's all right, then.' Charles, clearly relieved at the lifting of this household burden, grew more confidential. 'I telephoned Flint,' he said. 'He asked me round for a drink this evening, actually. Do you mind?' He made it sound like the most natural thing in the world, although she knew that he and Andrew Flint had not met since their days at university. Since that time Flint had acquired a reputation both as a novelist and as a biographer but Charles had rarely mentioned him, except as the subject of casual jokes with Philip. 'Just like old times, isn't it?' he was saying now to Vivien. There was a note of triumph in his voice, and it was clear to her that the discovery of the Chatterton manuscripts had given him a sudden access of confidence; but she knew, also, that this mood would eventually fade.

'Why don't you show him your poems?' she asked. 'He might help to get them published.' There was a silence and Vivien realised, too late, that this was quite the wrong thing to say. 'Don't forget Harriet,' she went on hurriedly. 'Do you want me to phone her for you?'

'I can do some things myself, you know.' And Charles rang off.

Cumberland's voice startled her. 'Whenever a man phones the gallery, someone becomes terrifying. He makes strange moaning noises and has to be taken to the park.' Both partners had silently entered the office.

'It was only my husband.' Vivien forced herself to smile.

'Ah, a husband! I knew a husband once.'

Vivien smiled, more naturally now. 'They still exist, you know.'

'We must move in entirely different social circles, Vivienne. I haven't seen one since the Festival of Britain. And that was in the dark.'

Maitland stuck out his tongue, apparently in distaste, and at this moment Claire came back into the office, half-whispering and half-giggling. 'There's a new boy out in the playground.'

'Oh God.' Cumberland sometimes tired of her allusiveness. 'Can someone translate for me?'

Claire seemed offended and added, more briskly, 'He said his name was Berk. Or Jerk.'

'Ah, Mr Merk.' Cumberland sailed out into the gallery, hand outstretched; he always prided himself upon making the right first impression. 'We were just talking about you.' Cumberland was clearly expecting him.

'Yes?' Stewart Merk took his hands out of the pockets of his baggy linen trousers and sauntered towards Cumberland. 'Hot stuff,' he said, looking at the pictures already hanging in the gallery. They were part of an exhibition of abstract art from Poland, which Maitland had organised. 'A lot of interest expressed, right?'

Cumberland did not detect any irony in his tone, but he could not absolutely discount it. 'Well, we like them. And Poland is so romantic these days, don't you think? With all those Catholics and their walrus moustaches?'

'You mean Lech Walesa?'

'I was thinking more of the women actually. Vivienne! Notepad!'

Vivien came out of the office and Merk did not bother to hide his interest.

'Nice chick, yes?' he murmured to Cumberland.

'I have never enquired into her origins –'

'I bet you haven't.'

'– but an egg is out of the question.'

And, when they were all seated in Cumberland's office, he introduced Stewart Merk as Joseph Seymour's last assistant, who

[66]

had worked with the artist until his death three months ago; it had been Merk who put up for auction the three oil paintings which Cumberland had purchased, and now he wanted to negotiate the sale of some more. 'And why,' Cumberland was asking him, 'have you avoided Sadleir? He was Seymour's dealer, after all.'

'Okay. Fair comment.' Merk was admiring Vivien, who was transcribing their conversation in shorthand. 'I'm not too fast for you, am I?' He smirked at her before going back to the question. 'Sadleir is a wally.'

Cumberland was not sure what this meant. 'That is *brutally* frank, I'm sure. But can I put my gallery owner's hat on?' His hands fluttered towards his head: he was already imagining something black and rather severe, with perhaps a brooch pinned to it. 'Can I be brutal too?'

'Go on. I might like it.'

'How did you acquire these paintings?'

Merk took out a packet of Sobranies, and lit one; Cumberland's nostrils quivered as he blew a smoke ring into the space between them. 'Okay. The old man gave them to me. We worked together for some time but you know that, yes?' Cumberland tried to feign surprise, but in fact he was quite aware of Seymour's working practices and of Merk's own role. 'When the old man died, Sadleir was round to the studio straightaway.'

'That is the trouble with dealers. Death holds no terrors for them. It merely represents a lump sum.'

'But there was nothing to give him, right? Seymour had left all his last works to me.'

'So naturally he broke down at the sudden bereavement. For Sadleir, crocodile tears and crocodile shoes are matching accessories.'

'I was given everything. For services rendered, yes? The old man never liked parting with money.' Merk blew another smoke ring towards the ceiling, and all four of them watched it slowly ascend before it shook slightly and faded away.

'But do you have proof . . .?' Cumberland was saying.

'Of ownership? Yes.' Putting the cigarette in his mouth, Merk took out from his pocket a wad of papers which had been tied with a length of blue tape. He tossed them at Cumberland, who gracefully caught them with one hand. 'You can check the numbers on the backs of the canvases, right? He was very methodical.' Merk settled back in the chair and smiled at Maitland, who seemed somewhat alarmed by this attention. 'I could have gone my own way, years ago. I could have set up on my own and done my own work. I gave him four years of my life, man.' He leant forward quickly, to stub out his cigarette, and Maitland retreated further into his chair. 'But I'm going to make it pay now.' For a moment there was a trace of menace in his voice but then he went on, in his bland London accent, 'That's my story, yes?'

'And what a good story it is.' Cumberland had been carefully examining the papers which Merk had thrown to him. 'Almost worthy of the Brothers Grimm.' He looked across at Maitland. 'And what does my colleague and dear friend think of it?' Maitland had taken out a handkerchief, and was wiping the sweat from his forehead. He puffed out his cheeks, and said nothing. 'Precisely my opinion. Mr Merk —'

'You can call me Stew.'

'Stew. We will buy your paintings. We will go on with your story, but only on condition that nothing happens next.'

### the sleeper awakes

Philip Slack stared at the rows of dark books; then he switched on the electric light above his head, and in its bright circle he could see the red, brown and green cloths of the volumes, their spines dulled and rubbed, many of their titles so faded that only certain letters could be recognised, their edges worn at the top where other people had taken them down to read them. And, beyond this circle of light in which he stood, the books cast intense shadows. He was in 'the stacks', the basement of the library in which he worked, where all the forgotten or neglected volumes were deposited. Some of these had been piled in corners, where they leaned precariously against the damp stone walls of the basement; but some were scattered across the floor, and it occurred to him that they had been dragged from the shelves by vermin before being eaten. Within this place there lingered the musty, invasive odour of decay; but it was a smell which soothed and pleased Philip.

He had come down to see if he could find any references to Thomas Chatterton and, since he suspected that in old books some forgotten truth might be recovered, he placed his trust in the principle of *sortes Vergilianae*. So now he walked along the narrow pathways between the shelves, turning on the lights as he went, lightly touching the damp spines of the volumes until eventually he took down the one on which his finger had come to rest; the red cloth of its cover was dusty, but when he brushed it with his hand he saw the title very clearly: *The Last Testament* by Harrison Bentley. It seemed appropriate for his search, and he opened the book. The pages of the novel were slightly soiled, with light brown

[68]

stains spreading across them in an arc, and when he turned to the frontispiece he saw that it had been published in 1885 by Sullivan and Bridges of 18 Paternoster Square. Philip held it up to his face, as if he were about to devour it, and turned the pages quickly; he might seem slow or hesitant in his dealings with the world, but he always read swiftly and anxiously. He knew that his real comfort was to be found in books.

And so the outline of the story soon became clear to him: the biographer of a certain poet, throughout referred to as K——, discovers that his subject, at the end of his life, had been too ill to compose the verses which had brought him eternal fame; that, in fact, it had been the poet's wife who had written them for him. The plot seemed oddly familiar to Philip but he was not sure if he had read this novel some years before, or if it resembled some daydream of his own. Distracted now, he turned to the last pages of the book and then to the endpaper which contained an advertisement for 'Mr Harrison Bentley's most recent publication'. This was entitled *Stage Fire* and the précis of its plot, in eight point type, summarised the history of an actor who believes himself to be possessed by the spirits of Kean, Garrick and other famous performers of the past – and who, as a result, has a triumphant career upon the stage. Once more this story seemed familiar to Philip; he recognised its shape so clearly that he was convinced that he had read it elsewhere and that this was not simply some trick of his imagination. He understood the phenomenon of *déjà vu* but he did not believe that it could be applied to books: how could he trust his reading, if that were so?

He was idly tracing the watermark on the last page with his finger when he remembered: he had read the story of *Stage Fire* in a novel by Harriet Scrope. He did not recall its title – that was not important – but it had concerned a poet who believed himself to be possessed by the spirits of dead writers but who, nevertheless, had been acclaimed as the most original poet of his age. And at once Philip remembered where he had read Harrison Bentley's *The Last Testament* before: Harriet Scrope had written a novel in which a writer's secretary is responsible for many of her employer's 'posthumous' publications; she knew his style so well that she was able effortlessly to counterfeit it, and only the assiduous researches of a biographer had uncovered the fakery. This was very close to the late nineteenth-century novel which Philip now held in his hand. He dropped it, and its fall echoed around the basement of the library.

Philip was surprised by his discovery, particularly since he admired Harriet Scrope's novels. When Charles had first told him that he was going to work as her assistant, Philip had read them avidly and with pleasure; he had been impressed by her combination of violence and comedy although, when he had mentioned this characteristic to Charles, his friend had merely shrugged and said, 'Fiction is a very debased form'. Philip felt bound to agree – Charles, after all, was more creative and imaginative than he was – but he was still content to enjoy this lower pleasure.

And so what did Harriet's borrowings matter? In any case, Philip believed that there were only a limited number of plots in the world (reality was finite, after all) and no doubt it was inevitable that they would be reproduced in a variety of contexts. The fact that two of Harriet Scrope's novels resembled the much earlier work of Harrison Bentley might even be coincidental. He was less inclined to criticise her, also, because of his own experience. He had once attempted to write a novel but he had abandoned it after some forty pages: not only had he written with painful slowness and uncertainty, but even the pages he had managed to complete seemed to him to be filled with images and phrases from the work of other writers whom he admired. It had become a patchwork of other voices and other styles, and it was the overwhelming difficulty of recognising his own voice among them that had led him to abandon the project. So what right did he have to condemn Miss Scrope?

He picked up *The Last Testament* and carefully replaced it on the shelf. Then, in order to calm himself after his strange discovery, he took down the small volume next to it. It was a selection of literary reminiscences, edited by the Dowager Lady Moynihan, and at once his attention was drawn to the engraved plates which illustrated the text and which were still protected by the thin, fine tissue common to that period of book production. He looked through them, eventually stopping at one scene which was familiar; and, when he looked down at the legend beneath the engraving, he read 'Chatterton's Monument in Bristol Churchyard'. There was a short text on the page opposite the illustration: it concerned the novelist George Meredith 'who, in the early months of 1856, in the utmost extremity, and with thoughts of self-murder after his wife's desertion, sat in the gloomy environs of St Mary Redcliffe in Bristol, lo, even in the shadow of Chatterton's Monument. He had purchased a phial of mercury-and-arsenic with which he intended to end his life but, as he was about to put the deadly flask to his pale lips, he felt a hand laid upon his wrist; looking up, he saw a young man standing over him and forbidding him to drink. When he put down the phial, the young man disappeared. Thus was the young George Meredith saved for literature by the intervention of the ghostly Thomas Chatterton. I do not believe my readers will know of a more chilling and yet more noble story.' Philip leaned back against the wall of the basement, and tried to imagine this scene . . .

He was aware that someone was watching him. It was Harriet Scrope and behind her, his face in shadow, was Harrison Bentley. Philip jerked forward and opened his eyes; his throat was dry from sleep, and he could feel the dampness of his shirt where he had been slumped against the stone. There were pools of light among the stacks, directly beneath the bulbs which Philip had switched on, but it was now with an unexpected fearfulness that he saw how the books stretched away into the darkness. They seemed to expand as soon as they reached the shadows, creating some dark world where there was no beginning and no end, no story, no meaning. And, if you crossed the threshold into that world, you would be surrounded by words; you would crush them beneath your feet, you would knock against them with your head and arms, but if you tried to grasp them they would melt away. Philip did not dare turn his back upon these books. Not yet. It was almost, he thought, as if they had been speaking to each other while he slept.

At last he was able to run up the stairs to the main library and, believing that his absence might have been noticed, kept his head bowed and looked down at the blue linoleum floor as he quickly made his way to his desk. Some recently acquired volumes had been placed there for him to catalogue and, as he gradually became absorbed in his work, his anxiety abated. The library was not peaceful but it was a place of somewhat precarious refuge, and by now he was accustomed to the footsteps, the coughing and the occasional muttered voices of those who came to sit here in the early afternoon. And why should he, who knew the comfort of books, deny it to others?

A vagrant was sitting on one of the green plastic chairs in the 'Reference' section, quickly turning the pages of a dictionary and talking to himself in a rapid, high voice (and, Philip wondered, had he done this as a child?). A middle-aged woman, with an old brown shawl thrown across her shoulders, was kneeling on the floor by the 'Fiction' section: she had two books open in front of her, but her tangled hair kept falling across her eyes and she moaned as she swept it back. The staff were used to her presence, however, and made no effort to move her. Close to Philip's desk was a long table, at one end of which a young man with bright red hair always sat; he had his elbows on the table (there were holes in the sleeves of his jacket, where the fabric had been worn away) and, as usual, he was staring down at an unopened book. Philip had once asked him if there was anything in particular he wanted to read and he had replied, very quietly, 'Oh no, nothing really.' And still he came every day. And the smell of the library was always the same – the musty odour of old clothes mixed with the keener scent of unwashed bodies, creating what the chief librarian had once described as 'the steam of the social soup'. Philip recalled a poem in which the world was compared to a vast hospital but what if it were a vast public library, in which the people were unable to read the books? And yet those now around him seemed resigned to this; they were quiet, helpless, and poor. It might have been better if they had risen up in a fury and destroyed the library but, no, they sat here and left at closing time. Even the most deranged of them seemed to be content with that.

Some publishers' catalogues had been left on his desk, since it was one of his duties to read all the announcements of new books and to order those which seemed most suitable. One of them was a slim list from a university press and, although it advertised books which the library could rarely afford to purchase, he glanced at it with some interest – an interest which turned to a sudden start of recognition when he read here of the forthcoming publication of *Thou Marvellous Boy: The Influence of Thomas Chatterton on the Writings of William Blake*. Immediately beneath the title was an illustration, no doubt by Blake himself, of a young man with his hair flaming, as an emblem of the sun, and with his arms outstretched in greeting. A précis followed: 'There have been many accounts of Thomas Chatterton's influence upon the Romantic poets, but Professor Brillo's study is the first to examine in detail the effect which Chatterton's 'Rowley' poems had upon the vocabulary and prosody of William Blake's epic verse. Professor Brillo also studies the devices by which Blake introduced the subliminal figure of Chatterton, the suicide, into his texts and discusses the influence of Chatterton's medievalism on Blake's own vision. As Professor Brillo states in his introduction, "This is the one subject which Blake scholars have seemed unwilling to address, for it assumes that Blake was influenced by the work of a forger and a plagiarist. But it would not be going too far to suggest that, without the work and the influence of Thomas Chatterton, Blake's own poetry would have taken a wholly different form". Homer Brillo is Professor of Advanced Information Studies at Valley Forge University, Wyoming.' Philip remembered the lines which Charles had quoted in the train from Bristol; they had been Blake's own words, apparently, but they had been signed T.C. But he could not think of this for long: there was a series of bleeps in the far corner of the library;

one of the computers had malfunctioned, and was signalling for attention like a wounded bird. The young man with red hair watched him as he rose to rescue it.

*and still the dream goes on*

'Ah welcome, Charles.' Andrew Flint greeted him at the door of his flat in Russell Square. 'Welcome to my dulce domum. My humble third-floor walk-up. Do you know what that signifies in English? I haven't a conception.' He had grown fatter in the twelve years since Charles had last seen him, but there was still the same nervous panic in his eyes. 'Where is the spouse?'

'Vivien's working late.'

'In durance vile, no doubt.' He ushered his old friend into a barely furnished room. 'This is the inner sanctum,' he said apologetically. 'Can I tempt you?'

'Excuse me?'

'Nunc est bibendum?'

'What?'

'A drinkie?'

Charles asked for a vodka martini, a choice which surprised him even as he made it. Although they had only been in each other's company for a few seconds Flint retreated to the kitchen with a feeling of relief and, before bringing the drink to Charles, he consulted a small card on which he had written down a list of topics for conversation. It read, 'Job, Poetry, The Past'; the first one sprang to his lips when he entered the room, bearing two glasses on an expensive beaten copper tray. 'So tell me about your occupation, Charles. Or are you *pre*occupied? Is the labourer still worthy of his hire?'

'There's nothing to say, really.'

Mentally, Flint scored a line through 'Job'; it was clear that Charles did not have one. 'And what does anyone *do* in particular? Mutatis mutandis, of course.'

'Of course.' There was a slight pause. 'Except that you're a success.' Charles said this as easily as he could bear.

'Not uncommon in the metropolis, alas. And, horribile dictu, generally a temporary phenomenon.' Whenever Flint's eyes seemed in danger of meeting those of Charles, they swerved away.

This made Charles uneasy, also. 'Do you still write poetry, Andrew?' They had met at a poetry reading in the basement of a Cambridge college; in the course of a long and drunken evening, they had discovered their mutual enthusiasm for certain contemporary French writers and as a result had decided to become friends.

[73]

'Hélàs, non. Departed. The Muse has taken her claws from my shoulder, if I may use a personification.'

'Why not? It's a free country.'

'Ah, a libertarian. Do you read Burke?' But Flint had noticed the irritation in his voice, and now said more gently. 'But what have we here?' He pointed to a brown envelope which Charles had placed on a small glass table by his chair. 'Have you composed a poem?' His tone was not as enthusiastic as it had once been.

'No, not a poem.' In fact Charles had brought with him a page of the Chatterton manuscript, and now he took it out to show Flint. 'I was wondering,' he said, 'if you could tell me its . . .' He could not think of the word he needed.

'Provenance?' At university, Flint had studied manuscript material of this kind.

'I remember you were interested in graph . . .'

'Palaeography?' Flint took the page from Charles and held it up to the light of a sculptured Italian lamp placed casually on a perspex stand in the corner of the room. 'The Durham lily,' he said.

'Like the Jersey lily?'

'No.' He was too interested to laugh. 'A watermark, actually. Distinct and unassuageable. Do I mean unassuageable? I don't believe I do. Do I mean ineradicable?' All the time he was examining the handwriting of this document carefully. 'It's an English round hand,' he said at last, 'but there are definite traces of an ornate schoolroom script. You can tell that from the ascenders. And here, in extenso, a secretary hand too.' Charles seemed puzzled. 'It was perfectly common, you know, for the same person to compose in more than one style. Think of the Bishop of Tewkesbury. Or perhaps, on second thoughts, don't. He was a Socinian, I believe.' Charles seemed even more puzzled. 'My amabilis insania. Don't worry, I have passed the contagious stage. And, oh look, a magnificent minuscule! This must be the work of an antiquarian.'

'I know.' Then Charles went on, pleasantly, 'I have a date. I just want to see if you agree.'

'The headlong rush, it seems.' But Flint was enjoying the use of his skills. 'The punctuation and the capitals have been rationalised but, on the other hand . . . Is that a pun? Gracious me. On the other *hand*, there is no real contrast between the thick and the thin strokes. Do I dare to give a date?' His old friend said nothing, and Flint was forced to continue. 'Yes, I dare. Experto crede, dear Charles, and not me. But I would suggest before 1830 –'

'Exactly.' He nodded, as if he had analysed the same evidence and was waiting only for Flint to confirm it.

[74]

'– and since the Durham watermark was not in use until 1790 . . .'

'Early nineteenth century! I knew it!' Charles lifted his glass, and drained the vodka from it.

Flint handed back the manuscript. 'Tell me more.'

There was a time when Charles would have explained everything to him, and together they would have exulted in this extraordinary discovery, but now he held back. He did not really know his friend any more. 'I will,' he said, 'I will when I can.' But he was embarrassed by his own discretion, and looked down into his empty glass.

'Attempt a second drink.' Flint had only been mildly curious in any case and, sensing Charles's unease, gratefully disappeared into the kitchen with the empty glasses. He consulted his list of topics, and put a small tick against 'Poetry'. 'Can I take it,' he asked as he returned into the room, 'that the laurel wreath is still somewhere on your brow?'

'What?'

'Are you still writing poetry?'

'Yes. Of course.' Charles seemed hurt by this question. 'I thought you might have seen my latest book.'

'Mea culpa –' Flint blushed.

'But I've got plenty of time,' Charles added, quickly. He cocked his head to one side, a gesture which Flint remembered very well. 'I'm in no hurry.' The movement of his head had provoked a sudden pain, and he shifted uneasily in his seat. 'I've got all the time in the world.'

'Patience is certainly a prerequisite for the serious artist, although sometimes it can acquire the quality of –'

'Can I have another drink?' Charles had swallowed the rest of his vodka, wanting to drown the pain, and now he held out his glass eagerly.

'Thirsty work, I take it?' Flint was happy to retire to the kitchen yet again; he drew a line through 'Poetry' and, when he returned with two more drinks, launched into his third subject, 'The Past'. 'The years are incorrigible, aren't they? They never cease. Was it Tennyson who said that? No. Horace. It was Horace Walpole.' He looked up to see if Charles had caught his joke, but he was staring ahead at the wall. 'It only appears like yesterday when –' he hesitated, not having prepared a specific example; Charles looked at the wall steadily as Flint took another large swig: '– when we were young. No longer the juvenile leads, I know, but where are we being led? What is the prognosis, physician?'

'I never have any trouble,' Charles replied, glancing at Flint.

'I'm just fine.' The pain was going but, unaccustomed as he was to vodka, he was feeling a little confused. 'But what about you?' he went on. 'What have you been doing recently?'

'No comment.' Flint was rubbing his eyes, looking blearily around the room when he had finished. 'I mean, I have considerable difficulty. Difficulty in –' It was not just that he was unwilling to talk about himself: he seemed unable to do so.

Charles had not realised this. 'But what are you working on now? After the novel?'

Flint scratched his face, and then examined his fingernails for evidence of dead skin. 'I'm writing the biography of George Meredith,' he said, quickly, 'the English poet and novelist.'

Charles, now feeling more comfortable, stretched out in the chair. 'I knew you had it in you.' For a moment he enjoyed the luxury of pretending that they were both back at university, with Charles himself still in the ascendant. 'You were the one who worked hard. You were always ambitious.' This surprised Flint, who did not realise that he possessed any marked characteristics at all. 'I'm very pleased for you.' And at this moment, as it happened, Charles was.

'Oh no,' Flint cried, suddenly animated by the vodka. 'I'm just a hack!' He looked at Charles for a reaction. 'I'm just a fraud. Did I sell out? Did I compromise?' He seemed elated at the thought.

Charles drained his glass and made a point of gazing at Flint very seriously, although his eyes seemed to have some difficulty in focusing on him. 'Do you want me to justify you to yourself? Is that it?'

'No, nothing. I want nothing!' Flint lost the thread of whatever it was he had intended to say. 'I admire you, Charles. Charlie. You adhered to the poetry. You haven't changed!' Charles was delighted at these sentiments, but Flint's enthusiasm disappeared as quickly as it had come, and he lapsed into pensiveness. 'But in the long run,' he muttered, 'it doesn't matter, does it?'

'You mean because, in the long run, we're dead?'

Flint nodded gloomily. 'Do you know,' he went on, animated once more. 'Do you know, there are times when I go through that door.' He waved in the general direction of that object. 'When I go through that door, and I think to myself. I think, well now, Andrew Flint Esquire, novelist and biographer, who's to say you'll ever come back again? Who's to say you won't be *dead*?' He intoned the last word before getting up very quickly, rushing into the kitchen, ticking 'The Past' on his list and coming back into the room with the half-finished bottle of vodka. More drinks were poured.

[76]

Charles was bowed over his glass, trying to remember what he wanted to tell his friend. 'You've lived alone too long,' he said. 'You work too hard. You shouldn't work too hard.' He paused. 'I've been married eleven years now.' He stopped to consider his next thought. 'It's been fun.'

'Yes, I know.' Flint put out his hand to comfort him, and knocked over his glass.

'And it does matter. It does matter. Think of them all around us, watching us, Blake, Shelley, Coleridge –'

'And Meredith.'

'– And Meredith. All of them influencing us.' Flint looked suddenly depressed. 'And do you know what, Andrew, do you want to know something? It's a secret, but I can tell you. You're a great friend. They got it all from Chatterton. Did you know that? I do.'

'It wouldn't surprise me.' Flint seemed only vaguely interested in this piece of information, and suddenly he leaned forward. 'It's amazing how much money you can make out of writing. Do you want to know how much I got for my novel?' Charles shook his head, and at this moment the pain returned. 'Go on. Guess.'

'I don't want to.'

'Go on. Be a sport.'

'I really don't want to know.' Charles could not control the pain, and he felt a sensation very close to vertigo. He looked down and he noticed that the button on his left shirt-cuff was hanging only by a small thread. He clutched at it, but it fell to the floor.

'Let me show you my word processor then,' Flint was saying. 'It cost a fortune.'

'No, seriously –'

'Come on. You'll like it.' Charles got up unsteadily, and Flint led him into his small office where a computer was perched upon his desk. 'Four thousand pounds,' Flint said proudly. He switched it on and, as a vague hum filled the room, he pushed three or four keys in succession; the word 'Library' appeared in the top left-hand corner and a series of Latin phrases passed across the screen, glowing with an amber light.

'I have to go now,' Charles was saying. 'My wife –'

'Oh, right. Yes. Of course. The happy family.' The sight of the computer seemed to have sobered Flint a little, and he led Charles towards the front door of his apartment. 'We must do this again soon.' He looked away as he said this. 'We really ought to keep in touch.' Then he noticed the expression on Charles's face and, with some alarm, he took hold of his arm. 'How are you feeling?'

Charles leaned against the side of the door, thinking that he had heard the words, 'I am your humble servant'. But he saw Flint looking at him anxiously, and murmured, 'I'm fine. What did you say in the old days? It must have been the salmon.' He felt the wall throbbing against him. 'Do you remember the salmon?'

'I'll call you a cab. And don't forget your manuscript.' Flint went down into the street, and it was only when Charles was being led towards the taxi that he remembered he had very little money on him. But he allowed himself to be placed in the seat, and the door to be closed; he even managed to smile and wave as he was driven away.

Flint went up to his apartment, relieved that the meeting had come to an end. He washed the glasses carefully, threw away the now empty bottle of vodka, rearranged the chairs on which they had sat, and then went back into his study. He switched on his computer, and for a while he stared at the bright screen.

*

'Stop!' Charles said, about a mile from his own flat. And then he murmured, almost to himself, 'I'm sorry. That's all I can afford.'

He was about to pay when the driver opened the window. 'That's all right. Your friend took care of it.' He drove off quickly.

And so Charles walked the rest of the way home. It was dark now and the streets were misty; the vapour wrapped itself around him and, when he looked down, it seemed that his limbs were covered with snow. But he was also treading on the mist, and his light steps had no echo. 'There is a pain,' he said out loud, 'but it belongs to everyone.' There was someone walking beside him who heard this, and who nodded in agreement; Charles turned to his invisible companion. 'The dream unfolds,' he said. 'The sleeper awakes, but still the dream goes on.' And he realised at once that these were not his words, but those of someone other.

# *Part Two*

This ys mie formaunce, which I nowe have wrytte,
The best performance of mie lyttel wytte.
(To John Lydgate. Thomas Chatterton.)

Strayt was I carry'd back to Tymes of yore
Whylst the Poet swathed yet yn fleshlie Bedde
And saw all Actyons whych han been before
And saw the Scroll of Fate unravelled
And when the Fate mark'd Babe acome to Syghte
I saw hym eager graspeynge after Lyghte.
(The Story of Wyllyam Canynge. Thomas Chatterton.)

# 6

THESE ARE circumstances that concern my conscience only
but I, Thomas Chatterton, known as Tom Goose-Quill,
Tom-all-Alone, or Poor Tom, do give them here in place of
Wills, Depositions, Deeds of Gift and sundry other legal devices.
Take then the folowing Account for what it is, tho' a Better, I
believe, could not be given by any other Man: for who was present
at my Birth but my own self, tho' it may be that this was one of
the few Occasions when my Mother had a better conception than
my Mother-wit. I was born in Pile Street, in the month of April,
in the year of Our Lord 1752, in the shit-hole of Bristol, in the sure
and certain Hope of being revil'd, abus'd, contemn'd by the pious
and admirable natives of that City who, like the Androcephalogoi,
carry their Heads where their Pricks should be. My Father being
dead, all around me at that time were Females, which fact may
account (as I explained to my Mother, and made her quite Cry
with Laughter) for my sudden Hysteric fits as a small Boy: for why
should I, the great Parodist, not coppy the softer Sex? But if it were
not the Females, then it was the Spleen which o'erwhelmed me.
One of my first Satires, writ when I was seven years old, was upon
this Topick.

My Father had been the singing master of St Mary Redcliffe, the
which Church was opposite to our house in Pile Street and so close
that I could number the very cracks in its Stone; and since he
expir'd only three months before my own Birth, it has often occur'd
to me that I must have heard his singing while I was yet in my
mother's Womb: hence my own love of Musick, even of the
discordant Airs which waft from the Publick Gardens and leave
me weeping. My Mother was a good woman, who never tired of
instructing me in the Virtues and Qualities of my Father: 'Your
Papa,' she would say, 'so loved this Church he might have built
it with his own Hands.' Then she would sigh, and then she would
laugh, putting down her Thread and Needle to embrace me. 'Why
so serious now?' she would ask me as I gazed up at her, 'Lord

what a boy is this, to be swayed by his Mother's poor memories!'

In the evenings I would sit with her, and twine my Arms around her neck, as she told me old stories by the Fire. 'Three hundred years ago,' she would say, 'the Church-steeple was struck by a Lightning rod and down it fell, tumbling among some cows in the neighbouring Field, where the Pie-shop and the Bookseller are now.' Three hundred years ago! The words were like a Spell upon me: a time before my self, and even before my Father, this same Church stood here! I was but a small Boy then, and yet from those Dayes forward I haunted St Mary Redcliffe. Whenever I entered its Porch it was with bowed head; being a fantastic, forlorn and fickle little Fellow it seemed to me that I was entering my father's own house (that in no Pious sense), and to my Fancy all the funerary monuments there became Images of him straitened in the death from which I wish'd to pluck him. So you see how I came to be so great a lover of Antiquity.

In those far-off Dayes, I would put on my brown cloth coat, and my round hat, and wander into the Fields in the hope of finding hidden Tumuli or inscriptions upon Stones. I would lie down upon the cropped grass, or lean against a tree, and look with wonder upon the Church which so dominated the fields and alleys beside it. 'There,' I would say to myself, 'there is the spot where the lightning hit the steeple – and there is the place where they formerly acted Playes. On the west side, there, the old monks blessed the well on the feast-day of St Mary – and there it may be that my Father used to sit on an evening, when he was tired of Singing.' And all these things came together, so that I fell into a kind of Ecstacy.

About this time I was put into a Dame-school, where I was taught how to calculate the price of Corn and other such Bristolian necessities (for there is no Love except for Lucre in that Jakes, that Privy, that Burial-Ground for Merchants and for Whores), and after that I advanc'd to Colston's School in Redcliffe Street. There is nothing so sordid or so obstinate as the Schoolboy, and it was all I could do to restrain my immoderate Laughter when my companions prattled on about their Brothers and their Sisters, their Parents and their Pet-mice, their Ball-games and their Writing-lessons. They called me Tom Chanticleer, or Chanty, because of my red hair; but they never guess'd the Names by which I knew them. They also called me Tom-all-Alone because of my solitariness: but I was not alone, since I had as many Companions as I required in my Books. My Father had purchased a hundred dusty Volumes, and these I would take from their Shelves (scattering the Mice) with as much Reverence as if they had been written in his own Hand: I read heraldry, English antiquities, metaphysical disquisitions, mathematicall researches, music, astronomy, physic and the like. But nothing enthralled me so much as Historicall works, and indeed I could not learn so much at Colston's as I could at home: I had not books enough at School but in my Closet I studdied Speight's Chaucer and Camden's Britannica, Percy's Reliques and Miss Elizabeth Cooper's Muses Library; then I was at Peace, because my Father's world had also become like to mine.

I never stopp'd my reading but yet there came a time when I chang'd it, and this on the winter Morning when my Mother showed me an old manuscript in French with illuminated capitals and all its antique Finery preserv'd. 'Tom,' she said, 'Tommy, look at this musty Parchment lodged in one of your father's Singing-books. The colouring is very pretty for such an old thing, do you think? Shall we sell it, and turn this paper into Fire-wood?'

I was amazed, for the manuscript was perfect of its kind. 'You have found a treasure,' I said, hugging her, 'which may kindle more than a winter's fire. Nothing can be like it!' And I put my fingers across the intense golds and greens of its Capitals, which glowed like a Tapestry or like a Field of Flowers.

'Oh,' says she, surprised by my Enthusiasm. 'No doubt there is plenty more such Stuff in the Church. Your poor Father used to tell me of it.'

'My dear Dame and Relict,' said I, thus making her laugh despite herself, 'do give me an exact Description of the place or I will surely die.'

'Well, well, Tom, you are too young to die yet. I must save you.' And then she set herself to thinking where my father had found the Parchment: 'Was it in the Vestry? No, not there, not with old Mr Crowe in attendance with his dirty Snuff . . . was it in the Tower, no, too high for him . . . was it, no . . . I have it, Tom, it was in the locked room above the north Porch, where there was talk of Bats and such like. All the old Coffers and Cabinets are there.'

I hugged her again. 'Mother,' said I, 'you are worth a thousand Vestal Virgins!' (For I had lately been reading Mudie's *History of Rome*.)

'I hope I may be modest, Tom,' she replied, 'but I am no Virgin, unless there is to be another Age of Miracles.'

'I will perform a Miracle,' I said. 'I will bring the Past to light again.'

And at once I set off across the path to find Mr Crowe, the verger of St Mary Redcliffe, an old and rambling party who never could leave off his Snuffing and his Sniffling. 'Mr Crowe,' I said when finally I found him in the Vestry, brooding over his sadly arranged Accounts, 'may I trouble you for the key to the little room above the north Porch?'

He knew me well, and knew me in every respect to be my Father's son. 'There is nothing there but Dust and old Ragged things, Tom,' says he. 'Nothing for a Boy.'

'My Father found Parchments there,' I replied. 'I came to find some others of a like kind.'

'Oh there are Papers.' He sneezed and wiped his Nose with his Sleeve, as was his Custom. 'But they are Tattered and Rotten ones. They are no use except as Thread-papers or as Fools' Caps for Boys such as you.' He laughed, and gave a little Sniff.

'Venerable Mr Crowe,' I began, and he laughed again. 'If I am a Fool then pray humour my Folly. For they say that a Man out of his Wits is close to being Wise.'

'Thomas Chatterton,' said he, 'you have an old Head on young Shoulders.'

'Then old Papers are mine by Right of Primogeniture.'

He gave me a Look and then smil'd. 'Well,' said he, 'it is true that the church has no further use for them.' So he led me, by way of the winding stair beside the north Porch, to the old Muniment Room; he unlock'd the thick wooden door and then left me with great Despatch, the Cold entering his Bones (or so he thought).

It is said that there comes an Instant when any Man may see his whole Fate stretching in front of him, as it were in a Vision, and so imagine my own Astonishment and Joy when I saw within the bare stone Chamber two wooden Chests. I hasten'd to open them, and there all higgledy-piggledy were old Papers, Parchments, Accounts and Bills which were thrown together like so many Leaves fallen after a Hurricanoe. With much delicacy and gentleness did I hold them up, the Parchments seeming to burn my Hands so great was my Delight in them; some were inscrib'd in Latin or in French, while others had numbers scrawled across them as if they might be Church Accounts or Tables of Interest. But there were some Fragments that I could easily make out to be in the English tongue (although curiously writ) and, leaving the other Papers in the Chests for the moment, took these away with me homewards. With trembling Fingers I laid them out in my Closet and, tho' much decay'd and composed in the native Gothick of that time, I could read them pritty easily: in truth there was not much to decipher, being the peeces of Words or sentences only, but it was enough; my Imagination was all on Fire, and I began to transcribe them in my own Hand. Here were such phrases as

[84]

'Sendes owte his greetings', 'ye have gyvyn me a grete charge', 'the nombres therewythalle' and it seemed even then that the Dead were speaking to me, face to face; and when I wrote out their words, coppying the very spelling of the Originals, it was as if I had become one of those Dead and could speak with them also. I was brought to such a Pitch that, when I left off transcribing, I found that I could continue in my own right; there was a pritty little Sentence, *viz* 'And so they toke him by every parte of the body', to which I then added, 'and bare hym into a chambir and leyde him a rych bedde'. The very words had been called forth from me, with as much Ease as if I were writing in the Language of my own Age. Schoolboy tho' I was, it was even at this time that I decided to shore up these ancient Fragments with my own Genius: thus the Living and the Dead were to be reunited. From that very moment, I ceased to be a meer Boy.

And so I, Thomas Chatterton, at the age of Twelve, began my own Great Ledger of the Past. My first task was to give myself as good a Lineage as any Gentleman in Bristol, and this I did by combining my own knowledge of Heraldic devices with a document which, as I put it, was 'just newly found in St Mary Redcliffe and writ in the language of *auntient Dayes*'. All this issued from me so freely that I could not bridle my bursting Invention, and speedily I composed *Trew Histories* of Bristol and of the Church itself. My Method was as follows: I had already around me, in Volumes taken from my Father's shelves or purchas'd from the Booksellers, Charters and Monuments and such like Stuff; to these I added my Readings from Ricat, Stow, Speed, Holinshed, Leland and many another purveyour of Antiquity. If I took a passage from each, be it ever so short, I found that in Unison they became quite a new Account and, as it were, Chatterton's Account. Then I introduc'd my own speculations in physic, drama, and philosophy, all of them cunningly changed by the ancient Hand and Spelling I had learn'd; but conceeved by me with such Intensity that they became more real than the Age in which I walked. I reproduc'd the Past and filled it with such Details that it was as if I were observing it in front of me: so the Language of ancient Dayes awoke the Reality itself for, tho' I knew that it was I who composed these Histories, I knew also that they were true ones.

But it was not enough for me to Write. The cunning citizens of Bristol calculate only by outward Show and so, to confound and to outwit them, I learned how to give my own Papers the semblance of Antiquity. Into my Closet I smuggl'd a pounce bag of Charcole, a great stick of yellow ochre and a bottle of black lead powder, with which Materials I could fabricate an appearance of great Age as closely as if my new invented Papers were the very ones from the Chests of St Mary Redcliffe. I would rub the ochre and lead across the Parchments and sometimes, to antiquate my Writings still further, I would drag them through the Dust or hold them above a Candle – which process not only quite chang'd the colour of the Inke but blackened and contracted the Parchment itself. I was a willing Student but, at first, there was more madness than method in my labours; and my Mother, hearing sundry Groans and Curses coming from my Chamber on the first Day that ever I tried them, entered and found me in a clowd of Charcole. I was so cover'd in ochre and in lead that she threw up her hands, saying 'Lord, Tom, do you colour yourself to join the Gypsies?'

'Worthy Mother of a worthy son, I am a strolling Player and this Chamber is my Theatre.'

She sniffed the Air. 'This musty Stuff is no play. Pugh! I blame Mr Crowe for it!'

'Dear relict and bounteous Dame of Bristol,' said I, 'you are too curious and sharp-nosed for your poor Son. I wish you would go out of my Room – it is *my* Room.' But, seeing that she was somewhat offended by this, I went on hastily, 'This musty stuff, as you put it, will make our Fortune. I have stumbled upon, with the help of the venerable Crowe, I admit it, I have stumbled upon true Narrations of our fair City and several famous Anecdotes of our leading Families.' (So great was my Faith in my own Skill that I concealed the Truth even from her.) 'There will be many paunchy Citizens who will pay and pay again for these Memorials of their illustrious Ancestors.' And then I went on, embroidering upon this fair Trick and goodly Device even as I conceived it, 'It will delight our sweet Gentry at the same time as it will satisfy our Purse.'

Now my Mother, whose mouth was so open that she could catch summer-bugs even as she talk'd, was not long in spreading this News throughout the Town, *viz* that her dear and learned Son had found withinne the Church some old Papers which would be *of as much value as interest*, as she put it, to the amiable Citizens of Bristol. And pritty soon I was able to offer proof of this when I fabricated various Memorials to Master Baker, Master Catcott, Mistress Higgins, and what not, proclaiming the Virtues of their Bristolian forebears. And when they ask'd, 'how met you with this?', I replied, 'This is authentick evidence, found in an old Parchment Roll and discover'd in the Chests of St Mary Redcliffe. You may ask the Verger, Mr Crowe, who directed me thither.' And so fervent was their Hope, so froward their Belief, that they sprang from illustrious Stock, and not from the Sows and Whores which they resembled, that their Minds were soon put at Ease by this.

So I was not short of Coins to jangle in my Pocket, even tho' my own Tune was to be quite a different one. Poetry was my device. I invented my self as a monk of the fifteenth century, Thomas Rowley; I dressed him in Raggs, I made him Blind and then I made him Sing. I compos'd Elegies and Epicks, Ballads and Songs, Lyricks and Acrosticks, all of them in that curious contriv'd Style which speedily became the very Token of my own Feelings; for, as I wrote in Rowley's hand, 'Syke yn the Weal of Kynde', which is as much to say, 'All things are partes of One.' I put it in another sense with the following:

> Now Rowlie ynne these mokie Dayes
> Sendes owte hys shynynge Lyghte
> And Turgotus and Chaucer live
> Inne every line hee wrytes.

Thus do we see in every Line an Echoe, for the truest Plagiarism is the truest Poetry.

These ancient Verses I then despatch'd to various of the Journals, both in London and in Bristol, with the same Postscriptum appended: 'This Poem wrote by Thomas Rowlie, Priest, which I have discover'd in the Muniment Room of the Church of St Mary Redcliffe; I send the whole as Specimen of the Poetry of those Dayes, being greatly superior to what we have been taught to beleeve'. And so Antiquity, like the blind Prophet led by a Boy, was given over to my Care. I sold my Verses to the Booksellers also and, tho' I met with some Success in London, for the most part the fame of Thomas Rowlie was bruited through Bristol – and that to such an extent that the Trade in my Work was very brisk. There was one Bookseller who suspected the Truth, *viz* that these were Verses of my own Devising; this was Sam. Joynson, a young Man lately gone into the Trade, who had lent me Books and Pamphlets before Rowlie was ever created. He knew what a bright Spark I was, and what a Soul I had for Learning, but at this time he said nothing and he purchas'd my Verse without so much as a remote Allusion to its Origin. You may ask, why did you not stand forth as the true Author and thus proclaim your own Merit? But you forget the elegant Town of Bristol, a very Ship of Fools where only Rank and Gold are the Captains. Being a boy of obscure Birth and imperfect Education, anything that I produc'd myself would have been despised and neglected: I am a poet born, which is a greater thing than a Gentleman, and even in those Dayes I had too much pride to become an Object for the low Jests and carping Examinations of the sordid Bristolians.

And so it was that, even while I was caught fast in this Shit-hole and Whorehouse which I blush to call my Native town, all my Thoughts began running upon London where (or so I thought) my Genius might blaze and consume all those who saw it. I first projected this Scheme to Sam. Joynson, on a morning when I was standing beside one of his Shelves filled with sad modern Stuff. 'London is the lodestone which draws me,' I said, 'I am as uneasy in this place as a Drab in a Nunnery.'

'Well, well,' says Sam, with his bright Eyes upon my Face. 'Be sure you are not drawn towards the Rocks.'

'What Song was it the Sirens sang, Sam?'

He laughed at my Alliteration. 'No song of your devising, Tom.' Then he stopped short. 'Tho', of course, I cannot be sure of that.' He coughed a little and blamed the Dust for it. 'Well, well,' said he at last, 'at least in London you may work in secrecy, which will suit you.'

'Why should it?' I asked him sharply. But he gave me another of his bright looks, and said no more.

When I broach'd the matter with my Mother, and told her that I was resolv'd to go, she gave a little Moan and, sitting down heavily upon a Rush-chair, crack'd it. This made her laugh. 'You used to kick so hard in my Belly,' she said after a Moment, 'I knew that you would be eager to go on your way. But beware of the Pox, Tom. They say that the Females of London are meer Sluts.'

'Quite different, then, from the modest Maidens of Bristol?' She tried to smile at this, but then put her Apron to her Eyes to wipe off a Tear.

There was nothing more to be said, and so in the first week of April 1770 I coach'd it to London: each blast of the Horn seemed to be driving me closer to my Fortune, and tho' the Wind cool'd my Cheeks it also warm'd my Heart. When we entred Leadenhall and Old Jewry I was already considering my self to be a Citizen, and was lost in a Maze of Admiration long before I was ever lost in the Maze of the Streets. The sister of Sam. Joynson had a common Lodging-house in Holborn and, directing my Steps thither as Sam. had instructed me, I was greeted with much affection and taken to a small Chamber up three pair of Stairs: here in my aerial Abode I looked across the Chimneys and Rooftops, dreaming of my approaching Fame.

But if my Course was set upon great Poetry, the Race was hard enough; and, on the next Morning, when I visited the Offices of those Journals that had published my Work while I was a meer Boy of Bristol, I found that they had more need for Satires than for Songs. Of course these I compos'd willingly enough, for I hold that Man in contempt who cannot write to Measure: for the *Town and Country* I wrote political Satires against all Parties, Whig or Tory, Papist or Methodist; for the *Political Register* I compos'd meer Squibs, which they took up gladly tho' they did not know the true Range of my Shot; and, knowing my own Skill in the Art of Personation, for the *Court and City* I set myself to write the memoirs of a sad dog (a gentleman pursewed by Bailiffs), of a malefactor chain'd in Newgate, of an old Relict thirsting for a Man, and of a young ripe Girl about to be pluck'd. And these I related in their own Voices, naturally, as if they were authentick Histories: so that tho' I was young Thomas Chatterton to those I met, I was a very Proteus to those who read my Works.

Yet now I must invoke the weeping Muse and have recourse to Elegie for, to put it shortly, I could not live. I learn'd too soon that writing is all a Lottery, and Taste very changeable, for within a very few weeks I found my Rowley works to be despis'd (who was there in that frantic painted Age to have recourse to the Past?), my Satires scorn'd and my Squibs extinguished with Coldness. Indeed there were so many Barbs to my Pride, and Hindrances to my Progress, that I was like to be o'erwhelmed and to sink under them: in the morning I walk'd to the Booksellers and to the Newspapers, tho' I had too much pride to Entreat them to publish my Work; then, disturbed in my Mind, I went rambling in the Parks and the Suburbs with nothing so much as a Sheep's Tongue in my Pocket to satisfy my Hunger; then back again to my Lodgings in the Evening, to stare at the empty Grate. My landlady, Mrs Angell, being as I said the sister of Sam. Joynson, would often beg me to join them in the Kitchin or the Parlour where I might eat with them; but I am of an imperious and wayward Disposition, I admit it, and could not bring myself to show my Poverty or to accept another's Charity. Instead I sharpen'd my Quill and sat down to write, in the uncertain Hope that Poetry might ward off my Afflictions; but these were the Verses of indigence, compos'd in Inconvenience and Disquietude: they gained me nothing but the Coste of Inke. Indeed I had reached such a Pitch of Distraction that I had settled in my Mind that, having studied Physic from Books when I was a boy, I might become a Surgeon's mate on the Voyages to Africa. But such Travelling was not for me: my Voyage was to be of quite another kind, for it was at this Moment that Sam. Joynson (no doubt summoned by his Sister) called upon me. I was overjoyed to see him, tho' I took care not to show it. He gave me a quick Look, which I knew well, and first he asked me if I would care to take a Dish of Chocolate with his sister, an invitation which I declin'd with much Acknowledgment. Then he suggested to me that we should repair to the Potato-ordinary in Shoe Lane; this I declin'd again, knowing that he saw in my Face some marks of Hunger or of Faintness. 'I have just eaten,' I said, 'but I will watch you eat.'

'No, no, Tom. But can I perswade you at least to share some Wine with me? There is no Harm in that, I presume?'

After some hesitation I consented to this, and he called down to his Sister's Kitchen Maid for a Bottle and two Glasses. Then he settled himself upon the Edge of my Bed (there being little Furniture in my Attick room) saying, 'So how do you drive your Trade in London now, Tom?'

'Pretty good.' He was always of quick Perception, so I added at once, 'How goes the poet Rowley in your Bookshop?'

'The Monk is too prolific,' he said, looking directly at me. 'I cannot sell as much as I did before. There are some Voices raised against him.'

'Voices?' I got up from my Chair, and walked over to the little Window from where I could see the Rooftops of London and, above them, the great Dome of St Paul's.

'There are some who say that he is an Imposture.'

I turned around quickly. 'He is as real as I am!'

'Yes. I know. Rowley stands before me now.'

'I don't understand your meaning, Sam Joynson.'

'I knew it was your own work as soon as you brought it to me, so eager and impetuous were you for my Opinion.'

'No –'

'Come, Tom, there is no need for more Pretence.' He got up from the narrow Bed and put his Hand upon my Shoulder, so that we were both now gazing out of the little Window. 'When you are in such a Strait as this, where is the need for Concealment?' He paus'd, and then he added, 'The monk cannot last. You are riding him too hard.'

He was Correct: there was no point in further Masquerade and, with Catastrophe threatening, I could no longer restrain my self. 'But I must write,' I said, 'I need to live. I cannot eat air or grass for my Sustenance.'

'I know. That is why I have come to see you, Tom.' Then he said in a softer voice, 'You may live well without Rowley, if you choose to. I have no doubt that there are other Authors within you.'

'As Junius would say, your Discourse is a little Mysterious, sir.'

Joynson pac'd around the room before coming to a stop in front of me. 'Now,' he said, 'now is the white minute for other Discoveries. Think of it: Akenside is just now lying in his Coffin in Burlington Street, Gray is sick of a Cancer and not thought likely to recover, Smart is raving and tyed to a Chair. Do you understand me as yet?'

'Go on.'

'The verses of Dyer and Thomson are much admired and, tho' they have both been dead these twenty years, who knows if more of their work is not to be found?' He paused. 'Do you understand me now, Tom?'

'I think I understand your Drift, sir. You wish me to forge the work of these men.'

'I did not say Forge. Is the work of Rowley a forgery?' He hesitated, collecting his Words. 'Is it not, as the Platonists tell us, an imitation in a world of Imitations?'

'But why should I stoop to *imitate* –' I emphasised that Word – 'the Verses of Poets much inferior to me?'

He looked at me steadily. 'You cannot eat or drink Pride,' he said at last. Then he took my Arm and added heartily, 'And when at last you admit these Works to be your own, the Confession will bring you Fame.'

'The Fame of a great Plagiarist?'

'No, the Fame of a great Poet. You prove your Strength by doing their Work better than ever they could, and then by also doing your own.'

This was a clever Hit, and caught me unawares. 'I did such work once,' I said, 'when I was a Schoolboy. In Bristol I have copies of my poem, *The Seasons Upside Down*, after Thomson, and *The Water Closet Unveiled*, after Goldsmith.'

'I know. Your Mother showed them to me. If there is one thing finer in Heaven's sight than a dutiful Son, it is a dutiful Parent.'

'She is an old Mountebank,' I said, 'to prick you on thus.' But the Humour of it impress'd me, and I began to Laugh.

'Oh no,' says Joynson, laughing with me. 'It is my Plan, not hers.'

'And your Trade, also.'

'*Our* Trade.'

'And our Trade is this, is it not? I give you Verses so like the Originals that the Poet himself could not tell them apart, and then you sell them as the work of Dyer and such like?'

'The Profits to be divided equally.'

'The profits to be divided Equally.' But then another Thought

[91]

struck me: 'But my Name has long been known in Bristol. How, after Rowley, could we keep such a Secret?'

'I have thought of that,' he said solemnly. 'It may be necessary to hide you in Obscurity for a while. You should remain an Enigma, even to yourself.'

'And how is this to be achiev'd?'

'Why, you must vanish like a Spectre.'

'And this without Necromancy?'

'Well,' he said, putting his Head on one side. 'There is a way.' He grinned at me. 'I have been considering your Death, Tom.'

'I think I will have some Wine now.'

He poured me a Glass, right to the very Brim. 'For what, Tom, is so Close and so Secret as the Tomb?'

'I see that this is a grave Topick.'

'If you can impersonate others, why can you not impersonate your own Fatality?'

I was so taken Aback that I said nothing for a few Moments. 'You mean, to forge my own death?'

He laugh'd again, and refilled my Glass which I had drained. 'What better Protection might we have? Who could suspect you of Versifying after so severe a Change?'

It was a merry Jest indeed. 'And how shall I reach this happy state, Sam?'

'A suicide. My sister will spread it to the World that you are undone, and no one will suspect the Truth of it. The verdict of *felo de se* is easy to obtain in this Parish, where the Poor perish so fast they can hardly be counted. Of course you must moddell a death-bed scene, for the sake of Witnesses –'

He was about to outline the Remainder of his Plan, but I stopp'd him. 'And after that?'

'You work in Peace for as long as you chuse.'

And indeed after the Confusions and Injuries in which I had already been whirl'd, the notion of working silent and unseen pleas'd me – not less so because it would lead to my greater Triumph over those who now scorn'd me. The Booksellers and Publishers who call'd me a *meer Boy* would soon be applauding that Boy's work, albeit under other Names, and when I reveal'd myself as I truly was I would confound them, and break them, and prove my own Genius.

And so it was (to look forward a little) that after my untimely Departure from this Life I first began upon the *newly discovered Works* of Mr Gray, Mr Akenside, Mr Churchill, Mr Collins and sundry others: I even coppied Mr Blake, for my own love of his Gothick style, but this was for the Foolery only. A great Genius can affect anything, and I understood their Passions as soon as I imployed their Styles: it was not some cold Burlesque but rather –

'It ends there,' Charles Wychwood said, putting down the manuscript from which he had been reading. 'That's the lot.'

At this point Philip Slack discovered that he had slid off his chair and was now sprawled upon the floor, rubbing his eyes. 'I can't . . .' he began to say. He started to examine his knees, and muttered 'Real' to them.

'What was that?'

'Is it real?'

'Of course it's real. It's stupendously real. Incredibly real.' Charles paused. 'Didn't it seem real to you?'

'Yes, it seemed real.'

This was enough to confirm Charles's enthusiasm. 'They're going to cause a sensation.' He put the papers up to his mouth. 'I love them so much I could swallow them whole!'

Philip tried not to be alarmed by this, but he knew his friend's eating habits. 'They must be fragile,' he explained to his knees.

'Oh, these are just the copies. Vivien did them on her office machine.'

'Against my better judgment,' she said quietly, coming into the room now that Charles's recital was finally over.

'I thought it was against your desk.' Charles was delighted by his joke. 'I thought it was against the wall. I thought it was against the law.' He was laughing, and spinning himself around in the middle of the room. 'There has to be a copy,' he said to Philip in the course of these gyrations. 'How could we know that it was real without a copy? Everything is copied.'

Philip and his knees debated this point. 'I suppose,' he said finally, 'that you're right.'

'No, I mean that all the other documents are copied, too.' He stopped spinning and, swaying slightly, went over to his desk; he held up a sheaf of papers and handed them to Philip, who tried unsuccessfully to raise himself from the floor in order to read them. Even from a cursory inspection it was clear to him that there were poems in a number of styles, but all transcribed in the same handwriting. He gave them back to Charles. 'I can't,' he said, gravely. 'I have to be alone to read.'

'Ah, the solitary reader.' Charles grabbed Philip's hand and hauled him up from the floor. Then he took his arm and rapidly marched him around the room as he spoke. 'Some of them are by Crabbe, some by Gray, and some by Blake. There are some very famous poems here, but we know now that it is Chatterton imitating all of them.' He squeezed his arm as they walked in smaller and smaller circles. 'Do you see how it works? Joynson persuades Chatterton to fake his own death, then Chatterton forges the great poetry of his time, and then Joynson sells it. Elementary.' He stopped suddenly, and Philip stumbled forward. 'You know,' he went on, catching hold of him just before he fell, 'half the poetry of the eighteenth century is probably written by him.'

Philip leaned against the wall, breathing heavily after these exertions. 'He's the greatest forger in history,' was all he managed to say.

'No! He wasn't a forger!'

'The greatest plagiarist in history?'

'No!' In his enthusiasm Charles looked triumphantly at him. 'He was the greatest poet in history!'

'I'll make some tea,' Vivien said quietly. 'Philip looks worn out.'

As soon as she had gone into the kitchen, Charles's mood changed; he lay down upon the sofa and stared out of the window at the rain, his face very pale in the early evening light. 'Flint dated the handwriting,' he said, after a pause. 'He seems to know about everything.'

Philip was affected by Charles's thoughtful mood, and replied gravely. 'He's a lucky man.'

'Ah yes, but the lucky man is always nervous. He never knows when his good fortune might end.' All the animation seemed to have left him, and he turned towards Philip with a sigh. 'Consider the lilies of the field, and so forth.' A sudden gust of wind blew the rain through the open window, and Philip went across to close it; Charles's face was wet, but he did not notice this. 'Did you find anything about Chatterton in your library?'

'No. Do you want to wipe your face?' Charles shook his head and Philip, unnerved by his sudden silence, felt it necessary to carry on talking. 'It was curious, but I was reading some novels by Harrison Bentley –'

'Typical.'

'– and they were very much like Harriet Scrope's books. The plots were the same. Not that it matters,' he went on hurriedly. He was annoyed at himself for mentioning this; he had resolved to say nothing about it. 'It doesn't matter at all.'

Charles seemed neither interested nor surprised. 'There you are, you see. It's catching.'

'What is?'

'Chatterton.' Vivien came back into the room, and Charles sprang up from the sofa. 'We were just planning our next move,

Vivie.' Philip blushed. 'Philip says we must find a publisher. He's convinced this will make us very rich!'

Vivien said nothing and Charles went on, 'I'm working for Harriet tomorrow, so I'll ask her advice. We can always trust her.'

*

That night he could not sleep and, as Vivien lay beside him, images of Chatterton's handwriting floated across him. He stretched and put out his arms, so that he resembled a 'T'; then he curled up in the bed and became a 'C'. But it was in the darkest and most silent part of the night that he rose from his bed and walked softly into the other room. He turned on the light and, blinking, looked over the papers which he had shown to Philip that evening. When he came to these lines, he stopped and read them out loud:

And you who soon will join th'unhonoured Dead,
    Closing your Eyes to Fate's unjust decree,
Who took you to this place where now you hang your Head
    In sorrow, and drink Ambition to the lees?

He put his head upon his arm, and wept.

Vivien came into the room, and was bending over him. 'Is it the same pain?' she asked him.

'Yes,' he said. 'Yes. It's the same pain.'

# 7

HARRIET SCROPE was trying to examine her gums in the ormolu mirror above the mantelpiece; she was craning her neck and leering at her reflection, almost toppling over as she did so, but she could see nothing. 'Never again!' she said out loud. 'I'll never have that man in my mouth again!' The door-bell rang and, since she had just had a long telephone conversation with Sarah Tilt about the iniquities of her dentist, she half-expected her old friend to materialise on the doorstep. So she opened the door quickly, screaming 'Hello, darling!', and saw at once that it was Charles Wychwood. 'Oh, good morning,' she said in a lower voice. 'I thought you were someone else.' She had forgotten that Charles was supposed to be working for her today.

'No,' he replied. 'I think it's me.' His manner seemed jaunty, in spite of his somewhat haggard appearance.

'Just so long as you're sure. I wouldn't want a stranger in my lovely house.' She led him through the hallway into the sitting room, and then pointed in a marked manner at a vacant chair. 'I was in the hands of a butcher earlier,' she said as soon as she had sat down opposite him.

'Oh! What's for dinner?'

'No, not that kind. A real *butcher*. My so-called dentist. I hate the things he puts in my mouth. Hard things, horrible things. I felt like a rag doll, Charles, slumped in his so-called surgery. And don't ask me what he did to my poor gums.' She rearranged her fingers upon her lap so that both hands were locked together. 'So how are you?' she added, quite casually, as if her previous diatribe had never taken place.

'I'm managing.'

Harriet nodded solemnly at this piece of information. 'And I'm managing too.' There was a silence between them. 'I see,' she said, 'that Christmas is coming.' She pointed to an object wrapped in brown paper which Charles had brought with him, and which was now propped against his chair. Beside it there was a plastic bag filled with papers. 'I'd love a new fur coat.'

'This is something I want to show you, Harriet.' Charles made an effort to rise from the chair but the cat had leapt upon him and now seemed to be pinning him down. 'Do you know anything about Thomas Chatterton?' Mr Gaskell left him with a strange cry, and Charles could now lean forward to pick up the bag.

'Chatterton?'

'Shall I let you into a secret?'

'Oh yes. I love secrets.' She always assumed that the secrets of the young concerned sex, and she ran her tongue across her upper lip.

'He didn't die.'

'That is good news.' The idea seemed to please her. 'What did he do instead? Hibernate?' She got up quickly and walked towards the alcove, where she poured herself a gin. 'Medicine,' she said, brandishing a small spoon, 'Medicine for my poor gums.'

'I'm serious. Thomas Chatterton didn't die.'

'Oh, go on. Pull the other one.' She put her right leg in the air and waved it about. 'Go on. Pull it.'

Charles gratefully declined her offer. 'No, I mean he did die. But not when he was supposed to. Not when everyone thinks he did. And I've got proof.' He took the wrapping off the canvas and, as he did so, Harriet noticed how slow and clumsy his movements had become. 'Do you recognise the face?'

'Search me.' She held up her hands, as if she was offering herself to be frisked.

'It's Chatterton in middle age.'

She took another spoonful of gin, trying to remember something of her conversation with Sarah Tilt. There was a line about a bough, or a branch, being cut . . . 'But wasn't he the boy who committed suicide?'

'That's just the point. He didn't kill himself. He carried on writing in other poets' names.'

'You mean, he was a plagiarist?' A change had come over Harriet's face, and she turned away for a moment. 'This medicine is bitter,' she said to the alcove. But, when she turned back to face Charles, she took the portrait from him and scrutinised it. 'He looks like Matthew Arnold,' she said. 'Not my cup of tea at all.' She put the painting down. 'Did they catch him?' Charles was obviously puzzled by her question. 'Did they expose him?'

'Who?'

'You know. The guardians of the town, of course.' It was an

odd phrase, and Harriet had crossed her fingers behind her back as she said it.

'No, it wasn't like that. He wasn't doing anything wrong –'

'I know!' she said loudly.

'   and in any case he confessed everything. You see, this is really what I wanted to show you.' And he handed her the photocopies of the manuscripts which he had discovered in Bristol.

She held them out at arm's length. 'They look,' she said slowly, 'as if they were written in the year dot.'

For a moment Charles had an image of a blank television screen. 'He wrote them about 1810.'

'Well,' she said, very seriously, 'that's before my time.'

He ignored this. 'I was hoping to find a publisher quite quickly.' Oh God, another book, was Harriet's first thought as Charles continued. 'It will destroy all the academic theories. They were all completely wrong.'

'Really? That is good news.' Harriet had always been angered by the marginal attention which academic critics paid to her; in fact, she considered anyone teaching at a university to be a personal enemy. 'Let them eat cake,' she said.

'Don't you mean humble pie?'

She waved the empty glass at Charles. 'What do they know of Harriet Scrope who only Harriet Scrope know? I mean *cake*. Now tell me the story again.' And so Charles explained once more the history of Thomas Chatterton and his forgeries. In her excitement, Harriet put her hands between her thighs and squeezed them – with such vigour, in fact, that when Charles came to the end of his narrative they emerged bloodless and shrunken.

'. . . I'll be rolling in clover,' Charles was saying.

'Who's Clover?'

'– that is, if I can publish them.'

She got up with a shriek. 'Of course we can publish them! They'll never be able to ignore us now!' Charles was not quite sure what she meant by 'us' and then she added, almost as an afterthought, 'Why don't you leave all the papers with me, Charles? I'm very good with old things.' Charles was about to turn down her generous offer, but in any case the momentary look of alarm on his face was enough to warn Harriet that she had said too much. 'Silly me,' she added. 'We can talk about the trivial details later.' She smiled reassuringly at him as she changed the subject. 'Don't you think, dear,' she went on, 'that we ought to have a session on my book now? It will cheer us both up.'

Charles had forgotten that he was supposed to be helping Harriet with her memoirs, but now he assumed a look of pleasurable anticipation. 'That would be very nice,' he said. He was still wondering what Harriet had meant by 'us'.

She walked into her study, which was on the opposite side of the hallway, and after a few moments called out, 'Perhaps Mother is another Chatterton! Perhaps I go back thousands of years!' She returned as suddenly as she had left, carrying in front of her a pile of typewritten pages which she dumped on Charles's lap with a look of distaste. 'That silly bitch typed them out but –' and here she imitated her previous assistant's high quavering voice – 'it *seemed* to her, *actually*, that she didn't know what to *do* with them. As it *were*.' And all the time she spoke she was looking at the bag filled with the Chatterton manuscripts.

Charles began leafing through the papers she had given him. On some of them there were paragraphs or sentences, while on others only certain names and dates had been typed. 'You should keep it as it is,' he said. 'It could be a poem.'

'But I don't want to write a poem. I want to write a book.'

Charles put his head to one side and smiled at her. 'What's the difference, really?'

She stared at him for a moment. 'You ought to know.' Instantly she regretted her tone and added, sweetly, 'You ought to know what I mean. You've managed to do both, haven't you?'

'What was it Montaigne said, I no more make the book than the book makes me?'

'What a lovely thought, Charles.' She paused, uncertain how to go on. 'I'm sure you're right.'

'Not me, Montaigne.'

'Well, who's counting?' She glanced down at the Chatterton manuscripts again and, as she stood over Charles, tried surreptitiously to move them towards her with her foot. But the bag fell over and Harriet said, quickly and loudly, 'Now go on. Ask me something about the notes I dictated to the silly little bitch. Oh look, your bag has fallen over. You should take more care of it. Let me pick it up and put it somewhere safe.'

'It's fine, Harriet. It's quite safe here.' He beamed up at her and she turned away, scowling, to find a chair.

'Go on then,' she said. 'Ask me a question.'

Charles extracted a page of the typewritten notes and read out, in an uncertain voice, '1943. The Collage. John Davenport. T.S. Eliot. The Hotel Russell.'

'I was drunk every day then, and twice on Thursdays.' She was delighted by her memory of this, although in fact it was only a line from one of her novels.

'Who was Davenport?'

[99]

'I can't remember. Some nobody, probably.' She was beginning to feel the panic again – the panic which was aroused whenever she was questioned about the past. 'Now Eliot was a sweetie. He published my first two novels.' She was trying hard to remain calm. 'Not that he knew anything about fiction, of course. Are you taking this down, dear?' Charles had been doodling on the paper – dead faces, with no eyes – but now he began to write as she talked. 'It was Djuna Barnes who recommended me. She was a dreadful woman, really.' Harriet sighed. 'She was a lesbo, you know. And an American.' She shook herself, as if her old-fashioned Chanel dress had suddenly grown too tight for her. 'She tried to tongue me once. I don't mind a few kisses and cuddles from my own sex – you know Sarah Tilt, don't you? – but I draw the line at tongue. It's the roughness I can't stand. It makes me vomit.'

Charles wrote down 'tongue' and then stopped. 'Do you want me to mention this?'

'Well, I hope she's dead by now.' Harriet had another moment of anxiety. 'She is dead, isn't she?'

'I'll look her up.'

'That's where you'll come in so handy, Charles. Looking things up.' She yawned, and hastily tried to cover her mouth. 'And then Eliot took me to the Hotel Russell. But only for tea, you know.' She closed her eyes and her fingers quivered slightly on her lap; it was her customary way of conceiving her fiction. 'Not that I wasn't a very beautiful young woman. Oh yes. People used to stare at me in the street.' She opened her eyes suddenly, and looked at him. 'They would come from miles around just to see my legs.' Charles was astonished by this, and she laughed. 'Don't worry, dear. Mother's only joking. She never was an oil-painting.' Then she sighed. 'But Eliot took me under his wing.'

Charles stopped writing for a moment, and looked up at her. 'Why should the aged eagle?'

'What?'

'It's a quotation from Eliot.'

'It sounded like Shakespeare to me.'

'It was Eliot.'

'Well, you know these writers. They'll steal any . . .' And her voice trailed off as she looked down at her trembling hands.

'Anything, that's right.' He leant back in his chair, and smiled benevolently in her general direction. 'It's called the anxiety of influence.'

'Is it?' She seemed consoled by the phrase. 'That's right. Anxiety.'

'Of influence.'

'And of course it must be true of novelists, too.' She paused, and licked her lips. 'No doubt,' she went on, 'there are resemblances between my books and those of other writers.'

'You mean like Harrison Bentley?' Charles only just remembered Philip's remark of the previous evening, and now brought it out triumphantly as an indication of his wide reading.

'What was that?' The colour had gone from Harriet's face, and Charles could see the grains of rose powder on her cheeks. She seemed to have some difficulty in speaking. 'I don't, you know. Is it?' She got up from her chair. 'I've lost something,' she said and hurried from the room. She ran upstairs and went straight into her bedroom, stopping before the full-length mirror on her wardrobe. 'Mother's in trouble,' she said to her reflection. 'Mother's in big trouble.' Then she unzipped her red dress, flung it onto the bed with a cry of derision, and took out from the wardrobe an old brown skirt and sweater which she hastily put on. 'You're adorable,' she said. 'But now you must think. Think!' She went out to the top of the stairs and called down to Charles, 'I'll be a few minutes!' Then she added, 'Female problems!' But Charles did not hear this. He was gazing out of the window, the papers falling from his hands, his attention as wide and as blank as the sky to which he longed to flee.

Harriet sat on the edge of the bed, watching the creases in her leather shoes as she curled and uncurled her toes, wondering how it was that Charles had found the connection between her work and that of Harrison Bentley: this was the discovery which she had always feared, this was the revelation which she had suppressed but which had provoked so much anxiety in her. It was inconceivable that Charles had learnt this for himself, he was far too lazy. Someone must have alerted him . . . perhaps there was an article about her in the *Times Literary Supplement* . . . perhaps she was about to be exposed. She kicked the wardrobe door shut with her foot, and in its mirror the room swung violently around her.

This is what had happened: her first novel had enjoyed a modest success when it was published in the early Fifties. It was the work of a stylist, and had been praised by other stylists; kind words from Djuna Barnes and Henry Green were printed on the back of the American edition. It had taken Harriet six years to complete (while working as a secretary for a small literary magazine) since she wrote very slowly, sometimes composing no more than a sentence or even a phrase each day. She told herself that words were 'sacred', however, gradually forming their own associations and gathering in their own clusters of significant sound; when they were ready, they informed Harriet of their presence and she was content to transcribe them. As far as she was concerned,

[101]

that was all. The only continuity which her novel possessed lay somewhere within the workings of her own consciousness.

And so after the first novel she could see no further ahead: she had brought her consciousness 'up to date', as she put it, and she was not at all sure that she could expect any more progress from it. The words had vanished just as mysteriously as they had once arrived. Her friends and colleagues expected another novel from her, she knew, but the prospect of writing it bewildered her: she could not find within herself any strong connection with the world, and so she could find no method of describing it. Even when she did manage to write something, her inspiration seemed random and inconsequential; she would have an 'idea' when shopping, or when sitting on a bus, but then it became clear to her that if she had not needed to shop that day, or travel in that particular direction, the idea or phrase would never have emerged. This made her work seem frail, even worthless. And, really, she had nothing whatever to write about.

It was then that the notion of adapting a plot from some other source occurred to her. For two weeks she read all of the most interesting stories in the newspapers, but she found anything even remotely connected with actual life baffling. She even tried following people in the street, to see where they went and whom they met, but one unpleasant scene (when an old man had rounded on her and called her a 'tart') convinced her that this was not wise. Then one late afternoon in May, bored by herself and by her failure, she walked into a second-hand bookshop off Chancery Lane. Normally such places depressed her since she could easily imagine her own work lying forgotten on their shelves, but now she found a strange comfort in the rows of dusty books which surrounded her. She picked out at random *The Last Testament* by Harrison Bentley and, even as she began to read it, she realised that here was the answer to her problem. Since she believed that plots themselves were of little consequence, why should she not take this one and use it as a plain, admittedly inferior, vessel for her own style? So she bought the old novel, and set to work. And, with the story of *The Last Testament* to support her, she found that the words came more easily than before. Where phrases and even syllables had once emerged as fragments of a larger structure which she could neither see nor understand, now she could make her own connections; she went on from sentence to sentence, as if she were carrying a lamp and moving from room to room in a large mansion. And she looked about her with wonder, sensing her ability to describe what she was seeing now for the first time.

This second novel, *A Finer Art*, was also a success; once again she was praised for her style (the *Manchester Guardian* called her a 'lepidopterist of language') and the fact that the plot of the novel was described only in the vaguest terms encouraged her to use another Harrison Bentley narrative for her next book. But her confidence had increased with her ability, and in *The Whipping Post* she adapted only the beginning of his *Stage Fire*. She altered the characters, changed their relationships, and, by the end, only the barest outline of Bentley's initial situation remained in place (of course, this was all Philip Slack had understood from the précis which he had read in the damp basement of the public library). The experience of employing a plot, even though it was the invention of some other writer, had liberated her imagination; and, from that time forward, all her novels were her own work. But in recent years even this originality had begun to bore her. Once she had derived enormous pleasure from seeing her characters move and develop through time, but the spectacle no longer charmed her. She recalled with pleasure only the writing of her earliest novel, with all its obliquities and discordancies; and, for the first time, she began to admire her own nervousness and isolation during that period. She had allowed the language to carry her forward; she had not tried to direct it. She had been a serious writer then, a proper writer: she had not known what she was trying to say.

It was this new sense of her own life which had intensified her anxiety about the use of Harrison Bentley's novels. She had forgotten the early episode – at least, she had dismissed it as of no particular account – but, when she began to contemplate the writing of her memoirs, this act of plagiarism acquired a prominence which she had not since been able to challenge. She could see no way around it. She could not bring herself to admit the borrowing, and this mainly for reasons of pride; but, even if she did not herself confess to it, the plagiarism might in any case be discovered and an unwarranted suspicion cast over the rest of her work – even over her first novel. Anxious reflection had so nourished the problem that it seemed to encompass the whole of her past. There was no escape from it. So now she sat upon the edge of the bed, her hand clasped to her forehead as the wardrobe door slammed shut.

But it was with a noble calmness that she eventually descended the stairs. 'Mother's back!' she shouted when she was half way down. 'She was straining her greens,' she added, rather grandly, as she entered the room.

Charles did not know this phrase. 'For dinner?'

She was so intent on what she was about to say that she answered quite factually. 'No, not for dinner. I'm thinking of spaghetti tonight.' Roused from his day-dream by her voice, Charles started making random pencil marks on the side of the pages she had given him. She watched him with apparent fascination and then asked, very sweetly, 'What were you saying about Harrison Bentley?' She scratched her arm viciously and then left her hand poised in mid-air as Charles continued to be preoccupied with her notes.

'Oh. Nothing.'

'Nothing!'

Something in her voice made Charles look up, and he noticed how her left eyelid was trembling. 'I just meant . . .' He hesitated. 'I just didn't think that it was very important.'

'No, you're right. It isn't important.' She put her hand up to her trembling eye, and Charles tried not to laugh as the remaining eye stared calmly at him. Slowly she pulled her hand down across her face, the eyelid peaceful now, and then wagged her finger at him. 'You've been a naughty boy, you know. You've found Mother out. Bentley did influence me once, but that was a long time ago.' She spoke without thought since these were words she had rehearsed many times before. 'In any case novelists don't work in a vacuum. We use many stories. But it's not where they come from, it's what we do with them. I've found lots of material elsewhere but no one –' and here her voice rose slightly – 'no one has ever accused me of plagiarism!'

'No. That's right.' He did not quite know what to say. 'That's why it wasn't important. I didn't accuse you.'

Charles's benign reaction was unexpected, and at once his unconcern began to remove her own fears. The telephone rang, but she ignored it for a few moments as she stared at him in relief. 'You mean, it doesn't matter? You haven't read about me anywhere?'

'Of course not. Why should it matter? Everyone does it.'

Her telephone answering machine had already whirred into action. 'This is Harriet Scrope. I am not here –' In her profound and sudden relief Harriet dashed to the telephone, switched off the recording and shrieked, 'It's me! It's Harriet Scrope in the flesh!' It was Sarah Tilt. 'Oh darling, I was just talking about you!' She winked at Charles and, putting her hand over the mouthpiece, whispered, 'One of my happier white lies.' She turned her attention back to Sarah's voice. 'Don't tell me now, darling. If you're just around the corner, come over. Charles is here. He's dying to meet you.' There was a pause. 'Charles Wychwood. The poet.' She put down the receiver.

'Who am I dying to meet?'

'Oh, it's only Sarah. I always tell her that. It makes her feel less uncomfortable with people.'

'I really ought to go now. My wife . . .'

'Oh yes, how is she?' Harriet picked up the bag containing the

Chatterton manuscripts and, with apparent absent-mindedness, began patting it with her hand. 'Is she married?'

Charles, slightly alarmed by her action, had not properly heard the question. 'She's working in a gallery for the moment. I don't know why. Have you heard of Cumberland and Maitland?'

'Ah yes, Cumberland and Maitland.' She had put the bag onto a small ebony table in a corner of the room, and was beginning to examine its contents. 'Cumberland and Maitland.' She was taking out pages and scrutinising them carefully, calmly repeating the phrase as she did so. 'Cumberland and Maitland. That's right.' Then she held up a batch of manuscripts. 'Shall I keep these safe for you, dear?'

'It's very kind of you,' Charles began to say. 'But I really need to do more work on them –'

The doorbell rang. 'Fuck her,' Harriet muttered under her breath and, as she rose to let in Sarah Tilt, Charles hastily replaced the papers in his bag, picked up the portrait, and followed her into the hall. 'What's the French for pilgrim?' she suddenly asked him.

'Pélérin, isn't it?'

'Ah,' Harriet said, as she flung open the door to her friend. 'Ma pélérine triste!'

'I don't know what you're talking about. I was just passing.' Sarah sidestepped Harriet and fled from her down the hall. But she collided with Charles, who was standing back in the shadows, and she gave a little shriek.

'Yes, that's right. Scream.' Harriet was standing with her hands on her hips. 'It's a man.'

Sarah muttered something about needing new glasses and, with the sheer effort of 'making way' for each other, she and Charles found themselves backing into Harriet's study. In the light which filtered through some antique blinds there, Sarah could see the portrait of Chatterton which Charles was carrying. 'Oh,' she said, 'who is it?' Her interest in painting was quite genuine, and she was about to take the picture in order to examine it more carefully.

Harriet was suddenly beside them. 'Did I introduce you? Sarah Tilt. Charles Wychwood.' She rattled off the names, as if they did not belong to anyone in particular. 'Charles has to go now, darling. He's married.' Then with a coquettish smile she took his arm and led him towards the front-door.

'It's Thomas Chatterton,' he called out over his shoulder. 'He's very sorry not to have been able to talk to you longer.'

Harriet almost pushed Charles out of the door, but she muttered to him on the threshold, 'Are you sure that everyone does it? You know what I mean?'

'Yes, everyone copies.'

He was about to say something else but she cut him off by waving goodbye in her most agreeable manner and then, when he had gone, she slid down onto the floor of the hallway. 'I thought,' she said, 'that he would never leave.'

'What was all that about Chatterton?'

'He's demented, dear. He'll say anything.' She seemed to have spread herself between the wall and the floor, her legs splayed out in front of her. 'Will you help Mother up, please?' With an expression of grim determination Sarah walked towards her and, putting one hand beneath Harriet's arm and another around her neck, attempted to haul her to her feet. This operation took longer than was strictly necessary, however, since Harriet's right foot and part of her arm became entwined around an umbrella which had been left beside the door. 'It keeps on poking me!' she said. 'Look at it!' Eventually she managed to reach an upright position and the two old women leaned against the wall, panting. Then Harriet gave a parting kick to the umbrella before leading Sarah into the sitting room. She went straight to the bottles in the alcove.

'Yes, I'll have one too,' Sarah said in a loud voice. 'Charles seems very nice,' she went on, having at last been handed a gin-and-tonic. 'Not at all demented.'

'That was just a figure of speech.' In fact Harriet, now reassured about the effect of her plagiarisms, was thinking once more of the Chatterton discoveries: already it seemed to her absurd that such an important matter should be left to Charles, and it was with considerable indignation that she reminded herself that the manuscripts which she had seen were not the property of any one individual. In any case, the academics would be more interested in her than in some obscure young poet. But how was she to get the papers from Charles? 'There I was,' she said suddenly, 'like a cross between Cleopatra and Old Mother Hubbard –'

'The balance rather falling on one side?'

'There I was sitting on my lovely Regency sofa.' She pointed to a piece of mid-century provincial furniture.

'The stained one.'

'You would be stained, too, if you'd been sitting upright for two centuries covered in blue silk!'

'Sometimes I think I have.'

'When he arrived.'

'Who?'

'Charles Wychwood, of course. The so-called poet.' Then she asked, very suddenly, 'And how are *you*?'

Sarah settled back for a lengthy discussion. 'Well, my thighs –'

[106]

'Your thighs are your cross, of course.' Harriet did not sound particularly sympathetic. 'Perhaps there's something strained in the bikini area?'

'I get these little shooting pains.'

Harriet broke in again. 'You know, I suddenly realised why Irishmen say Mother of God when they're in trouble.'

'Oh yes?' Sarah was very cool.

'It's their way of calling for Mother without appearing to.' She sighed and looked out of the window at the turbulent sky. 'I suppose that's what Pascal meant by the fear of infinite spaces. Another drink?' Harriet raised her spoon and clinked it against her empty glass.

'Why not?' Sarah seemed mollified. 'You only live once, don't you?'

'Well, in your case, let's hope so.' She approached, and returned from, the alcove at remarkable speed. 'Shall we have a look at the box?' Without waiting for Sarah's approval, she went over to the television set, switched it on, and settled in her wicker chair close to the screen.

Two women, one old and one young, were sitting on a park bench. 'Oh look,' Harriet said, 'they're just like you and me when we're depressed!' The older woman was discussing the affairs of an absent friend. 'Oh, she sounds exactly *like* you! Exhausted, somehow.' Harriet stared eagerly at this scene as the much younger woman began to say something in reply. 'And that's just the way I talk, isn't it? Don't you think she looks like me, with her hair piled up like that?' Harriet patted her own hair and then crowed with excitement as the two women rose and left the bench. 'I don't believe how close this is. Do you see the way the older one is having so much trouble with her walk? That's you!' The young woman was laughing. 'Well, this is really uncanny. I *always* laugh like that. It's so musical, isn't it?' But then, tiring of this game, she picked up her remote-control device and changed programmes. She moved quickly, glimpsing a face, an action, a phrase, an explosion as she switched from channel to channel; but the resulting combination seemed to her to be making perfect sense and, for a while, she was happy to watch the screen. Sarah was growing bored, however, and had started inspecting the contents of her handbag while at the same time muttering something under her breath.

'You sound like an old tramp, dear. Talking to yourself.' Harriet had turned off the television set and was watching her old friend with amusement. 'You'll end up licking the vomit off your dress.' She could not help laughing at the image she had created.

'I wasn't talking to myself. I was talking to you.' Sarah had become very grand. 'I came to show you this.' From her bag she

[107]

brought out a small pamphlet. 'Your favourite painter is up for sale.' It was a catalogue of recent Seymour acquisitions. 'Just the sort of thing you like, dear.' And she snapped her handbag shut.

'So you know what I like, do you?' Harriet took the catalogue from her, and began to leaf through it. 'How nice. Lots of colour.'

'If you say so.' Sarah was no longer surprised or even particularly amused by the vulgarity of Harriet's artistic judgments.

'Oh no, I must have seen this one before.' Harriet bent over the catalogue, and put her face so close to the page that she seemed to be sniffing or eating it. 'I know this one.' Sarah got up, and went to look over Harriet's shoulder: she saw the reproduction of the painting in which a small child was looking out from the interior of a ruined building. Something seemed to be touching his shoulder. 'What's it called?'

Sarah took the catalogue from her, and turned to the back. 'Bristol Churchyard,' she read out, 'After the Lightning Flash. What a perfectly pointless title.' She had no very high opinion of Seymour's work.

'Well, at least,' Harriet began, and then stopped. 'At least he knows where the bodies are buried.'

Sarah refused to interpret this remark. 'Why don't you go and see it? It's still at Cumberland and Maitland.'

'Is it? Cumberland and Maitland. Now where have I heard that before?' Of course. Harriet remembered what Charles had said about his wife working there; and she wanted to meet this little wife. 'Why don't we go together, Sarah dear? You know how I value your opinion.' Vivien, that was the name, Vivien might have some influence in persuading Charles to hand over the manuscripts to a *real* writer. 'Yes. You've twisted my arm.' She put one arm behind her back and opened her mouth wide, as if she were about to scream. 'We *will* go.' And she sprang out of her chair.

'I ought to telephone them first, you know.'

'Give them a tinkle while I'm putting on my face.' She was about to leave the room. 'And don't talk for too long. You know how it mounts up.'

'Your face?'

Harriet went out, stumbling over Mr Gaskell, who emitted a short howl of protest, and a few minutes later came back wearing a bright blue hat with a small budgerigar pinned to it. 'I'm present and correct,' she announced. 'All done and docketed.'

'I've warned them you were coming.'

Harriet tipped her hat to one side, at what she considered to be a rakish angle. 'Then we mustn't disappoint them, must we? Come on.' She pointed at the device on her hat. 'Follow the bird.'

# 8

'AND WHO is this, looking divine in lilac and grey? It *can't* be anyone I know.' Cumberland had heard Maitland's familiar, nervous cough and had turned just in time to see his partner's back disappearing into a small office. 'Poor thing. Did you see the thinning hair?' he asked Claire. 'I could read a copy of *Art News* through it.'

'But the Deputy seems happy, sir.'

'A virgin's bliss, I think. When you look like Mr Maitland, it is folly to be wise. And talking of folly –'

He looked around at the gallery. The Polish show was coming down, and an exhibition of Art Brut was taking its place; already on the walls were drawings covered with nothing but cramped handwriting, the same words repeated over and over again; brightly coloured pictures of men and women with no eyes, and with wild crayon marks covering their limbs; maps of the world disfigured with hieroglyphics; forests of dark trees in which small human figures could only faintly be seen; and, in various corners of the gallery, sculptures made out of wood or straw with bottle-tops for eyes and string for hair. 'Oh,' said Claire suddenly, 'that one looks like the Deputy Head!' And indeed one figure made out of cardboard, cans, crumpled newspaper and pieces of broken glass did bear a faint resemblance to Mr Maitland.

'Isn't it lovely? I particularly admire the beer can, which symbolises Mr Maitland's commitment to the male sex.' He looked for the sculpture in the catalogue. 'Down a Chicago Alley I Wept and Wept Again, by Grandma Joel. Well I think that says it all, don't you?' He read out the rest of the description. 'Grandma Joel, known only as Grandma, was a prolific and versatile artist despite her mental instability. She thought herself condemned to death without knowing why. I sometimes feel that way, Claire, don't you? She was interned in an asylum, where she painted and made sculptures without stopping. That must have been where she met Mr Maitland. She wanted to explain the entire material and spiritual world in terms of imitation, and kept on repeating "The blind are fathers of the blind". She was obese and of rigid deportment. Do you think she *was* Mr Maitland? And at times of anger or discouragement she destroyed all her work. Well, in London,' he said, handing the catalogue to Claire, 'we will let the critics do that for her.'

'What does it mean?'

'It means absolutely nothing. Have you heard the expression, kind hearts are more than pass degrees and simple faith than aspirates?' He gaily caressed the large wart upon his cheek, and Claire felt it necessary to look away. 'That's all it means. Where there is no tradition, art simply becomes primitive. Artists without any proper language can only draw like children. It's so –' he heard movement behind him – 'so empty. Isn't that right, Vivienne?'

'Good morning.' She looked exhausted, and barely returned Cumberland's greeting before going into her office.

'Someone,' Cumberland murmured, 'must have slept on a pea last night. Claire, why don't you –' He gestured towards Vivien.

She followed Vivien through the back of the gallery. 'You didn't say anything about the Head's new paintings.'

'I'm sorry. I didn't really notice them.'

Claire sat upon Vivien's desk, and dangled her legs against its side. 'What's up, head girl?'

That morning Charles had complained of a headache, and his movements had seemed to Vivien to be particularly clumsy; now she could think of nothing else. 'It's nothing. I'm just tired.'

'How's Edward?' Claire always mentioned Vivien's son rather than her husband.

'Oh, he's fine. He just sits and watches television.' Since Charles had become ill, Edward had withdrawn more and more into himself. She forced herself to smile at Claire. 'And how are you today?'

'I'm fine, too.' She popped a Polo mint into her mouth. 'But Mummy's in a panic. She thinks she might be pregnant again.'

'Doesn't she know?'

'She doesn't know anything.' Claire's 'Mummy' was a constant item of conversation in the gallery: she was a divorced woman who, in her daughter's unconsciously lurid accounts, resembled some rouged doll careering around London. 'But she has a pretty good idea who the father is. She says she's going to join the Girl Guides and set up camp on his doorstep.'

'Until he marries her?'

'No, until he gives her money for the thingummy. You know, when you pay to have babies taken away.'

'Adoption?'

'Oh, no. I think it's called an abortion. But she says if the worst comes to the worst she'll pay for it herself. She's an old softy, really, when it comes to things like that. But you know,' she added loyally, as if to counteract this image of feminine weakness, 'she's the best three-day-eventer I know.'

Vivien was not particularly interested in her horsemanship. 'But does she know what an abortion would be like at her age?'

'Oh yes, of course. She's had some before.' Claire tossed her hair back. 'Mummy was always in demand, at cocktail parties and things. I think I came out of some kind of party.' She laughed but, catching sight of Cumberland prowling uneasily at the other end of the gallery, she slid off the desk. 'I can't stay here chatting all day. The Head will bring out his cane.'

Vivien went back to her work, distracted from her own problems by Claire's account of her mother and ready to be soothed by the routine of duties which she now had to undertake. But still she found it difficult to concentrate and from time to time she heard herself sighing . . . when she looked up, Maitland was in the room. He was taking a handkerchief out of his pocket. 'I was wondering,' he said, 'I was wondering if you were all right?' He mopped his forehead. 'You seemed depressed and I didn't . . .' He stared at her, not quite knowing how to go on. 'If there's anything I can do to help,' he added. But then he faltered again; he started walking backwards out of the room rolling the handkerchief around in his hands. 'You see, I don't understand,' he was saying as he walked backwards into Grandma Joel's effigy.

'Famous Five to the rescue!' Claire bounced across the gallery in order to save the sculpture just as it rocked dangerously upon its pedestal and, by some miracle of timing, she managed to catch it before it fell to the floor.

'Oh dear.' Maitland looked at her and blew his nose.

'It didn't hit the playground sir!' Claire was delighted by her agility. 'Do I get top marks?'

She looked around to see if Cumberland had witnessed her triumph, and in fact he was already standing behind her; his hands were outstretched as if he had been prepared to catch her when she fell backward with the precious object. 'Sometimes,' he said, 'I feel like slapping that man. One hard slap, just enough to get someone's blood moving.' He was about to add something else when Vivien came out to inform him that Mr Sadleir, Seymour's old dealer, urgently wished to speak to him.

With a sudden display of energy Cumberland rushed into the office and lunged for the telephone. 'Oh yes?' he said very calmly.

[111]

He listened for a moment and then the corners of his mouth turned down; for Vivien's benefit, he mimed a look of alarm. 'You mean?' He raised one foot from the ground and held it there for a moment before putting it down again. 'I see.' He sat upon the desk. 'Really?' He got up and executed a few dance steps, all the time gazing, wide-eyed, at Vivien. 'Is that so?' He lay down upon the carpet, with the telephone clutched to his chest. 'Of course I reserve my position.' He kicked his legs in the air, as Vivien looked down at him in astonishment. 'I would like to see your proof!' With difficulty he half-raised himself from the floor. 'Shall we say three o'clock?' Then, exhausted by the effort, he collapsed on the carpet again and put the telephone next to his ear. 'Goodbye.' He lay very still for a moment, and then he said to the ceiling, 'Sadleir says that my Seymours are fakes.' After a few seconds he added, 'You can pretend, Vivienne, that I never said that.' Then he yawned, and put his hands beneath his head. 'You had better contact our friend, Mr Stewart Merk, and tell him to come here at three as well.'

Claire was about to enter the room but she stopped, astonished, at the threshold. 'What's the matter with the Head?' she asked Vivien, as if Cumberland's recumbent posture had removed him from the sphere of ordinary conversation.

'The Head,' Cumberland replied, 'is waiting for Salomé. When she comes, would you give her a dish?'

*

At precisely three o'clock, Claire rushed into Vivien's office and whispered, 'It's him! It's the school bully!'

Sadleir had come to a halt in the middle of the gallery; he held his arms down by his side, and was staring straight ahead. Because of his pronounced military bearing, in fact, he was generally known as 'the colonel' and he was still standing at attention when Vivien came towards him. 'Sadleir' was all he said, and he kept his eyes fixed on the wall behind Vivien's head. She led him towards Cumberland's office, and it was with a definite effort that he shifted his gaze fifteen degrees to the east: this was in the direction of Cumberland's door, and he stared at this point on the compass after he had entered the room. 'Sadleir,' he said again.

Cumberland bowed slightly and tightened the knot of his tie, Maitland stood at attention and blushed, Stewart Merk lounged in a chair and smiled. 'Won't you,' Cumberland was saying, 'sit down? If you can.'

Sadleir lowered his eyes in the direction of Cumberland. 'Those paintings are fakes.'

[112]

'No social niceties, I see.' Cumberland looked back at him grimly. 'What a breath of fresh air.' Vivien had been standing in the doorway, uncertain whether to stay, but at this point he turned his wart towards her and she closed the door. 'I'm sure you know,' he went on, very agreeably, 'Stewart Merk who was Seymour's *assistant*.' He emphasised the last word.

'I know Merk.'

'Now Mr Merk, who *was* Seymour's assistant, assures me that the paintings are quite genuine.'

Sadleir's eyes swivelled towards Merk, who gave a little wave to them. 'He is mistaken.'

Merk laughed. 'Oh really?' He took out a cigarette but forgot to light it. 'Is that right?'

'Those Seymours are not genuine.'

Merk spent some time finding a match and then striking it, while the others watched him. 'Let me put it this way. They are as genuine as all his other recent paintings.' He blew a smoke ring towards the ceiling, and settled back into the chair.

Sadleir continued to stare at him. 'I have been Seymour's dealer for twenty-five years.'

'Ah.'

'I know all his work.'

'So do I.'

'He kept a photographic record of all his paintings.'

'I know. I took the photographs.'

They were both staring at each other now. 'They're fakes.'

Merk laughed. 'But who is to say what is fake and what is real? You're sure you know the difference, yes?'

Sadleir stiffened perceptibly and for a moment his eyes did not seem to be focusing on anything in particular. 'I know what I know.'

'Oh yes, and what *do* you know?' Merk had suddenly become more animated; he stubbed out his cigarette and bent forward in the chair. Then he laughed, and sat back again. 'Did you know, for example, that Seymour was suffering from arthritis in his hands?'

'His hands . . .' Sadleir was looking straight ahead.

'And did you know that he couldn't hold a newspaper, let alone a brush?' Sadleir made an effort to look in Merk's direction but he could not, while Cumberland ran his fingers across his highly polished desk as if he were playing the piano. 'And did you know that he was in despair, that he didn't want to paint any more, that he wanted to die?' Merk paused. 'You knew that, right?'

'I don't see . . .' Sadleir began.

[113]

'No, you don't see.' He leaned forward again. 'You don't see what's staring you in the face. You don't see that *I* painted all of Seymour's last pictures.'

In the silence which followed this, Maitland heard the sound of drilling in the road outside the gallery. 'I'm sorry,' he said. 'I'll close the window.' But the others paid no attention to him and he stood, with his back turned towards them, staring out at nothing.

Sadleir was moving his head from side to side, and his eyes were swerving wildly with it. 'You may claim that you painted them,' he was saying. 'Very well. But I would like to see your proof.'

Merk unzipped the portfolio beside him and took out a small canvas: it was clearly an example of Seymour's late style, with its combination of abstract shapes and small figurative objects as well as the characteristic stippled texture of its paint. 'I finished this last week.' He looked at it with admiration. 'Good, isn't it?'

'Unfortunately,' Cumberland said, 'there are no critics in this room.'

Sadleir could not take his eyes off the painting. Then, with the flourish of a conjuror, Merk turned it around and showed the reverse side to Cumberland. 'There is the canvas number, yes? And there is the supplier's mark. Am I right? Just like yours –' Now he looked at Sadleir. 'And just like yours.'

Sadleir blinked nervously. 'How do you . . .'

'I kept the books. I know what canvases you have. You have sold only three paintings in the last two years, and you have kept fifteen. You knew that Seymour's death would push up the prices –'

'Gruesome,' Cumberland murmured.

Merk took off his neat gold-rimmed spectacles and polished them on the sleeve of his jacket. 'Now you don't want to accuse me or anything, do you? You don't want to ruin a good trade.'

Sadleir closed his eyes. There was a long silence. 'I'm sure,' he said at last, 'that we can come to some kind of arrangement.'

And for the first time Cumberland laughed – a loud, long laugh which echoed around the gallery.

*

Harriet Scrope turned into New Chester Street; she was walking a few paces ahead of Sarah Tilt, and with so purposeful an air that a casual observer would have been forgiven for thinking that she was leading her companion forward. In fact she had no idea where

[114]

she was meant to be going. 'Come on dear,' she said in a fever of impatience. 'Mother hasn't got all day!'

'It's my legs!' Sarah screamed across the heads of several people who had already come between them. 'I can't help it!'

'*I can't help it.*' Harriet mimicked Sarah's plaintive voice; she looked back at her with a vicious smile, and at that moment collided with Sadleir who was just leaving the gallery. He did not notice; in fact he did not seem to be noticing anything, but stared blindly ahead as he made his way through the crowds. 'Cunt!' Harriet called out after him. Then, realising that she was now outside Cumberland and Maitland, she adjusted her hat and proceeded into the gallery.

'I'm Harriet Scrope,' she announced to Claire. 'And this –' she waited until Sarah had followed her into the gallery. 'This is Sarah Tilt. The famous art critic. Take us to your leader.'

Sarah, still breathless after her forced march down New Chester Street, managed to intervene. 'Mr Cumberland,' she said, 'is expecting us. I telephoned . . .'

Claire went into the office. 'Is the Head around?' she asked Vivien. 'There are two old bats to see him.' Their voices had in fact penetrated some way into the gallery, and when she had heard Harriet's name Vivien had panicked. Had she called with bad news about Charles? Had he collapsed at her house? But, no, she knew already that they had come to talk to Cumberland about the purchase of a Seymour painting. There was nothing at all to worry about. She came out to greet them. 'Miss Scrope,' she said. 'I'm Vivien. Charles's wife . . .'

Harriet stepped back in astonishment. '*Are* you? I had no idea that you worked here! Charles is so secretive, isn't he? But such a dear.'

They smiled at each other and Sarah, who was slightly nervous at the thought of Harriet's prospective interview with Cumberland, added, 'And such a coincidence.'

Harriet gave her a baleful look. 'There is no such thing. This was *meant*. Do you know Sarah Tilt? The famous art critic?'

After another round of introductions Vivien left them in order to find her employer, and for the first time Harriet looked around the gallery. 'What's all this?' she asked.

Sarah had walked up to one painting which showed several rows of human figures, each one linked to the next so that they resembled lines of hieroglyphic writing. 'Innocent Art. Art Brut. Naïve Art.'

Harriet rolled her eyes. 'I know all about that.'

'Of course you do.' Sarah sniggered. 'All these mad artists.'

[115]

'Really?' Harriet was suddenly more interested, and she peered at the various objects around her. 'Were they truly mad or were they just pretending?'

'Seeing is believing,' Sarah replied and took her up to a canvas which showed a girl sitting upon a wall: behind her, floating in the air, was her double and the second image was gently touching the first image on the shoulder. The colours were very bright. Sarah took up a catalogue, found the painting, and read out the summary as Harriet gazed at the two identical girls: 'Fritz Dangerfield's composition, The Opium Dream. He painted the same picture over and over again but he would not be parted from the canvases, which he kept in his bedroom until his death. He did not speak, and he did not write except with an alphabet of his own invention.' She closed the catalogue. 'Now that really *is* madness.'

'I see what he meant, though.' Harriet had become serious. 'He wanted to be separate from everything. He had his own alphabet because words made him feel unclean. He wanted to start all over again.'

'But that's just the point. As a result, he was unintelligible. No one can start again.'

'So there's no choice. You have to carry it all around with you.' Harriet adopted the stoop of a stage hunchback, and began limping through the gallery just at the moment when Cumberland emerged from his office to greet them. He looked at her, astonished, but she straightened up and said, 'There was a stone in my shoe.'

'How reckless. May I take your hat?' He was delighted by the small budgerigar which was pinned, through the breast, to the blue cloth. 'Or does it fly off by itself?'

'I don't know,' Harriet replied. 'Why don't you tempt it with some seed?'

Already she felt quite at ease with him, and she approached with her hand outstretched; Cumberland resisted the impulse to flee. 'I'm Harriet Scrope. And of course you know the famous art critic, Sarah Tilt. I mean Sarah Tilt, the famous art critic.'

'I know both ladies very well.'

Harriet laughed at his joke, principally because it seemed to be directed against her old friend, but stopped suddenly when Maitland entered the gallery. He was carrying a small brown parcel and, when he saw the two old ladies, he took a step backwards. Cumberland spotted him. 'Do you know my partner in crime?'

Harriet noticed that, for some reason, both men blushed at this. 'Is he Burke or is he Hare?'

'No, I believe he is one of the bodies.' Cumberland was very gracious. 'Miss Scrope,' he said, 'would like to buy one of our

Seymours.' Maitland dropped the parcel, and there was a muted sound of breaking glass. With a thrilled little laugh Claire rushed forward to help him as he stood there, looking down at it and biting his lower lip. In that moment of confusion, Harriet observed Vivien Wychwood closely: she could see the anxiety printed upon her face, and she wondered from where it came.

'Tell me,' Cumberland was saying to Harriet as he led her now into his office, carefully excluding Maitland, 'have you visited the gallery before?'

'Oh no.' Then she added, in an effort to be more diplomatic, 'But I'm *always* passing it.'

'It must be the gypsy in you.'

'Where?' She turned round, alarmed, as if some swarthy gentleman were about to penetrate her.

Cumberland tried not to laugh. 'And where are you living now?' It was as if he had known her all his life.

'Well, I call it Tyburnia.'

'What does the world call it?' Harriet did not answer this; she had become fascinated by the large wart upon his cheek and she was raising her hand in its direction, apparently with every intention of touching or stroking it, when Cumberland took shelter behind his desk. 'I gather,' he went on, more nervously, 'there was one particular Seymour?'

Sarah Tilt decided that it was time to intervene. 'Miss Scrope was particularly interested in Bristol Churchyard After the Lightning Flash. You know, the one with the glorious colour field.'

Harriet smiled at her foolishness. 'It wasn't a field. It was a building.'

Cumberland merely nodded and Sarah knew that he was measuring the precise degree of Harriet's ignorance. 'Let me show it to you,' he said, and pressed a button on his desk.

Claire must have been standing outside the door, since she immediately came into the room, with a small oil painting resting against her chest. 'The Deputy told me he wants to keep his hands clean,' she was saying, 'but I don't see any dust on it.'

'Just show it to them, Claire dear, and don't say another word.' So she held it up for their approval.

In the afternoon light the child and the ruined building seemed more clearly defined, and Sarah Tilt was impressed by the confidence with which this 'realistic' scene had been placed in a more abstract setting. The face of the child was still indistinct, but the building now seemed to swirl around him; it was the vortex into which he was about to be sucked. 'I do prefer Seymour's later style,' she said. 'As he grew more abstract he became bolder.'

[117]

Cumberland smiled but said nothing. 'He's such a recognisable artist, isn't he? Each work is unmistakably his.'

'I couldn't agree with you more.'

Now, in the actual presence of the painting, Harriet panicked, believing that she might be obliged to purchase it at once. 'It's not quite large enough,' she said. 'For my mantelpiece.' She appealed for support. 'You know, Sarah, with all that lovely marble I have.'

Strangely enough, Cumberland seemed pleased by her response. 'Would you like to think about it a little more?' Harriet touched the bird upon her hat, as if to confirm this. 'Of course. Don't worry. Claire will now take the canvas away.' He waited impatiently until she had left the room, and then turned back to Harriet. For a moment they looked at one another silently. 'I expect that you're writing another novel, Miss Scrope.'

'I'm thinking about it.' She leered at him. 'Got any ideas?'

'There's not an idea in my pretty little head at the moment. But our Mr Maitland, as you saw, is almost entirely fictional.'

'And what are you, brute fact?'

'Something very primitive, at least.'

He rose from his chair, but Harriet did not yet seem inclined to leave. 'So perhaps,' she went on, 'I could buy you instead?' She emitted a low laugh.

'I might look nice over your mantelpiece.'

'Not until you were stuffed.'

Sarah decided that it was time for both of them to go, and hauled Harriet to her feet. 'It's been so nice,' she said. 'Thank you so much.'

'The pleasure was all mine.'

'Don't say that,' Harriet told him. 'It always gives me a headache.'

And, when they got into the street, Sarah turned upon her. 'That was a disgusting exhibition you made of yourself in there!'

'I thought art galleries were meant for exhibitions.'

Sarah pursed her lips. 'You could have shown a little more interest in that picture.'

'It was too expensive.'

'Oh, don't be so ridiculous. You didn't even ask the price!'

'I know what I know.' She adjusted her hat as she spoke. 'I am what I am.' And, as she looked at her reflection in the window, she saw Vivien standing at the back of the gallery. 'Oh dear, Mother's left behind her handbag. Don't wait. I know how busy you are.' Sarah realised that Harriet, for reasons known only to herself, wanted to be alone; and it was with a certain amount of relief that she gave her a perfunctory kiss on the cheek before returning home. Where her book, *The Art of Death*, was waiting for her.

Harriet lingered until she had turned the corner, and then went back into the gallery. 'I wonder,' she said to Vivien, 'if anyone has seen my bag?' In fact she had carefully placed it in a corner, where it would remain unnoticed until she came for it. 'Ah, there it is! Isn't it sweet, just hiding there from me?' She rummaged around in it before extracting a large bunch of keys, which she proceeded to rattle in front of her. 'Just to prove it's mine,' she said. Then she snapped the bag shut and added, almost as an afterthought, 'How's Charles?' She seemed to have forgotten that she had seen him only a few hours before.

'It's difficult to say . . .' Vivien hesitated, not knowing how much of her own fear to express. 'You know, don't you?'

'Oh yes.' Harriet had no idea what she meant, but she took an inspired guess. 'He was looking a little pale, I thought.'

'Thank God you saw it too!' Vivien could no longer hold back her anxieties. 'He won't see anyone about it! He needs help!' But the relief she felt at finally admitting this seemed to her like a kind of oppression: it made her fears more real.

To Harriet she seemed dangerously close to tears. 'Don't tell me any more,' she said quickly. 'Until we go for a little walk. It always works with me.'

'I must just see . . .'

Vivien hurried back into the office and asked Claire to take her place for a few minutes; when she returned Harriet grabbed her arm and together they walked along New Chester Street, across Piccadilly and down St James's Street.

'Whenever I see street signs,' Harriet said confidentially, 'I think of Moll Flanders, don't you?' She stopped suddenly beside an automatic cash dispenser. 'Hang on. Miss Flanders needs some more silver.' With practised gesture she punched in her PIN, as she had learnt to call it – she liked these machines, and she greatly enjoyed the idea of her money being guarded by numbers. A vagrant lurched past and she sheltered the five pound notes, even then emerging from the dispenser, with her body. 'So near and yet so far,' she murmured as she watched him pass down the street.

'What was that?' Vivien had been preoccupied with her own thoughts.

'Nothing, dear. Nothing at all.'

But something of their sudden intimacy had disappeared, and Vivien was not sure how to proceed. 'Did you buy anything from the gallery?'

'Oh no. I don't believe in hastening to destruction.' Harriet ran nimbly across St James's Street, just avoiding a taxi which hooted at her. 'I don't believe,' she explained when Vivien had caught up with her on the other side, 'in impulse buying.' They walked through the gates into the park, and a gentle breeze brought the fresh scent of lilac bushes towards them. Harriet sniffed the air. 'Ah, jasmine. My favourite flower. I'd know it anywhere.' They were on a path which descended towards the lake and Harriet again took Vivien's arm, squeezing it perhaps a little too hard. 'And so how *is* Charles?'

'He doesn't say much, as you know.'

In fact he rarely stopped talking when he was with Harriet. 'I know, dear. He's a veritable sphinx.'

'But I must do something.' Vivien's pace increased to keep up with the increasing urgency of her thoughts, and Harriet trotted beside her. 'He's been having these headaches for the last two months, and there are times when he looks so ill. Sometimes he just sits and waits for the pain to go. Then he carries on as if nothing had happened. He doesn't seem to care. He saw a doctor once, but that was ages ago. But you know Charles. He never likes to hear bad news.'

'Of course not.' The path had taken them between some flower-beds, and the smell of freshly turned earth mingled with the scent of wallflowers and late hyacinths; a wind started up and shook the highest branches of the trees around them, and in the green protected light they walked forward. 'So,' Harriet said softly. 'He is really ill.' It was clear to her now that Vivien had been brooding on these matters for some time, and that this had been her first opportunity to express her anxieties. 'His poetry is very important –' she began.

She was going to add 'to him' but Vivien interrupted her. 'Oh yes! He's a wonderful poet! I'm so glad you see that, too! If only –'

The wind grew stronger, and some fallen leaves blew around their feet. Harriet kicked them away, happy that her opportunity had come so easily. 'You know,' she said, 'we're going to have to take charge of him. We'll have to take him in hand.' She squeezed Vivien's arm again, as if they were already accomplices. 'He must get plenty of rest.' Vivien was not sure that 'rest' was enough under the circumstances, but she was too grateful for Harriet's support to contradict her. 'Of course he can write his poetry, but he really shouldn't be doing more than that. Does he have anything else –' she hesitated, and looked down at the path – 'on his mind?'

'There is this other business . . .'

'What business is that?' They had reached the end of the gardens and now stopped to look out at the lake; a fine mist was moving across the face of the water, and Harriet shivered. 'Is it something important?'

'Oh no. He has some theory about a poet who died.' From her tone it was clear that Vivien disapproved of Charles's preoccupation with the Chatterton manuscripts, and that she did not understand their significance. The mist came towards them; a duck moved behind some fern.

'You mean, a friend who died?'

Vivien tried to laugh, but could not manage it. 'Have you heard of someone called Chattaway or Chatterton?'

Harriet looked puzzled, and put a forefinger up to her cheek in pensive mood. 'Wasn't there a very minor poet with a name like that? Some kind of forger?'

'That's the one! Charles has some theory that he faked his own death –'

Harriet seemed astonished at this news. 'What on earth would be the point of that, dear?' The mist passed across them, and for a moment she thought she tasted the brackish salt of the sea.

'Don't ask me. But it's all he ever talks about.'

Their voices seemed to echo across the surface of the dead water, and Harriet led her back into the gardens. 'You see, Vivien.' She took her arm again. 'May I call you Vivien? I feel as if I've known you for years – you see, it could be that all this Chatterton nonsense is affecting his health. He might be obsessed with it.' She paused. 'It wouldn't be the first time.' Vivien's look of surprise momentarily unnerved her. 'But don't tell Charles. Not yet.'

'Of course not.' Vivien looked down at the ground, reflecting on what Harriet had said. 'You could be right,' she said. 'Charles has certainly got worse since –'

Harriet pressed home her advantage. 'And I suppose that it's been keeping him from his poetry?'

'Oh yes.'

'Well.' Harriet stopped upon the path, apparently prevented from moving forward by the force of a sudden idea. 'Why don't you and I take these papers away from him, without him suspecting anything?'

It was clear from Vivien's expression that she approved of this idea. 'But how?'

'Leave all that to me, Vivien darling.' In her enthusiasm she had become effusive. 'If you look after Charles, I'll take care of the manuscripts. Papers.' She gave a little jump in the air. 'Won't it be fun working together? Oh shit!' She had felt a familiar pressure beneath her foot as she landed and, lifting it up, peered at some dog excrement smeared across the sole of her right shoe. 'I might have gone blind if that had gone in my eye,' she shouted. 'It might have flown up at me!' She sat down, very gingerly, upon the low green railings which surrounded the flower-beds. 'Hand me that leaf, will you?' Painstakingly she wiped off the mess, as Vivien passed her a number of wet leaves. Eventually she rose to her feet and glanced accusingly at her shoes. 'They should be shot,' she said. 'Shot and then buried in unmarked graves.' For a moment Vivien thought that she was planning the fate of her own footwear, but then Harriet pointed towards a small black poodle. 'They're nothing but animals!' The dog barked back at her, and this seemed to restore her high spirits. 'Well,' she said, 'how do we get out of this hell hole?'

They began walking across the short grass and Harriet, in her new role as a confidential friend, was almost girlish. 'I didn't like that Seymour painting, after all,' she was saying. 'It was too, you know, bright for my taste. Too ghastly.'

Vivien was still thinking about Charles, and was not really listening. 'Oh they've been talking about Seymour all morning. They think those paintings might be fakes.' Then she realised what she had said. 'Forget I mentioned that. It might just have been a rumour.'

'But I love rumours!' She saw the alarm on Vivien's face and added, 'Although of course I never believe them.' But now she understood why Cumberland had seemed so unwilling to sell that painting; and why both men had blushed at the phrase 'partners in crime'. They walked in silence for a few moments, until they came to the edge of the park. 'Don't worry,' she told Vivien, thinking of her indiscretion about the paintings.

'I'm much less worried now.' She smiled at Harriet. 'I'm glad that you're his friend.'

'So am I.' Harriet allowed herself to be kissed on the cheek before adjusting her hat and exclaiming, 'I go that way!' Vivien, thinking of Charles once again, slowly went back to the gallery.

Harriet was exhausted, too. 'Mother's fucked!' she said out loud, to the amusement of a flower-seller whose stall was on the corner of Jermyn Street. She smiled graciously at him. 'It's a dog's life, isn't it?'

It was beginning to rain and, as she proceeded up Piccadilly, she ducked beneath an awning to protect the small bird pinned to her hat. In fact she had taken shelter beside a cinema entrance and, as she peered inside, she could see a poster with the legend 'Swiss Maids in a Row'. She had not visited a cinema for some years and, seized with a sudden curiosity, she walked across to the small booth. 'One please,' she said to the old man who was sitting there disconsolately. She put up her finger. 'A single, s'il vous plaît.' He turned back to his newspaper while she rummaged in her bag for the proper sum.

'Five pounds *and* a membership fee does seem rather a lot,' she was saying. 'Even for modern life.' She patted her bag. 'But never mind. At least I've brought my own chocolates.'

When she entered the tiny auditorium the film had already started and in the darkness she stumbled over a man standing at the back. 'Excusez-moi,' she said. 'This is like the war.' She found a row and, groping her way to the middle, with a sigh fell into an empty seat. Vivaldi's *The Four Seasons* was issuing from loud-speakers on either side of the screen, and Harriet watched fascinated as two young women tossed a beach-ball to each other. She slipped off her shoes, took the chocolates from her bag, and stretched out. When a middle-aged man left his own seat and came to sit beside her, she was not at all alarmed: she assumed that modern cinemas had somehow acquired a party-like atmosphere, in which she was only too happy to join. 'You know,' she said companionably, 'I haven't been to the pictures since the Fifties. Would you like a choc?' She held out the box. 'They're lovely and bitter.' He gave her a wild look and at once moved away.

Somewhat surprised by his rudeness, she watched him for a few moments and then turned her attention back to the screen, just in time to see the setting change from the beach to a bedroom. The two girls were lying naked together, and Harriet was reminded of the picture which she had just seen in the exhibition of Art Brut: how one girl had been touching the shoulder of her double, before floating away. There was a sudden cut, and a man came in; he was wearing a traffic warden's uniform, and he began taking off his peaked cap and black jacket as soon as he entered the room. Harriet started to laugh but, when she saw all three on the bed together, they looked so tired and helpless that she shook her head in disbelief. Now she regretted not having seen the beginning of the film, since she wanted to know what had brought them to this point: the sex did not interest her, but the plot did. Even these couplings were the consequence of a story and, as far as she was concerned, that was the most interesting part. After all, everyone needed a story.

The scene had changed once again, and now the two girls were dancing together at a party. Harriet watched them for a while, but then her attention was drawn to the people around them. She saw a face which reminded her of a friend long dead, and then another, and another. They were all there together, all of her dead friends, as she had once known them; they had fallen back from the dancers and were now standing together silently, looking out at Harriet from the screen. She wanted to get up and talk to them, but a sudden terror kept her in her seat. That is why people go mad, she thought, they go mad from the fear of death. But she could sense the tears running down her face, and in bewilderment she put her hand up to her cheek.

The film was over. Dim lights came on above her head, and she looked around at the dirty room in which she had been sitting: there were cigarette butts and empty plastic cartons on the floor, the red carpet was frayed, the seats torn and stained. And over it all hovered the familiar, sharp smell of dust and cigarette ash. The same man was still standing at the back and, as he looked at her, he moved his hand in his pocket. She gathered up her bag and walked slowly towards him; he took out his hand and stood there sheepishly. She noticed how thin and white his fingers were but she only said, apologetically, 'I like a good cry before I go to bed.' Then she added, before hurrying out into the street, 'It's not real, you know. It's only a film.'

# 9

CHARLES WYCHWOOD was trying to read a copy of Meyerstein's *Life of Chatterton* but there was a patch of darkness on the left hand page, as if someone were standing over him and casting a shadow across the words. He closed the book and, fighting back his panic, called out, 'Edward!' There was no answer, only the sound of the television. 'Edward the Unfriendly!' He rose unsteadily to his feet and crept into the bedroom, where his son was at that moment trying to balance upon his head. 'Don't!' Charles said. 'Don't do that!' And with sudden anger he pushed him onto the floor. 'You could kill yourself like that!'

Edward was astonished. 'How?'

'You could injure your brain.' Charles pointed at his own head. 'You could shake it out of place.'

'But I like to see things upside down.' He glanced sullenly at the television screen. 'Everything looks better like that.'

'But the world isn't upside down, is it, Edward the Unrepentant?'

'How would you know?'

Charles grabbed him and, to his son's embarrassment, started rocking him on his knees. 'Have you been to the toilet today?'

'Yes.'

'Big jobs?'

'Oh, Dad.' Over the last few days Charles had become obsessed with his son's health, which had the effect only of irritating him.

'And you do eat all your meals at school, don't you?'

'I suppose so.' Edward turned away to make a secret grimace, but then his father leant across him and began picking over his hair as if he were looking for lice or fleas. 'Leave me alone, Dad.' Edward rolled away, and ended up on his stomach.

'You know I worry about you.'

'Your breath smells. You're sick.'

'I am *not* sick.' Charles was enraged but he could think of nothing

[125]

else to say. 'There isn't anything the matter with me.' He got up, with some difficulty, and left the room.

Edward muttered, 'Well, I'm sick of you.' But he was looking at his father anxiously.

Without thinking, Charles went over to the telephone and called Philip at the library; when his friend came to talk to him, however, he could not remember what it was he meant to say. 'Hi, it's me, Wychwood. Charles.'

A vagrant in the reference section was shouting, 'It wouldn't take more than a couple of puffs to blow you out of the water!' and Philip could not hear what Charles was saying. 'What was that?'

'I said Chatterton's going fine. And you know what, we ought to halibut. Celebrate. We ought to arrange a dinner.'

It sounded to Philip as if Charles had been drinking, so slurred and uncertain were his words. 'That's good.'

'Is that all you can say, that's good!' Then Charles realised he had raised his voice. 'No. I'm sorry. Listen. I'll invite Andrew Flint. I'll invite Harriet. And then I'll read them my bare face.'

'What?'

'Preface. I'll read them my preface. It's all in my head.' Charles licked his lips, which had suddenly become very dry. 'All I have to do is write it up. Down. Chatterton.' Edward was standing in the doorway and noticed that, as his father talked, he was moving his head very slowly from side to side. 'Look, Philip. I have to go now. Thanks for calling.' He put down the telephone, and stared out of the window. He still had his back turned to Edward, but the child could see his head swaying and dipping. Then he picked up the receiver and dialled another number. 'Andrew? This is me. Your Chaucer expert. Chatterton.' As Charles talked, he was forming his left hand into a fist and beating it against the side of his leg. 'Did we mention dinner? That's right. Let's make it next week. My day. Friday. I know, we shouldn't lose touch . . .' When eventually he put down the receiver he unclenched his fist and, with bowed head, stood in the middle of the room. Eventually he turned and looked towards his son, but for a moment he seemed not to know who he was. Edward said nothing, but gave a low whistle and went back to the television.

Charles had in fact hardly noticed his son's presence and now, with sudden urgency, he went over to his desk and began writing on the first piece of paper which he found there: 'Thomas Chatterton believed that he could explain the entire material and spiritual world in terms of imitation and forgery, and so sure was he of his own genius that he allowed it to flourish under other names. The documents which have recently been discovered show that he

[126]

wrote in the guise of Thomas Gray, William Blake, William Cowper and many others; as a result, our whole understanding of eighteenth century poetry will have to be revised. Chatterton kept his own account of his labours in a box from which he would not be parted, and which remained concealed until his death. The sad pilgrimage of his life . . .' Charles stopped, uncertain how to continue with the preface. He could not now remember whether all this information came from the documents themselves, or from the biographies which Philip had lent him. In any case he noticed that each biography described a quite different poet: even the simplest observation by one was contradicted by another, so that nothing seemed certain. He felt that he knew the biographers well, but that he still understood very little about Chatterton. At first Charles had been annoyed by these discrepancies but then he was exhilarated by them: for it meant that anything became possible. If there were no truths, everything was true.

Charles went back to his preface but, when he read 'The sad pilgrimage of his life', he stared at the words with incomprehension. Where had they come from? He closed his eyes for a moment, as a shadow passed across him, and then almost at once he started writing furiously again. The biro he was using had run out of ink, but he was so eager to continue with his thoughts that he merely pressed deeper into the paper in order to print the outlines of his words. All at once he saw the entire pattern of Chatterton's life, and with redoubled pressure he wrote it down with his empty pen. He had just completed the last sentence when the telephone rang and, in his enthusiasm, he answered it with a loud 'Hello! Hello!', in the manner of a music-hall comedian.

Or so at least it seemed to Harriet Scrope, who replied 'I say! I say!'

'Harriet?'

'Yes, what is it?'

Charles was very relaxed now. 'No. I think *you* were calling *me*.'

'Well, that is a coincidence.' Harriet was standing on one leg while with the other she kicked out at Mr Gaskell, who was about to spring upon a side-table covered with what Harriet called her 'knick-knacks'.

'Isn't it a lovely day, Harriet? April with his showers sweet.'

'Get off it!' Harriet was addressing the cat.

'It is. Really.'

'I know it is.' She tried to explain. 'I was just talking to Mr Gaskell.'

'Did he tell you about it?'

Harriet gave a loud laugh, but she stopped very suddenly. 'I wanted to talk to you, Charles dear.' She hesitated; she was not sure whether she ought to admit having seen Vivien the day before, especially since she was about to act upon their conversation. 'I think we ought to rest on our laurels for a while. The memoirs can wait, don't you think? We're both a little bit tired.'

'Tired?'

'Yes, you know, weary, exhausted, bushed, clapped out, fucked.' Then she added: 'Of course I'll still pay you.'

Charles was so delighted by his sudden ability to write about Chatterton (for the last few days he had done nothing except stare out of the window or sleep) that he was hardly listening to her. 'That's entirely up to you, Harriet.'

'Yes, I suppose it is.' She hesitated again. 'How's Chatterton?'

'As a matter of fact –' Charles was smiling at Edward who, hearing a change in his father's voice, had come back into the room. He beckoned his son over and placed an arm around his shoulder as he continued talking to Harriet. 'As a matter of fact, I'm planning a celebration. I've almost started. Spinach. Finished. I've almost finished.' He hugged Edward tighter as his son tried to break free.

'That is good news.'

'I was thinking of dinner at the local Indian. Friday week.'

'I'll be there. I adore hot things.' Harriet stuck out her tongue in disgust. 'I like them to burn me.'

Edward had struggled free of his father's embrace and, sensing his excitement, was marching around the room and shouting 'Friday the thirteenth! Friday the thirteenth!' But he became silent when Charles, having put down the telephone and returned to his desk, groaned softly to himself. The words which he had inscribed deeply into the page had already faded, leaving only a few hollows and striations behind; all of his thoughts about Chatterton had disappeared. With deliberate slowness he opened a drawer and took out another pen; very carefully he placed a fresh sheet of paper on top of his desk; calmly he settled himself in his chair; and all the time he was trying to remember what it was that he had written before. 'Chatterton,' he wrote; and then he stopped. Children were playing in the street outside, and they shouted out small words which rose towards the sun. The old house trembled beneath its own weight.

When Charles looked up he saw Edward standing by his desk; he must have slept again. 'Hi, kid. What's the problem?'

For a moment neither of them spoke. 'Let's go out, Dad.' He held his arms stiffly down by his sides, and then solemnly repeated a phrase he had often heard his mother use. 'We need some fresh air.' He marched back into his room, and Charles followed him; it was then that he saw Chatterton lying on the bed.

After the first moment of blank fear he realised that it was the portrait of Chatterton: Edward must have removed it from behind his desk as he slept, and placed it here at the top of the bed. He was about to retrieve it when his son put out his hand to stop him. 'I wanted him to fall asleep,' he said.

Charles was genuinely interested by this. 'Why must he fall asleep?'

'Because he was staring at you.'

'And how do you know that?'

'Can't you see?' Edward pointed at the portrait, and for a moment Charles was alarmed. 'Can't you see he's trying to hurt you?'

Charles went over to the canvas, and turned it to the wall. 'He can't hurt me. He's dead.'

'How do you know, Dad?' Edward spoke slowly, as if his father was a child whom he had to convince with very clear arguments. 'He's alive in the picture, isn't he?'

'Seeing is believing,' Charles said, almost to himself. He seized Edward's hand. 'I'll tell you what. I'll make a deal with you: if I showed you a picture of him dead, would you believe that?'

Edward hesitated, suspecting that this was a trick question. 'I might do.'

'Come on. Make a deal.' His father was very insistent. 'Would you believe he was really dead?'

Edward looked at the canvas and then back at his father. 'Okay.'

'All right then, Edward the Uncertain, we're going on a journey.'

*

'No, it's true. Your hair can stand on end, Eddie.' They were holding a serious discussion on the top deck of the bus which was taking them towards the Tate Gallery. 'When you're afraid, the little muscles on the hair-root contract. And then the hair stands up. Look. I'll show you.' Charles screwed up his eyes, trying by an effort of will to raise his hair; and, in fact, he could feel his scalp quivering with the strain. But then there was some larger disturbance beneath his skull, and he leaned back quickly against his seat.

'You did it!' Edward was very excited. 'You made your hair stand on end!' They were approaching the river from Oakley Street and, as the bus turned the corner onto the Chelsea Embankment, Edward pressed his face against the grimy window. 'Look at that bridge, Dad! It's moving!' There was a strong wind, and the Albert Bridge was swaying slightly between its two banks. 'How can that be safe?'

[129]

And Charles himself was aware how fragile it seemed: it looked to him to be on the point of collapse, ready to crack or break beneath the strain, and he had a sudden image of the cars and pedestrians falling helplessly into the water. 'Don't be silly,' he said. 'Of course it's safe. Nothing can happen.'

He looked around, almost apologetically, at a young man who was sitting across from them. He was wearing an olive green jacket and a pair of flared brown trousers: old, frayed clothes which hung so awkwardly on him that it looked as if he had been dressed by someone else. He had lank hair, and his eyes protruded slightly so that he gave the impression of being in a state of permanent surprise or shock. He seemed to be smiling at some private joke but then, noticing Edward's interest in the bridge, he said, 'You know when that was built, don't you?' Edward shook his head. 'In 1873. There are four hundred separate pieces of ironwork on that bridge, and each piece was made at Boulter's Foundry in Birmingham. It took two years to finish and it cost seventy thousand pounds.' He seemed to take as much delight in imparting this knowledge as he did in possessing it. 'It was part of the great improvement. You know, there was a time when all this was just wasteland. The poor people came here and searched for coal or wood. They needed fires, you see.' He had a curious, engaging smile but Charles noticed how nervously he pulled at his frayed cuffs as he spoke. 'And the river banks were just mud, although the very poor still lived here some- how. We should count our blessings, shouldn't we?' He looked earnestly at them both. 'This is my stop. Goodbye.'

'I hope we see you again,' Charles said. When the bus pulled away he watched as the young man, in his shabby, ill-fitting clothes, started walking towards a block of council flats beside the river.

'That man knew a lot of history, didn't he, Dad?'

'Yes, he did.' And he saw at once how he must have looked out at that bridge all his life. 'Some people like history.' Then, to his son's embarrassment, he put his arm around Edward and hugged him. 'It's cosy up here, isn't it? It's like being on a plane above the clouds.' He was about to say something else when he saw the Tate Gallery approaching on the left. 'Come on, Eddie! No more day-dreaming.' He jumped up enthusiastically. 'We're here.'

But when they reached the steps of the gallery Charles held back: he seemed reluctant to enter the building until Edward put his hands against his back and pushed him upwards. As soon as they walked into the front hall, however, Charles knew the way. 'Now,' he said. 'We have to get through the nineteenth century first.' Edward did not know what he meant but he followed his father into the first gallery; crooked streets of whitewashed houses with pink blinds and grey roofs stretched away from him on the right side, and on the left purple and emerald landscapes glowed upon the wall. In front of him he could see the interiors of small rooms, some of them looking out onto gardens where the flowers seemed to breathe colour into the air; and when he turned suddenly he saw the shimmering surface of a lake quietly reflecting the evening light. Charles had turned a corner and he hurried to catch up with him, his shoes squeaking on the green marbled floor. His father was standing in the middle of a gallery filled with much larger paintings and Edward took his hand as the prospect of gorges, ravines, abysses and wild oceans surrounded the man and boy. 'Is this it, Dad?' he whispered.

'No, not really.' Charles turned slowly, absorbed by these images of extinction. The violent colours seemed to be detaching themselves from the canvas and floating towards him. 'No. We have to go further back.'

'Go back?'

'We want Chatterton.'

But Charles made no effort to move away; he stood there, gazing at the paintings, as Edward left his side and walked up to an attendant. 'Please could you tell me about Chatterton?'

The attendant looked down at the thoughtful, anxious child. 'That's a painting, isn't it?'

'I think so.'

He called over to a colleague, lounging against a door. 'Chatterton?' And he in turn shouted to another, 'Chatterton?', until the question echoed around the white walls. And, when the answer came, Edward was directed to Gallery Fifteen – down the right-hand side, fourth on the left. And he went back for his father, taking him by the hand once again and leading him forward.

They passed through an exhibition of portraits, and in the first room of modern acquisitions Charles noticed large human figures in various brooding or unquiet configurations, some of them carrying heavy burdens and some of them sitting dejected. In the next room he saw eighteenth century portraits in which solid, complete figures dominated the landscape like trees; in the third room there were seventeenth century faces, looking out from dark corners of panelled interiors or smiling in the shadows. Charles could see in each face the life and the history; he did not want to leave the world in which his own face was their companion.

They had reached Gallery Fifteen, and Edward turned around to see his father hesitating. 'Come on, Dad. This is our one.' Charles took a deep breath and then walked quickly past him; he did not glance at the other canvases but went straight up to a painting hanging on the far wall. When Edward joined him, he saw a man lying down upon a bed with one arm trailing upon the floor.

'There it is.' His father bent down and whispered to him. 'Do you believe me now?' He pointed at the title beneath the canvas, 'Chatterton. By Henry Wallis. 1856.'

But Charles himself did not want to look at the actual body, not yet. Instead he looked out of the window of the garret in Brooke Street, towards the smoking rooftops of London; he examined the small plant upon the sill, with its thin translucent leaves curling slightly in the cold air; he saw the burnt-out candle on the table, and his eye travelled upward along the path of its fading smoke; he turned his head slightly towards the wooden chest, lying open, and then he started to count the torn pieces of paper which lay scattered across the boards of the floor. And, at last, he looked at Thomas Chatterton.

But was there someone now standing at the foot of the bed, casting a shadow over the body of the poet? And Charles was lying there, with his left hand clenched tightly on his chest and his right arm trailing upon the floor. He could feel the breeze from the open window upon his face, and he opened his eyes. He was able to look up and, her face in shadow beside the garret window, he saw Vivien standing above him. She was crying.

'That's not our face,' Edward was saying. 'Our face is different!'

'Oh no.' Charles was swaying slightly, and he held onto his son's shoulder for support. He was finding it difficult to breathe, and for a moment he could not speak. 'Oh no. That's George Meredith. He was the model. He was pretending to be Chatterton.'

'So he's not dead yet!' Edward was triumphant. 'Chatterton isn't dead! I was right!'

'No,' Charles said softly. 'He's not dead yet.'

\*

> 'You like not that French novel? Tell me why.
> You think it most unnatural . . .
> Unnatural? My dear, these things are life:
> And life, they say, is worthy of the Muse.'
>                    (Modern Love. Sonnet 25. George Meredith.)

'How can it be unnatural?' Meredith took out a handkerchief from the pocket of his lilac trousers, and draped it across his face. His voice was slightly muffled by the cloth. 'Now you can see the common features of mankind, free from individual expression. So how can a mask be unnatural?'

[132]

'But I want you as a model. Yourself. Your face.' Wallis blinked as the winter sunlight flooded the room, and the enamelled Chinese vases suddenly caught fire on the mantelpiece.

'My face, but not myself. I am to be Thomas Chatterton, not George Meredith.'

'But it *will* be you. After all, I can only paint what I see.' Wallis looked around for support to Mary Ellen Meredith, but for a moment she seemed abstracted; she was examining her palm as she clenched and unclenched her right hand.

Meredith laughed and raised himself from the sofa on which he had been lounging. 'And what do you see? The real? The ideal? How do you know the difference?' The two men had been debating like this all afternoon and, much to Mary Ellen's annoyance, her husband would not let the argument rest. 'When Molière created Tartuffe, the French nation suddenly found him beside every domestic hearth. When Shakespeare invented Romeo and Juliet, the whole world discovered how to love. Where is the reality there?'

'So this is how you see your own poetry, I take it?' Even as Wallis said this he could not help but glance again at Mary: with the light upon her hair, her cheek, her shoulder, she seemed to him to resemble a Giotto, whose paintings he had just been studying in Tournier's *History*.

'Not at all. I don't aim so high. I can only lay claim to a small enclosed room, a little narrow space of observation where I set my pen. Of course there *is* a reality –'

'Ah! The tune has changed!'

'– But, I was going to add, it is not one that can be depicted. There are no words to stamp the indefinite thing. The horizon.' Meredith stretched out on the sofa again, and seemed to scrutinise his wife.

Briefly she returned his look. 'My husband thinks more of his poetry than he will tell us, Mr Wallis. He is very proud.'

'Yes, Wallis, why don't you paint that? Pride Dying in a Garret. It would be worthy of the Royal Academy. Or you could place it there, beside the other true fictions.' Meredith was pointing towards an ebony book-case, already decorated with groups from Chaucer, Boccaccio and Shakespeare.

No, she is not a Giotto, Wallis thought, but an Otto Runge. 'I must go,' he said softly. 'I must work before it gets dark.'

Mary got up from her chair, and the rich blue colouring of her dress swirled around her as if she were some goddess rising from the Mediterranean sea. 'You must walk Mr Wallis to the stand, George. He will lose his way in this fog.'

'What fog is that, my dear?'

[133]

She rang for a servant to bring Wallis his ulster and, while they waited, Meredith was capering on the carpet behind them; he was lunging at his friend's back with an invisible sword. 'I will put him at a stand,' he said. 'Take that, and that, and that.'

*

The two men left the house in Frith Street and, as they walked slowly towards the cab stand, Wallis noticed how Meredith lost his artificial manner when he was no longer in the presence of his wife. He was talking about some paintings from the Nazarene School, which he had seen in the St James's Gallery the day before, and Wallis was impressed by his enthusiasm. 'I like details,' Meredith was saying as they turned into Soho Square. 'I detest the grand effect, unless it springs from small things. The Stanfields and the Maclises are mere theatre, mere Dickens on canvas.' The rays of the setting sun touched for the last time the warm bark of the trees which stood in the Square, and the light brushed against the grey stone of the houses around it. There was a vague fog in the air, but it seemed only to broaden the light – as if its milky veins were spreading outward and turning into smoke. Two high window panes glittered, and Meredith pointed towards them: 'Is that what you call electro-typing?'

Wallis's thoughts had been elsewhere, and it was only with an effort that he understood his friend's remark. 'It has quite a Cuyp effect, doesn't it?' They walked on in silence for a moment until Wallis added, 'You see how the twilight makes all the colours fade into one another.' He pointed towards a piece of wrapping paper which was blowing among the trees: 'Only blue and white can keep their luminosity in this light.'

'Yes, dear Henry, everything fades.' Meredith's sepulchral tone made them both laugh, but then he added in the same mournful voice, 'And no doubt it is true that we see nature through the eyes of the painter.'

'Only if you are content to be a copyist. But look.' He took Meredith's arm and crossed the square. 'Do you see how the light becomes blue as it is filtered through the leaves? No one has caught that effect before on canvas. Put it in a poem, George, and it will be yours.'

'I never know what is mine any more.'

There was only one cab waiting at the Oxford Street stand, the breath of the horse steaming visibly around the hunched figure of the driver. 'To Chelsea!' Meredith shouted, as he closed the door upon his friend. The driver was sucking on a clay pipe and turned around only briefly before raising his whip. Meredith looked in at

[134]

Wallis through the half-open window. 'Of course it is all an illusion,' he said. 'Art is just another game.' But Wallis was thinking once again of Mary Ellen Meredith; he stared at her husband without hearing what he said, and then the horse drew him away.

Without company now, Meredith's face lost its brightness and he turned back from the cab stand with a puzzled expression. He did not want to return home, not yet, and so he wandered along Oxford Street. In the gathering darkness the faces of those he passed seemed more vivid, and in all their clothes and their movements they seemed to be showing him their histories, beseeching him to understand them. The city had become one vast theatre – not the theatre of his imagination, either, but that of Astley's or the Hippodrome, tawdry, garish, stifling, real. He tripped against a stray gas-holder, ready for the pole of the lamp to be fitted into it, and two small boys screamed out in delight. 'Do yer mother know yer out?' one of them called over to him, and the other took up the refrain with ''Ow's yer poor foot?' Meredith laughed with them and, in sudden exhilaration, he took several small coins from his pocket and tossed them towards the two boys. As they scrambled for them on the pavement, he returned with lighter tread to Frith Street. He slowed down at the corner, however, and began determinedly to whistle as he approached his house.

As soon as Mary heard him she went across to the chimney piece, carved in Grecian form, and kept her back turned to him as he entered the room. 'What are you doing?' he asked. But he asked her gently.

'Nothing.' Then she added, 'I was thinking.'

'What were you thinking about, my dearest?'

'I don't know. I can't remember.' She still had her back turned to him, and in that instant he realised how little he really knew of her. Two horses passed in the street outside and with a smile she faced him. 'I was thinking about that,' she said. 'I was thinking about sound.'

*

It was this moment that Meredith remembered when, two weeks later, he received a letter from Henry Wallis. He read it aloud to Mary as they sat at breakfast: 'My dear Meredith, I hope you are still game to sit to me (he is not a stylist, my dear, but shall I go on?). I ask you so soon after our conversazione because I have had a great good stroke of luck. Do you remember Peter Tranter who joined us in the Blue Posts on one convivial occasion? It was he who chucked his waistcoat into the Thames if you recall –' Meredith looked up to see if his wife had enjoyed this aside but she merely raised her eyebrows.

'It is the life of the male, my dear,' he said; but not apologetically. Then he went back to the letter: 'Well it happened that I fell into conversation with him a few nights back and quite by chance he informed me that his very particular friend, one Austin Daniel – this Daniel is a scene painter at Astleys and may not be unknown to you. It was he who used the figures of Michael Angelo for the pantomime of the Enchanted Palace, and the proprietor said they were too small. But I digress (yes, you do, dear Wallis). In any event, it transpires that this very Daniel now occupies the lodgings in which Chatterton expired. I asked Tranter to call upon him at once, to request my use of this room *pro tem*, to which the said Daniel has readily agreed. My dear Meredith, I trust you will understand how important this may be and, if I could be assured that you are still ready to sit to me, I believe I will be able to create a work which would be worthy of those ideals which we have discussed. I do beg of you to write to me this day, with your answer. My respects to Mrs Meredith, who I hope may be persuaded to join us at Chatterton's fatal lodgings. Yours very truly, Henry Wallis.'

Meredith put down the letter. 'He signs with a flourish.'

'What were those ideals which he mentions?' Mary was about to leave the table, but she stayed for the answer.

'He wants to be modern. He wants to paint a new world. Poor Wallis has his fancies, you see.'

'I wish,' Mary replied quietly, 'that you had some.'

*

Meredith climbed the staircase of a tenement in Brooke Street, Holborn, preceded by the servant girl who had opened the door to him. 'Mind how you go, sir,' she called out – although he was immediately behind her – 'There's a looseness somewhere in these boards. You could take a nasty tumble.' Meredith laughed, and she jumped. 'Oh sir,' she said, 'I didn't know you was so close.' With a giggle she ran on ahead, and was now briskly rapping at the door on a tiny landing at the top of the house. 'Here's a gentleman!' she shouted and then, with another giggle, brushed past Meredith and ran down the stairs, tightening the strings of her cap as she did so.

He waited for a moment and then, hearing no noise from within, gently opened the door; but he stepped back quickly when he saw Wallis's body lying on a bed, one arm trailing down upon the floor. But the body spoke: 'Don't be alarmed, George. I'm rehearsing your part.'

'Oh, my apologies. I had no idea this was a theatre. A private one, I trust.'

[136]

'The better I impersonate you, dear George, the better I paint you.' Wallis got up and sat on the edge of the bed. 'Has Mrs Meredith not come with you?' He asked this casually, as if the answer could be of very little importance to him.

'No, she could not come. Her dear father called, and insisted on driving her through the park like some superannuated Phaeton.' In fact Mary had not mentioned the sitting again after he had read out Wallis's letter, and he presumed that it held no interest for her.

Wallis got up quickly. 'Now tell me how you like my garret.' He put out an arm as if introducing him to the room – which, indeed, was so small that for a moment Meredith saw himself as an intruder in a dolls' house. 'You came just in time. I've completed my first sketches.'

'So this is where the poor poet died.' Meredith turned in a circle, his boots scraping against the worn wooden boards of the floor. 'How does Shelley put it? Rose pale, his solemn agony had not yet faded from him? Nonsense, no doubt.' He felt the bed with his hand and then knelt upon it to look out of the window, across the roof of Furnivals Inn and towards the blackened dome of St Paul's. 'Your friend's bed is very hard,' he said.

Wallis was scattering small pieces of paper across the floor. 'Austin Daniel lives downstairs. This is his servant's room.'

'That girl?'

'Her name is Pig. Don't ask me why.' Meredith had no intention of doing so; he was watching in amusement as Wallis continued dropping bits of paper around his feet. Wallis caught his glance. 'In Catcott's account of Chatterton's death,' he went on, 'we are told that pieces of torn manuscript were found beside the body. I'm glad that you're amused by my poor attempts at realism.'

'Call it verisimilitude.'

'Call it what you will. It is the same thing.'

'Well, it is the same room.' Meredith put his elbow on the window ledge and leaned upon it, his pale face and red hair silhouetted against the winter sky. 'From poet to Pig. But this room is no sty.' He looked around at the chair and table placed neatly at the foot of the bed – carefully dusted and polished although, to judge by the antiquity of their style, they might have been used by Chatterton himself. The bed was of a similar age: it was unlikely that Pig knew she slept upon a bed of death, but was it possible that she had bad dreams? There was a small plant on the ledge beside him and, as he examined the way in which the thin and pliant stalk curled against the window pane, he realised that this must be her only possession.

Wallis was dragging a battered wooden chest from beneath the

[137]

bed. 'This is not Pig's box,' he said. 'But she has given us gracious permission to use it.' He opened the lid; there was nothing inside, but he filled it with manuscript papers before pushing it against the side of the whitewashed wall. Then he stepped back into the opposite corner, and surveyed the scene. 'Something is missing,' he muttered to himself.

'Me?'

Wallis had not heard the question. With quick movements he walked towards Meredith, leaned across him and opened the window. The cold November air filled the small room. Then he moved the small wooden chair a few inches, and flung his own coat upon it. He went across to the chest and put it at an angle to the wall. Then he stepped back into the corner again.

Meredith had been watching all this activity with interest. 'Is it becoming more real, Henry?'

'When you are lying dead upon the bed. Only then will it be real.' He examined Meredith now for the first time. 'Could you remove your coat and boots?'

'Then I will become a perfect Chatterton and surely die. Do you feel the draught from the window?'

Wallis had sat down upon a stool, and put a wooden board across his knee. 'Then shut it up, shut it up,' he said, distracted. 'I know how it was. I will be able to recall it.' He had taken a large sheet of rough drawing paper and placed it on the board, fastening it at the top with two pegs. 'Throw your coat and boots to me, George. They will be out of sight.' Meredith did so. 'And now lie down upon the bed.' Wallis's manner was peremptory, but already he was absorbed in his work. 'Now move your head towards me. So.' He turned his own head so that he was staring down at the floor. 'No, you look as if you are about to fall asleep. Allow yourself the luxury of death. Go on.'

Meredith settled more deliberately onto the bed, and at once felt something digging into his back. 'Did you ever read,' he asked, 'the story of the princess and the pea?' He got up for a moment, and found a small red button lying on the sheet beneath him. He put it into his trouser pocket and then lay back again. 'I can endure death,' he said into the air. 'It is the representation of death I cannot bear.'

'Let your right arm trail upon the floor. Thus.' Wallis put his own arm down and his fingers brushed against the wooden boards. 'And clench it. Clench it as if you were holding something. I must see the motor movements in your hand.'

Meredith followed these instructions, but he was silent only for a moment. 'I seem to be clutching thin air, Henry. Is that some emblem of the poet's life? Some symbol, perhaps?'

[138]

But Wallis was now drawing the scene he had devised; he used black chalk, fastened on a port-crayon, and said nothing at all until he managed to sketch the curve of Meredith's arm. 'I can add the details in the studio. I just need the general effect now.'

'I see. So the greatest realism is also the greatest fakery?' Again Wallis did not reply but continued rapidly to sketch. 'May I . . .' Meredith began, but Wallis put up his chalk to stop him.

'Please stay quiet for a few moments, George. I need that expression.' He worked in silence for two or three minutes. 'Now you may speak.'

'Now I have nothing to say.' But he was silent only for a moment. 'Did I tell you, Henry, that I dreamed of Chatterton the other night? I was passing him on some old stairs. What does that signify?'

'I believe stairs are an emblem. Was that your word? Stairs are an emblem of time.'

'But why was I showing him a puppet?' Meredith gazed up at the ceiling, noticing for the first time how decayed it was, how blackened with soot and grease, and how one dark stain had taken on the lineaments of a face. With a sudden sense of oppression he realised that this may have been the last thing Chatterton saw on earth, like the prisoner looking at the walls of his dungeon before he is led away . . . he closed his eyes and tried to imagine that last darkness. But he could not. He was George Meredith. He knew only the things George Meredith knew. There could be no escape for him yet.

'Hold still. I need that light upon your hand.' Wallis's tongue protruded slightly from his lips as he worked upon this. Then with a sudden flourish he wrote something in the right-hand corner, put down his chalk and leaned back against the wall. 'I am so pleased we came here,' he said. 'This is the room. This is the actual bed. This is the London light. There is no reality, George, except in visible things.' He looked around, clearly delighted with everything he saw.

'Can I move now?' Meredith sat up, and rubbed his right shoulder. 'I presume you have finished?'

'For the moment.'

'A moment! It seems like an age.' Wallis blushed and Meredith added quickly, 'Not that I object to it. I enjoy it. It is a delightful way to spend one's morning. Then in a few days I will call on you in your studio, you will dress me and you will make a small painting. Am I correct?' Wallis nodded. 'That will be delightful, too. Then you will transfer that small picture to a larger canvas. At the end of some weeks, or even months, the painting will be complete. Delightful once more.' Wallis had been looking curiously

[139]

at the light which was falling across Meredith's face, and now he took up a fresh sheet of drawing paper to begin sketching again. But he was smiling, as Meredith continued. 'It will be lovely, but there is no need to talk of reality. You will have created a costume drama, a tragic scene worthy of Drury Lane. These visible things are stage props, mere machinery.'

'Stop!' Wallis held up his chalk. 'Stop in that position! Close your eyes and think of nothing. Evacuate your mind as I draw you.'

'Nothing could be easier.'

Wallis worked on in silence and Meredith seemed to sleep, the stillness broken only by the angry buzzing of a fly which was trying vainly to escape through the closed window. But there was a sudden rap at the door and the painter, annoyed at the interruption, called out, 'Who is it?' After a few moments they both heard muffled sounds, as if someone were speaking confidentially to the door itself. 'Who's there?' Wallis shouted out again.

The door opened very slightly, and the tip of a nose emerged from behind it. Meredith sat up and laughed out loud. 'Pig, dear Pig, do come in!'

She entered warily. 'Excuse me, sirs. I didn't know if you was decent so I told her to wait.' She jerked her head back in the general direction of the stairs.

'Pig, dear Pig, are you by any chance related to Francis Bacon?'

'I am a Trotter, sir. A Trotter from Hammersmith and always have bin.' She straightened her cap slightly and stared at Meredith, as if daring him to disagree with her. 'And all of us Trotters in service, I'm glad to say.' Then she recalled her business with Wallis. 'There's a lady downstairs wishing very graciously to come up if you would be so obliged, sir. Are you wishing that she be brought up directly or left exactly where she is?'

'Did she give her name?' he asked, and at this moment Mary Ellen Meredith walked into the room. Wallis rose suddenly from his stool, and knocked his drawing board onto the floor.

'I'm sorry,' Mary said. 'I seem to have come at an inconvenient time, as always.'

'No. Not at all. No.' Wallis and Pig were both kneeling on the floor, rivalling each other in their efforts to pick up the sketches which had slipped from the board. 'We have quite finished.' Wallis waved Pig away. She rose to her feet and, looking at each one of them in turn, proceeded backwards out of the room.

Meredith lay upon the bed, his hands cupped beneath his head, and smiled at his wife. 'Forgive me, my dear, but I cannot move. I am the dead or dying poet.'

'I know. Or, rather, I know that you are posing as one.' She turned to Wallis who had got up from the floor and was now, with bowed head, placing his sketches in order. 'Is my husband a good model, Mr Wallis?'

'Ah –' Wallis looked at her in confusion.

'I am a model poet, at least. I am pretending to be someone else.'

'So this is the famous garret.' She seemed to ignore her husband, but Wallis noticed how nervously she played with the string of amber beads at her wrist; she was twirling them around and the sunlight from the window caught them, sending flashes of colour across the small room.

'And think of all the passions that heated it, my dear. Even here on this bed.'

'I thought you were dead, George.'

'But dead men still tell tales.'

'May I see the sketches, Mr Wallis?' She turned hurriedly towards the painter, and he stood beside her as she looked at the work which he had completed that morning.

'You see here,' he was saying, 'how the shadow falls. But forgive me.'

'Forgive you? Forgive you for what?' She had said this involuntarily, and played still with the amber bracelet.

'I mean that you already know about such things. George is so fluent –'

'No, believe me, I know nothing. George never speaks of serious things. Not to me.' She was scrutinising the sketch of her husband lying dead upon the bed.

As they spoke together Meredith once more adopted Chatterton's pose and, with his head twisted in an even more uncomfortable position, whispered to his wife, 'Why not look at the great original rather than the impressions of him?'

'You always told me to rely upon first impressions, George.'

All three of them laughed at this, no one louder than Meredith himself. 'But am I not an object to set your soul on fire? I am, as Henry says, so real.'

'You are hardly real at all.' She spoke very softly, still examining the drawings.

'You think me unnatural, my dear?'

'I find you more natural on paper.'

'My own, or the sketches here?'

'Both, no doubt.'

'So I am a forgery but my writing is not?'

'You must ask your looking glass that question.'

[141]

'But you are my looking glass.'

'No. I am only your wife.' Wallis was startled by the frankness with which they talked in front of him, but Mary turned to him again as if nothing particular had been said. 'Tell me how you will proceed with these sketches, Mr Wallis. I like to have every detail, you know, so leave nothing out.' She glanced briefly at her husband who, from his still recumbent position, was surveying them both with a small smile. 'George will pretend not to listen, of course, but he will hear everything. That is his way.'

'It is the way of the world, my dear.'

But she was already attending to Wallis, who was holding his last sketch up to the light. 'When I have finished the drawing I will need to saturate it with water, and then I can use a grey tint to block in the shade. After that I put on my colour and allow it to dry: when it is firm, I can use a hair pencil for all the details. As for the lights –'

'Out, damned light!' Meredith was staring at the ceiling once more.

'– As for the lights, I need only touch the drawing with water and then rub it with a little piece of bread. That is my method, at least.'

The small bed creaked as Meredith turned upon it. 'Bread and water always kept poets alive. Did you know that, my love? You have heard of love in a hutch, I take it?'

But they were too deep in their theme to pay any attention to him. 'You cannot beat the reality, Mrs Meredith. This is Chatterton's room, precisely as it was . . .'

'Is everything the same?' Mary surveyed it, steadily taking in her husband as she looked around as if he, too, were part of its old furniture.

'Yes, it is!' Wallis was so enthusiastic now that even this simple enquiry elicited his strong assent. 'Yes, exactly! And, you see, if I can depict the room now I will have fixed it for ever. Even the poor plant, of all things the frailest, that too will survive!' In his excitement he had touched her arm, and he withdrew his hand quickly from her. But she had not moved away. He went on, not quite knowing what he was saying now. 'I sat down here and looked at the entire scene. I was doing this for hours before you came, George –' He swung wildly towards him. '– But I told you that. And the room somehow became brighter as I watched it. Can you conceive of this?'

'Yes,' she said. 'Yes, very well.'

'And if I can place that brightness on my canvas, it will never fade.'

'Unlike the poor poet.' Meredith pretended to groan.

[142]

'But the death will be realised too, don't you see?' Wallis had moved away from Mary, and now talked equally to husband and wife. 'I need the reality of the room for the greater reality of the death. I cannot paint the taking of the arsenic, the convulsions, the foaming at the mouth. Not unless I gave you poison, George –'

Mary sat down heavily on the chair at the foot of the bed, and Meredith laughed. 'You must not lead my darling through too much reality, Wallis. It can be dangerous for those who are not accustomed to it.'

'It was not the reality, George,' she said. 'It was the closeness of the room.'

Meredith leaned up from the bed and opened the garret window, before continuing. 'I would be happy, Henry, to foam at the mouth if you wish me to. I am very understanding of tragedy, is that not right, my dear?'

'You understand what you want to understand, certainly.'

'But tragedy is my forte.'

'And comedy is your vice.'

It seemed to Wallis that this was some theatrical performance they were displaying for his benefit, but then at the same moment he realised that they were also in earnest. Suddenly Meredith rose from the bed and, muttering 'I will bring some water for you', left the room.

Wallis picked up the sketches and began busily to rearrange them, although they were already in order. He brushed his drawing board with his sleeve and then placed it carefully in a corner. At last he stood up and faced Mary. 'George is a wonderful model,' he said. 'He lay so quiet upon that bed –'

He stopped as Mary rose from the chair, leaving a large crease in the ulster which Wallis had draped there, and began pacing up and down the room. 'I do like it here,' she said, almost to herself. 'It seems to be such a secret place. It is like a spot buried within oneself.' She went over to the window, stretching across the bed to reach it. 'And if I grew bored with my own secrets I could look down on the streets below and wonder about the secrets of others.' She turned to Wallis. 'Do you ever think about such things?'

He hesitated. 'I wonder about your secrets.'

'Oh no. You must not do that.'

'Was he offering to paint you, my dear?' Meredith came back into the room, carrying a glass of water, and had apparently heard her last words. 'Wallis has an eye for beautiful form, whatever he says about brute realities.' Hurriedly she moved away from the bed and took the glass of water from him, but she did not drink from it. 'It is not poisoned, my darling.'

[143]

Wallis could bear it no longer. 'I must leave you,' he said. 'I have to collect my colours from Bellew's.' He picked up his board and sketches. 'I am sure that Mr Daniel will be happy for you to stay and rest here together.'

'No –'

'No, that will not be necessary, Mr Wallis.' Both of them had spoken at once.

Meredith laughed, embarrassed at their unwillingness to be left alone together. 'Do not leave me to the mercies of Pig, Henry. She talks of nothing but Trotters and Hammersmith.'

Wallis was eager to leave. 'So I can expect you in my studio next week, then?' He took one last look at the room before opening the door. 'There you will be comfortable at least, George.'

They descended the stairs, Mary leading the way down the narrow staircase. 'Do with me what you will Henry,' Meredith answered. 'I am entirely at your disposal.'

'He means that he has nothing else to do, Mr Wallis.'

There was a sharper note in Meredith's voice as they turned at the first landing. 'How would you know, my love? I never see you.' But then he laughed, and put his hand lightly upon her shoulder. 'Don't be alarmed, Henry. This is modern love, you know. Secretly we adore each other. Is that not right, Pig?'

The servant girl was waiting for them at the bottom of the stairs; as soon as she saw them, she giggled and rushed to open the front door. She curtsied to each of them as they crossed the threshold and then, murmuring 'It must be a fine day for it', closed the door very firmly behind them.

They walked down Brooke Street into Holborn Hill, but Wallis was so careful of his sketches that he hailed a cab as soon as they had entered the main thoroughfare. He hesitated as he opened the door. 'Can I take you back to Frith Street?' he asked them. 'It is on my way.'

Meredith seemed about to accept when Mary shook her head. 'No,' she said, stepping away from the warm interior of the cab. 'No, we must walk.'

'We need more air,' Meredith explained. 'After all, I have just been poisoned.'

Wallis watched them from the back window of the cab as he was driven away. They seemed to be deep in conversation as they walked down into Holborn, or it may simply have been that both their heads were bowed. The cab turned the corner into Gray's Inn Lane and, with a great sigh, Wallis took out his last drawing of Chatterton upon the death-bed. But he could not concentrate upon it. He turned back again, but the Merediths were lost from sight.

# 10

T HE MUTTON TANTRAS are very nice.' Charles Wychwood
was addressing the others as they sat, on the appointed
day, in the Kubla Khan restaurant. 'Some people prefer the
Bhagavad-Gita, but it's very hot.'

Harriet Scrope ran her finger down the list of dishes on the tattered
menu. 'I don't see anything like that.'

Charles laughed. 'I was making it up. Have you never heard
about poetry being the food of love . . .'

'Ah, ignis fatuus,' Andrew Flint murmured, to no one in particular. 'An interesting dish, don't you think, for a strong stomach?'

'Give it to me hot,' Harriet was saying. 'I like it hot and strong.'

'Korma,' Philip Slack replied to the red paper napkin folded
neatly beside his plate.

'What was that, dear?' Harriet had decided to be particularly
nice to this young man, who seemed to be a close friend of the
Wychwoods.

'The Korma is hot.'

'Oh, I bet it is.' She winked at him. 'You must come here often.'
The piped Indian music was suddenly very loud, and she waved
her arms above her head. 'The goddess Kali used to do that,' she
said, 'in the old days.'

Flint was still studying the menu. 'Que faire?'

Harriet gave a little shiver after her sudden exercise. 'I've decided
already. I'm going to have the mutton dressed as lamb.' She turned
in her seat. 'But where's my gin?' In fact the waiter had just come
up to the table and was immediately behind her with her drink.
'Oh, you scared me. I thought you were the Lord High Ex-
ecutioner.' The waiter did not understand this, but he bowed and
smiled. 'Now can I have a teaspoon?' she asked him.

'I'm sorry, please. Ice please, is it?'

'No. A spoon.' She repeated the word very slowly and precisely,
carving the shape of a spoon in the air. 'Sippy sippy.'

Flint was now so embarrassed by her behaviour that he leant

across the table to Vivien and, in a determined voice, said, 'I gather you work in a gallery?'

Vivien Wychwood was very quiet. Charles seemed faint and dizzy just before leaving for the restaurant, and she had been watching him all evening for signs of strain or sickness. 'Me?' she seemed surprised by Flint's interest. 'Oh, I work at Cumberland and Maitland. You know, in New Chester Street . . .' Her voice had trailed off.

'Do you *really*? I didn't know that.' Harriet spoke very clearly, to remind Vivien that they were not supposed to have met there – let alone to have discussed the possibility of taking the Chatterton manuscripts from Charles. 'In a *gallery*, of all places!' The tone of her voice made it sound like an abattoir, but Vivien had not heard. Once again she was looking anxiously at her husband, who was moving his head from side to side in obvious discomfort. Harriet followed Vivien's glance. 'You seem,' she said to him, 'to have some kind of bee in your bonnet.'

'Oh no. Nothing like that.' Charles smiled and waved his hand, as if dismissing his headache. 'I like honey, but not bees.'

'Ah, a hedonist.' There was a narrow band of sweat across Flint's forehead as he leaned forward eagerly to speak. Charles said nothing, and Flint turned nervously to Vivien. 'Pity my ignorance, but did I see some Seymours in your gallery?'

'Ha!' Harriet put down her menu, with which she had been fanning herself. 'I'd be careful if I were you.' But then, sensing Vivien's alarm that her indiscretion about the paintings was about to be revealed, she added, 'He isn't cheap, you know.'

'Caveat emptor, I take it?'

'What does that mean? Beware of the dog?' Without realising it, Harriet had bared her teeth slightly.

He cleared his throat. 'Well, yes, mutatis mutandis.'

'Ad nauseam,' she murmured. In a sudden depression of spirits she looked around at the garish green-and-gold wallpaper, the violet drapes which concealed the entrances to the kitchen and to the two tiny lavatories, the red carpet stained with food and wine, the grey tablecloth already damp from the gin she had spilt in her excitement. 'Do you know my friend Sarah Tilt? The famous art critic?' she asked, and the others fell silent. 'She knows all about painters.' Harriet brightened visibly. 'But what she really needs is a toy boy.' She brought out the phrase with great aplomb, having recently come across it in a copy of the *Daily Mail* which she had picked up in her dentist's waiting room. They looked at her astonished. 'Let's not mince words,' she went on. 'Let's face a few facts. She's no oil painting.'

Philip coughed, trying to announce the fact that the waiter had been standing by the table ever since Harriet had decided to denounce her old friend. And in a sudden flurry of activity they all picked up their menus once again. 'Now let me see,' Flint began. 'Do I dare to eat a peach?'

Charles put out his hand. 'No,' he said. 'Let me order. This is my treat.'

'I'll have another gin then,' Harriet said quickly to the waiter, who had now entered the spirit of the proceedings and was smiling broadly.

'With a utensil, please?'

'Someone's getting *fresh*,' she said. But she continued smiling and nodding at him as he took Charles's order for Chicken Tikka, Tandoori Mutton, Chicken Korma, two vegetable biryanis and a side-order of papadoms. 'And don't forget the wine,' Charles added.

'And the gin! Ginny, ginny, no waity.'

When the wine came, Charles raised his glass. 'Here's to Chatterton!' he said. 'Here's to the poet and all his works!'

Flint leant across to Vivien. 'What's this about Chatterton? Thomas, I take it?'

Harriet shot her a warning glance. It was as if to say (and Vivien understood it quite well): if we are to save Charles, if we are to relieve him of the Chatterton material, we must keep it to ourselves. So Vivien said merely, 'I don't know, really. I don't know what he means.'

'A discovery.' Philip spoke in a low tone to his empty plate. 'A great discovery.'

'What?' Flint strained to hear.

'Tell me, Andrew.' Harriet had turned to Flint very quickly. 'May I call you Andrew? What are you working on now? I would love to know.'

The question unnerved him, as it always did. 'Mea culpa . . .' he began to say.

'What is that, a novel or a biography?'

'Well, I am writing a biography.' He swallowed; he found it difficult to discuss any of his activities, which seemed to him no more than the hole through which he was falling. 'Of George Meredith, you know –'

'Yes, I know very well. Didn't his wife have an affair with that painter? I always thought he was a terrible fool, to let her go like that.'

'I wouldn't go so far as to say that.'

Harriet was very grand. 'I don't suppose you would go so far as to say anything.'

[147]

Flint blushed and was about to reply, when a metal dish filled with some brown liquid was placed in front of him. He could see one or two peas floating on top of it, and a dribble of tomato revolved slowly as the waiter stirred it with a fork. 'Biryani, sir,' he said. 'Very good.'

Harriet cackled. 'Bury my heart at wounded knee? That's about Indians too, isn't it?'

The waiter laughed with her and, now considering the meal a great joke, eagerly watched the reactions of the others as he brought them a succession of dishes.

Harriet leant across the table and sniffed the platter of Chicken Tikka, putting her nose so close to the meat that they were for a moment indistinguishable. 'This food,' she said with some satisfaction, 'looks as if it's been to hell and back.'

Vivien put some rice on Charles's plate: he looked at her and smiled, but he paid no attention to his food and seemed content to watch the others as they ate. He held up his glass of wine and looked at them through it, for a moment seeing their faces red and distended. 'You see –' he seemed to be talking to his wife – 'you see, poetry never dies. Here is a biographer writing about George Meredith. The poet lives.' His words were slurred and he paused for a moment before going on. 'That's what I've said about Chatterton. You know, Harriet, I've managed to finish the introduction now –'

But she started talking across him, in Philip's direction. 'I hear you work in a library, dear. Tell me, how many of my books do you actually have? In round numbers, I mean.' She had come to this dinner expecting only Charles and Vivien – she had accepted the invitation as a further stage in the plan she had made with Vivien in St James's Park – but the presence of both Andrew Flint and Philip Slack unnerved her. So she was drinking more than usual.

'We have them all, Miss Scrope.'

'Harriet. A librarian can always call me Harriet. So you won't think of me as just a book.' At this point she put her hands stiffly by her sides, sucked in her cheeks and closed her eyes. Philip was alarmed, and looked wildly around at the others for some explanation, but they were talking together. Then Harriet opened her eyes and smiled at him. 'I was pretending to be a slim volume, Philip. May I call you Pip? It's more literary, don't you think?' The waiter had brought her a third gin, without any prompting, and with a magnificent gesture she handed him the teaspoon and put the glass straight to her lips. It seemed to stay there for rather a long time. 'They love me,' she said eventually, handing the empty glass back to the waiter. 'The public has taken me to its beating heart and will never let me go. I've tried, God knows I've tried to pull away. But no. They must have me! They must have all of me! They can't get enough of me.' She touched herself. 'And I never slapped my public in its face. Never! Might I just have one more little drink, please?' Philip had no real idea what she was talking about – no more than she herself had – but he gestured furtively for the drink she had requested. 'Tell me, Pip, do you write? Gin!' The waiter had misunderstood Philip's gesture, and had brought over a saucer of mango chutney. 'Mummy's ruin!'

Philip was scrutinising the unwanted chutney. 'I tried to write a novel once,' he said.

'That is good news.' Everybody seems to be writing them these days, was her thought.

'But I failed. I stopped . . .'

'Let me see your hands, dear.' Hesitantly he held them out for her inspection and she grabbed them, squeezing his fingertips very hard. 'I knew it,' she said triumphantly. 'They're a writer's hands. Just look at that heart line.' With her finger she traced the crease in question. 'It doesn't know when to stop, does it?' She rolled her eyes.

The waiter had brought a full bottle of gin over to the table, and was refilling Harriet's glass while listening to this brief conversation. 'I have novel,' he said. 'Good book.'

'Who wrote it?' Harriet asked sharply.

'No sir. This my idea.' And it occurred to the horrified Harriet that the waiter had a story to tell also. 'Nice modest man, correct?' He stood up straight, and flashed a smile at her. 'Now this nice man does not want to stand out from others, do you see? Too modest.' Harriet held out her glass, and he refilled it as he spoke. 'But still he is odd. Very odd man.' He shook his head. 'And do you know why?' He could hardly contain himself. 'He is very odd because he tried to be exactly like everyone else. Precisely like. Good story, is that so?'

Harriet was astonished. 'I suppose,' she said, 'that's what is known as magic realism.'

'Exegi monumentum aere perennius . . .' Flint was quoting.

'No, Andrew, it is true.' Charles was in the middle of a heated discussion with him. 'Poetry *is* the finer art.'

Flint was suddenly very angry. 'And what does that mean, really?'

'It lives.' Charles closed his eyes for a moment.

'This is essentially a Romantic attitude. I am not a Romantic.' Flint had never wanted to come to this dinner, and had accepted only from fear of seeming discourteous to Charles; but now he was furious at himself for attending. 'Don't you realise,' he said, 'that nothing survives now? Everything is instantly forgotten. There is no history any more. There is no memory. There are no standards to encourage permanence – only novelty, and the whole endless cycle of new objects. And books are simply objects – consumer items picked up and laid aside.' In his anger, Flint was speaking freely for the first time that evening. 'And poetry is no different. Poetry is disposable, too. Something has happened during the course of this generation – don't ask me why. But poetry, fiction, the whole lot – none of it really matters any more.'

'If I thought that,' Harriet said, 'I'd shoot myself!' She put her thumb and forefinger up to her right temple. 'Mummy go bang bang,' she added, for the waiter's benefit.

'No,' Charles said, softly. 'Some things do survive.'

But Flint was eager to pursue his own argument. 'Yes, they survive. But don't you realise that it's just another kind of death? Five hundred books of poetry published in any one year – they're piled up in the library stacks, or they gather dust on the shelves.' Philip looked down thoughtfully at his hands. 'They are preserved, yes, but only as reminders of all that remains unread, will never be read. A monument to human ambition and human indifference. When I see all that waste of paper, that waste of time, I want to be sick.' As Flint continued talking, Charles got up and walked uncertainly towards one of the curtained alcoves. He held one hand up to his forehead and Vivien half-rose from her chair, looking anxiously around after him. 'Any contemporary work has a life of about three months. That's all.' Flint was quieter now. 'We can't think of posterity. There is no posterity. At least I can't see it.'

'Do you think Charles will remember that he's paying?' Harriet whispered to Philip. 'He seemed a bit squiffy just then.'

But Philip was staring at Flint, his hands clenched tightly together. 'What *do* you see, then?'

Flint paused, and for the first time took in Philip's lean and sombre face. 'What do I see? I don't know.' He was apologetic now. 'I see nothing really.' He took out a handkerchief and wiped the sweat from the sides of his nose.

'Don't be so gloomy, Andrew.' Charles had returned and was patting him on the shoulder.

'I'm sorry.'

'No. Don't be sorry. There's nothing to be sorry for. We can all have our day in the sun.'

'Wrong.'

'What was that, Philip?'

[150]

'I said he's wrong. Andrew is wrong.' Philip was still very tense, and Harriet watched him with amusement as he strained forward in his seat.

'I know he's wrong.' Charles frowned, and seemed to shield his eyes from the restaurant's weak lights. 'Of course words survive. How else could Chatterton's forgeries become real poetry?' He paused again, rubbing his hand slowly across his forehead. 'And there are lines so beautiful that everything is changed by them.'

'Name two,' Flint whispered to Harriet. They had both been drinking heavily, and were now entering a kind of complicity against the others.

'The Brighton Line is one,' she whispered back.

'A child can read a poem, and his whole life can be changed too. I remember this.' Charles looked at Vivien as if he were talking only to her, and she put her hand upon his arm. 'That is why it is such a wonderful thing to have the vocation of a poet, since it's a vocation from childhood that nothing can ever change. No poet is ever completely lost. He has the secret of his childhood safe with him, like some secret cave in which he can kneel. And, when we read his poetry, we can join him there.'

'I thought,' Flint whispered once more to Harriet, 'that eloquence was supposed to be a dead art.'

'It is.'

Charles was looking around the restaurant with a look of intense concentration. 'And there are true poems because there are true feelings, feelings which touch everyone. Do you remember this?' He put his head back, and began quoting in a strange sing-song voice:

> 'But it's not the selfsame bird
> Perished to dust is he . . .
> As also are those who heard
> That song with me.'

Then he laughed, and rubbed his eyes. 'And if poetry doesn't matter, Andrew, why is it that there are people who find their only comfort on earth in reading it? Why is it that some poets are the only companions of lonely or unhappy people? What is it that they find in books which nothing else in the world can show or tell them? Do you know?' Flint looked across at him and said nothing. 'And why is it, Andrew, that some people try all their lives to become writers or poets, even though they are too ashamed to show their work to anyone? Why do they keep on trying? Why do they write and write, putting their poems and stories away as

[151]

soon as they're finished? Where does *their* dream come from?'
Vivien took his hand, but he did not notice her movement. 'I'll tell
you what it is. It is a dream of wholeness, and of beauty. All the
yearning and all the unhappiness and all the sickness can be taken
away by that vision. And the vision is real. I know. I've seen it,
and I am sick.' Vivien looked at him in astonishment, because he
had never before confessed to the sickness which she could now
see clearly upon his face. He turned towards her and smiled. 'I'm
sorry, love,' he said. 'I'm sorry you were stuck with me. I tried my
best but it wasn't good enough, was it?'

His attention was distracted by someone standing behind her;
he made an effort to rise from his chair, as he muttered, 'Yes, of
course. I know you very well.' But then he collapsed, falling
sideways from his chair onto the carpet of the Kubla Khan.

*

'. . . it must be sleep, when low
Hangs that abandon'd arm towards the floor:
The head turn'd with it. Now make fast the door.'
(Modern Love. Sonnet 15. George Meredith)

Henry Wallis was standing at the window of his studio as the
Merediths came down Paradise Walk; it was a large window on
the second floor, looking down onto the Chelsea street, and the
winter sunlight filled the room behind him.

The house itself might have been especially designed for a
painter, in fact – it was newly built and the high-ceilinged rooms,
the broad expanse of the windows and the general airiness were
precisely what Wallis needed although, when the wind came from
the Thames a hundred yards away, some of its scents made him
retch. He feared the cholera even here. But the light was the
especial thing – that brilliant light which glanced off the surface of
the water, spilling across the housefronts and the fields like some
wave which has travelled inland from the sea; a light which, in
this suburb of London, was free of the smoke which even now
could be seen hanging over the city.

Meredith was walking a little ahead of his wife, peering at the
numbers of the new houses in obvious confusion. Wallis noticed
that Mary looked neither at the houses nor at her husband, but
kept her gaze on the ground as she walked towards the river. Now
Meredith was standing in the middle of the road and waving up
to him: 'We're here,' he shouted. 'Your dead poet and his consort
are here!' Mary's face was still averted but, just as he was about

[152]

to turn away from the window, she looked up at him and smiled. Meredith was knocking wildly on the door. 'Take me in!' he called. 'Take me in or I will die on the streets of Chelsea!'

Wallis hurried down the stairs into the long hallway. He prided himself on having no servants, although in fact he still retained a cook; but she rarely ventured from the basement, and lived in constant fear of meeting one of her employer's female models. Occasional shrieks or groans from the kitchen were the only tokens of her presence in the house, and Wallis had already christened the basement area of the house Tartarus. He opened the front door and Mary was standing there alone. He took a step backwards; neither of them said anything; and then Mary inclined her head slightly to the left. Wallis peered over the threshold and saw Meredith lying sprawled upon the dusty ground, apparently choking. 'The poet has taken poison for a broken heart,' he was saying, clutching at his throat with his hands. 'The poet has taken poison!' He looked up at them. 'You are the giants in the land of Cockaigne. Please help me.' Mary entered the house without speaking, as Wallis grabbed his arm and lifted him to his feet.

She was waiting for them in the hallway. 'These flowers are so real,' she said. Wallis had hung a sunflower pattern on his walls, and its colours glowed against the white staircase and the polished wooden floors.

Meredith touched a small terracotta bust beside the stairs, and felt the coolness of its head beneath his hand. He clutched it tightly as he spoke. 'This is modern living, my love.' And then he added, 'Everything is so bright.'

Wallis looked from one to the other, not certain if they wished to continue their conversation here; but they fell silent, and he began leading them upstairs to his studio. 'Here,' he said, over his shoulder, 'is a scene of antique living. Not so bright, as you will see.'

Meredith laughed out loud when he entered the studio: the bed, the wooden chest, the small table and the chair were exactly as he had last seen them in Brooke Street. They were arranged against the far wall of the studio, beneath a window which looked out upon a long garden; and, on the window-sill itself, Wallis had placed a small rose plant just as it had been in Chatterton's garret. Then Meredith noticed a body lying on the bed. It was only when he came closer to it that he saw it was a costume. 'I rented the clothes from Nathan's,' Wallis said.

Meredith fingered the light grey shirt and the purple breeches, wondering who had last worn them. 'I suppose,' he said, 'that they will fit me?'

[153]

'I have measured you like an undertaker, George. I know your size as if it were my own.'

'A small thing, but it *is* my own.' Meredith seemed exhilarated at the prospect of dressing up in this costume. 'And what will you do with my body when I am found dead in this?'

Wallis laughed. 'I intend to varnish it. It will give the flesh a greater look of nature.'

'I thought I could smell the embalming fluids of the Nile.'

'No, that is the spirit.'

'So there are spirits, too, in this resurrection.'

Mary had walked away from them, and was in fact sniffing the clay bottles of Martin's Spirit as they talked. Then she glimpsed her reflection in a tall gilt mirror propped against a corner of the studio, and she stood up quickly; she turned around, examining the paint brushes, mixing bowls, phials of paint and palettes which were scattered across two old wooden tables. There were several sketches pinned to the walls of the studio and, as she wandered across to them, she noticed many of Wallis's old canvases racked on their side behind a faded Japanese screen. A tall studio easel had been placed just in front of the screen and she ran her fingers down its side, feeling the grain of the wood beneath her hand. The canvas upon it had been freshly stretched, and an undercoat of brilliant white already applied: it was so bright that Mary could not look at it without blinking, and small whorls or spirals were appearing in front of her eyes. No one can perceive blankness, she thought; the eye is forced to create shapes as the mouth forms words.

'If the cap fits,' Meredith was saying, 'then I must wear it. But where is the cap?'

She stared once more at the whitened canvas, trying to imagine how the fabricated image of Chatterton's room could be transferred to it. But she could see nothing. All the time she had been conscious only of Wallis's presence, and now she moved behind the screen as if she were shielding herself from a source of heat. She picked up one of the abandoned paintings stored there, and saw a female nude, the upturned breasts pink and glowing.

'These breeches are too tight,' she could hear her husband saying. 'Too much Nature and not enough Art.'

Very deliberately she put down the painting, and came out from behind the screen. 'Be thankful, George,' she said, 'that Mr Wallis is not painting you without breeches.' She saw the surprise on the painter's face, and she faltered slightly.

'Go on, my dear. Go on.' Meredith was grinning at her. 'Now that you have mentioned the unmentionable, I am eager for more.'

[154]

'I was only going to say –' She hesitated. 'I was only going to say that I must leave you both. I have to go now.'

'But –'

'No, Mr Wallis. I came only to point George to the right house. He has no sense at all, really, no sense.' She turned at the doorway and said very quickly, 'Goodbye, George.'

'Adieu, Mrs Chatterton.'

Wallis hurried after her in order to open the street door, and she paused before walking out. 'I hope,' she said, not quite knowing what she was saying, 'I hope that I didn't shock you . . .' She regained her self-possession. 'I hope that I didn't surprise you by arriving with my husband. It was on my way . . .'

'No, of course not. I'm only sorry that –'

'I must go now. Goodbye, Mr Wallis.'

Before he could complete his sentence, she had turned away and started walking towards the river. 'You are going in the wrong direction!' he shouted at her, 'Mrs Meredith! The road is that way!' She looked at him and then – as if she had not heard what he said – she merely shook her head and smiled before turning the corner towards Chelsea Wharf. She will yield to no one, Wallis thought, as he went back to the studio.

Meredith was now completely dressed in the mid-eighteenth-century costume which Wallis had found for him. 'How do I look?'

'You are Chatterton to the life.' Wallis walked over to one of the wooden tables; he had already prepared his colours in several clay mixing bowls, and now only needed to place them on his palette. He thought he heard Meredith laugh. 'No, truly, you do resemble him. Did you know that you both have red hair?'

Meredith was silent. 'How did you persuade Pig,' he said after a few moments, 'to give up everything for art?'

'Pig?' Wallis was still bent over the table.

'How did you persuade her to lend you her poor furniture?' Meredith was bouncing up and down upon the bed.

'I'm sorry to disillusion you, but these are not Pig's. I purchased everything. Can't you see the difference?'

Meredith pressed his finger into the pillow which lay against the bed-head. 'I suppose it makes everything more real? When you buy something, when it is your own, does it acquire a deeper reality?' Now he lay down upon the bed itself, wriggling his feet in the air and inspecting the buckled shoes which he had just put on. 'Don't you think so?'

Wallis took the large canvas from the studio easel and put in its place a smaller one, on which he had underpainted his final composition. Above this he pinned two sketches, already marked with his colour notes for the finished work. He carried the easel into the centre of the studio. 'Do you remember how you were lying in the garret, George?'

'No. You must ask Chatterton that question.'

'You were so.' Wallis brought over to him one of the sketches.

'You *are* a Resurrectionist, Henry. You can bring the dead to life, I see.'

Wallis went back to his easel. 'Put your head to the side. Let your left hand lightly clutch your chest. Good. Now allow your right arm to trail upon the floor. Good. Very good.'

'Was I meant to be clutching some poison?'

'The phial looks better on the floor. It helps the composition.'

'In that case, let us banish reality. Throw it out of the window. Abjure it.' But, as he spoke, he adopted the position which Wallis had shown him; in fact he remembered it so well that he took on Chatterton's last attitude without thought.

Wallis selected a horsehair brush and dipped it into his mixture of ochre and veridian red: this for the colour of Chatterton's, and Meredith's, hair. He worked quietly and intently; his mood of pervasive concentration seemed to affect his sitter, also, who closed his eyes and with his head on one side seemed to sleep. But Wallis understood the lineaments of the human face, and he sensed that Meredith was thinking – thinking in perplexity.

Neither man spoke, and Wallis was soon so absorbed in his task that he saw not the individual face but the general human image on his canvas. He was uncertain how to throw light across the small room when it occurred to him that he should come upon the body as the others must have done – the garret forced open when the servants woke and smelt the bitter arsenic seeping beneath the door, the dead poet discovered just after dawn in late August. Wallis was now entering the room with the others and at once he could see how the slanting rays of the early sun brushed the body of Chatterton, how the guttering candle had been snuffed out by their entrance and how, in the sudden draught, the scattered papers drifted uneasily across the floor. Now he was painting the pale face of the poet. 'Have you passed Chatterton on the stairs again, George?' he said at last.

'What was that?'

'In your dream. You told me how you saw Chatterton.'

'No, I dream of other things now.'

'Suddenly, George, you are very solemn.'

'I was dead, remember.' The words had sounded too harsh, and Meredith quickly went on to say, 'Actually, I was thinking of bringing poison into a love poem.' He opened his eyes. 'But I think

[156]

that for once the woman ought to take it, don't you, Henry?'

For some reason Wallis was embarrassed by this. 'I wonder why you talk so little of your poetry.'

Meredith laughed. 'Because I talk so much about everything else?'

'No, I mean that you speak so eloquently about painting –'

'Your painting, at least.'

'– And yet you are always so reticent about your own work.' Wallis was blocking in some shadows as he spoke.

'There is nothing really to speak *about*.'

'You mean it isn't real?'

'No, not that. There is nothing more real than words. They are reality. It is just that everything I do becomes an experiment – I really don't understand why and, please God, I never shall – and until it is completed I never know whether it will be worth a farthing.'

Wallis was at that moment trying to fix the colour of the smoke, which was about to issue from the expired candle. 'But how can you experiment with what is real? Surely you have only to depict it.'

'As you do? But what about your phial of poison, which miraculously changed its position?'

'But the phial was a real object. *That* did not change.' He had found the right mixture of Naples white and cobalt blue, and began carefully to paint the smoke with a sable brush.

'And I am in the same boat. Do you know that phrase? I said that the words were real, Henry, I did not say that what they depicted was real. Our dear dead poet created the monk Rowley out of thin air, and yet he has more life in him than any medieval priest who actually existed. The invention is always more real. May I get up now? My arm aches.' Wallis nodded and then stepped back to see the effect of the candle smoke upon the canvas. Meredith, inspired by his theme, jumped up from the bed and began prowling around the studio, taking care not to look at the painting as he talked. 'But Chatterton did not create an individual simply. He invented an entire period and made its imagination his own: no one had properly understood the medieval world until Chatterton summoned it into existence. The poet does not merely recreate or describe the world. He actually creates it. And that is why he is feared.' Meredith came up to Wallis, and for the first time looked at the canvas. 'And that is why,' he added quietly, 'this will always be remembered as the true death of Chatterton. Can you smell burning?'

Wallis looked up in alarm, and at once saw thick smoke billowing across the window. 'Oh my God,' he shouted, 'there must be a

[157]

fire outside!' Yet at the same time he noticed how darker and lighter patches of smoke crossed each other in succession.

The fire seemed to be coming from the direction of the river, and the two men ran out of the house. One of Meredith's buckled shoes came off on the cobbles (he had forgotten that he was still in costume) and, by the time he had bent down and refastened it, Wallis had joined a small crowd at the corner of Paradise Walk and Chelsea Wharf. A workman was pointing towards the back of an eighteenth-century house beside the river: 'It was in that garden,' he was saying. 'It went up quick but it came down again ditto.' The smoke was now slowly clearing as the wind changed direction, sending the ash and debris across the water.

'Was there no danger?' Wallis asked.

'No, not a bit of danger.'

Meredith had come up behind him and Wallis thought he heard him whisper, 'Let it burn, let it burn,' but, before he could turn to look at him, he saw Mary emerging from the house with a small child in her arms. 'Mrs Meredith!' he called. 'Mrs Meredith! Over here!' For one single instant of fear, he believed that for some reason she had started the blaze. Mary had given the child to a young woman, who seemed to be a servant of the house, and now started walking towards Wallis. She was smiling happily, and he assumed that she had seen her husband beside him; but now, when he turned, Meredith had gone. 'I didn't know you were still here,' he said. 'I . . .' He noticed a small dark smudge on her left cheek, like a shadow. 'Are you hurt?'

'No.' She laughed. 'Not in the least. It was only Miss Slimmer's chalet.'

Miss Slimmer was a poet who lived in this house beside the river, but she insisted on writing in a small wooden shed, her chalet, at the bottom of the garden. She did not often leave the house, but Wallis had occasionally seen his neighbour wandering down Paradise Walk with her bonnet half-tied and her skirts sometimes trailing in the muddy road. She was a large woman, whose somewhat hectoring manner was not expressed in her delicate and pathetic verses.

'Why were you carrying the child?' He blushed as soon as he asked the question and Mary, sensing his sudden embarrassment, tried not to smile. 'Why, Mr Wallis, did you think it was my own?'

'No, not at all. Of course not. I merely wondered . . .'

'It was the daughter of Miss Slimmer's housekeeper. The little girl was enjoying the drama so much that she did not want to leave the house, but I was afraid the smoke might choke her. What is the saying, no smoke without fire?'

The unaccustomed and unexpected physical excitement had enlivened her: Wallis had never seen her so happy. A sudden gust of wind sent the smell of charred wood towards him, and he did not know what to say next. 'The study of Chatterton is well under way,' he muttered. And then, in a more confident tone, 'Will you come and see it?'

She became quieter now. 'No, not yet.' She put her hand under his arm for a moment. 'I would rather see the final painting. May I?'

'Yes. Of course.'

'Write to me when it is finished, and then I will come.' Wallis did not know how to respond to this. 'I would prefer to see it without my husband dancing attendance –'

'He was just here . . .'

She ignored this. 'He thinks he is my prompt book. He thinks I cannot speak for myself. So of course in his company I am as mute as any other palace servant.' Wallis had never known her talk so freely but, then, he had never before been alone with her.

'Mary! Mary!' The deep voice of Miss Slimmer prompted them to move further apart, although in fact they were holding only an ordinary conversation. 'You are an absolute heroine, Mary dear. You saved the life of that poor, poor child!' Miss Slimmer was sweating profusely, and was holding a linen handkerchief up to her forehead.

'There was no danger, Agnes.'

'No danger! Just look at me!' And indeed she did look as if she had been rescued only moments before from some natural disaster. Her bombazine dress was torn in several places, and her face was streaked with ash and soot: where the sweat had run down her cheeks, furrows of white flesh could be glimpsed beneath the patina of grey. In fact she had torn the bombazine with her own hands. 'If you painted me, Mr Wallis, it could only be as Lot's wife or some Harpie.'

This seemed to be a challenge rather than a statement. 'You look very well, Miss Slimmer. I see you more as Ophelia.'

She smiled at this, but rather grimly. 'At least,' she went on, 'my manuscripts are safe. I had already sent my last poem to *The Examiner*, and everything else has been given into the care of the public. My Muse has been scorched, but she has survived the burning.' She turned her back on them for a moment to examine the scene once more; the little crowd had dispersed, and a thin column of smoke could be seen drifting towards the river. 'But my chalet! My poor chalet!' She twined her fingers together. 'How does one wring one's hands?' she demanded. 'I could never do it properly, not even as a child.' Then she turned around abruptly. 'We were discussing you, Mr Wallis, just before the catastrophe. You know that Mrs Meredith –' Miss Slimmer looked pityingly at her – 'that Mrs Meredith is a great admirer of your work.'

Wallis was delighted by Mary's approval, which he had not suspected, and was about to thank her when Miss Slimmer held up her hand. 'No, before you say it, Mr Wallis, I confess I am of the old school. I dwell in the realms of the Ideal.' At the last word she lifted her dress slightly. 'That is why I cannot endure your new subject, Chatterton.' Mary blushed, as if in describing Wallis's latest painting to her friend she had betrayed some confidence. 'That medieval style offends me, it is all artifice. What is it that you painters say? *Pasticcio*. It is all *pasticcio*. For me poetry must be direct and it must be inspired. It will be simple and it will be true. And I know. I have a public. Is that not right, my heroine?' Mary nodded, although in fact she was considering the possibility that Agnes Slimmer's poetry might be rather more interesting if it did truthfully reflect her forceful personality. 'It must come from the heart, where all our feelings start.' She seemed to be searching for evidence of that organ as she pressed her hand against her bosom, but it was only to bring out a fresh handkerchief. 'It must be real,' she went on. 'What is the reason for the imitation of an imitation?'

'I don't agree, Agnes.' Mary was smiling at Wallis as she said this. 'Sometimes reason does not seem to be so very important. Sometimes one should do exactly as one pleases.'

'I call that hedonism, Mary, and it is not becoming in a young woman.' She turned her stare upon Wallis. 'Where is Mr Meredith? He is your model, is he not?'

Mary intercepted the look, which was growing more suspicious. 'My husband is in his costume, Agnes, and he is no doubt hiding from you. You would not be pleased to find an eighteenth-century poet outside your door.'

'Mr Meredith in masquerade! I never would have believed it.'

'But he is always in masquerade. What was the word you used? He is always *pasticcio*.'

'Well then you had better go and find him. Go and wake him up.' This rather surprising response was delivered in her absence, as it were, since she began walking back to her house as soon as she had started speaking.

They were alone again. 'Will you come back with me?' was Wallis's question.

Mary looked at Miss Slimmer's retreating back. She seemed about to join her, but she hesitated. 'What do you mean, come back with you?'

[160]

'Will you come back with me now to see George? He must be waiting for us.'

Mary seemed relieved. 'Oh, no. George waits for nobody, not even for himself. He is very proud. But you know that, don't you?' She turned to go. 'I think Agnes needs me more.' She left him just as the wind changed direction once again, sending the smoke billowing around Wallis as slowly he made his way to the studio.

Meredith was sitting on the bed, dressed in his own clothes. 'You had finished with me, Wallis, hadn't you?' He sounded dispirited. He picked up the costume and solemnly handed it to him. 'I was growing tired of my part.'

Wallis wondered why he did not mention his wife's appearance or his own sudden departure from the crowd. 'Yes, George. Your part is finished.' He flung the clothes into a corner, where they lay in a crumpled heap. 'But don't worry –'

'I never worry.'

'It will be a fine picture.' He paused. 'Did you know your wife was in that house?'

Meredith seemed to pay no attention to this question, but walked around to survey the preliminary painting once more. 'I will be immortalised,' he said, brightening a little. 'Not with a kiss but with a brush. When all our little feelings are forgotten, I will be there still. Now that *is* immortality.' He pointed at the body on the canvas. 'But is it Meredith or is it Chatterton?'

'There will come a time when even you will not know the difference.'

'You mean I will have been swallowed up by time?' He laughed out loud, as if this were precisely the fate he most wished for himself. 'But after forty years, after four hundred, even four thousand years, what will I – what will he – what will *it* look like then?' A sudden crash and a squeal echoed from the basement kitchen; Wallis's cook had broken a dish.

Meredith was gazing intently at his own image, and Wallis put his hand upon his shoulder. 'In time of course the flesh tints will fade. Is that what you mean?'

Meredith laughed again. 'But you see how pale I look already.' And then he added, 'Mary is pale, too. Have you noticed?'

He was squeezing the side of the canvas with his hand and Wallis gently took it from him. 'Be careful with your picture, George. It is fragile still.' He took the painting over to the window and scrutinised it in the light. 'Of course in time the vegetable colours will fade as well. But, even after centuries, the mineral colours should remain the same.'

'My vegetable love.' Meredith joined him beside the window,

and saw the last traces of the smoke rising from the ruined chalet. 'Annihilating all that's made, to a green thought in a green shade.' He looked upwards, at that point where the smoke was fading into the brightness of the sky. 'And so I too will one day become a thought. Whoever sees this painting will somehow be thinking of me. I must go now,' he said. 'My wife may –'

'I will walk out with you.' Wallis seemed relieved that he was leaving, and made no effort to detain him. 'But we must try to avoid Agnes Slimmer. I was just talking to her, you know.'

'I know. I saw everything.'

Wallis had his back to Meredith: he was bending over to pick up his ulster, and he stayed in that position for a few moments longer than was strictly necessary. Then he turned towards him and showed him the coat. 'Is this mine or yours?' He held it out still further, as if demanding that Meredith take it. 'They are both so alike that I never see the difference.'

'It is yours, Henry. I have no ulster.'

Wallis put it on very quickly. 'Do you never feel the cold?'

'No. Never.' But Wallis noticed, as they went out into the street, how he seemed to shrink a little in the wind. They walked towards the river in silence. Meredith had decided to take the paddle steamer from the Chelsea jetty to Westminster and, as they passed Miss Slimmer's house, Wallis looked towards it anxiously; and yet he was not sure why he felt ashamed to meet her again. Meredith was contemplating the rough surface of the road: 'The effect of that painting,' he began to say quite suddenly, 'will be quite different from anything we can understand now. Certainly quite different from anything that you intend, Henry. It is the same with a poem or with a novel.' Wallis thought he saw a face at a ground-floor window, and he was startled for a moment. 'The final effect it has upon the world can never be anticipated or measured or arranged.' Meredith was looking across at the turbulent surface of the water. 'That is what I mean by its reality' – a door was opened and closed somewhere – 'It can only be experienced. It cannot be spoken of.' He paused, as if listening to the sound of the hurrying footsteps. 'And yet the words for it still haunt us, pluck at us, fret us.'

'Mr Meredith, a moment please.' It was Miss Slimmer, still a few yards off but coming up quickly.

'There is my steamer, Henry. I must make haste. Goodbye.' He ran off towards the jetty and Miss Slimmer, breathing rather heavily, came to a sudden halt.

'I only wanted to give him this,' she said, and held out a volume of her poetry entitled *Songs of Autumn*. Wallis shrugged his shoulders and then, with a polite bow, hurried away from her.

But he felt too uneasy to return to his studio, and instead he went towards the river. Along its bank there was a lane where he often walked in the early evening; it was known as Willow Passage, because of the pollard willows which sprang up on each side of it, and here he would sometimes sit or sketch. He considered the trees to be highly picturesque in their perspective, and often lost himself in contemplation of their general lines, but on this particular evening they seemed to dip and weave in the wind, disharmonious, incomplete, merely confused matter against the sky. He usually sat in the same spot, where the grass bank rose into a small hill, and now he hurried towards it, hoping to find some rest there from his own distracted thoughts. He lay down against the soft slope, wrapping his coat around him; and idly, without his usual curiosity, he gazed at the willow on the opposite side of the path.

But even as he lay here he began to perceive patterns in the bark of the tree, its cracked and mottled surface taking on shapes and contours which he could not help but recognise. But the patterns themselves no longer seemed to him to be sufficient: their texture and colour came from their place upon the whole tree, and from the line of trees to each side, just as their shade and tone were borrowed from the changing lights of the world itself. But if all this could not be painted – for what hope was there of capturing the general life of the world upon a canvas – how was he to depict the human form itself? Then another thought disturbed him: how could he invoke the soul of Chatterton when he believed that his own soul was now stained? He had come with such restless impatience to Willow Passage because he believed that he had acted furtively or even deceitfully towards his friends – how could a man such as he portray the human body in all its glory?

He looked across the darkening fields of Chelsea, and it was only after a few moments that he noticed the figure of a woman; she was bent over, cutting the willow wands which grew by the side of a ditch beyond the trees. She must have felt his eyes upon her, for at this moment she straightened up and looked across at him: Wallis could see her sweep her red hair back from her face. And then Mary Ellen Meredith was running towards him, and she was saying, 'I knew you walked this way. I have been waiting for you.' Yet he was alone. The woman was still looking at him but then she gave a harsh laugh and, taking up her basket of willow wands, hurried away towards Pimlico. His imagination had been deceived or, rather, he had deceived his imagination.

\*

On the following morning he began. He had prepared the canvas; its glue and plaster ground was now perfectly smooth and, as he touched it, he could feel the outline of the projected images already guiding his finger . . . here the body would lie, and here the arm would fall. He began mixing the flake white with the linseed oil until he knew that it was of the right consistency, then he placed the paint on blotting paper to remove the excess oil. Nothing is pure, he thought, everything is stained. He took a French brush, dipped it into the paint, and began to cover the canvas with a brilliant white ground, working from left to right until the underpainting was complete. He stepped back to examine the freshly painted surface, looking for cracks or patches of uneven brightness, but it was quite smooth. This was the stage before all colour and for a moment Wallis wanted to strike out with his brush, to slash it or to make wild and indecipherable marks upon it until the brightness was torn and then dimmed for ever.

But as he watched that absolute white drying slowly on the canvas he could already see 'Chatterton' as a final union of light and shadow: the dawn sky at the top of the painting, softening down the light to a half-tint with the leaves of the rose plant upturned to reflect its grey and pink tones; the body of Chatterton in the middle of the painting, loaded with thicker colour to receive the impact of that light; and then a principal mass of darkness running below. Wallis already knew that he would be using Caput Mortuum or Mars Red for the coat of Chatterton, thrown across the chair, and that he would need Tyrian Purple for the strong colour of his breeches. But these powerful shades would stay in delicate contrast to the cool colours beside them – the grey blouse, the pale yellow stockings, the white of the flesh and the pinkish white of the sky. These cooler colours would then be revived by the warm brown of the floor and the darker brown of the shadows across it; and they, in turn, would be balanced by the subdued tints of the early morning light. So everything moved towards the centre, towards Thomas Chatterton. Here, at the still point of the composition, the rich glow of the poet's clothes and the brightness of his hair would be the emblem of a soul that had not yet left the body; that had not yet fled, through the open window of the garret, into the cool distance of the painted sky.

It was all of a piece and, in his recognition of the complete work, Wallis knew that it could never be as perfect upon the canvas as it now was in his understanding. He did not want to lose that perfect image, and yet he knew that it was only through its fall into the world that it would acquire any reality. He took up his palette and, with a quick intake of breath, he began.

# 11

WHEN HE woke up he was sitting beside an open window:
he could see the rooftops gleaming after a sudden shower
of rain and, curling above them, a large dome which was
slowly turning into smoke. In the street beneath him, a blue horse
stiffened and then collapsed. As Charles opened his lips to speak,
with a roar the sunlight broke against the side of a white building;
in front of it stood a young man smiling and pointing to a small
book which he was carrying in his right hand. 'Like the painting,'
he said and everything moved away. Charles turned his head in
surprise, and realised that he was being carried forward on a bed
or stretcher. There was a conversation going on to one side of him
and he distinctly heard, 'He was dressed in old clothes, like
everyone else.'

He opened his eyes and saw Edward standing at the foot of the
bed. 'Hello,' he said but he could not hear his own voice. Then
the left side of his son started to disintegrate, as if the boy were
going through the stages of youth, age, death and decay in front
of him. Charles tried to put up his hand, to shield himself against
the sight, but he could not raise it. So he closed his eyes. But this
could only have been for a moment because, when he looked up
again, Edward was still standing there. 'Mum,' he said, 'he's
awake now.'

Vivien was bending over him, but he could see her only indis-
tinctly; it was as if the left hand side of his face had been plunged
into shadow and he could only peer out hopefully. 'The doctor
has seen you,' she was saying. 'They found you a bed.' Charles
strained to hear the words: it seemed to him that several voices
had whispered, 'He was found in your bed', and he looked up at
her in horror.

'Are you still in pain, love? They injected you.' And as she spoke
he understood how unique she was: it had taken the whole
universe to spin her together, just as now it was spinning him
apart. I tried, I tried to hold on. I didn't know how easy it was to

let go. But his mouth was very dry, and he had not spoken.

'Here, Dad, I brought you your papers.' Edward held out the pages on which he had seen him writing: he had brought them because he did not know how else to help him, and because he knew that they had been the most important thing in his father's life.

Vivien took them from him. 'Not now,' she said. 'Not yet. He has to rest.'

But they reminded Charles of something left unfinished. 'Chatterton,' he tried to say.

'Your tongue, love? What's wrong with your tongue?'

'His mouth has gone all funny, Mum.' Edward spoke very slowly, trying to control his panic at the sight of his father helpless upon the bed.

'Don't worry.' Vivien sounded very calm. 'He's going to be all right.'

'He's not, Mum.'

She put her finger up to her lips, to silence him. 'Help me put the screen around him now.'

There is no past and no future, only this moment when I see them talking quietly together, my wife and my child, the number two can be used of them, they are called alive. 'A light,' he seemed to say.

There was a window above his bed, and Vivien leaned forward to pull up the blinds; the dawn light stirred through the hospital ward.

*

When Charles had murmured 'I know you very well' in the Kubla Khan restaurant, Harriet Scrope looked up for a moment and saw the outline of a young man who smiled and bowed towards him. She was so astonished by this that, in the confusion which followed Charles's collapse, she snatched the bottle from the waiter's hands and helped herself to two more large gins. Vivien was staring in horror at her fallen husband, but Philip got up at once and knelt beside him, feeling his pulse. All the activity of the restaurant was arrested and, in the sudden silence, Philip said to the waiter, 'You had better call an ambulance.'

'At once sir. Nine nine nine.'

Vivien knelt down beside Charles now; she took her jacket and gently placed it beneath her husband's head.

Harriet was still staring at that spot where she thought she had seen the image of a young man and it was only when Charles was placed upon a stretcher, and carried out to the waiting ambulance,

[166]

that the reality of the situation began to affect her. She put down her empty glass, and followed him out of the restaurant. 'The women should be with him,' she said to Flint in a loud voice. 'He needs a mother's care!' Besides, she had never been driven in an ambulance before and was curious to see its interior.

'Look after Edward,' Vivien called out to Philip before she, too, entered the waiting vehicle.

As soon as they came to St Stephen's Hospital, Charles was wheeled away. Like a dessert trolley, Harriet thought. I wonder what they had for pudding in that ghastly restaurant? 'Follow him,' she said to Vivien, who was in fact already hurrying away after her husband. 'I'll guard the fort.' And with a certain melancholy stateliness she settled herself in an almost empty waiting room. She started to leaf through an old copy of *Woman's Realm*, left on the seat next to hers, with an increasingly grim expression.

'What are you here for?' She was startled by the question, and looked around to see an elderly woman sitting in the row of seats behind her. 'Drink, is it?' She sniffed the air around Harriet.

'Certainly not. I only allow myself the occasional glass of sherry.' She leaned forward. 'Actually, I'm here for a sex change.'

She was about to add something else when Vivien came running over to her. 'He's having a brain scan,' she said desperately.

'What's the matter with him?'

'They don't know. They think it might be a stroke.'

'A stroke?' Harriet had a sudden image of the way her cat arched its back when she ran her hand through its fur. 'How could he have a stroke?'

A child was crying somewhere down a corridor, and Vivien put her hands up to her face for a few seconds. 'I think Edward should be here,' was all she said when she looked again, wide-eyed, at Harriet.

\*

'He always waits up for them,' Philip whispered to Flint as they climbed the last stairs and turned towards the Wychwoods' apartment. They had come straight from the restaurant. 'They're never late. Usually.'

'Who is it?' Edward must have been standing by the closed door when Philip knocked.

'It's Philip.' He cleared his throat, uncertain how to conduct the forthcoming interview.

Edward opened the door a little and, after peering curiously for a moment at Flint, asked 'Where's Dad?'

Philip made a determined effort to sound cheerful. 'He was feeling a little sick, so Mum has taken him to the hospital.'

And Flint added, 'He should be back soon.'

Edward looked at them suspiciously and then, opening the door wide to let them enter, he went back into his room without saying anything else; he had been watching television and Flint could see an open mouth, and then an arm, passing across the screen. With only mild curiosity he examined the rest of the apartment, and was reminded at once of Charles's rooms at university. The posters on the walls, the cheap pine table, the sagging sofa with an Indian rug draped across it – all of these things depressed him still. Then he saw the portrait, propped up against Charles's desk, and something about its face intrigued him. 'Who is this?'

Philip was slumped on the sofa, looking towards Edward's room. 'It's Chatterton,' he answered without turning around.

'He can't be. He's far too old.'

Philip suddenly felt weary. 'That was the point. You see, Charles found some papers –'

At this moment Edward came back into the room. His face was very pale. 'What time did Dad say he would be coming home?' He scratched the side of his leg.

'He didn't say exactly.' Philip cleared his throat again. 'But Mum said that she wouldn't be very long.'

'How long?'

'Not too long.'

Flint, paralysed by the look of distress on the boy's face, was holding the portrait awkwardly in front of him. 'It's him!' Edward was pointing towards Flint. 'He started it!'

'What, me?' Flint's voice went up half a register in alarm.

'No. Not you. Him in the picture.' Flint looked astonished at this, and Edward appealed to Philip for confirmation. 'We saw him in the gallery, too. Didn't Dad tell you?' Edward stepped forward and grabbed the canvas from Flint. He was about to fling it into a corner when Philip got up to stop him.

'No don't, Eddie. Don't do that. Your Dad will need it.'

'So he's not very sick?'

'No.'

Edward smiled in triumph at having extracted this admission from him. 'I knew it!' he said. It was then that Vivien telephoned from the hospital.

*

Charles reached down with his right hand and touched the bare wooden floor; he could feel the grain of the wood, and with his

[168]

fingers he traced the contours of the boards. His knuckles brushed against something, something light like the skeleton of a mouse or a dead bird, something gathering dust, but then he realised that it was a piece of the rough writing paper he had been using. There was another piece beside it, and another; these were the torn fragments of the poem which he had been writing. In that poem he had been trying to describe how time is nothing other than the pattern of deaths which succeed one another, forming an outline of light upon a dry, enormous plain; but other voices and other poems kept on interfering, kept on entering his head.

He had torn up the poem and allowed the pieces to drift across the floor where now, with his outstretched hand, he could touch them . . . and, when the pain returned, he wept. His face was turned to the wall but, with difficulty, he moved it so that he might look at his last room on earth: and he could see it all, the garret window open, the dying roseplant upon the sill, the purple coat thrown across a chair, the extinguished candle upon the small mahogany table. And he was seized with terror as the others stood around him: 'No!' he shouted. He was ready to plead with them. 'This should not be happening. This is not real. I am not meant to be here. I have seen this before, and it is an illusion!'

'His eyelids moved, Mum.'

'I think he's waking up now.' Vivien was watching the face of her husband, and put out her arm to hold onto Edward. Charles opened his eyes and stared at her; and his eyes were of such an intense blue that, for a moment, she was frightened.

He could see her outline as she bent over him, and she was encircled by light; the boy burned brightly also and, as Charles's soul left the world, their souls were shining in farewell. At that instant of recognition he smiled: nothing was really lost and yet this was the last time he would ever see them, the last time, the last time, the last time, the last time. Vivien. Edward. I met them on a journey somewhere. We were travelling together.

'I'll miss you,' he tried to say; but his lips had not moved. Charles died, and in the library Philip was writing 'Yes' on a memorandum; Charles died, and Flint was sitting with bowed head over a paperback copy of *Confessions of an English Opium Eater*; Charles died, and Harriet was holding up her cat in triumph; Charles died, and Pat was jogging around St Mary Redcliffe; Charles died, and Mr Leno was whistling while dusting a brass figurine of Don Quixote astride Rosinante. His right arm fell away and his hand trailed upon the ground, the fingers clenched tightly together; his head slumped to the right also, so that it was about

[169]

to slide off the hospital bed. His body arched once in a final spasm, quivered, and then became still.

*

> What are we first? First, animals; and next
> Intelligence at a leap; on whom
> Pale lies the distant shadow of the tomb,
> And all that draweth on the tomb for text.
> Into which state comes Love, the crowning sun.

(Modern Love. Sonnet 30. George Meredith.)

'Chatterton' was finished. He took a sable brush and, dipping it into a small pool of ivory black, wrote 'H. Wallis. 1856' in the lower right-hand corner of the picture. And there was a resurgence of power at the moment of its completion, at least this was the sensation that Wallis had: the painting became very bright in one last effort towards life, and seemed to glow before assuming the solemn quietness of its natural state. And Wallis knew then that it had indeed been infused with the soul of Chatterton – a soul not trapped but joyful at its commemoration, lingering here among the colours and forms before escaping through the window which Wallis had left open for it. When it had fled – and he knew that it would be gone as soon as others came to look at it – this work would take on a different life as another painting in a world of painted objects. And it was with a kind of pity that Wallis looked at the face of Meredith, which had become the face of Chatterton in death – not pity for himself at finishing the work, but pity for the thing he had created. This garret he had painted had become an emblem of the world – a world of darkness, the papers scattered across the floor its literature, the dying flower its perfume, the extinguished candle its source of light and heat. He had not realised until now that this was his true vision. But then he laughed out loud at his own sorrow: this was his triumph, after all. This was his unique creation. Neither he nor Chatterton could now wholly die. He looked once again at the face which he had depicted, and then quickly began to cover the canvas with copal varnish.

And at this moment George Meredith was examining with curiosity the effigy of Punch, with its miniature beadle's hat and red coat, the white cravat tucked beneath its chin. The puppet was singing:

> 'My wife is surely an ass, sirs,
> To think me as brittle as glass, sirs,

[170]

But I only fell down on the grass, sirs,
And my hurt – it is all my eye.'

Meredith touched his wife's shoulder and whispered, 'Do you think I could learn to write poetry like that?'

'No. There is too much feeling in it.' Mary looked straight ahead at the stage as she answered him; she was preoccupied with the performance as Judy reappeared and Punch savagely swung his stick at her.

'How do you like my teaching, Judy dear?'

Meredith whispered to her again. 'But I have feelings, too.' She seemed to shake him off, moving a few steps closer to the booth as Judy slid from one side of it to the other.

'Oh pray Mr Punch. No more!' The high voice of the puppet squeaked in mock fear.

'Yes, one more little lesson. There! There! There!' Judy fell across the stage, her head over the front of it, and as Punch continued to hit her she put up one limp arm to protect her head. 'Any more, dear wife?'

The small crowd laughed at this, and then laughed even louder as Judy lifted up her head and in her miserable voice pleaded, 'No, no, no more.'

Meredith walked up to Mary. 'She is a model wife, is she not?'

And Punch added, 'I thought I should soon make you satisfied!'

Mary suddenly turned away and her husband, with one last look at the little wooden stage, followed her. They were in Houndsditch. It was a cold Saturday morning in February and, with nothing to occupy them at home, they had decided to visit Rag Fair – or, rather, they had been so eager to leave their house that they had no real destination, and it was only when they saw the omnibus to Bishopsgate that they had boarded it and travelled here. And, as Punch crowed in triumph over the prostrate body of Judy, Mary entered the small court which led to the Fair itself. Some cheap carpets and hearthrugs were hanging here on a dirty rope, and Mary stopped to look at them, taking a piece of grimy fabric between her fingers. Meredith resisted the temptation to caution her about the filth ingrained in it. 'Can you imagine,' he said, 'how many Punch and Judies have walked across this?'

She was about to reply when the owner of the carpet stall came up to her; he was a tall man but his voice was unusually soft. 'Madame –' he lengthened the word, so that it sounded like a sibilant. 'I'm the only party breathing that's got these goods.' He put his hand close to hers, and she drew back.

[171]

Meredith, muttering 'We have no hearth for the hearthrug', took her arm and led her out of the courtyard.

When they entered the cobbled alley outside, she started to laugh. 'My saviour,' she said. 'You have saved me from a carpet beater!'

They walked down some steps into the main section of the Fair, picking their way carefully through the slippery patches of oyster juice which lingered in the hollows of the stones. Meredith at once became high-spirited in the noise and tumult of the market itself; he stood between two piles of hats and, taking one hat in each hand, began to juggle with them. But this gaiety clearly annoyed Mary, and she walked ahead of him towards a selection of old gloves heaped upon a stall. She seemed to be inspecting them in some detail because her head was bent across them but, when he caught up with her again, he could see that she was crying. There was a wooden box of rusty keys next to the gloves and, in his astonishment, Meredith picked up one of them and began to rattle it as he spoke. 'What is the matter?'

She was still looking at the gloves, turning them over and over with her right hand. 'Nothing is the matter. What could be the matter?'

A small child appeared from beneath the stall, an old blue choker tied loosely around his neck. 'Lovely gloves, Miss. Lovely delicate gloves for a lovely lady. No blemishes at all.'

Mary smiled at him and turned away, her husband following close behind; she walked down a side-alley where several rows of old calico dresses were hanging, some of them with a faint lustre of their former glory, others faded and their flounces stale or withered. To Meredith's alarm, they resembled lines of hanged women swaying slightly in the breeze. She walked behind one row, momentarily out of sight, and he parted the dresses in order to talk to her: the rough material brushed across his face, and for a moment he could sense the odour of rotting cologne. 'Something must be the matter. Tell me.' She moved down the aisle between the dresses, and Meredith followed her on the other side, watching her feet. 'Tell me!'

She reappeared at the end of the row, and took his arm as if to comfort him. 'I want to go away for a while.' They walked quickly out of the alley, both of them afraid of each other for the first time.

'I don't understand what you mean.'

He sounded almost fierce with her, and she withdrew her arm from his. 'I want to go away from *you*. Can you understand that?'

He stopped, fighting for breath. He thought he was going to

vomit here, among the common people. 'I thought you were happy.'

'Happy? No. I've never been happy.' Without seeing anything except her own resolution to leave him, much stronger now that she had at last given it expression, she was staring at a pile of old trousers. They were heaped upon a plank and an old man, sitting behind them, saw her intense glance and raised his little finger as if to catch her attention. She was startled by the movement, blushed, and walked on. Meredith was still by her side, trying to keep up with her rapid pace. 'That's not true,' he said. 'We've always been happy.' She said nothing and, accepting her silence as acknowledgment of the truth of this, he went on, more quietly, 'So why are you crying?'

'I'm crying for you, George.'

'What was that?' He pulled her beneath an old shop-front, out of the glare of the day. He did not want to see her face too distinctly, not yet.

'I have to leave you.'

He stepped away from her, and entered the doorway of the shop. 'What's his name?' She seemed to shake her head. 'What's his name? What's his name?' He made it sound like a comic patter from the Cremorne Gardens, but then he turned round and blundered into the shop. He knew one name but he could not say it in her presence; he had some fear that, if he spoke it out loud, the bearer of it would suddenly appear in front of them. 'Look at those paintings,' he said, although his back was turned to her, 'lying discarded there.' He was pointing into a corner when Mary followed him into the shop, towards a number of old or dirty canvases which were propped against a wooden trunk. He walked over and picked up one of them. It was of a middle-aged man, without a wig, sitting beside a candle; his right hand rested lightly upon some books, the titles of which were indistinct. 'This face is familiar, Mrs Meredith,' he said. 'Is it a poet, I wonder?' With trembling hands he held it up against the light which streamed in from the open doorway, and for a moment Mary saw Meredith's own face depicted there – lined and furrowed in a desolate middle age. 'What do you think, Mrs Meredith, is he the original or merely a model?' He put down the painting, and wiped his fingers on the sleeve of his jacket. 'I suppose only the painter will know.'

'It is too close in here,' she said and walked out of the shop.

'Shall I see you later?' he called out after her, sullenly. But he did not want to follow her. He did not want to walk out into the light, and he turned to the owner of the shop who had been watching them intently from behind a small oak counter. 'Take care of that picture, my friend,' Meredith said. 'It is a valuable piece of work.'

'Do you know the artist, sir?'

'Oh yes, I know the artist. I know the artist very well.'

*

'No, I don't wish to see it.' But then she added in a quieter tone, not wanting to offend him, 'Not yet. Will you show it to me later?' She did not care to see her husband lying dead, now that she had left him, even though his death was only an image upon a canvas. But Wallis was so delighted by her unexpected arrival that nothing she said really seemed to matter.

When he opened the door, Mary had been standing in the street with her back to him. 'Agnes's chalet has been rebuilt, I see.' Then she turned around suddenly, and the astonishment was so visible upon his face that she had laughed out loud. 'I told you I would come, you know.'

'Yes. Of course.' Then he added, without really knowing what he was saying, 'I always knew that you would come.'

They stood on the threshold together, neither one moving, until Mary looked past him into the house. 'May I?'

'Oh, yes. I'm sorry.'

He did not want to stand too close to her, not yet, and so when she entered the hallway she took off her cloak herself and handed it to him with a smile. But he could not remember what he was supposed to do with it, and he was still holding it as he led her up to the studio. She was the first to speak. 'The painting goes on display soon?'

'At the Hogarth Gallery.'

'He will like that. He often talked of it.'

Wallis said nothing: the Merediths' separation was well known to the younger artists, but was she aware that he knew of it? 'Some tea?' he said at last. And without waiting for her answer he got up and filled the tea-kettle from a standing tap in the corner of the studio. He needed this opportunity to collect his thoughts. 'I am a primitive here, you see, Mrs Meredith.' He blushed; he had not meant to call her this. 'I mean –'

'What is it?' She was still smiling.

'What?'

'What is the tea?'

'Oh.' He was relieved. 'Only Souchong, I'm afraid.' For some reason they were now both laughing.

'I thought Souchong was a style of painting, Mr Wallis.' She used his name very deliberately.

'No, you are thinking of Marikomo.'

'Really, I wasn't thinking of anything.' They sat in silence until the whistle of the tea-kettle brought him swiftly to his feet, and his hands were still shaking when he carried it over to her. She sipped it, and grimaced. 'Are you sure it is *not* a painting?'

He sipped his. 'I'm sorry.' He poured the rest of the tea into a small wooden bowl. 'I can taste the mastic, too. I must have been using the cups for varnish.'

She put down her own cup. 'I'm ready now.' He stared at her. 'I'm ready to see the painting.'

But he was no longer so eager to show it to her: not because he was anxious about her reactions to the picture itself, but rather because he feared her response to the sight of her husband lying upon the bed. 'I'll bring it down here,' he replied, very carefully. 'I have put it in my own room.'

'No. No, take me to it. I want to see it just as it is now. No formal introduction.' She was clearly as nervous as he was.

He led her upstairs to his study. The curtains were drawn, to protect the newly-varnished canvas from the daylight. 'Let me part these,' he said, hurrying towards them. 'You will be able to see it more clearly.'

'May I see it in shadow first? I am a little afraid of it now.' Wallis took her into a far corner, where the painting was propped upon an ebony night-table; in the shadows, its violent colours seemed all the more fierce, the whiteness of the flesh the more luminous. The soul of Chatterton had not yet left it.

'Don't be frightened of it,' Wallis was saying. 'After all, this painting helped us –' He hesitated, not certain how to go on. But she was not looking at the canvas; she was looking at him. There was a small nervous movement in his left eye-lid. She wanted to put out her hand to soothe it, to touch his face. And now, across 'Chatterton', this is what she did.

[175]

# 12

ANDREW FLINT had arrived early at the Finsbury Park Crematorium. The service for Charles Wychwood was to be held in the West Chapel, a plain red-brick building which reminded Flint of a municipal baths; but its doors were still locked. Someone might still be burning inside, and it was with a certain relief that he turned away and walked beneath an arch into some gardens which, with their freshly mown lawns and carefully laid-out flower beds, promised to soothe him. Then he saw the sign beside some rhododendron bushes: 'Disposal Area Three. Please Keep Off the Grass.' Charles's death had been so unexpected that it still seemed to Flint to be a sort of practical joke – if he suddenly appeared from behind one of these bushes, laughing, he would not have been in the least surprised. In fact, he expected it. And he waited on the gravel path between the chapel and its lawns.

A sudden movement caught his eye and, when he looked more closely, he saw a woman kneeling beside a flower-bed, apparently plunging her hands into the damp, cold soil. When she straightened up, awkwardly wiping her hands against her black dress, Flint realised that it was Harriet Scrope. She saw him at the same moment and called out, 'Don't let me touch you! My hands are unclean!' When he came up to her he saw that she was holding a geranium by its roots. 'I just wanted a cutting,' she said, and popped it into her handbag.

Flint smiled and nodded, as if this were the most natural thing to do in the grounds of a crematorium. 'Flos resurgens, I suppose? What lovely gerania.'

'They should be, dear. They spring from the ashes of the dead.'

'Ah yes.' Flint sighed. 'Suspiria de profundis.'

They walked down the gravel path in silence until Harriet said, 'This reminds me of the scene from *Villette*.'

'Does it?' Flint was very cautious, never having read that particular novel.

[176]

'You know, when Lucy Snowe walks around the gravel path in search of the ghostly nun.'

'How apt.' He hastily moved on to another subject, and pointed at the closed and shuttered West Chapel. 'A forbidding edifice, n'est-ce pas? Almost Babylonian.'

'I wouldn't know, I've never been. I never got beyond Brighton.'

'Ah, but there you have the lachrymose Royal Pavilion.' He stopped, and picked up a piece of gravel. 'This is my first –' He hesitated, searching for the delicate word.

'Cremation.' Harriet took evident satisfaction in uttering it for him. 'I'm always coming here,' she added, with equal satisfaction. 'It used to be cocktail parties, and now it's funerals. Still the same people, of course.' She took the piece of gravel from him, and threw it down upon the path. 'I know every inch of this place.'

'Sunt lacrimae rerum, don't you think? Mentem mortalia tangunt?'

'Does that mean, *they're dropping like flies*?' She adopted a solemn voice for this phrase. 'Well, they are.'

'Exeunt omnes –' he began to say.

'In vino veritas.'

She was clearly parodying him, but he did not mind; in fact he welcomed it. He positively invited it. 'Dies irae,' he added.

She knew only a few select Latin tags, and had to think for a moment. 'Veni, vidi, vici.' They both laughed and progressed arm-in-arm down the gravel path, passing a young woman who was carrying a small black book. 'Whenever I see anyone reading a Bible,' Harriet said, 'I always assume they must be slightly mad. Don't you? Oh look, here's another one.' A clergyman walked across them and she smiled graciously towards him.

'What a charming morning,' Flint said, rather loudly. 'Quite rosy-fingered, if not precisely dawn.'

There were three puffs of white smoke from a chimney at the back of the West Chapel, and Harriet took this as some kind of signal. 'Someone's up and away,' she said, rubbing her hands gleefully, 'but we had better go back now. The others may be coming.'

'Yes, I hear an English sound.' There was a noise of car-tyres crackling across gravel and, just as Flint and Harriet walked back into the courtyard of the Chapel, Vivien and Edward were stepping out of a black car.

Flint, embarrassed, hung back while Harriet put out her arms and went over to Vivien. 'I *know*,' she murmured, with tears starting in her eyes, 'yes, yes, I *know*. I've been there.' Where, precisely, she had been she did not say.

[177]

Vivien embraced her. 'You both came. You're both here!' She said this so gratefully that Flint pitied her and he noticed how frail she seemed when he, too, embraced her. Edward would not move from his mother's side, and clung to her dress as she stood with them. 'You were his true friends,' she told them, looking from one to the other. Flint blushed.

'Here's Philip,' he said quickly; and indeed Philip was getting out of a second car, together with three others. Edward left his mother and ran towards him; Philip lifted him up in his arms, and kissed him. Why is it, Flint thought, that I am the only one who does not know how to behave?

And slowly, with subdued voices, they proceeded into the West Chapel – Vivien and Edward leading the way, with Harriet following close behind. Flint sat down in a back pew, and watched as the other mourners entered. And how many would bother to attend my funeral? The idea of extinction itself did not alarm him, for this he simply could not imagine, but the thought of all the work he would have to leave unfinished was intolerable. It seemed to him to be a kind of humiliation. And yet what did it matter? All activity must cease and, in any case, was it not all just a motiveless revolution of the wheel? We turn the wheel simply in order to turn it, to hear it turning and to break the silence which would otherwise destroy us. At the back of the West Chapel Flint experienced a kind of nausea.

The service was beginning and, as a priest entered from a side door, Flint for the first time noticed the pine coffin half-covered by flowers: it was resting on a ramp, also festooned with flowers, just in front of two small wooden doors. 'You all knew Charles well . . .' The priest had started his sermon, and at once Flint's attention wandered towards Harriet who was sitting behind Charles's family in the second pew; she seemed to be weeping, and she was kissing something which dangled from her neck. At first Flint thought that it was a pearl necklace, but then he saw that it was a large crucifix suspended on a thick silver chain. She must have kept it in her handbag, next to the uprooted geranium, until she thought the time had come to display it.

The priest had shifted his stance and was now looking over the heads of the congregation. 'Charles was a poet, as you all know, and he was, from what I have been told by his family gathered together here today, a very fine one. It may seem to you a tragedy that he has died before he could fully explore those gifts, but we must thank God for those gifts themselves and quote with the great poet Wordsworth, and declare that God's will has been done, even though we do not yet have the skill to discern it. O God, through Whose mercy the souls of the faithful find rest . . .'

The stupid idiot has got the words of the poem wrong, Harriet thought, but then she settled down to enjoy the rest of the familiar ceremony. She closed her eyes and tried to visualise all the pulleys and trap-doors beneath her feet, like Don Giovanni descending into hell . . . a sudden burst of sound, from the tape of an organ playing Vivaldi's *The Four Seasons*, woke her from her pleasant slumber; and for a moment she thought she was back in the sex-cinema where she had last heard the music. But then the small wooden doors opened and the coffin slid through them, leaving only the flowers behind.

'Ave atque vale,' Flint murmured.

The music ceased and the priest – with a quick, nervous smile – took Vivien and Edward with him through the side door. Harriet was watching Edward: their eyes met briefly, before the door was closed behind him, and she was reminded of his silent presence in the hospital when Vivien had shown her the X-ray picture of Charles's tumour. She had looked at the bulbous grey shape lodged in his brain, and it seemed to her to have the lineaments of a human face.

The mourners came out under the cloudy sky and stood in small groups, uncertain what to do next. Then an elderly couple started ushering the others towards some flowers which had been laid upon the flagstones beside the chapel: Flint presumed that these were Charles's parents, and he was surprised how drab they seemed. They were ordinary even in their grief. Then he heard Charles's mother say, 'The cars are booked, ain't they?'

'Don't worry yourself. It's all been accounted for.'

Harriet, who had been the last to leave the chapel, was now hastening to join the others; she was fumbling in her handbag and for a moment Flint believed that she was about to fling the stolen geranium, roots and all, upon the pile of more conventional floral tributes. But she took out a handkerchief and put it to her eyes. Then she saw Flint, and came over to him quickly. 'I'm not really crying, dear,' she whispered. 'It's rheum. Rheum at the top.' With an appropriately mournful expression she was steadily examining Charles's parents, and then whispered to him again, 'Isn't it amazing how many poets are born common?' Flint had an over-whelming desire to laugh and he put his sleeve over his mouth for a few seconds, as if he were wiping it. But when he looked around he saw the strained and stricken faces of Charles's relatives, as they started moving back to the cars; he lowered his arm.

Vivien and Edward, with Philip just behind them, had now come out into the courtyard. Harriet went towards her and kissed her on both cheeks. 'You're being so brave,' she said. 'So brave. But that's Nature.'

Philip looked on as she embraced Vivien for a few seconds longer than was strictly necessary. There is something wrong here, he thought, something strange. I don't trust you.

*

On a rainy evening, soon after the funeral, Vivien and Edward were sitting together. She was compiling a shopping list, making the calculations of prices as she went along; and then going back over them, checking them very carefully. She was making such lists all the time – for food, for clothes, for rent – and, as soon as she had finished one, another item of income or expenditure would occur to her and she would begin all over again. She still bought all the things that Charles had liked – a special kind of scented soap, a certain brand of butter, a particular variety of cheese. All these now had enormous significance for her, and it would have been unimaginable for her to live without them. Not that she ate very much; indeed she found it difficult to eat at all, and Edward had got into the habit of preparing his own meals. He was trying to carry on with all those small jobs which he had seen his father do before, but all the time it was as if he were acting out a part for the benefit of his mother. 'Don't forget the washing up liquid!' he was saying now, triumphant at having remembered something so important.

'Yes. Of course. Excuse me a minute, Eddie.' Her throat felt dry once more, and she went into the kitchen for a glass of water. But she found herself drinking glass after glass, and as she put her hand under the tap she saw how it trembled: she watched herself with interest, since there were times now when she no longer seemed to be real. Then she remembered another item to add to the list, and she hurried back into the sitting room where Edward was anxiously waiting for her. 'I forgot the sugar,' she said; for some reason she was out of breath, and she sat down for a minute to regain it. Both of them were quiet; in fact both of them had already discovered that there was a new kind of silence in the world.

She started writing down prices in the margin of her list, and Edward suddenly called out to her, 'Lipstick!'

'What would I need that for?' She was about to add 'now', but did not.

'To beautify yourself, Mum.' This was a phrase he had often heard her use, jokingly, to Charles.

'No, Eddie. Not when it's just the two . . .' She could not carry on with what she was about to say.

Suddenly the boy felt afraid for her; he could hear the rain falling heavily across the roofs and streets of the city. 'But *why* don't you want it?'

He almost shouted this, and she looked at him in alarm. 'Don't make so much noise,' she said. 'The neighbours might hear.' She had never concerned herself about such things before, but now it seemed to Edward that everything worried or frightened her. And, as she looked anxiously at the partition wall, it was almost as if she had conceived a horror for the apartment itself. '*Why* don't you want it?' he persisted in asking her.

There was a sudden bang – a car had backfired in the street beneath them – and she flinched. 'What was that, Eddie?'

'Nothing, Mum.' But he could see how tired she was, and with a sudden rush of affection he knelt beside her and kissed her on the cheek. The night before, unable to sleep in her own room (although she still called it 'our room'), she had climbed into Edward's bed for warmth and comfort. He found her there when he had woken up that morning, and instinctively he stretched out his hand to stroke her hair; and both of them, just after the moment of waking, were thinking of Charles's death. 'Do you know what I'm going to do?' he said, getting up from the sofa.

'What's that?'

'I'm going to make you a nice cup of tea.' She tried to smile but she seemed to Edward to be on the point of crying, and he added quickly 'Do you know what Dad would have said? He would have said, *then go and do your worst, Edward the Undrinkable.*' He had imitated Charles's voice exactly, and Vivien looked at him in surprise; Edward, astonished at his own feat of recollection, was smiling benignly at her. And in his expression at that moment she could see the lineaments of Charles's face: her husband was dead and yet he was not dead. With a sudden sensation of happiness she got up and followed Edward into the kitchen. 'What time is it?' he asked as he stood on tip-toe to find the tea-cosy on the shelf above the sink.

'Half past kissing time, and time to kiss again.' She bent down and kissed the back of his head.

'And what time is Philip coming tomorrow?' Philip had just bought a second-hand Ford Cortina and tentatively, with extreme

[181]

embarrassment, he had invited them to 'go for a spin' in the country; in fact he had bought the car specifically for them. 'As early as he can, Eddie. He says he wants to drive as far as possible.'

'Great! We can get away!' He hesitated. 'I mean, we can have a good time.'

Her son's high spirits lifted her own; there was a knock at the door and, in her new mood, she no longer feared it. 'I wonder,' she whispered, 'who that can be?'

'Go and find out, Mum.' He was urging her forward, giving her strength.

It was Harriet Scrope, accompanied by Sarah Tilt. 'We were just passing,' she said. 'And I just had to see you. I'm dying to know how you've been getting on.' Perhaps realising that this was an unfortunate phrase, she turned quickly to Sarah. 'This is Vivien Wychwood, my very great friend and *confidante*.' She turned back again. 'And this is Sarah Tilt. The famous art critic.' Even as she was making these introductions, Harriet was carefully examining the room. She stopped short when she saw Edward staring at her from the interior of the kitchen. Instinctively she stuck out her tongue. 'And this is little Edward, Sarah. You've often heard me talk about him, haven't you? He's an absolute angel.'

Edward addressed his mother. 'She stuck her tongue out at me!'

Harriet tried to laugh. 'I didn't stick it out, darling.'

Sarah interjected. 'She must have put it out.'

'Yes, that's right. I put it out to dry.'

Edward appealed to his mother again. 'It was dry already. And it was all funny and green. Look, there it is again!'

Vivien turned but Harriet had assumed a prim expression, her lips firmly sealed. 'I'm sorry, Harriet,' she said. But she could not bring herself to be angry with Edward. With an apologetic smile towards the two old ladies, she steered her son towards his room. 'I won't be long,' she said.

'Goodnight, darling!' Harriet blew a kiss towards Edward as he was led away. 'And remember, boys will be boys.' But, as soon as Vivien had closed the bedroom door, she whispered to Sarah, 'In a fairy tale he would have been eaten by now.' She looked furtively around the room again, and then nudged her old friend. 'There it is!' she said, and inclined her head towards the portrait of Chatterton. 'And I wouldn't be surprised if his papers were still there.' She sensed, correctly, that Vivien would not yet have wanted to clear out Charles's desk, or remove the preface which he had been writing on the day of his death. Sarah was about to speak but Harriet put her fingers up to her lips and crossed over to the desk. She opened the first drawer, saw some typewritten poems, and closed it without interest. But then in the second drawer she found a large brown paper envelope with 'Chatterton' written across it – and, lying beneath it, Charles's typed preface. She glanced quickly at the bedroom door and then peered into the envelope; there were some notes in Charles's handwriting, but also more bulky papers which seemed to her to be written in a different and more ancient hand. Meanwhile, Sarah had been examining the portrait.

There was a muffled sound of 'Goodnights' from behind the closed door, and in an instant Harriet had moved from the desk back to the sofa. 'Hurry up!' she whispered to Sarah who, at a slower speed, was joining her. They were sitting together amicably, discussing the recent elections in Australia, when Vivien came back into the room.

'Edward has had a hard time recently,' she said apologetically. She did not notice the thin trickle of perspiration which was even now making its way down the side of Harriet's nose. 'He's been under a lot of strain.'

'And so have you.' Harriet leaned forward and touched Vivien's knee. 'Hasn't she, Sarah? You look like a woman who's suffered. And I should know,' she added grandly, 'I have suffered, too.' Sarah looked at her in astonishment as Harriet continued. 'That's why we've come to help.'

'That's kind of you.' Vivien was not sure how to respond. For some weeks she had been using phrases like 'That's kind of you' or 'It's very good of you', but it was as if she was performing the role of the person she had been before Charles's death. She no longer knew what she meant.

Harriet sensed her uncertainty. 'The important thing, as Sarah and I were *just* saying, is that we must do what Charles would have wanted.' She resisted the temptation to look over to his desk. 'The important thing is to get his work published.'

'Oh, do you think you can?' Vivien was delighted. 'I have all his poems here.'

'That is good news. I always said he was a very fine poet, didn't I, Sarah?' She hesitated. 'And is there anything else?'

But Vivien had not heard the last question; she had gone over to his desk and was looking through the drawers. 'Charles had finished a new poem about his illness, if I can find it.'

'Really?' Sarah's attention was caught by this. 'May I see?'

Harriet was annoyed with her for changing the real subject. 'As far as my old friend is concerned, Vivien, a poet's illness is very interesting. She is *supposed* to be writing a book about it.'

But once more Vivien was too preoccupied to be listening carefully. 'And the strange thing is,' she said as she brought over the

[183]

typescripts to Harriet, 'I didn't know he was writing it. He kept it from me.' Once more her grief threatened to overpower her. 'I'll get the tea,' she added very quickly. 'Edward just made it.'

As soon as she had left the room Sarah leaned across to Harriet. 'You really are a bitch, aren't you? I'm writing a book about death, not about illness. And you might have some consideration for her feelings.'

'Why do you think I'm being so nice?'

Their frantic whispers were interrupted by the sound of Vivien opening the door. And, by the time she had entered the room, Harriet was examining Charles's poems with delighted attention. 'This is good,' she was murmuring to Sarah, apparently not having realised that Vivien was now standing above her. 'Oh yes, this is good. Wait until I tell dear Vivien.' She gave a little start when she looked up. 'My dear, you frightened me. I didn't see you come in. Sarah and I love the poems. We've just been talking about them.' She laid them flat on her lap. 'And is there anything else?'

'Oh, you know.'

'I know?' She managed to control her impatience.

'Just the wild goose chase. Just the Chatterton papers we discussed in the park. Are you sure you really want them?'

Harriet gave a light-hearted laugh. 'Well, let me take them anyway. I might be able to interest someone in them eventually. Sarah thinks it's the least we can do, don't you?' Sarah sipped her tea, and glared at her. 'Of course if no one *is* interested in them, I'll return –'

'No. You can have them. I never want to see them again.'

Harriet could no longer restrain her suppressed wish to rise, and she sprang to her feet. 'Shall I get them, dear?' she asked very casually. She was about to rush over to the desk, but she checked herself. 'Do you remember where you put them?'

'In the second drawer.'

Harriet moved quickly over to the desk, opened the drawer with a surprised 'Oh, here they are!', took out the original Chatterton manuscript with Charles's own notes and then began to stuff the papers into her capacious handbag. She had brought a particularly large bag for this purpose.

Vivien was watching her fondly. 'It really is good of you to help like this,' she said. 'I don't know what I would have done without you.'

'There's no need to thank her.' Sarah put down her cup, as Harriet returned her glare. 'Harriet will do anything for literature. She's well known for it.'

'I know.' Vivien was very grateful: grateful not only because her husband's work might be published now, but also because Harriet obviously shared her own recognition of Charles's genius. 'You've been so good to me,' she went on. 'I don't know how to repay you.' Harriet smiled and said nothing. 'I must give you something. Something to remember him by.'

'I have his poetry. That's the important thing.' She patted her bag, although in fact the typescripts of the poems were still on the sofa where she had left them.

'No, I mean something of your own. Something to keep.'

'Really I don't want anything. I'm only a humble hand-maiden . . .'

But the more tentative Harriet seemed, the more insistent Vivien became. 'There must be something.'

'Well, I don't know . . .' With an almost subliminal movement, Harriet glanced for an instant at the portrait.

'Will you take this?' Vivien went over to the canvas and held it up. 'Charles was very fond of it.'

'No, I mustn't, dear. It might be valuable.' She paused. 'You never know.'

'No, not at all. It's just something he picked up in a junk shop.' It was clear to Harriet that Vivien still did not understand the significance of Charles's discovery; that, in fact, she wanted the painting removed altogether. 'Please say you'll take it. I know Charles would have wanted you to have it.'

Harriet was enjoying the luxury of feigned indecision. 'Well, I don't know. If you put it like that . . . I'm such a sentimental old thing, really.' She wheeled around to face Sarah Tilt, who seemed to be on the verge of laughter. 'And what does the famous art critic have to say?'

'Well, you know, dear,' Sarah replied, 'the value is always in the eye of the beholder. What is worthless to one person may be *very* important to someone else.' She smiled very sweetly at Harriet.

'Thank you for those few kind words, Miss Tilt.' Harriet turned away from her. 'What she is trying to say, Vivien, is that this picture is probably worth more to you than it is to me.'

'No, I insist you have it. It's yours.'

'In that case you should put it in writing.' Harriet saw the surprise on Vivien's face and she went on, hurriedly, 'I mean, we should put all this on paper. What –' and here she hesitated – 'What if I should die tomorrow, and Charles's poems were found on my desk?' She looked towards Sarah for support, which was not forthcoming. 'Everyone would think that *I* had written them.'

The prospect horrified Vivien. 'But surely they would know they were by someone else?'

'Nobody knows things like that.' Harriet took the portrait from Vivien's hands, and held it up in front of her; her face was obscured by it as she went on to say, 'So we ought to make it clear who owns what.'

Edward, unable to sleep, had quietly opened his bedroom door and was looking at Harriet as she spoke. Only Sarah had noticed him. 'Isn't this nice,' she said. 'See what your Mummy has given to Auntie Harriet.'

Edward turned to Vivien. 'That was Dad's.'

'I thought you hated it, Eddie.' Vivien was sitting at the desk, writing out a list of everything she had given or lent to Harriet.

'But it was Dad's.'

Harriet slowly lowered the portrait from her face, so that she could see the boy. 'Your father has gone away,' she said wistfully. 'He has gone far, far away into the silent land.'

'I know. He's dead. And that was his.'

'Please, Edward.' Vivien was embarrassed now. 'I've given it to Miss Scrope as a present. For being so nice to us.'

'What has she done then?'

'She's going to look after your father's work.'

'Why is she doing that?'

Vivien had completed the inventory, and Harriet quickly took it from her. 'I think, Sarah dear, we must make our move.' She seemed a little flustered by Edward, who continued to stare at her. 'You look exhausted. It must be all that art criticism. Hold this for me while I gather my odds and ends.' She thrust the portrait into Sarah's hands and then picked up her handbag, now filled with the Chatterton papers, and her dark fur coat which Vivien noticed for the first time.

'That's a lovely fur,' she said.

'It's rat.' Vivien jerked her hand away from it, and Harriet laughed. 'No, I'm only joking. It's raccoon. One of my favourites. They have such lovely white teeth. Have we got everything, Sarah dear?' She put out her cheek for Vivien to kiss, and made a little sucking sound in exchange. Then she moved towards Edward, but he backed away from her into his own room. She wagged her finger at him. 'There, there. You are shy, aren't you? But Mother loves you just the same.'

She turned to leave with Sarah and they had in fact stepped out into the corridor when Vivien called after them. 'Miss Scrope! Harriet! You've forgotten Charles's poems!'

She had left them on the sofa. 'My dear,' she said. 'Silly me.

And they're the reason I came!' She snatched the typescripts from Vivien and, as soon as she had turned the corner of the stairs, she stuffed them into the pocket of her coat.

Vivien suddenly felt very tired when she came back into the apartment and for a moment she leaned against the door, her eyes closed. 'You shouldn't have given her the picture, Mum.' Edward was standing by his father's desk. 'That was a mistake.'

*

'I can't go by public transport,' Harriet said as they entered the street. 'I'm not in the mood for common people.' She stepped into the gutter to flag down a taxi but her eyesight was so bad that, for the most part, she was hailing passing cars.

'You know,' Sarah said, 'that this picture might be a fake?'

'Don't tell me that. Not now.' But then she added, 'How do you know?'

'There's something wrong. I can't tell you what exactly, but there is something . . .'

'Well, never mind.' As far as Harriet was concerned, the documents were of far more importance. She knew what to do with the papers, with the writing, and the image on the canvas could be left for others to resolve. 'I can always consult the experts, Miss Art Critic,' she added very grandly. And she already knew which experts she would choose: Cumberland and Maitland might authenticate the picture or, if Vivien's indiscreet remarks about the Seymour forgeries had any truth, they might even be persuaded to alter it. Already the vision of her triumph engulfed her. 'Of course,' she said, waving wildly at a black object on the horizon, 'Hello! There's an old woman here! Of course I will have to give something to that poor girl. Or would that be too silly?'

'Of course you should. And you should acknowledge her husband's work. After all –'

'After all what? He's dead, isn't he?' The taxi had pulled up beside her, and she took the canvas from Sarah. 'Do you want a lift?'

'No. I think I'll just be quietly sick into my handbag.'

'That's rather taking coals to Newcastle, isn't it, dear?'

*

'If you were real, I would love to give you one hard *slap*.' Harriet was addressing the portrait, which she was trying unsuccessfully to hang in her sitting room. She had rested the canvas on the mantelpiece but it had slipped down, almost breaking the death mask of Keats; she had tried to suspend it from a metal bracket,

[187]

last used for a Hogarth print of 'The Distrest Poet', but the bracket had come away from the wall, leaving a small cavity behind; then she had started to hammer in a nail but Mr Gaskell had entwined himself between her legs. 'Excuse me,' she said, 'I was up here first.' She kicked the cat away but she was so precariously perched upon her wicker chair that, as she did so, she almost fell and in her effort to right herself the painting slipped from her grasp; it crashed down heavily upon her head before hitting the floor. Fortunately she was still wearing her fur hat but, although she was not injured, the canvas knocked off the little stuffed bird which had been fastened to it. Mr Gaskell immediately pounced on it. 'It's not real,' she shouted. 'It's only an imitation!' But it was too late: the bird's stuffing was now strewn across the carpet.

She readjusted her hat and, with a sigh, got down from the chair. 'Oh well, darling,' she murmured, 'you wouldn't know the difference anyway, would you? You're not really human, after all.' She extended her arms. 'So come and give your Mother an animal's kiss!' But it would not kiss its mother, and with another sigh she lowered her arms. The portrait was lying on the floor, the painted side upwards. Harriet Scrope was tired now, and she sat down. If I were a poor person, she thought, I could be sleeping beneath the trees. I could be part of Nature . . . and then, when eventually she opened her eyes, Thomas Chatterton was staring at her.

# Part Three

Since we can die but once what matter it
If Rope or Garter, Poison, Pistol, Sword,
Slow-wasting Sickness or the sudden burst
Of Valve Arterial in the noble Parts
Curtail the Miserys of human Life:
Tho' varied is the Cause the Effect's the same,
All to one common Dissolution tends.

*(Sentiment.* Thomas Chatterton.)


Within the Garret's spacious dome
There lies a well-stored wealthy room . . .
When in the morn with thoughts erect
Sly Dick did on his dream reflect;
Why faith, thinks he, 'tis something too,
It might – perhaps – it might – be true,
I'll go and see – away he hies,
And to the Garret quick he flies . . .

*(Sly Dick.* Thomas Chatterton.)

# 13

ON THE morning of the twenty-third of August, in the year of Our Lord seventeen hundred and seventy, Thomas Chatterton wakes feeling unusually merry. This summer dawn is very bright; the sun hovers above the rooftops of London and already the mist has dispersed over the adjoining fields, driven away by the encroaching heat. A warm breeze stirs the tops of the trees and the birds rustle on the branches, preparing to sing. Many of the citizens hurrying through the narrow streets look up in surprise at the bright air, as if it were a quality in themselves which they were seeing for the first time: at least this is Thomas Chatterton's vision, as he gets up from his bed and stares down at the rooftops from the window of his attic room in Brooke Street.

He has never lived so high above the streets before, and it is still with a feeling of wonder that he surveys this scene. In my aerial abode, he wrote to his mother as soon as he arrived in London, I enjoy *high* spirits. I am *elevated* beyond expression, and have *lofty* thoughts of my approaching *eminence*. Soon you will see me on the *pinnacle* of glory, dear Mama, far removed from the *prostrate* and *debased* Bristolians of our acquaintance. He has lodged here for five weeks and each day he has felt the same exhilaration, waking above the city and then descending into it, wandering lost through its courts and alleys, savouring its smells, feeling the excitement of its crowded thoroughfares and then, at night, walking back to Brooke Street by the light of the flares and to the sound of the fiddle or the barrel-organ. He is seventeen years old and this is his new world.

He opens the window wide, breathing in the air. He can hear the sound of the cattle bellowing in Smithfield, and already the carriages are hurrying down High Holborn, but these noises delight him. They accompany the rush of his own pride and ambition as he faces the summer day, and in a strong melodic voice he sings out across the rooftops the latest comic song from the Vauxhall Gardens:

I came up to town scarce four months ago
An awkward country clown, sir, but now quite a beau.

A small boy down below, selling old shoes which are tied around his neck, gives a little scream of recognition and yells up to Chatterton the refrain: Too ral loo ral loo!

Chatterton waves to him and falls back upon his bed, scratching himself and yawning. Then he remembers that, last night in the coffee-house, he heard of the death of Alderman Lee who was set fair to become one of his patrons. Well, what of it? One patron dead, but more to fill his place. He takes up the paper and lead pencil which he always leaves by his bed before he sleeps (for his poetry often comes to him in dreams), and writes:

Lost by Alderman Lee's death in promised work . . £1.11.6
Will gain in elegies for Lee. . . . . . . . . £2. 2.0
Will gain in satires against Lee . . . . . . . . £3. 3.0
Thus . . . . . . . . . . . . . £5. 5.0
So am glad he is dead by . . . . . . . . £3.13.6

In fact he has already written part of one elegy and, as for the rest, they will soon be commissioned and speedily completed. Chatterton is to be relied upon in such matters and, despite his youth, certain booksellers are already prepared to pay him small sums in advance of his finished work. Lee, he says idly to himself as he stares up at the blackened ceiling, Lee, Lee, twig from the City tree, which does not grow but springs unnaturally, its roots in consanguinity, its fruit mere fantasy. He laughs at his own invention, warmer than the warmest breeze, closer than his breath, brighter than the sun; he stretches out again upon the bed, and writes words in the air with his lead pencil: Dearest Mama, my *rise* through life proceeds apace. I am *exalted* in London and will no doubt soon reach the pitch of *sublimity.* Your loving son, Tom.

Nothing now disturbs his high spirits, not even the suspicion that he has caught a dose of the clap from the fair mistress of the house, Mrs Angell. He leaps up from his bed, though, to inspect his night-shirt; and he gives a low whistle when he sees the stains upon its rough cotton. This is no fantasy, he says out loud, but the seed of propinquity, for I have lost my virginity, and now stand in perplexity. What is to be done? Last night he told a particular coffee-house friend of his adventure, one Daniel Hanway, a compiler of miscellanies.

Do you ever make love, Dan?

No, I buy it ready made! Hanway laughs: he is equal to anything, and always has a riposte to hand.

Well, may I tell you of my last act of darkness? (It was also his first, although he says nothing of this.)

Do. I am at home in the dark, Tom.

It was my landlady –

Ah, it is always thus.

I was leaning from my window, savouring the night air, when I heard a woman singing. You know the song which goes, I put my hand into a bush?

And pricked my finger to the bone. An Irish ditty, Tom, a low one.

So she is singing this and, when I look down, I see my Mrs Angell, drunk to the last degree, knocking upon the door of her own house and demanding admittance.

Oh, Tom, she was to be had.

So I slip down the stairs, not wishing her to wake the street –

Or wake in the street.

And no sooner do I unlatch the door when she falls into my arms.

You scoundrel, you. You took her at once?

Oh Mr Chatterton, she says, oh Mr Chatterton. I am infinitely obleeged. And she hangs on to me like ivy around a tower. Then you know what begins to stir?

Your prickle, naturally.

It begins to stir con amore. And when she feels it against her she whispers to me, oh Mr Chatterton, you may lodge in me tonight. And so.

And so?

I obliged her infinitely. I did not creep back to my own apartment until dawn.

Crawled rather than crept, I presume?

No, I was still strong. It was that morning I wrote the Panegyric on the King's Water Closet. Do you remember it?

The lines on the *Privy* Council?

Yes, the very same. Chatterton brightens at this memory of his own verses, but now he lowers his voice a little. But I must tell you this, Dan, I believe I have some issue from my encounter with Mrs Angell.

A child so soon?

No, no, I mean an issue from my you know what. And, and, there is a pain when I piss. Is it –

The clap! You have the clap! This calls for more wine.

Chatterton assumes a merry expression but, after the potboy

[193]

has left a fresh bottle, he bites his nail and asks, What cure is there, Dan?

Hanways laughs again. I have heard good reports from the lime tubs, but those are only for the sorely afflicted. And, if you have missed the pox, the surgeon need not be called. The clap is nothing at all, Tom, nothing at all. Chatterton plainly shows his relief as his companion goes on, but catch it now before it grows. Employ our illustrious London kill-or-cure.

Kill?

No, a mere hyperbole. But it cures.

And what is this famous antidote?

Arsenic and opium mixed together. The arsenic removes the contagion, the opium allays the sourness and the pain. It is the speediest removal in the world. You need only four grains of arsenic to one dessert-spoon of opium. Hurrah, finished, the clap departs. And all the while you will have had sweet opium dreams.

And there is no danger?

No, no danger in the world. You will fare much worse at the hand of the surgeon. You know, how, with his knife . . .

Chatterton recalls this advice now as he stands perspiring in the summer dawn, his night-shirt still clutched in his hands. I am young yet, he says, this is nothing. A mere bagatelle. Bag of nails. All the great poets have suffered it. And he remembers his words as a child: paint me an angel, mother, paint me an angel with wings and trumpets, to spread my name all over the world. This clap is nothing at all. I have fallen a prey to Venus but Orpheus still directs my steps.

And with this he begins scribbling again, wishing to complete the elegy in praise of Alderman Lee before his breakfast: it has been ordered by *The Town and Country*, to be delivered that morning. And then perhaps another verse, a satire against Lee, for the *London Gazette*. He works on, naked, his night-shirt tossed upon the bed, shielding his face from the rising sun as the attic room slowly fills with light. When he is finished he writes the lines over in blue ink and signs them. And as he inscribes his name with a flourish he is filled with a wild joy; he jumps up and dances around the room in his exhilaration, his bare heels thudding against the wooden boards, the sun catching his red hair as he leaps at the centre of the turning world. He does a somersault upon his narrow bed. The world turns upside down. Then he stops as suddenly as he had begun, and takes out his pocket-book to write: One elegy and one satire completed, before eight this morning.

Now for beef and coffee. The household servant has left a jug of water on the top landing outside his door, and he fetches it to clean himself. Then he puts on blue breeches, a green waistcoat, and a dove-grey tail-coat: a gentleman of parts, a young gentleman of substance. As he puts up his hand to part his hair he notices a wafer of candle grease upon the right sleeve of his jacket and, with a sudden fierce energy, he scrapes it off with his fingernail as shards of wax drop onto the floor. Now he is complete. He takes his hat and opens the door cautiously; he descends the stairs softly, for fear of waking Mrs Angell from her slumbers. But, as soon as he walks out into Brooke Street, he gives a little skip and runs to the corner of High Holborn: under this summer sky he could run to the ends of the earth. But in Holborn he checks himself, and on an impulse turns back to enter the druggist's at the corner.

Mr Cross is sitting behind the counter, wiping the top of a glass jar, when Chatterton enters and in a loud voice asks for fifteen grains of your best arsenic and some tincture of opium.

And how much of that last particular item, sir, would it be? Cross keeps on polishing the jar, which has something floating in it.

Chatterton grows more hesitant. Enough, he says, enough to give me relief from my stomach cramps.

Ah, replies the druggist, this is a matter of philosophy, for how can I measure the intensity or duration of your pains?

They are very severe. Chatterton makes a face: he is enjoying this masquerade. They attack me in the night, and I roll in agony until the morning.

Oh dear.

They are like the burning of a poker, red hot from the fire, and like the stinging of bees.

What martyrdom. Cross rises from his stool, puts down the jar and leans over the wooden counter. Shall we say five hundred drops of laudanum? I could offer you grain pills, but the liquid laudanum is always to be preferred. I boil it myself, sir. I banish the impurities. I bid them to be gone.

Chatterton tries to recall Hanway's advice on the constituents of the London kill-or-cure. And I can measure it with a spoon?

Oh, my good sir, there are spoons and spoons. There are your dessert-spoons and your tea-spoons, your dinner spoons and your cooks' spoons.

Just a spoon.

Oh, *just* a spoon. Cross takes down a large coloured bottle and, with his back turned, becomes confidential. And that is how I take it, good sir. *Just* a spoon. For cramps, naturally. Laudanum stops the nausea and soothes the pain in the bowels. He measures out

[195]

the tincture into a glass phial. Ah, opium, opium, he continues, wiping the side of his mouth with his hand, the happy cordial, the ruby fountain of dreams, the great procurer of bliss. And, of course, physic for the sick. He taps in the stopper of the phial with his forefinger. Fifteen grains of arsenic, did you say? Or did you wish for fever drops?

Chatterton clears his throat. No, white arsenic, if you please. For the rats. They disturb me with their squeaking and gnawing.

What nights you must pass. And with your stomach, too. Cross goes over to a high shelf, and takes down a linen bag. Arsenicum album. A sure death, sir, but a lingering one. The arsenic never works hastily. It burns slowly, you might say. Chatterton laughs at this, and Cross gives him a quick look. You are in good spirits yourself, are you, sir, despite this unfortunate stomach?

Oh yes, perfectly good.

Yes, you look to be well, you look to be well. Cross measures out the grains of arsenic. A curious combination, sir, arsenic and opium. He filters the grains into a smaller bag. Did you know of the suicide seven doors from here? Chatterton shakes his head. A Prussian gentleman it was, by the name of Stern. Francis Stern. They found him the next morning, all his limbs and features twisted out of shape. Arsenic convulsions, you see, sir. It acts on the prima viae and frequently proves eccoprotic.

What was that you mentioned? Chatterton takes out his note-book, in which he keeps new-found words.

Eccoprotic, dear sir. A purgative. An evacuation. Often fatal. He leans over and touches Chatterton's little book. *And* they found a piece of writing on the unfortunate corpse.

Yes? Chatterton is intrigued by this.

The victim had written, O Lucifer son of the morning, how art thou brought down to Hell, the side of the pit. Almost a specimen of poetry, sir. Cross ties up the small bag of arsenic with a double length of cord. But no doubt the literature sprang from the opium, which was discovered by his bed. And the verdict was felo de se. Suicide. As the worthy Friar says of the poppy, does he not,

> Within the infant rind of this small flow'r
> Poison hath residence and medicinal power –

Chatterton finishes the quotation for him,

> For this being smelt, with that sense cheers each part,
> Being tasted slays all senses with the heart.

[196]

But I have a clear conscience, Cross goes on, the German did not buy the arsenic here.

Again he gives Chatterton a quick look, which the young man interprets correctly. I can assure you, I have no such intention as the gentleman you speak of. He laughs. I am at war with the grave, and have no desire to be vanquished by it. Not yet. I am just beginning, you see.

Yes, you are a young man still. Shall we say sixpence? Cross takes the small silver coin which Chatterton gives him and, the business complete, grows confidential again. I take it from your accent, sir, that you are not from this place?

No, Chatterton says hastily. From Bristol.

Ah, the fair city.

Yes, very fair. As fair as a sepulchre.

Cross does not know how to decipher this remark, and returns to his original theme. So you may not know, sir, how in this city sudden grief or great misfortune often urge young people to destroy themselves. We read of it every day.

The druggist's words intrigue him. You speak of the young, Chatterton tells him, but is it not true that none of us, young or old, can really do wrong to ourselves? We must have power over our own existence, or else we are nothing at all.

But to take one's own life, is it not irrational?

From his schooldays Chatterton has always enjoyed debate, and now he proceeds upon his argument. Irrational, perhaps, but it is a noble insanity of the soul. The soul is released by death, after all, and takes on its proper shape.

But surely, sir, for the good of society –

When we neither assist nor are assisted by society, we do not injure it by laying down our own load of life. Chatterton is pleased by his newly found opinion, and makes a small bow to Mr Cross before taking up his bag of arsenic and his phial of opium. Your servant, sir.

And yours, sir. Cross smiles at him, and then goes to the door of his shop to watch him hurrying down High Holborn. Remarkable, he thinks, for such a young man. There is something remarkable there. He does not forget their conversation about suicide and later he will recite it, with appropriate embellishments, to anyone who cares to listen.

Chatterton crosses High Holborn and, with his curious long stride, walks down Shoe Lane to the small coffee-house there. He orders his beef and coffee, and eats with an appetite. I have just been talking of suicide, Peter, he says to the pot-boy, so fill my cup again. It is thirsty work.

[197]

The boy sits down with him for a moment. Suicide?

Yes. Chatterton puts the linen bag of arsenic down beside him. Death by poison.

Peter gets up again very quickly. Take it off the table, please, take it off the table.

Chatterton laughs but then puts his hand up to his neck, making strange noises in his throat. He rolls his eyes, and adopts a series of savage and unearthly expressions as if he were being poisoned on the very spot.

The pot-boy sees his game; he is a fat, jolly boy and soon begins to laugh. Oh, stop them faces, he says at last, or I shall die, Mr Chatterton. Stop, Mr Chatterton, please do.

*

'Mummy used to live on your street!' Claire was talking to Harriet Scrope in the gallery. Harriet had brought the painting to be examined by Cumberland and Maitland, having first established that Vivien herself was still on leave after her husband's death. 'Mummy was between Daddies then.'

'Mothers always live alone, didn't you know? It's Nature's way of saying she's sorry.' Harriet gazed with a certain pleasure at this plump, rather plain, young woman. I don't suppose, she thought, that *you've* ever been sexually harassed. 'Of course I have Mr Gaskell. But he's just a cat.'

'And Mummy had a cat, too! What a coincidence! Well, it was a parrot actually. But Mummy used to call it her green cat. It was a great hoot.'

'You mean it had a large beak?'

'No, you know. Hoot. Fun. You're thinking of hooter. Anyway, it went into a decline. Mummy never knew why.'

'Perhaps it swallowed a fly?' Harriet opened her mouth very wide, and then pretended that she was yawning.

'No. It just moulted.'

'Oh dear, I am sorry.'

'It just used to sit there.'

'Shivering?' Harriet made an expressive little gesture.

'Yes, just like that. There wasn't a feather left in the end. It was like a little Christmas turkey.'

'Ah, Miss Grope. Scrope.' Cumberland had come out of his office, and was advancing towards her with hand outstretched. But he stopped short and pointed to her hat. 'What happened to the divine bird?'

'It flew away.'

'The other hat is always greener, isn't it?'

[198]

Harriet refused to laugh. 'No, actually it fell off. The cat ate it.'
'One small swallow?'
'I don't know what kind it was.'
During this brief exchange Cumberland had been leading her towards his office. 'My secretary is away,' he said. 'Like an anchorite, I'm living in my own filth.' In fact the room seemed as clean and as neat as it had been on Harriet's last visit. 'Her husband died very suddenly. It's a sad story.'
'Really?' Harriet was determined to give no sign of recognition or even of interest: for what she planned to do, there must be no connection between Vivien and herself.
Cumberland stepped quickly behind his desk. 'But then all stories are sad, aren't they?'
'If you say so. I wouldn't know.'
'But surely?' He was about to say something else when Maitland appeared on the threshold, rocking slightly on his heels as if he were not sure whether to move forward or to retreat. He was wearing a light brown suit which was a size too small for him, so that he seemed to be held upright by it rather than in it. 'Oh,' exclaimed Cumberland when he saw him, 'can this be Patience smiling at Grief? He seems to be looking in your direction.' Maitland was about to leave, when Cumberland put up his hand to detain him. 'Miss Lope. Scrope. Has brought us a painting. Something very romantic, if I know her.'
Harriet had covered the portrait with an old beige shawl, which in winter she used to line Mr Gaskell's box, and now with a flourish she removed it to reveal the image of the sitting man, his right hand hovering above his books, the candlelight upon his face. The three of them remained silent, and Cumberland took a step backwards: there was something about the face which intrigued him, as if he had seen it before in quite different circumstances. 'Well . . .' He hesitated. 'It's awfully good, isn't it? For that type of thing.'
Harriet was disappointed by his tone. 'But is it genuine? Is it what it's supposed to be?'
'And what exactly *is* it supposed to be?'
Harriet faltered; she was not sure if she wanted to explain the significance of the portrait to him, and she was no longer even convinced that the painted object she was now holding could endure all the imaginative life which had already been invested in it. 'It's supposed to be real,' she replied.
Cumberland went up to the canvas and examined it closely. 'So you believe that it's early nineteenth century? Or, rather, you believe what you see.' He pointed towards the inscription in the

[199]

upper right hand corner, *Pinxit George Stead. 1802.* 'But just look at those thick legs.'

'You can't see his legs!' For some reason, Harriet was annoyed.

'The legs of the table, Miss Scrope. Ugly furniture was just as popular then as it is now. Maitland, you know more about ugliness than anyone. I am right in thinking that this piece of furniture is from the 1830s?' Maitland nodded, sat down, took out a paper handkerchief and mopped his forehead. 'And the hair is quite wrong. Men's hair was the greatest tragedy of the eighteenth century, with the possible exception of George Stubbs's animal paintings. This hair is too carefully arranged. Strictly not done in the period.'

'I thought they wore wigs.'

'Precisely.' Cumberland looked for a moment at Harriet's head. 'A wig can cover a multitude of gins.' He took the picture from her and carried it over to the window. 'Just look, I knew it. There is something behind that face. There *is* another face. Maitland, you little chatterbox, come and see this Janus.' Maitland rose slowly and joined his partner by the window: and there, as Cumberland traced it with his finger, he could just see the faint outline of another face beyond the painted mouth, nose, eyes and hair; and, as the sunlight touched the canvas, it seemed to Maitland that this anterior face gleamed slightly.

'What do you mean, two-faced?' Harriet was indignant, almost as though she believed Cumberland's comments had been directed at her.

'I mean that it's a fake.' He gently lowered the canvas to the floor. 'That is, if it's meant to be what you think it is.'

Harriet opened her handbag, examined its contents with apparent curiosity, and then closed it. 'It is so hard to tell,' she said, viciously snapping the bag shut, 'what is real and what is not real, don't you think?' Ever since Sarah Tilt had informed her that there was 'something wrong', Harriet had prepared herself for the knowledge that the painting might have been forged; and she had laid her own plans accordingly.

'There are experts, Miss Scrope.'

'Whenever I hear the word expert,' she replied, 'I reach for my gun.' She opened her bag again as if in search of that particular weapon, and Maitland backed away from her.

Cumberland leaned gracefully against his desk. 'The greatest experts do tend to be the ones who agree with their clients. They are inveterate diners-out on other people's expectations.'

'And these experts are so often wrong, aren't they?'

'Certainly only very rich people can afford to take them seriously.'

'May I take an example?' Harriet was almost coy.

'You may take anything you like.'

'Just suppose, for example, that you had been exhibiting the work of a modern painter. And then, just supposing again, that you found out that his pictures had been systematically forged.'

Maitland sat down heavily upon his chair, but Cumberland managed to remain upright. 'Oh, you do have an imagination, Miss Scrope. The critics were right.'

'These experts would never know, would they? They would have nothing to judge them by, so the forgeries would never be discovered.' She was smiling now at Maitland as she spoke. 'I was thinking about that when I saw your lovely paintings by Seymour.' Maitland had just taken out another paper tissue and was about to apply it to his forehead when he froze. 'Of course I would applaud the forger,' Harriet went on. 'It is a great talent. Anyone with that kind of skill should be rewarded rather than *imprisoned*, don't you think?' Maitland gave a low moan, and bit off part of the tissue. 'And someone like that could work wonders with other paintings, couldn't he? Just for the sake of argument, of course –'

'Of course.'

'A good forger might even be able to solve the problems of this old thing.' She gestured towards the painting. 'This hypothetical person could take out all the little blemishes you mentioned, couldn't he?' Maitland had stuffed the rest of the paper handkerchief into his mouth, and was now chewing on it.

Cumberland looked at her steadily. 'And they were,' he said very softly, 'only blemishes after all.' He bent over to pick up the canvas again. 'I knew at once that this was a very remarkable portrait. How old did we estimate it to be, Maitland?'

Maitland still had the tissue in his mouth, and Harriet answered for him. 'It says 1802.'

'And paintings never lie, do they?'

'Not to my knowledge.'

Cumberland unbuttoned the collar of his blue striped shirt, and moved his neck slowly from side to side. 'We must get an expert,' he said, 'to *authenticate* it properly.'

'Of course I will trust *your* expert implicitly.' Harriet was eager to leave now, and rose from her chair. 'So when shall we three meet again?'

Cumberland gave a short, high-pitched laugh. 'Should I say something about being steeped in blood?' There was a brief silence. 'Well, Harriet. May I call you Harriet?' She gave the briefest of nods. 'Do you think you could leave the painting with us? Now that we've discovered how valuable it is.' A motorbike accelerated

[201]

in the street outside and Cumberland grimaced, putting his trembling hands up to his ears.

As soon as she had left, he slumped against the door as if he were physically trying to prevent someone from entering the room. 'So how,' he asked, 'did the old bitch find out?' Maitland was removing the last pieces of his tissues from his mouth. 'No. Say nothing, Frank. Don't tell me she was just guessing. She knew. Someone told her.' For a moment Maitland believed that this might have been through some indiscretion of his own, and nervously he took out another paper handkerchief. Cumberland was pondering on the problem. 'Merk. It must have been Mr Stewart *Merk*.' Maitland was relieved that he, at least, was blameless; he blew his nose very loudly. 'No, don't try to defend him. Mr Stewart Merk has been boasting about his success in the salons of London –' Cumberland waved in the general direction of Chelsea '– and the old cow found out.' At this point he seemed to come to a decision; he buttoned up his shirt and turned to his partner. 'I know what you're going to say, Frank, but we can't go back. We can only go forward. Merk will have to fix this – this –' He would have been happy to put his brightly polished shoe through the face on the canvas – 'this *thing*. He will have to alter it to please that bitch. No, don't ask me any more questions. I'm too depressed to talk to you now.'

\*

It is time. Time to deliver the verses on the late lamented Alderman Lee, and Chatterton hurries from the Shoe Lane coffee-house to his lodgings. The elegy must be printed at once, but should the satire be kept over for another death? He recalls his dialogue with the druggist, Mr Cross; how strange that I should be obliged to think of death in this summer heat. To expire on a hot day, in the midst of a prodigal summer, beneath an infinite brightness: this is a mystery which I do not yet understand. But his reverie is broken at the corner of Brooke Street where a cadaverous pale man is standing on one leg and turning slowly; Chatterton stops, and reads the sign propped up beside him: 'The Posture Master. Extraordinary Exhibition of Postures and Feats of Strength.'

As he turns, he sees Chatterton. I am a model for the globe, he says. I spin upon my axis and bring forth the patterns of Nature. He comes to a halt and, keeping his eye still upon Chatterton, makes the sounds of a nightingale and then of a bull.

Chatterton is intrigued by this, and throws a penny into the wooden box by the sign. Can you do forms as well as noises?

The posture master winks at him and calls out, in a high voice:

> Pray here use your eye
> And you'll not ask for a Y.

Then he stands upon his head and opens his legs wide, so that he makes the very shape of the letter.

> Now these limbs strive to show
> They can make a good O.

At once he links his hands and feet together, assuming a circular form; and he rocks dangerously, as if he were about to roll away down the street.

> Only one soul in view
> But sufficient for U.

He unties his limbs and arches his back into the shape of that letter, still swaying upon the ground. Then he springs up and points at Chatterton. And what do these human symbols form but YOU, sir? You! You!

Chatterton laughs at this, but for some reason he is afraid.

Yes, sir, you laugh but be sure of where your laughter comes from. He puts his hand across his lips, and when he wipes it away his mouth seems to have disappeared and the lower half of his face is a blank. Chatterton studies him for a moment, and then performs the same trick. The posture master scowls, and starts spinning upon his heels so fast that neither his front nor his back can properly be seen. And with a laugh Chatterton imitates him exactly, both of them spinning together upon the rough ground. The posture master is the first to stop; he puts his arms out to Chatterton in a gesture of entreaty and murmurs in a low voice, You are a mad boy indeed.

Not so mad, no. He does not like to be called a boy. Not so mad that I need pity from one such as you.

The posture master rocks upon his heels and puts both arms above his head. A proud one, I see, as proud as Lucifer.

Chatterton recovers his good humour. So you will remember me then, if I am so proud? He starts walking forward to the door of his lodgings and calls out over his shoulder, You *will* remember me!

*

'So this is it, yes?' Stewart Merk held the painting up to the light. 'This is the little beauty.'

Cumberland repressed a shudder. 'So I am told, Stewart.'

'Just call me Stew, right? All my friends do.' He was examining the portrait carefully as he spoke. 'It's time for the old Nescafé then.'

Cumberland telephoned Claire for some coffee, 'Oh,' he said, his hands gently placed over the mouthpiece, 'Stewart. Stew. Do you like it black or white?'

Merk took off his wire-rimmed glasses, shook his head slowly, and laughed. 'Oh, that was a joke, yes?' Cumberland was perplexed. 'I need the coffee for the picture. If you mix the grains with the paint, you get the right effect of ageing.'

'How fascinating. Until now I have been as protected from knowledge as an infanta. Should I start drinking tea?'

'Old things have to be treated carefully, you know.' Merk was looking across at him, with a sly grin. 'They can break.'

'At their age only confidences, I'm afraid.' He was beginning to suspect Merk of a sense of humour.

'You don't like old things, am I right? You prefer young things.'

At this moment Claire bounced in, carrying a tray with three cups of coffee. 'Where's the Deputy?' she asked, peering around the door in case Maitland were hiding from her there.

Cumberland was annoyed by her intrusion at this particular moment. 'Perhaps he's seeing Matron, Claire.'

'Matron?'

'I really don't know where he is. He went to powder his nose a moment ago.'

'Shall I try his office?'

'Rather a Pandora's Box, don't you think?'

Merk was still scrutinising the canvas and now broke in with, 'Some of these cracks are just on the varnish, here and here –'

'– I think we should discuss this after we have tasted Claire's delicious coffee. Even though it may age us terribly.'

He was leading her out of the office, but she stopped suddenly. 'Oh, Vivien phoned. She's coming round this morning, just to say hello.'

'That is good news.' He pushed her out of his office, blew her a kiss, and closed the door.

Merk was crouched on the floor in front of the canvas, and Cumberland eyed his slim buttocks apprehensively as he turned back into the room. 'You look as if you are about to be spanked, Stewart. Stew.'

'I've been a bad boy, have I?'

'Oh, I'm quite sure of *that*.'

He took a step towards Merk but the young man was more interested in the canvas. 'It's not so much the varnish that has cracked, right? It's the paint. There are so many different layers.'

Cumberland came over and stood behind him. 'Could it just be the underpainting?'

'No. There's definitely another painting behind this one, and there may be more. You see here, yes?' Merk traced the outline of the face. 'Someone has changed it. The flesh tints are too bright.'

Cumberland considered this. 'And if the original painting *is* much older, we could strip this off and keep the one underneath?'

'So you want me to strip, do you?' Merk was sitting cross-legged on the floor beside the canvas. 'You want me to touch it up?'

'I'm in your hands, Stewart. Stew.'

'I'll do anything for you. Of course I will. Now that we're partners.' In fact Merk had realised at once that the painting contained the residue of several different images, painted at various times: the flesh tint of the hands had faded but that of the face was still bright, the white lead of the candle flame had become slate-coloured while that used for the titles of the books had retained its tone. The face itself seemed to have acquired the characteristics of three or four different images: he assumed that this was why it had such an unsettling effect and why the eyes, in particular, had depth but not brightness. He had already realised that it would be necessary to strip the paint altogether and, using the outline on the canvas, begin all over again. But he was still trying to determine which painter of the period he would use as his model: as Seymour had known, Stewart Merk was a fine and subtle painter but one who was preoccupied with technique. For him the pleasure of painting rested in formal execution and not in imaginative exploration, in mimesis rather than invention. And now he was saying to Cumberland, 'I can restore the finished outlines, but I can't revive the lost colours. I'll have to use fresh pigments.' There was a knock on the door, but both men were too preoccupied to hear it. 'Don't worry. I can darken the paint with coffee and dirt. And then pop the canvas into the oven.'

'The oven?'

'Just for the cracks, yes? And then I finish them off with a needle. It will be the best fake you ever saw. Better than this one, anyway.' There was a sharp intake of breath behind them, and a sudden movement; they both turned around at the same moment, to see Vivien Wychwood falling in a faint upon the floor.

\*

Chatterton enters his room and locks the door behind him. Posture on, my master, I have a different world to win. I shall kill or cure. Then for a moment he searches frantically in his pockets for the arsenic and laudanum; but they are there, in his coat, the spinning has not dislodged them. You stick to me as to a lodestone. I am the Arctic region and you shall be my ice and snow. But, for now, hide yourselves. He climbs upon a chair and places the bag and the glass phial upon a high shelf, behind a copper warming pan. Unless Mrs Angell has wings, she will not find them. But what was it he used to say over and over to himself, in the shit-hole of Bristol? God sent his creatures into the world with arms long enough to reach anything, if they choose to seek it. So the slut may discover my remedies, but what of it? She may cure herself, also, though no doubt she will spurn the poison for the laudanum.

It is time to deliver the elegy. The songs of Apollo must take precedence over the joys of Morpheus. He jumps down from the chair, shaking the floorboards as he lands, and snatches up the poem which he has left on the table. This is a pretty verse, he says out loud, a very moving piece of work. Then he sits down on the side of his bed to read over the satire, and he smiles at his own invention.

Mr Chatterton! Mr Chatterton! He hears the heavy footsteps of Mrs Angell climbing the last flight of stairs. Mr Chatterton! He springs to his feet and tip-toes over to the door, saying nothing but putting his ear against it. Mr Chatterton! She knocks softly and then tries the handle. It is your Sarah, Mr Chatterton. Did I hear you fall? Is there something heavy upon you, Mr Chatterton, which I may relieve? He keeps his ear to the door and says nothing, hardly daring to breathe. I know you are there, she says in a harsher voice. I saw you enter.

He hears her taking out the keys which she keeps tied to her apron, and suddenly he is overwhelmed by anger. It was always thus as a child, when his mother disturbed him at his composition. Let me alone, Mrs Angell. Leave me!

But why lock your door against me, a poor relict who has shown you so much kindness? And that in more ways than one.

His fury mounts. I must be alone! I must work! I must write!

Oh, she says, disappointed, you are always at your devotions. I hear you pacing above my head. But all work and no play, as the saying has it . . .

His anger has abated a little, and he lowers his voice. I must work to live, Mrs Angell. Sarah. So please leave me for a little. I will come to you later, and I will bring something that will mightily please you. I will bring her the arsenic and the opium, so that we may be cured the same night.

Oh, so you will show your poor Sarah poetry of another kind? She gives a little laugh. What are words compared to deeds? I will be waiting, Tom. And with a shake of her head she descends the stairs.

Chatterton sighs with relief and then goes back to his satire, reading it over and over again until his own words calm him. *If I have Mrs Angell beneath me, I still have the world before me: no one can touch me now.* In his new mood he takes up a pencil and on a small fragment of paper he inscribes two fresh lines against Alderman Lee:

> Have mercy Heaven, now that he has ceased to live
> And this last act of wretchedness forgive.

But the printers are waiting for the elegy. This satire can wait, and he puts aside the new lines; they fall from his table onto the floor, where they will be found the next morning.

He is about to leave when he stops at the door, and takes down from its pin his brown cloth great-coat; it is in the latest style, with its long buttonholes and deep pockets, and despite the heat of the morning he puts it on. Now he is defended against the world. He opens the door slowly and creeps down the stairs, whistling softly as soon as he enters the street and sees that the posture master has gone.

The office of *The Town and Country* is above a printer's shop in Long Acre, so from High Holborn he turns left into Chancery Lane and crosses through Lincoln's Inn Fields. Then, pausing before the tenements of Clare Market where the stench assails him, he turns left down Duke Street and walks briskly up Great Wild Street where the lime pit has been but lately dug. The alleys and houses all around here have been cleared of their tenants, because of the danger of subsidence, but as he passes one of the empty houses he senses a sudden movement in one of the bare, stripped rooms. He stops, peers around the door half-torn from its hinges, and for a moment he thinks he sees a child, standing in one corner with its hands outstretched. But a cloud passes across the sun and, after the sudden change of light, there is nothing there. This may be a phantom of his imagination: he knows its tricks and he knows, too, that the only inhabitants of this place are the labourers who, with their leather caps tied to their heads and their faces streaked with white and grey ash, look like so many spirits of the earth.

Chatterton turns the corner of Great Wild Street into Misericord Court, and sees two horses tethered to the iron posts there. The horses dip their heads, and in the silence of this place he can hear them quietly breathing. *This is the breathing of the world,* he thinks, *its rise and its fall.* But just then there is a roaring, a

[207]

splintering and a cracking which turn him around like a fierce wind. The ground shakes beneath his feet and the horses rear up toward him in fright: looking back from where he has just come he sees the old house shaking as if with a fever, the air quivering around it, before part of the building falls. With a shriek he rushes towards it, until he is stopped by two workmen who wipe their eyes and grin at him. There is a child there, he shouts, I think I saw a child.

Oooh noo, no cheeld. An eempty hoose, sur, an eempty hoose. Eet moste fall.

No house is empty, he replies, and they laugh at him. But now he runs towards it, shouting.

*

Chatterton's house had gone. Harriet Scrope had travelled to Brooke Street, to find the attic where the young poet committed suicide, but a computer centre had been built along that side of the street and on its bright red brick was fastened a blue plaque: 'Thomas Chatterton died in a house on this site, 24 August 1770'. She sat down on the edge of a concrete flower-tub, and glanced up at this small memorial. 'I wonder,' she said, 'if they'll put up anything for me?'

A middle-aged couple passed her, giving only the briefest glance in her direction, but Harriet heard the woman distinctly say, 'Poor old dear, talking to herself like that. She ought to be in a home.'

And suddenly she felt very tired, tired of Chatterton and tired of herself for pursuing him. At first his memoir, or 'confession' as Charles Wychwood called it in his introduction, had intrigued her; eagerly she had read all the papers which Vivien had given to her. But it was the element of mystery which had appealed to her. Now that everything had been explained, she was losing interest. She always preferred stories in which the ending had never been understood. And what did any of it matter, anyway? 'The caravan moves on,' she said out loud again, half remembering a poem from childhood, 'chuck the stone into the bowl and spit.' She wriggled her toes. 'And there's some spit in the old girl yet.' But she was getting old. She would soon be joining Chatterton under the ground, so why try to find him now? Why should she concern herself with the dead when she could see the living all around her? She got up from the flower-tub, and started walking back along Chatterton's street. But it was not his street. He had left it centuries ago, and why should she follow *him*?

# 14

CHATTERTON STOPS in front of the ruined house. The front and one side have already collapsed, and he chokes on the dust still hovering in the air; in the momentary silence after the fall, he can hear the carts rattling down Long Acre. And there, in a jagged corner of the front room, close beside a stairway which sags but has not yet snapped, he notices a cheap wooden doll lying among the debris – a doll without a face, the limbs and torso held together by rusting wire. And this is the corner where he thinks he saw the child. The sun beats down upon his head, and he can smell the sourness of the old house as a thin pillar of smoke rises like a libation from the rubble into the bright sky. He hears something moving in the space beneath the stairway and, fearing vermin, he steps back. But then he bends down and peers into the shadows; and he sees the face. Come out, he says. For God's sake come out. The stairs will fall. Come!

The face of the child opens, and from it emerges a strange high note. To Chatterton it sounds like the call of some animal which has lost its young, and for a moment he is afraid. Come now, he says, before we are both pressed to death. On a sudden instinct he picks up the doll and holds it in front of him; slowly he retreats, waving the doll, and the child creeps after it, wailing. Chatterton reaches the street and then stops, while the child waits in the ruined doorway: although he is partly in shadow, Chatterton can see that he is wearing a mouldy shirt and breeches that are no more than rags. He seems to be about ten, or eleven, and then Chatterton notices how large his head is, how small his body. Hydrocephalus. An idiot boy.

Come, take your doll. I mean you no harm. He stretches out his hand, and holds it in front of him.

The child comes out from the shadow of the house, and speaks. Passey me.

Chatterton gives it to him. What is your name? See, my name is Tom. Tom. He points to himself. Who are you?

Whoyoo? The boy kisses the doll, and then presses it against his cheek.

Tom. I am Tom. Who are you?

Tom. The boy points to himself, in imitation, and smiles. Tom.

For some reason Chatterton is ashamed. You must leave here, he says, or you will die. The house will fall.

Dyen? He puts his head to one side, and looks at the doll carefully. Dyen?

Without words, Chatterton thinks, there is nothing. There is no real world. Without words I cannot even warn or protect you. Look, he says, taking a coin from the pocket of his great-coat. Look, this is for you. Food. He holds up the sixpence, and it gleams in the sunlight. But the boy is still crooning to the doll. Without words you are in a different time. You exist in some other place, where you are calm. The boy notices the winking coin, and snatches it from his hand. Food. You must buy food with it. Chatterton makes motions as if of eating. Do you understand that word?

Worlds. The boy puts his hand into his mouth. Wordso. Woods.

Well, Tom, you can learn, I see. How the boy lived Chatterton could not imagine, but he had heard stories of deformed children abandoned by their parents and left to wander the streets. And did they then become like the city itself – brooding, secret, invulnerable?

The boy offers him the wooden doll to hold. You. Dolly. You.

No, he says, no. It is your own. And if he had been abandoned, too, would he have become as this child now was? For a moment, as he looks at the boy, it is as if he were looking at himself.

The two labourers pass by. Ees eet the cheeld then? Ees he oonharmed by the fall?

Yes, yes, he is safe now. Chatterton does not want them to come too close. He wants them to go on their way.

A parish-cheeld, is he? Sure he ees a ragged one. The labourers laugh, and the boy laughs with them – holding out the doll for them to see. Ees Mr Punch ees he? And they walk away, still laughing.

Better to give him arsenic, Chatterton thinks, than to leave him undefended against this harsh world . . . but there is no more time now. The elegy must be delivered at once. I must go, he says. I must see someone. He turns to leave and the boy lets out a wild cry. Oh no. Don't let him need me. Chatterton turns around. He does not want to touch him – he sees the filth encrusted upon his skin – but he takes a step towards him. I will come to you again. Tomorrow. I will come here tomorrow. He makes a movement

[210]

with his hands to suggest the next day. Tomorrow. I will be here. Your friend. Tom comes here.

Chatterton hurries away towards Long Acre and the office of *The Town and Country*, where he describes the idiot boy to Mr Crome, editor, publisher and printer of that esteemed journal.

But what can we do? The mobile vulgus, Mr Chatterton, the mobile vulgus. In any case, better the streets than Bedlam.

Where lies the difference, Mr Crome?

Ah, sir, I see you are not happy in our enlightened age.

When I first came to London I thought I had entered a new age of miracles, but these stinking alleys and close packed tenements seem to breed only monsters. Monsters of our own making . . .

But you seem to take pleasure in it, Mr Chatterton. You see the poetry in it, do you not? There is a smile playing about your face.

And, indeed, Chatterton bursts out laughing.

On the next morning, the boy waited by the ruined house; he stayed there all that day, crooning to his doll, but Chatterton was not to be seen. And he returned there each day, looking for the red-headed stranger who had given him the bright coin, but no one ever came. Gradually Chatterton faded from his memory, and the street itself was changed, but the idiot boy was always known as Tom.

*

'But why did Harriet give them the picture?'

'Well, perhaps –'

Edward interrupted them. 'Philip, why is the field green *and* yellow?'

'Some parts of the grass are living, and some parts are dead. But they're all part of the same field.'

Edward contemplated this for a moment, and then thought of something else. 'Look,' he said, 'the rain is like a ghost isn't it?' He pointed across the field, as a sudden shower drifted slowly towards them. It was their Sunday in the country. For the last few weeks the three of them – Vivien, Philip and Edward – had climbed into Philip's beige Ford Cortina and had been driven on what he called a 'mystery trip'. On this particular afternoon they were in Suffolk; they were walking along a path between two fields, and had now come to the edge of a small pine forest. 'Come on,' Edward shouted, 'the ghost can't get us here!' He ran ahead of them into the forest, across the fallen pine needles, and his laughter wavered among the slender trees.

'Why *did* she give them the picture?' Vivien repeated her question. It was now two weeks since she had seen the portrait in

Cumberland's office and had heard Stewart Merk say, 'It will be the best fake you ever saw. Better than this one, anyway.' And she had fainted. She had known at once that it was the painting which Charles had brought home in triumph, but in these unfamiliar surroundings it seemed flimsy, unreal: it became for her yet another token of Charles's death. And the sudden realisation that it was a forgery – that Charles had been wrong – so overpowered her with a feeling of helplessness that she had fallen to the floor. All the misery since his death had come to a point.

They followed Edward into the pine forest. 'Harriet probably wanted to have it authenticated,' Philip told her. In fact he suspected her of less honourable motives, but he knew that any hint of this would distress Vivien still further. 'She was just checking. Or, more likely, she gave it to them for restoration. You know, to clean it properly. And they discovered that it was a –'

'A fake. A cheap forgery. How could we have it for so long and not realise?' There seemed to be a note of accusation in her voice, and Philip blushed. They walked on in silence while Edward ran ahead of them, kicking a blue football between the trees. 'I remember how much it meant to him,' Vivien said after a while, her tone changed now. 'He always kept it by his desk. Sometimes, you know –' and she laughed at this – 'sometimes he used to talk to it.'

Philip looked away for a moment. 'I think,' he said, 'that his poetry changed after he found it.'

'Perhaps it found him.'

'I know.' The wind stirred the tops of the trees, and he noticed how some of the pine needles had fallen from them and were suspended on the lower branches like clumps of hair.

'But if the painting is a fake,' she went on, 'does it mean –'

'The manuscripts?' Philip had already considered this possibility, that the Chatterton documents were not what Charles believed them to be; but he had not known how to suggest this to her.

'And you remember,' she was saying, 'how convinced he was. He was so excited about those papers.' It seemed to her that Charles himself was being removed from the world once again, sliding towards the fire which would consume him. She could not allow this to happen – the truth he had found in his discoveries, the trust he had placed in them, must not be seen to have been false. It was necessary to protect him, even in death. 'We have to get them back,' she said. 'Before any more harm is done.'

Philip knew what harm she meant: it was best to let the manuscripts be, to leave them as they were at the time of Charles's

[212]

death and make no further effort to prove or to disprove their authenticity. Had he not always said to Philip that there is a charm and even a beauty in unfinished work – the face which is broken by the sculptor and then abandoned, the poem which is interrupted and never ended? Why should historical research not also remain incomplete, existing as a possibility and not fading into knowledge?

'I should never have given them to Harriet,' Vivien was saying. 'But I didn't know what I was doing. I was so shaken by Charles's death. It was so difficult for us –'

'There's a hole here!' Edward shouted. 'A hole for a rabbit! It's like Alice in Wonderland!'

'Everyone thought I was bearing up. That was the phrase they used. But I wasn't. It was just that everything seemed to be happening to somebody else. Even when I cried, it was as if someone were crying in my place.'

'Don't . . .'

'No. I want to remember it all. I want to remember everything.' She took his arm as she continued. 'Even Edward was playing a part. We were both of us waiting, waiting to make the first move. But I didn't know how –'

'You should have said something to me.'

'But what could I say? That nothing seemed real? That everything threatened me? You couldn't protect me against my own fears.'

'I suppose not. And I didn't know how to help,' he replied. 'I thought of so many things but –' he bent down to pick up a branch – 'but there's no need to worry now. I'll get everything back from Harriet Scrope.' He swung the branch against a tree, and the sudden impact sent a shower of rain drops down upon them.

'But how can you? I gave her the painting, after all. I can't just ask for it back. And she was so excited about the manuscripts, about having them published . . .'

'Come on up here,' Edward shouted. 'There's a stream!'

They walked on, Philip swinging the stick savagely into the air. 'But how do we know,' he said, 'that they actually belonged to Charles?'

'How do you mean?'

'I never knew what happened in Bristol. He just came out of the house with all the papers in a carrier bag.'

She laughed. 'He never was very good at explanations, was he?'

As Vivien said this, Philip realised that he and Charles had never really talked properly – not because they were ill at ease with each other but because each conversation had seemed provisional, one in a succession which would go on. There had been no sense of

[213]

an ending. 'I don't even know,' he said, 'how Charles found that painting.'

'Edward can tell you all about that. He went to the junk shop with him.' But she was still intrigued by his previous remark. 'What difference does it make, about Bristol?'

'It's very simple. What if the papers don't belong to Charles, and what if the real owner wants them back? Harriet would have to return them. Do you see?'

'And no one else would ever know?'

'No one.' He threw the branch into the air, and it seemed to disappear among the trees.

'But how will you find out who *does* own them?'

'I'll follow the trail. I'll go back to Bristol, and talk to the man who gave them to him. There is something wrong, I can feel it. I should have known it before –'

'No, there was no reason –'

'But I'll discover the truth. I'll find out what these manuscripts really are. And then I'll pay a visit to Harriet Scrope.'

Edward ran back towards them. 'It's like a wood in a dream, isn't it, Mum? It's so quiet.' He ran off again.

'That boy,' Philip said, laughing, 'is going to be a poet.'

'He misses his father.' The stick fell back to the earth, having brushed against the branches of the trees, and Vivien picked it up. 'But he doesn't say anything.'

'Oh, boys are very resilient. They learn to compensate.' Philip had never talked so directly to her before, and he was just beginning to realise that he *could* talk: now that there were two people who had come to rely upon him, he was no longer deflected by nervousness or embarrassment. 'Events which are tragedies for us –' he hesitated for a moment – 'are just changes for them.'

Edward was kicking the blue football through the trees. 'Have you noticed,' Vivien said, 'how difficult it is to see blue in this light?'

'No,' he said. 'I never noticed that.' Suddenly he felt a great love for her, and he ran towards Edward, shouting at him to pass the ball.

*

I hold that writer to be incompetent who cannot write on both sides of the question, Dan. He is not worthy of his –

His hire?

His Muse.

Oh, now that you talk of Muses, you have me at a disadvantage. I know nothing of them.

[214]

Daniel Hanway, compiler of miscellanies, epodist, and hack, is sitting with Chatterton in a wine-drinking booth in the Tothill Pleasure Gardens; they have come here at Hanway's insistence, since he is eager to review the ladies of the night, but already Chatterton has embarked upon more elevated subjects. When I write in praise of the late lamented Lee, he says, it is a true relation; and, when I write damning him to the pit of Hell, it is true also. He takes up his glass of brandy and hot water. Do you know why, Dan?

Why, Tom?

Because this is an age of poetry, and poetry cannot lie! Here is to the Muse! He raises his glass, and spills a little brandy on his cravat.

And you are a child of this age, are you, Tom?

No, no child. Here, more brandy! Do I seem like a child? As the boy brings them another pot, the band of musicians in the rotunda strikes up an air; and all at once the torches are lit beside the avenues and booths. Chatterton sits back and surveys the scene. A sudden transformation, Dan, worthy of the pantomime.

And you are the imp, I presume? Hanway is also in his cups. Look, Tom, do you see the female behind the trees there? He points towards a covered walk, with some trees at the end of it. Steady your prick, and aim at her.

But Chatterton is dazed by the torchlight: all bright things remind him of his approaching fame, and he can feel the warmth upon his face. I am looking into the flame, and I see everything before me. He turns to his companion. Dan, Dan, tell me of the poets you have known.

Reluctantly Hanway takes his eyes from the lady. Ah. Poets. Well, there was Tookson, a crabbed old body with a pen of vitriol. He used to frequent the Hercules tavern, do you know the one in Dean Street? He was there so often that he became known as the pillar of Hercules.

No, not such men as he. The real poets, Dan.

Hanway smiles at him. And who am I to say who is real and who unreal?

But you knew Cowper. And Gray.

Curiosities. Both of them. Gray used to drink until he fell down helpless upon the ground, and then wake up as cheerful as an infant upon his mother's breast. But no one laughed at him. There was something about him . . .

Something? What was that? Chatterton is eager for this knowledge of the poets before him.

Hanway fills his glass. He walked among us, you see, but his thoughts were elsewhere. But this is no news to you at all.

No?

Well, you are the same. No one laughs at you. Even though you *are* but a boy. Hanway puts down his glass, and the glare of the torchlights reveals the deep furrows in his face. There is so much ahead of you, Tom. My own day is done.

You may outlive me yet, Dan –

No, it is so. I have made nothing of my life, but you – you may do great things yet. He fills his glass again, and then fills Chatterton's. Let me shake your hand, sir. Their hands join across the small oak table. See, here is one going forward and one passing away. We have met for an instant on our journey. And now I let you go. He takes away his hand, and laughs.

Chatterton is solemn still. There is no need to talk of passing, Dan, since all life is uncertain. Did I tell you of the idiot boy I found this morning by Long Acre?

Not yet, Tom, not yet. Hanway is preoccupied. And, now that we talk of journeys, I must make my own. He nods towards the lady in the covered walk. That little doe is waiting for me, yet I must go closer to her before I may shoot. He rises from the table, but before he leaves he turns again to Chatterton. I forgot to ask about your physic. Your kill-or-cure.

Oh, I take it tonight. Chatterton laughs, although the thought of it makes him uneasy. I will be sure to leave a residue for your use, Dan. You may need it before the night is done.

And I am undone. Hanway, laughing, goes on his way.

Chatterton fills his glass again. Dan is right. No man mocks me. I am Thomas Chatterton, and there will come a time when I will astonish the world. No man knows the things I will write now. He rises unsteadily from his chair, and walks between the torches towards the entry-gate. But there are no cabs in Abingdon Street. Shanks's pony, the old grey pony, will see me home. So he wraps his great-coat around him and hastens through the streets of the city toward High Holborn and Brooke Street. And, as he walks, certain words come to him in the form of a song.

*My syllables, the remnants of antiquity.*

The line rises from him into the night air, and he watches it fade. Then he sings out again.

*Will come back as shadows for posterity.*

Everything is coming to a point: it is in front of him and he keeps on walking towards it as he sings.

[216]

*Let this my song bright as my vision be.*

He stumbles into an alley, and can smell the excrement around him. My feet are in the shit, but my home is elsewhere. He could walk for ever.

*As everlasting as futurity.*

And then he stops singing. On the corner of St Andrew Street and Mercy Lane, he sees a hooded figure leaning against the old stone wall there which keeps the timber from spilling onto the street. He checks his step, and walks more slowly as he hears the sounds of retching. Even in his drunkenness he crosses to the other side, but the hooded figure straightens up and turns around towards him, arms outstretched: the flies are coming out of me! The flies are coming out of me! See how they stream from my mouth and eyes. I am dumb and blind with flies. Then he retches again, and Chatterton sees the black bile flowing against the stone wall.

On such a night as this the world may go awry, and Chatterton hurries away from the contagion. A gust of rain blows against him. The face of the idiot boy. Tomorrow by the ruined house. The single bell of St Damien rings out. It is one quarter past midnight. The twenty-fourth of August. All well.

Chatterton reaches his house in Brooke Street. Rain. He fumbles and drops the key. Posterity. Antiquity. The words are still in his head. Finds the key. Opens the door and mounts the stairs. All well.

\*

The sign outside Bramble House, in Colston's Yard just behind St Mary Redcliffe, had been changed since Philip last saw it. Now it read: 'No Vagrants. No Tramps. No Sluts. Polite Notice.' As he approached the house he glimpsed a face at the front-window, and before he could reach the door it was opened very wide; an elderly man in a purple track-suit stood on the threshold, his hands upon his hips. 'She's inside.' He jerked his head back, to indicate one of the rooms. 'Don't let her smoke.' Then he raised his voice, for the benefit of the person within: 'It is a dirty habit, it is a smelly habit, it is a disgusting habit.' And then, more softly, to Philip: 'I'm Pat, of course. I hope you like a giggle. Your *friend* did.' He ran upstairs, leaving Philip alone in the hallway.

'Come and join me.' From behind one door came a deep voice. 'Unless you think I'm a hallucination in which case you'll need a bell, book and candle. Not to mention the Jesuit priest.' Tentatively

[217]

Philip pushed open the door and there, rising to greet him, was a short, elderly man wearing a green silk smoking jacket and very narrow black trousers. He could have been no more than five feet in height, but his white hair was piled up and coiffed: it looked like a piece of wood which had been clumsily nailed to his head, but it did at least give him a resemblance of normal height. 'So you are the one with the papers, are you? Or am I utterly mistaken and need to be taken outside and unceremoniously knocked into the middle of next week?' Philip agreed that this would not be necessary since, indeed, he did have the Chatterton manuscripts.

After his conversation with Vivien in the pine forest, he had written to Joynson at the Bristol address; he had explained how the papers and the portrait had originally come into Charles's possession and, perhaps ingenuously, had merely requested further information. Two days later he had received his own letter back, with 'Sunday at 4' scribbled in its margin. So he had travelled to Bristol once more, and had now arrived at the appointed time.

'I haven't actually got the papers with me.' Philip was thoughtfully tugging at his beard as he spoke. 'Someone is examining them.'

'Is someone? That *is* nice to know. Now I suppose I can die in peace and be buried in an unmarked grave. Why don't you get a spade and do it?' His voice grew louder with each phrase but Philip noticed that, when he stopped talking, he always smiled broadly.

'Someone called Harriet Scrope. The novelist?'

'It's a woman, is it?' This seemed to amuse Joynson even more, and he shouted towards the ceiling. 'Did you hear that?' The sudden movement had displaced a strand of white hair, and he patted it back into place. 'They're mine, you know, not hers. Or yours. Either that or I'm an impostor about to be unmasked to civilised society in the *Bristol Daily News*.' He pushed his face towards Philip. 'What do you think, is this a mask? Pull it off with your bare hands, I dare you.'

Philip declined his kind offer. 'I can get the papers back,' he hastened to say. After all, this was why he had come. 'I can get them back at once.'

'I should hope so.' Joynson took an ivory cigarette-holder out of the pocket of his smoking jacket. 'Would you care for a fag?'

'No thanks.'

Joynson seemed disappointed. 'Not even a little one? Little ones can be the best, you know. They can be the strongest. They can give you pause for thought and wonder what life is really all about.'

[218]

'No. I don't smoke.'

'Neither do I.' With a sigh he put away the cigarette-holder. 'It's a filthy habit, isn't it?' Then he settled back in his chair, sinking so low that for a moment Philip could only see his white hair bobbing up and down, like a handkerchief being waved in distress. 'They're not genuine,' he said, after he had struggled back into view.

'The cigarettes?'

'Oh yes, I meant the cigarettes. I brought you all this way to talk about the merits of tobacco. I own a plantation in South America and I want you to have it for Christmas. No, dear, not the cigarettes. The manuscripts.' Philip had been expecting this but, still, the confirmation of his suspicions suddenly depressed him. '*My* manuscripts,' Joynson went on. '*My* papers. They were never meant to be shown to anyone. Or given away by *a stupid old cow*.' He bellowed the last phrase at the ceiling, before politely resuming his conversation with Philip. 'They're fakes, you see. I take it you know the word? It was in Roget's Thesaurus and in the Chambers International Dictionary when I last looked.'

'But Charles had the handwriting analysed.'

'She had it analysed, did she?' This seemed to cause Joynson even more amusement, and his hair vibrated for a few moments.

'No, Charles did. Not Harriet . . .'

'Yes, I know. Your *friend* did.' He gave the word the same emphasis as Pat had before. 'I said they were fakes. I didn't say they weren't real.'

Philip was becoming confused. 'Are we talking about the same thing?'

'We're talking about the Chatterton manuscript, or am I raving mad and about to make a lunge at you and bite off your lovely snub nose? Is my hair in tufts and clumps? Tell me, I would really like to know.' He stretched out comfortably in his chair, his feet just touching the floor.

'No –'

'That is good news. Now.' Joynson sat upright again. 'Would you like to hear a story?' He put his hands together, as if he were about to pray. Philip, already exhausted by his interrogation, merely nodded. 'Well then. I suppose you know the history of Thomas Chatterton's poetry, and how he forged his medieval verses? Very clever. Very cunning. Top marks. And you must have guessed that there was a real Samuel Joynson, a bookseller, just as it says in the memoir?' He started to slip down in the chair, and struggled upright again. 'Otherwise why should I have the same name? I didn't just pluck it out of the air, did I? If I did, you can lead me off to the Tower of London and behead me. I give you my full permission. You can strip me, too, and tear out my vital organs for the ravens. Fair deal?' Philip was unsure how to respond to this, and merely contrived to look thoughtful. 'Now, Samuel Joynson did actually print and sell Chatterton's poetry. They worked together. They may even have been *friends*.' Joynson wriggled his toes. 'So the Chatterton manuscript is correct as far as that goes. Are you still with me, or am I chattering into the air and about to be carted off to the Sunshine Home for the Elderly and Infirm of Mind? No? You give me a second chance? Good. Now. Chatterton did die. As far as we know, he committed suicide at the age of eighteen. A mere chicken. But you know the story?' Philip nodded. 'It was a very famous suicide, and it made Chatterton's name . . .' He broke off suddenly. 'Did you hear a noise?' Philip had heard nothing. 'I think I heard a noise.'

Joynson jumped out of his chair and scurried across to the door, throwing it open to reveal Pat standing behind it; he was carrying a pair of old plimsolls in one hand and, startled by his discovery, had put his other hand up to his heart. He jumped back and stared at Joynson. 'I wasn't stopping, I wasn't listening, I wasn't interested!'

Joynson mimicked his voice. 'I wasn't accusing you, I wasn't accusing you, I wasn't accusing you!' Then he slammed the door and, with a wink at Philip, went back to his chair. 'Miss Health and Beauty of 1929, she is. Last night she had yogurt all over her face and cucumber slices on her eyes. I could have cut off her head and sold it as a health food. Now where were we? Yes. So. Chatterton's suicide was a great success. Not immediately, of course. This was no overnight sensation. Shall we say twenty or thirty years? Oh, go on, let's say it. Twenty or thirty years. Then he became a phenomenon, glorious boy, bird thou never wert, the very houses seem asleep, and so on. So Joynson found that Chatterton's poems were in demand again. He published a collected edition. He began selling all the old manuscripts he had kept, and I wouldn't be surprised if he *discovered* a few new ones. Do you see? Kick me if I'm going too fast for you, kick me quite hard. Kick me till I scream for mercy and have to be taken to Bristol General by three big men in an ambulance.' Philip demurred, with a polite smile. 'But then my ancestor got a little bit of a shock. Some of Chatterton's letters were published, by a rival bookseller, and Joynson's name came up again and again. Thief. Scoundrel. Leech. Miser. Chatterton had accused him of buying up his work, and then of abandoning him. And these were the letters written just before his suicide.'

Joynson paused and Philip, eager for the rest of the history, said quickly, 'And so he –'

'Yes. Exactly. Precisely. You can read my mind and we should start an act together at the Alhambra, me in ballet shoes with a gag over my mouth and you with a whip. Precisely. Joynson decided to fight back. He had the evidence that Chatterton invented those medieval poems, so what could be easier than to prove he had faked everything else, including his own death? And what better weapon to use against a forger than another forgery? He decided to out-trick the trickster, do you see? So he began writing the manuscript which was given to your *friend*. By a piece of old slag!' He had screamed out the last words, in the general direction of the door, and Philip rose briefly from his chair in alarm; he was surprised that so much noise could come from such a small person. 'I don't think he intended to publish it,' Joynson resumed in his normal voice. 'He just wanted to leave it behind, to blacken Chatterton's name. It was a sort of joke. Just touch my funny bone, will you, and I'll be helpless on the Axminster carpet. Go on. I'll be putty in your hands, I promise.' But Philip was hardly listening to this latest offer: so that was it, after all, a joke. The memoirs had been forged by a bookseller who wanted to repay him in kind, to fake the work of a faker and so confuse for ever the memory of Chatterton; he would no longer be the poet who died young and glorious, but a middle-aged hack who continued a sordid trade with his partner. This was the document which Charles Wychwood had carried back with him.

There was a crash outside and Pat entered the room, wrestling with a vacuum cleaner as if it were about to strangle and devour him; smiling grimly to himself, he threw it upon the floor and began cleaning the carpet by Joynson's feet. 'I didn't have one!' Joynson bellowed at him. 'Look! Feast your eyes!' And he brought out the empty cigarette-holder.

'She can open her big mouth, she can rustle her big tits, she can scream blue murder.' Pat seemed to be talking to Philip. 'And what do I do? I smile, I give a delicate shrug, I behave like a lady.'

Joynson leaned across to Philip. 'She's more to be pitied than condemned, don't you think?'

Philip rose from his chair, eager to leave the company of these two elderly gentlemen. 'I'll get them back,' he said, raising his voice over the sound of the vacuum cleaner. 'I'll make sure that all the papers are returned to you very soon.'

Joynson smiled and, delicately stepping around Pat, accompanied him into the hallway. 'And don't forget the painting,' he said, 'which a certain old cow took up to London.'

[221]

'Was that your ancestor's, too?'

'Oh, his son painted that. It was part of the joke, you see. Tickle me and see me roar. Go on. It's your last chance. You'll be able to do anything with me.' But Philip had already opened the door, and was walking towards the iron gate. 'Don't forget,' Joynson told him. 'I want them back. They're my family heirlooms. My mementoes.'

'Yes, I know.' Philip turned back to wave and, as he stepped out into the street, he saw Pat at the window; he was pointing towards the sign on the railings, and giggling. Now it read: 'Let's Fantasise Together. Strict Bondage or Golden Showers. Enquire Within.' With a quick step Philip crossed the road, and walked into the shadow of St Mary Redcliffe.

# 15

CHATTERTON ENTERS his garret room and locks the door behind him; then he leans against it, laughing and wiping his mouth on the sleeve of his coat. All well. I am safe from the powdered Angell. He has just crept by her room, shoes in hand, and heard her snoring. I am safe here in my aerial abode. I am on top of the world. He goes over to the bed and drags from beneath it a wooden chest: he unlocks it, and takes out a bottle of Spanish brandy. Better here than in the Tothill Gardens, and cheaper too: I toast Dan Hanway, the first witness of my genius and first prophet of my fame. He opens the bottle, and puts it to his lips. I toast Mrs Angell, for ridding me of a shameful virginity. Another draught. He goes over to the small oak table at the foot of his bed, and pours the brandy into a dirty glass he has left there. I toast the posture master, for showing me an emblem of the world.

Here are the pen and pencil left from this morning's labours; swaying slightly, he takes the pencil and tries to write with it as he bends over the table. Posterity. Antiquity. He cannot recall the words of the song he has been composing as he walked home. I have lost the melody and, without the melody, there is no true meaning. Gone. Gone for ever. Returned whence they came. Ah, the empyrean. Now I am truly drunk. He draws a profile of himself upon the paper and, pressing down hard upon the pencil, traces lines of light from his eyes and from his hair; underneath he writes, in capital letters, APOLLO REDIVIVUS. Then he tears it up and scatters the pieces on the wooden floor.

The rain is blowing in through the half-open attic window, and he leans across the bed to close it: but he loses his balance, falls onto the bed, and lies there laughing. Then he yawns, brushing the spray of the rain from his face. He remembers. I must take my physic. He opens his eyes wide. Kill or cure. With difficulty he rises from the bed and drinks another glass of brandy before reaching up to the high shelf, where he has concealed the linen bag of arsenic and the phial of laudanum. Ah, the bag and the bottle, as it is in the fairy story. He takes them down, and balances one in each hand as if weighing them. Am I the prince or the pauper? He jumps down from the chair, crashing upon the floor. Hush, hush, I must not wake the giant. He carries the antidote to the table, carefully takes off his great-coat, and sits down. He loosens the bag and sniffs inside, savouring the slight aroma of garlic which rises from the arsenic grains. Then he uncorks the stopper from the phial, moistening the rim with his little finger. I see in front of me St Elmo's Fire and a Sahara, a rainbow and a fever, a crystal and a . . . now, what were the proportions Dan gave me? The phial is inscribed with measures on its side, and he sees that it holds two fluid ounces. Was it one grain of arsenic for each ounce of laudanum? Or four grains? Or two ounces? A little more brandy will aid the memory, and he pours some into his glass. Then he empties the linen bag onto the table and piles up the grains, rolling one of them beneath his finger. One for fame. He drops it into the glass. One for genius. He puts in another. And one for youth. He picks up a third grain, and adds it to the brandy. I can cure myself of all diseases, for we may rise above our natural state if the soul guides us. Then, on a sudden instinct, he pours most of the laudanum into the same glass: he holds back his head and swallows the whole draught.

Here is a strong blow. Oh. Very strong. But I will utterly defeat the clap, and rise in the morning purified. For a moment the bile waters his mouth, but he swallows it down. Yes. Yes. I feel it purging me. The cure begins at once. He rises unsteadily from his chair and falls upon the bed. I must remember the idiot boy. Tomorrow. He stretches out upon the bed, lying with his arm across his forehead. Hydrocephalus. He tries to sleep but something is touching him. He sits up, and the first thing he notices is the racing of his pulse. He looks down and, in this strange light, his hands seem to belong to someone else.

*

'Do you think that people could learn to call me Nelly Dean? I am a steady, reasonable little body, after all.' After his visit to Bristol, Philip had arranged to call on Harriet Scrope; now they were sitting together, with Mr Gaskell between them. 'My friends once knew me as Mistress Quickly,' she went on. 'But that was for entirely different reasons.'

'Oh. I see.' Philip, not sure how to begin, was chewing on the corner of his beard. He could feel himself sliding back into his old silence and embarrassed insufficiency, but he must stop, he must begin again: he was here for the sake of Charles and Vivien, he was their protector.

'You know, Philip, you look just like a renaissance knight with that little beard. Do you ever ride out to battle?'

He seemed to Harriet to be fighting for breath. 'No,' he said at last. Then he looked at her directly. 'No. I don't think I do.'

She put up her hands in a gesture of surrender. 'It was only a figure of speech, dear. I thought librarians were used to them. Would you care for a tiny drink?'

'No, I . . .'

'Don't tell me. You're driving. You're driving a hard bargain.' She laughed at her own joke as she went over to the alcove, and came back with a glass of gin. 'This reminds me of the lovely evening we had in the Indian restaurant. Wasn't it fun?' She seemed to have forgotten its conclusion but then she added, 'I think Charles enjoyed it, too, don't you?'

'Yes, I suppose . . .'

'Although it was unfortunate that his last meal on earth should be a chicken vindaloo. I want to go after some nice roast beef and potatoes.'

Philip sat up in his chair. 'Harriet, I really wanted to talk to you about the Chatterton manuscripts.'

'Do you?' She sipped some gin from her spoon. 'I expect Vivien wants them back, does she?' She had already guessed the purpose of Philip's visit, and was not unhappy about it. After her journey to Brooke Street, she had decided that she could do nothing with the papers – now that she had lost interest in Chatterton, not even the prospect of astonishing the academic world could revive it. As far as she was concerned it was a dead subject; and she wanted to stay with the living for as long as possible.

'Not Vivien,' Philip was saying. 'Their owner. Their owner needs them.' These were the lines which Philip had rehearsed to himself. 'The manuscripts belong to someone else, you see. They're a family heirloom.'

Harriet laughed. 'Whenever I hear the word heirloom,' she said, 'for some reason I think of crumpets.' She rolled her tongue around her mouth. 'Did Charles *steal* them?'

'No, of course not!'

She did not seem to have heard this. 'Do you think it was his cry for help, as the newspapers say?'

'He didn't steal anything. They were given to him.'

'I see.' Harriet was beginning to enjoy this conversation. 'So some kind of mistake was made?'

[225]

'I don't . . .' Philip did not want to admit that the papers were forgeries, and so betray Charles. 'I don't, you know . . .'

'What don't you know, Philip?'

'It wasn't a mistake exactly, just –'

Harriet watched with fascination as he tugged violently at his beard. 'Be careful you don't pull yourself down onto the carpet,' she said, very sweetly. 'You might frighten Mr Gaskell.'

'They were real,' Philip was saying, 'but they were not real . . .'

She put up her hand. 'Well, never mind. I really don't want to know.' She got up from her chair, smiling to herself, and was about to leave the room when she turned around to face him. 'If you want the painting back, too, you'll have to get it from that gallery. I never thought much of it, anyway.' She was gone only a few moments, returning with the pile of manuscripts which she deposited on Philip's lap.

But he did not want this meeting to end so abruptly. 'I suppose,' he said, choosing his words very carefully, 'that it was difficult to make sense of all this?' He flicked through the papers, surreptitiously checking that they were all there.

'Oh no. It wasn't difficult at all. It was all too easy.'

'I don't quite see –'

'*I* didn't quite see. That was the problem. None of it seemed very real, but I suppose that's the trouble with history. It's the one thing we have to make up for ourselves.' She could see his embarrassment. 'Of course I could still write it all down. I could tell the story much better than poor Charles.'

Philip had feared this. 'You can't do that,' he said, angrily. 'That would be a terrible thing to do!'

Harriet watched him with interest. 'For Vivien's sake,' she said at last, 'I agree with you.'

Philip was blushing now. 'It was all a mistake,' he said. He hesitated. 'But there's no point in going over the past.'

'You mean, over Chatterton?'

'No, over Charles. Now that he's –'

'Dead, dear. Let's not mince words.'

'Now that he's dead.'

'So the hand of time should turn the page?' She cocked her head on one side. 'What a pretty image.' She kissed her own hand. 'Thank you, Harriet Scrope, for that lovely sweet thought. By the way,' she added in a brisker tone, 'you'll find Charles's poems in there too.' She pointed at the papers on Philip's lap. 'I don't think I can do anything with them, after all.' Philip looked at her, disconcerted by her evident lack of interest, and she stepped back, defiantly putting one hand upon her hip. 'You think I'm grotesque,

[226]

don't you? But I'm not. I'm all too real. I might even bite.' She opened her mouth wide and, to Philip's astonishment, let her false teeth protrude for an instant before sucking them back in.

At this point the telephone rang. Philip, already in a somewhat nervous state, jumped at the sudden sound and scattered the manuscripts over the carpet. Harriet scurried out of the room, rubbing her hands together and grinning. It was Cumberland, sounding very grim. 'Miss Scrope, if you have a hat hold onto it.'

'Will a cat do?' She beckoned to Mr Gaskell.

'Do you recall the painting you wanted me to – to authenticate?'

'I remember it well.'

'Well, something rather ghastly has happened.'

*

The saliva fills Chatterton's mouth, a river overflowing its precious banks. There is a pain in his belly like the colic but burning so, my liver and spleen might roast in the heat. What is happening to me? He tries to rise from his bed, but the agony throws him down again and he rolls in terror to stare at the wall. Oh God the arsenic. He vomits over the bed, and in that same spasm the shit runs across his thin buttocks – how hot it is – and trickles down his thighs, the smell of it mixing with the rank odour of the sweat pouring out of his body. Everything is fleeing from me. I am the house on fire. Oh god the poison. I am being melted down.

*

Stewart Merk had cleaned the painting with a cloth soaked in hot water, starting in the upper right-hand corner and the dim inscription *Pinxit George Stead. 1802.* And he could see now that his original diagnosis had been correct: the flesh tints of the face were too bright, the residue of clumsy over-painting. The candle, which flickered beside the four volumes and shed an uncertain light on the side of the sitter's face, was also a later addition. And the hands were wrong: the left hand, gripping the manuscript, had been badly drawn and the other was too stiffly poised above the four leather-bound volumes. Yet the eyes were right. The eyes would have to be preserved. Merk picked up his camera from a low shelf, and began taking pictures of the canvas from every angle – each photograph would, in turn, help him to reconstruct the painting until it attained its final, authentic form. The sudden brilliant illuminations of his flash struck against the canvas like sheet lightning, altering its colours and sending so many deep shadows across its surface that it seemed to him to be moving. Merk put down his camera and sighed.

The cracks were not as deep as he had first suspected, since most of them occurred in the varnish rather than in the paint itself. So he mixed pure alcohol and water in order to remove this faded exterior and, as slowly he rubbed the dissolvent across the canvas, the newly-exposed paint seemed for a moment to glow in the unaccustomed light and air. With the varnish gone, the successive layers of paint became visible, and Merk could see the outline of some other object glimmering faintly behind the candle and the books. Inside the face of the sitter, too, another face could just barely be discerned; it was a younger face and, as it seemed to Merk, one that expressed suffering.

And then he cried out, in panic. The dissolvent was reacting with the freshly exposed paint. Small bubbles and creases were forming on the surface of the picture, and the image of the sitter seemed to shudder before beginning to shrivel, to bend, to drop away in flakes of paint which floated down from the canvas onto the tiled floor of Merk's studio. And as he watched in horror the dissolution acquired its own momentum: the top surface was being stripped away, and the various underpaintings were now crackling and bubbling. The face of the sitter dissolved, becoming two faces, one old and one young; as the paint decayed before Merk's eyes, the flakes becoming clots of colour which dropped onto the floor, these two faces recurred in a series of smaller and smaller images until after a few moments they had entirely disappeared.

He rushed up to the canvas and, uncertain what to do, lifted it from its easel. But it was too hot: the sides were burning in his hands, and with a cry he threw it down upon the floor where it shook and shuddered. He put his hands against his ears, to block out the whispers of the dissolving paint, and stared down at the portrait in the last stages of its decay. Within a few minutes nothing remained: except, curiously enough, certain letters from the titles of the books which now hovered in an indeterminate space. He touched it gingerly with his foot and then, in a sudden furious burst of anger and resentment, he stamped upon it, put his heel through the canvas, and kicked it into a corner of his studio. 'Dead? Yes?' he shouted, wiping away the spittle from his mouth.

*

a birth pain, my bowels ripped open to find the child, oh mother mother. Chatterton is being tossed up and down upon the sodden bed, the agony rising from him like mist into the attic room. Hold on oh hold on until this fit is past but my hands are nailed to the bed, my flesh being torn from me as I curve and break. His face is

[228]

swelling, his eyelids bursting in the heat. I am the giant in the pantomime oh God save me from melting, melting, melting

*

Edward passed a night-storm upon the ocean, its turbulent crest rising above his head and the spray all around him; then he stepped in front of a volcanic abyss, where travellers peered in horror at the chasms beneath their feet; then he entered a white gallery and made his way through a circle of polished stones which had, at their centre, a cubic pyramid made of shining bronze; he walked on quickly, impatient to reach Gallery Fifteen.

And the painting was still there: he had feared that it might have been concealed, or even destroyed, after his father's death. But 'Chatterton' remained, securely fastened to the wall, and to Edward it seemed even more real; it was brighter, perhaps even larger, than before. He walked straight up to it, and at first saw nothing but the texture of the canvas protected beneath the glass: he saw its cracks, and its patches of colour, and he was disgusted by it. He knew that 'Chatterton' had some connection with his father's own death: he remembered the precise expression with which Charles had first looked at the painting, and he would never forget his shadowy haunted look when he turned away. So where was its secret?

Folding his arms as he had seen his father do, he scrutinised the painting as if it were some hostile but silent witness. At first it seemed to him no better than a photograph, or a picture from a film; and an old one, at that. The colours were all wrong. But he watched it steadily, searching for a clue, and by degrees the painting relaxed also: to Edward the garret room became more real, and he noticed how it seemed to increase in size as he continued to gaze into it. The casement window was shaking slightly in the breeze, and he was just about to step forward and close it when he saw that two other people had entered the room. They were standing beside the body and the woman had put a handkerchief over her mouth and nose. He could hear them talking. What mischief is this, Mr Cross? I smell the arsenic, Mrs Angell, he is utterly undone.

Edward had not yet chosen to look closely at the man lying upon the bed but now, when he did so, he stepped back in astonishment: it was his father lying there. He was putting out his hand towards his son. Edward came forward, and held it for a moment before it fell away onto the wooden floor. He thought his father might be about to speak, but he could not raise his head and he only smiled. Then this picture faded.

[229]

Edward blinked three times, trying not to cry. He could not move and after a few moments he realised that he was staring at the reflection of his own face in the glass, just in the place where his father's face had been. And now Edward was smiling, too. He had seen his father again. He would always be here, in the painting. He would never wholly die.

*

The summer flies, in their terror, escape through the casement window. Chatterton is suffocating now, something is sitting on my chest and exulting, its head thrown back, I am the horse he rides. His body is plucked up and then thrown down in derision, the bed swaying and groaning beneath his convulsions. But he is suddenly quiet. No pain now the Arctic frost protects me from the dazzling sky and look my limbs are covered with snow. The air grows violet around me, violet and rose-coloured and steadily paler still. This is not dying this is forgetting to breathe. He seems to be looking around his room for the last time, but these are only the uncoordinated movements of the dying body: his left arm is pressed against his chest while his right arm slips from the bed, the hand clenching and unclenching as if trying to grasp the torn scraps of his writing which are scattered across the floor. Chatterton's neck has been twisted by the force of his arsenic convulsions, so that he lies at an unnatural angle on the dank pillow. His left foot is shaking but, eventually, it becomes still. Then he suffers a sudden blow inside his head and there is no pain but, rather, a sudden dazzling rush of light.

*

'So it's all over.' Philip gave an almost ceremonial bow to Edward who, presuming that this was a moment of great significance, bowed in return. 'I've sent all the manuscripts back to Bristol.' As soon as he had left Harriet's house with them, in fact, he had despatched them to Mr Joynson. He did not really even want to touch them.

'And the painting?' Vivien was clearly delighted.

'The painting has been destroyed.'

'Hoorah!' Edward got up and danced around Philip, butting him with his head and punching him. 'Chatterton's dead! Chatterton's dead!' Then he stopped suddenly and, putting one finger in his ear, went over to his mother. 'What about the other one?'

'Which other one, Eddie?'

'You know, the good one. That mustn't be killed.'

'There is no other one, Eddie. There was only one picture.' He looked at his mother with something very much like pity, but he said nothing. In any case, Vivien was more interested in Philip's news. 'And what did Mr Joynson say about the painting?'

Philip was smiling, enjoying the look of relief upon her face. 'He seemed pleased, actually. And Harriet was delighted. Don't ask me why.'

Harriet had come back into the room after her telephone conversation with Cumberland, and said to him, 'The painting is no longer with us. It has passed over to the other side.' She made the sign of the cross, and laughed. 'You know sometimes, Philip, I have thoughts which are far too deep for words. Or is it tears? I can never remember.'

'So it *is* all over,' Vivien said. 'At last.'

The three of them usually had dinner together, and on this special evening Philip had decided to celebrate by bringing over two bottles of Chianti.

Edward was particularly happy and insisted on trying the wine throughout the meal of asparagus soup, spaghetti bolognese and raspberry ripple ice-cream. By the end of it, he had a wide ring of wine and ice-cream around his mouth. 'You look,' his mother said, 'like a piece of Brighton rock.'

With a shriek of laughter he ran into his bedroom and then, after a few minutes, he started calling out, 'Philip! Philip!' He went in, and found Edward already in bed. 'Philip,' he said quietly, 'will you tell me a story?' So another story was told, and very soon the child was asleep.

Philip went back into the front room where Vivien was sitting, her legs tucked up beneath her on the small sofa. 'A penny for them,' he said.

'I was thinking of Charles.' And Philip blushed. 'No, not like that.' She stopped for a moment. 'Poor Charles. It seems a pity,' she added, 'that it should end like this.'

'You mean the papers?'

She nodded. 'In one way he was right, wasn't he? We all believed it.' In the silence voices could be heard in the flat above them. 'I wish it didn't have to be forgotten, Philip. It's such a waste.'

'But how . . .' He seemed to be staring into the distance as his question trailed off, but in fact he was looking at the chair where Charles had once sat. It was not an empty corner: he could still sense his friend's presence there, as if it were suspended in the air, remaining in the idea of Chatterton which Charles had created in this room. His belief had been the important thing. So the papers were imitations and the painting a forgery – yet the feelings

they evoked in Charles, and now in Vivien, were still more important than any reality. 'You know,' he said softly, 'they don't have
to be forgotten. We can keep the belief alive.' He looked at Vivien,
and smiled. 'The important thing is what Charles imagined, and
we can keep hold of that. That isn't an illusion. The imagination
never dies.'

'Oh, yes,' she said. 'Let's keep it alive.' She looked at Philip,
her eyes bright, waiting for him to complete his thought. But he
did not quite know how to continue; he rubbed his beard
and looked down at the ground. 'Look up, Philip,' she said. 'Tell
me.'

'You know,' he replied, slowly at first, 'how I tried to write? Life
seemed so mysterious to me – everything was connected and yet
apart. Do you remember I told you this?' She nodded. There had
been a conversation between them, the day after their walk in the
pine forest, when in order to comfort her Philip had explained his
own sense of insufficiency and loss; he told her how he, too, was
bewildered by a world in which no significant pattern could be
found. Everything just seems to *take place*, he had said, and there's
not even any *momentum*. It's just, well, it's just *velocity*. And if you
trace anything backwards, trying to figure out cause and effect, or
motive, or meaning, there is no real *origin* for anything. Everything
just exists. Everything just exists in order to exist. It was after this
conversation that Philip and Vivien had grown closer together.
'And you remember,' he was saying now, 'I told you how I used
to read novelists, to see if any of them had felt the mystery, too?
But none of them had, none of them seemed to feel how *odd* it
is that life is just the way it is and no other. Did I tell you this?'
She said nothing, waiting for him to go on. 'So I tried writing my
own novel but it didn't work, you know. I kept on imitating
other people. I had no real story, either, but now –' he
hesitated – 'but now, with this – with Charles's theory – I
might be able to –'

Vivien got up from the sofa, clapping her hands. 'That's a
wonderful plan! That's exactly what he would have wanted!'

'Of course,' he added, grave again, 'I must tell it in my own
way. How Chatterton might have lived on.'

'You could tell it in any way you want. It will be a wonderful
book!'

'And you know,' he said, smiling at her enthusiasm, 'I might
discover that I had a style of my own, after all.'

Edward, woken by the sudden noise, entered the room and
stood wondering in the doorway as Philip and Vivien hugged each
other. Philip saw him, and gently broke away from her. 'Do you

[232]

think,' he said, 'that I'm attempting too much? Do you think I should go and see Harriet Scrope first?'

Edward and Vivien shouted out in unison, 'No!'

*

rush of light around him his heart is beating like a hollow drum and Chatterton is being borne away; he is staring at the wooden boards of the floor and now, in his opium dream, the floor dissolves and the limitless sky is revolving beneath him. He has left his bed and his arsenic fear far behind and ah he is flying. Flying towards St Mary Redcliffe and the church is his father, lying on the short grass, propped upon his elbow and yawning as the sun rolls above him. Flying through the porch and through the west door, the sudden coldness of old stone changing the colour from light violet to aquamarine, which is the colour of dreams. The iron latch closes behind him and echoes for ever. Flying, into the church and seeing for the first time its vast spaces. Flying, past columns and circular stairways, past the exhausted faces of saints and the broken claws of griffins, past the upper arches and the clusters of pitted moulding. Flying, between the vaulting and the leaded roof, among the huge dusty roof timbers. Flying, along the narrow ledges of the galleries with abysses and cavernous depths to either side of him. The nave of the church has become a gigantic plain of smooth stone and when he looks down he sees his own monk, Thomas Rowley, with tonsured head, raising his hands to greet him; they stare at each other across the vast distance, and in the eternity of that look the light between them burns and decays.

Falling, and Chatterton is walking down a stairway of old stone where he passes a young man ascending on the other side; and he is always walking, always passing him, and the young man always shows him the puppet which he holds in his left hand. Falling, and Chatterton is standing beside a young man with his head bowed in pain; there is a fountain behind them, and the fountain is playing for ever. Falling, into the nave of the church where distant figures are trying to reach him and he waits with his arms outstretched. The idiot boy, hydrocephalic; the posture master; the Tothill whore; the pot-boy of Shoe Lane; the druggist bearing gifts. Each one of them in turn emerges from the shadow and greets him by name, 'Thomas Chatterton'. In turn he salutes each one with pride and gravity, and then kneels on the stone floor of the nave. 'We poets in our youth,' he calls to them across the infinite abyss, 'begin in gladness, but thereof come in the end despondency and madness.'

The silence that follows is never broken and now, when he looks

[233]

up, he sees ahead of him an image edged with rose-coloured light. It is still forming, and for centuries he watches himself upon an attic bed, with the casement window half-open behind him, the rose plant lingering on the sill, the smoke rising from the candle, as it will always do. I will not wholly die, then. Two others have joined him – the young man who passes him on the stairs and the young man who sits with bowed head by the fountain – and they stand silently beside him. I will live for ever, he tells them. They link hands, and bow towards the sun.

And, when his body is found the next morning, Chatterton is still smiling.